Dedication:

To the children of the world and to all those who are
responsible for their safety – may they always be vigilant.

Acknowledgements:

Mike Richardson for his editing skills.

Police Superintendent (retired) John Higgs for his tireless efforts in assisting me with the extensive research that went into this novel and for the various papers he gave me on the subject of paedophilia. Vanessa Rogers for her
editing skills. Jonathan Miller for his tireless encouragement.

My thanks to all of them for helping to produce this book.

A CIP catalogue record for this title is
available from the British Library

ISBN 978-1-909271-03-6

Published by
M-Y Books
187 Ware Road
Hertford
Herts SG13 7EQ

Front cover by Andrew Brechin

NEMESIS

by

VINCENT COBB

PROLOGUE

The man allowed the tear to trickle down his cheek as he laid out the naked body of the child before him on the dirt floor. She was a pretty little thing, with her locks of golden hair and pale, unblemished skin. She still looked pretty even now, in death, with her eyes closed and her thin, bloodless lips pressed tightly together. It was so sad that such a lovely child had to die; it always had the same effect on him when they left him like this – alone once more, with only the memory of his sexual satiation to sustain him.

He sighed. "If only it could be different," he thought, sorrowfully, as he gently stroked the naked body for the last time. Children, especially little girls, were his deepest love, and when he lost himself in the act of coition it was, to him, a divine moment – almost like a communion – and the cries of the child he was hearing were not screams of terror from a dying little girl, but the beautiful strains of a choir of angels.

The whole experience was so…so celestial. And then the uninvited, unwelcome God intervened and tore the life from the little girl right at the point of his ecstasy. He wiped the solitary tear from his cheek and said a silent prayer for the soul of his sacrifice. Then he gathered her in his arms and rose from his position on the floor; it was time now for the ritual burial. He had laid her clothes out carefully on the ground – an act of reverence rather than contrition. He had washed the stains of the baptism from her body and then cleansed himself of any residual evidence. Everything was prepared.

Carrying the body in his arms, he was making to leave the hut when suddenly he felt a jolt run through his body, like an electric current, coupled with a sense of intrusion that all but overwhelmed him. Someone, or something, was watching him. He could see nothing through the darkness, but he knew – from his heightened sense of intuition – that he was being observed, psychically, from afar; and it frightened him. Whoever, or whatever, it was knew; knew about his sacrifices – not just this one, but all the others too.

He felt confused, apprehensive; threatened, even. Who was it? Who could be watching him? And how? How was it possible?

He had been so careful to remain undetected. He had planned everything so meticulously, down to the finest minutiae, to ensure there was little chance of him ever being discovered.

And now someone knew – someone unknown but, like himself, with the metaphysical abilities to pierce the protective veil he had built around himself.

Suddenly, he was more scared than he had ever been in his life before. Was his world – a world so carefully constructed and defended – about to end…?

CHAPTER ONE

I was a 19-year-old newly recruited WPC at the Birmingham Central police station in Steelhouse Lane, when I first met Connie Rowden; not much older than she was, in fact. I remember the day well. It was a Saturday in the September of 1992 and I had spent that afternoon – with the benefit of overtime pay, I might add – on duty at the home derby match between Birmingham City and Aston Villa- evidently something called the Premier League had just started and, so I was told, Birmingham City were unbelievably fortunate to have qualified for entry. I wouldn't exactly describe myself as a football fan and even though the City won 3-0 I couldn't get excited about it. I was more concerned that afternoon with the behaviour of the visiting supporters, hoping against hope there wouldn't be any trouble. Thankfully there wasn't, and the forty or so uniformed police officers on duty at the ground returned to the station in high spirits – especially those City fans amongst us. Tell the truth I was relieved when it was over, not simply because it had been trouble-free, but more because I seemed to have passed my first test as a woman in a dominantly male world.

Later, I was taking a short break with some of my colleagues in the staff canteen when the call came that the DCI wanted to see me. I ignored the taunts from the other PCs, as I ignored the fact I was to go off duty, too worried at the time in case I had committed some serious breach of discipline that might cost me my career. That was me, though: always full of guilt.

I recall thinking, "What on earth Could a DCI possibly want from a naive young policewoman?" I mean, I was very lucky to have been assigned to Birmingham Central; the West Midlands Police Force has over seven thousand officers and covers hundreds of square miles over a very wide area, stretching as far as Wolverhampton in the North, my hometown, and Coventry in the South. So really, they could have posted me anywhere, and I couldn't believe it when Birmingham Central, my first choice station, came up positive. It was like winning the Pools for a newly graduated Constable, although I did learn, much later, that it was due more to my results at Police Training College than the luck of any draw.

The very thought of having to confront Detective Chief Inspector Templar, or Simple Simon as he was unkindly referred to by the rookies, frightened the life out of me. He was, to say the least, an extremely forbidding figure. It wasn't merely the size of the man, or the fact he was the detective chief inspector; it had more to do with his overpowering presence, and the sheer menace he projected, to say nothing of his abrasive manner, especially to subordinates.

But, after traipsing for what seemed like hours, along miles of corridors through the huge Victorian building, bumping into the scores of bodies in the corridors and passing various incident rooms filled with dozens of officers, either on computer terminals or manning the phones, interview rooms, the computer centre with its row upon row of terminals and processors, and senior CID officers' units, I finally arrived at the entrance to the office suite of the DCI. On the way I had stopped at the 'Ladies' to check my appearance and I wasn't too dismayed with what I saw. I was wearing little or no makeup- it was frowned upon at that time – but my face was presentable and the wind had caught my high cheekbones and added a little natural colour. I wouldn't describe myself as beautiful exactly, but the odd boyfriend had told me that I was more than attractive, and that my auburn hair and the depth of my eyes was – what was it one of them had said? Oh yes, 'incredibly appealing'. I think he meant fanciable! And being slim and having good legs helped a lot.

Of course I had been given the guided tour of the Steelhouse Lane Headquarters Building when I first arrived a few weeks ago, but it was so large, spreading as it did over five floors – and that excluded the basement cells area – that I felt it would take me years to find my way around. I was lucky to have remembered that the CID offices were on the third floor; what I did forget though was that three lifts serviced each floor of the building that could have saved me time and a lot of leg ache.

Much to my relief the tormentor actually smiled at me when I finally entered his office, a mannerism I was told later, that was completely foreign to him. He invited me to take a seat alongside an attractive but obviously very anxious woman who was already seated in front of his desk. I couldn't help noticing her striking blue eyes, whilst her hair was the colour of golden wheat. When I looked at her a second time I had the impression she was struggling to control some inner stress. Her face was taut, like an over wound spring, and those blue eyes had a haunted, almost desperate expression I had missed at first glance, as if she were pleading for someone to help her. Of course, I kept my feelings about her to myself, merely smiling 'hello', removing my hat, at the same time hurriedly attempting to rearrange my untidy hair, - something I had overlooked when I was in the loo - and taking a seat as commanded. Even so, I couldn't help noticing how she was unable to stop her hands from nervously rubbing together, as if she was wringing out a wet dishcloth. I guessed she probably wasn't as old as her demeanour suggested; in all, she was a woman who seemed to have had her fair share of suffering. I was curious, to say the least.

"Mrs Rowden," the chief inspector said; "I'd like you to meet Angela – Angela Crossley. PC Crossley's one of our newest recruits. Angela, this is Mrs Rowden."

"How do you do," I said formally.

"Sylvia, please," she urged, shaking my hand.

"I hope you don't mind my asking PC Crossley to join us, Mrs Rowden. I thought your daughter would find it easier to talk to a woman - specially one a bit nearer her own age."

"Yes... Yes she will... Does that mean you're willing to take me seriously? It's just that I had the feeling you were quite cynical about the whole proposition."

He frowned at the implied criticism.

"I'm sorry if I gave you that impression. If I hesitated it's only because I wasn't quite sure how to deal with the matter." He coughed, a little embarrassedly. "To be perfectly honest, Mrs Rowden, I'm not much clearer now... Except that I do think we need to have a chat with... Sorry, what's your daughter's name again?"

"Connie."

"Yes, quite; Connie. Well, under the circumstances, I don't think we've anything to lose by talking to her as long as we keep this strictly confidential - I really can't emphasise that too strongly. Is that all right with you?" He held out a hand to stop me from interrupting. I was only thinking aloud what an old-fashioned name Connie was and wondering what its source was.

"Fine, Chief Inspector. I don't think either of us wants to look a fool… And we could, couldn't we - especially if the press get to hear about it. When do you want to meet Connie? She's at home at the moment and I know she'd be happy to talk to you."

"Sir," I interjected determinedly – somewhat foolishly, I thought with hindsight.

"Can I leave you to sort that out with Angela here?" he said, ignoring me. "And, if you don't mind, you can brief her at the same time; as you can probably tell, she has no idea yet what this is all about."

He glanced towards me and scowled – somewhat condescendingly, I thought – and then rose from his chair as if to inform us that he was now terminating the meeting.

"Thanks for coming in, Mrs Rowden. PC Crossley will keep me informed of any developments."

We were dismissed, summarily, and he hadn't even had the good manners to explain what it was all about! I managed to return his rudeness by giving him a curt nod; if he noticed at all he didn't acknowledge it. Mrs Rowden – Sylvia – was still wringing her hands as we left the office and made our way to one of the station's interview rooms.

"He hasn't told you anything, has he?" she began.

"Well, he's a busy man, Sylvia. I'm sure you can understand we're all snowed under right now, trying to find the missing little girl. I don't think he meant to be rude - it's just a very worrying time for all of us."

The girl in question was nine-year-old Alice Newton. She had disappeared between her mother's house and the newsagents, a half a mile away, three days ago. The police and an army of volunteers were searching the whole area, but it was now feared that she had been abducted. I couldn't help wondering if this development with Sylvia wasn't somehow connected.

"I admire your loyalty, Angela, but I still think he's too embarrassed to deal with this himself."

"Why don't you begin by telling me what 'this' is exactly?" I said. "And how your daughter fits in with it."

Sylvia Rowden brushed the hair from the side of her face – another anxious gesture – then produced a small photograph from her handbag.

"This is Connie," she said, handing it to me across the table. "She's thirteen - and she's a very gifted child." She had a similar appearance to her mother: the same straw-coloured hair, the same blue eyes, and the same serious expression.

"You mean 'gifted' as in intelligent?"

"No. Not that, exactly." She hesitated, unsure whether or not to proceed. I stretched over and took her hand, trying to reassure her.

"How is she gifted, Sylvia?" I persisted. "You can trust me, you know."

"She's psychic," she said, simply, as if it was the most natural thing in the world. "She gets it from her grandmother – on my side of the family. I named her after my mother," she added, as though she had to explain herself.

"Psychic?" I repeated lamely, at the same time thinking: "Good God! No wonder the DCI wanted to dump it on me."

"Yes. But it's important you understand - she's no ordinary psychic. She isn't one of these people you read about who have flashes of visions that they don't understand." Nervously Sylvia brushed her hair away from her face again. "Connie knows exactly what she sees. I mean clearly, almost in perfect detail – it's like it's actually happening to her. And it affects her... Very badly, in fact. Can you understand that, Angela?"

I cleared my throat, not sure how to react. I mean, how the hell was I supposed to understand the mysteries of physic phenomena?

"Well, yes, I think so – but to be perfectly honest, I've had no personal experience with this kind of thing," I managed to say eventually – not in the least convincingly, I must add. "But what I don't understand is how this concerns the police. I mean, I take it she hasn't committed any crime?"

Sylvia then treated me to a patronising sigh of frustration. "You're very young, aren't you? Not much older than my daughter, I should imagine. Look, Angela, I came here because I believe my daughter can help the police to find that missing girl. But I think I should be dealing with someone more senior; someone with more experience. No offence, dear, but the fact they've dumped it on you says to me that your bosses aren't taking me seriously. Don't you agree?"

"On the face of it, yes," I acknowledged. "But the DCI hasn't actually passed it on to me, Sylvia. All he said, if you remember, is that we should certainly have a talk with Connie, and that I was probably the best person to do that because I'm nearer her age. When we've done that I'll report back to him so he can consider the matter further. It's fairly standard procedure," I lied, "and it doesn't in any way mean you're not being taken seriously." I could hardly admit to the DCI dumping her and her daughter on to me. Could I?

"Not being taken seriously in this place usually means you get nothing more than a polite 'good morning'. Now," I went on before she could deride me further, "why don't you tell me how you think Connie can help us find the little girl, and we can take it from there."

"Well, you'll have to talk to her yourself, of course - but she *says* she knows where the child is."

I wasn't sure how to respond to that. I mean, the way she just came out with it like that, it sounded so…what? Convincing? But, of course, it was quite ridiculous. The woman was obviously a nutcase and our beloved DCI must have already assumed that. The problem I was now faced with, though, was: how on earth did I deal with it? Or, more to the point, how did I get out of it?

"Not convinced, are you?" she said, after an interminable silence from me.

"I…I…I…" was all I could manage to stammer.

"Look, why don't you come and meet Connie? Have a talk with her. Listen to what she's got to say - and then you can make your own mind up whether or not we're a bunch of time-wasting nutters. Will you do that?" She looked at me with a kind of beguiling innocence. "You'll never know for sure otherwise. Will you?"

Of course I agreed. What else could I do anyway? The DCI had already instructed me, in effect, to meet and talk with her daughter. So I could hardly refuse, could I?

CHAPTER TWO

The sky was filled with dark, angry clouds, and a steady drizzle began falling as we left the police pound and set off in Sylvia's car, heading towards her home in Ladywood, on the outskirts of Birmingham. An officer from social services accompanied me as I wasn't allowed to interview anyone until I had graduated; he didn't say anything, I believe he was there simply as an observer. He introduced himself to me as Brian Horton, a quiet, well dressed man, who hardly spoke. It seemed to me a perfect day to be meeting up with a spook!

A half-hour later we arrived at the house in one of the many suburbs in the south of the city. Very little was said in the car during the journey, and I had to admit I was not looking forward to the meeting.

Connie, I soon discovered, was a quiet, rather shy teenager, who seemed to project wisdom far beyond her years. She was also on the frail side – almost skinny I would have said, as though she was undernourished and needed feeding up. In fact she made my own slender frame appear almost obese. But I also noticed – rather disturbingly, as it happened – that she had the same haunted look in her almond eyes as her mother, as if they shared some dark, unspoken secret.

They lived in a small terraced house, in Bromsgrove Street, a long narrow street of almost identical houses, the kind of neighbourhood you either spent your life trying to escape from or you retreated into when things were going badly wrong financially. Sylvia was quick to point out to me that the house was rented rather than owned.

Brian Horton still hadn't said anything and when I asked him did he want to take over he said he was just there to see how I handled the matter. It wasn't until we were seated in the equally small but comfortable lounge that I remembered to ask about the father. Until then no mention of him had been made, which struck me as rather odd.

"What about *Mr* Rowden? Does he know we're having this meeting?" I asked.

Sylvia looked decidedly uneasy at the question, and started wringing her hands again. All she said in reply was: "There is no Mr Rowden."

"You're divorced, then?" I asked, stating the obvious.

"No. He's dead. Actually, we were never married. I worked for him as his housekeeper – his live-in housekeeper. Connie was…"

"…An accident," Connie cut in. "It's okay, mum, you can tell her the story; it doesn't bother me any more."

"I'm sorry,' I murmured. This obviously explained their impoverished surroundings.

"It's okay,' she said. "My relationship with him was…. Well, one of those weak moments. He'd had too much to drink and I was lonely…" She shrugged philosophically.

"How did he die?" I asked Sylvia.

"It was an accident – car crash. He died intestate and as I was only a housekeeper…" She rolled her eyes, in distress I thought, "we were left without a penny."

It might have been a strange remark from a housekeeper except it was even more curious that her father hadn't left Connie anything for her upbringing. Still, it was none of my business except I thought she could have made a claim on his estate.

" I think Connie was about eight when we moved to this house. She barely remembers him…" Her voice tailed off again.

"Is there something wrong, Sylvia? I didn't mean to upset you."

Me and my big mouth, I thought.

"No. It's alright, really," she insisted – too strongly, I thought. Her face paled and her lips noticeably narrowed; she was also wringing her hands once more. " As Connie told you, that night together was a mistake although I've never once regretted having her. Now it's something we don't like to talk about – Connie and I, that is. Do we, Connie?" she said, turning to her daughter.

The girl merely nodded her agreement, although it occurred to me that the subject seemed to be as correspondingly distasteful to the daughter as it was to her mother.

I couldn't say very much because it wasn't dissimilar to my own background. My father had walked out on us only a few months after I was born; I had neither seen nor heard from him to this day. Essentially, my mother – a single parent – brought me up, though I can remember having a succession of 'uncles'. Thinking of my mother invariably caused me to smile; she was the bright diamond in my life, and had she not decided to move in with her latest 'boyfriend' I'm sure I would still be living at home instead of having to rent my own flat. I did make a point though of meeting up with my mother at least once a month for a coffee, or sometimes a meal, and a chat about the latest gossip. As far as I could tell she seemed to be happy, and I was glad for her.

"So," I said, breaking the ensuing silence, "shall we move on? Connie, your mum's been telling me about your special gift. And that you might be able to help us find young Alice. Are you up to talking about that?"

"No!" she said flatly. "I don't want to talk about it."

"Oh!" was all I could think of to say, although Connie's response seemed to confirm my opinion about the family being nutters. "I'm sorry; I must have misunderstood. I thought your mother was sure you knew where Alice could be found, and you were going to help us. Have I got it wrong?"

Noticeably, Sylvia never said a word during this exchange, which reinforced my view. I was already rehearsing my exit when Connie said: "No. I didn't say I wouldn't help you. I *will* tell you where she is, but I don't want to talk about it."

"Oh! Right. Where is she, Connie? Is she with some friends of yours?"

"She's dead!" she stated in a flat voice, lacking in emotion. "Buried! I know the place – well, I'm pretty certain I do – but don't ask me to take you there because I won't. It's too scary."

I remember falling back in my chair at this revelation, too shocked to say anything. "Dear God," I thought. "She's serious; deadly serious."

How in heaven's name was I going to deal with this? I imagined myself ringing the station and informing the DCI not to expect me back for a while as I was on my way to locating the body of the missing child. I shuddered at the thought. Bang would go my career! And Brian Horton wouldn't help either – he was just there to take notes.

"You're obviously shell-shocked," I heard Sylvia saying from what appeared to be a long way away. "Would you like a glass of water – or something stronger? Connie, bring the constable a glass of water, would you, and a wet flannel."

"No! Thanks but I'm all right – really. I'm just… As you said, a bit shocked."

"Connie," Sylvia continued, "could you draw us map or give us some directions to where the little girl is buried?"

"Well, sort of. She's buried in a forest, the one near the old quarry. There's a kind of glade, with a disused workman's cottage. She's in a pit behind it. But it's very dark there, and, like I said, it's scary. I think there might be other bodies there as well. Alice isn't the first one he's murdered."

I looked at the teenager intently, trying to recover some composure. "Connie, this is a very serious matter; you do understand that, don't you?"

"Of course," she said, indignantly tossing her head. "Don't you think I know that already? I'm the one who has the nightmares."

"Is that what they are – nightmares? Bad dreams?"

"You'll be telling me next I imagined all this," she snorted angrily. She spread her arms as if to illustrate the point, then turned to her mother. "See, I told you they wouldn't believe me. I said it was a waste of time you going to the police."

Sylvia sighed then rested her chin in the cup of her hand. Turning to me, she said: "I did tell you this was difficult for her, didn't I? But I do know, better than anyone, that these… *visions* aren't dreams; they're very real, and Connie suffers terrible traumas afterwards. The last time she had one of these 'episodes' it affected her so badly she had to have treatment afterwards for months from a psychiatrist. That's why she won't, or can't, take you to the actual place. You have no idea of the damage it would do to her psychologically."

"Look, Connie," I said, as gently as I could. "As I told your mum, I've experience with this type of phenomenon; and I can't just go back and tell my bosses what you've said and expect them to accept it just like that. They're bound to ask me where the proof is. They're policeman - that's what they do: look for evidence. Surely, you must see that?"

"Yeah; I guess. But I don't like people suggesting I'm some kind of nut, because I'm not. Like Mum say, my visions are real – and they're totally scary." She shook her head again and frowned. "Okay," she went on, "I'll draw you the map. I don't know the exact name of the place but you should find it okay. It's about three or four miles from here. But, like I said, the glade where Alice is buried won't be so easy to find. It's dark and creepy in there, and when you do find it you're not going to like it."

"But can you give me something more solid, Connie?" I almost whispered. "Anything that might convince my superiors? You know – something unique?"

She shot me a look that had 'dummy' written all over it. "Yeah. Tell them Alice has a scar where I think she had her appendix out. It kinda looks like that anyway. Oh," she continued thoughtfully, "one other thing. She's got a mole on her stomach – looks like a half-moon – but light brown. Is that the kinda thing?"

"God!" I thought. "What if this is for real, and she's not making it up or hallucinating?"

"Thank you, Connie," I said. "That's great. Now, if you can draw me the map I'll have something solid to take back to the station. But don't be surprised, will you, if my superiors want to talk to you?"

"That's okay. I don't mind talking to them. Just as long as they don't expect me to lead them to that horrible place."

CHAPTER THREE

Less than an hour later, Brian Horton having persuaded the police car pool to collect us from Sylvia's in a passing patrol car for the journey back to Steelhouse Lane, I was again knocking at the DCI's door, this time feeling a little less apprehensive than beforehand. He nodded at me, and then pointed to a chair as he replaced his telephone.

"So how was your little excursion?" he said curtly, "Seen the Second Coming yet, have you?"

He was his usual sarcastic self, but, undeterred, I cleared my throat and said: "Sir, I know you're going to take the piss – but she was really convincing. Honest."

"Yeah, to you maybe – no surprise there. You're not s'posed to be taking these nutters seriously – you're just meant to get 'em off my back. Don't tell me you reckon these 'psychic visions' are for real! Jesus wept, if you're that fucking gullible you want a change of career girl. This is a police station, not a bleedin' spiritualist church!"

I felt my face reddening at the barb. It was unkind and unnecessary, I thought. "I realise that, Chief Inspector... And – no – I wasn't 'taken in' by either of them. I did what I've been trained to do - listen, objectively, without prejudging the issues, and then report the findings to my superiors. That is precisely what I'm trying to do – if you'll give me a chance... Sir."

"All right, go on then," he said gruffly. "You've got my attention."

By the time I got to the part about the map his face was suffused with anger. Obviously he'd had enough, and, in fact, he was on the point of exploding. I didn't give him the chance. When I submitted the evidential information he frowned, trying to appear cynical, but without doubt he was suitably impressed.

"Hmm. All right – maybe that *is* interesting. I don't suppose you've checked it out have you?"

"Yes, sir; I have. I asked DS Robbins to talk to Alice's mother. And she's confirmed that Alice *has* had her appendix removed, and she *does* have a half-moon mole on her stomach."

"Jesus! What the hell are we dealing with here?"

"A genuine psychic, maybe?" I suggested.

"Not so quick, constable. She could've found out about that in any number of ways. For instance, this Connie might have a little chum who knows Alice… Knows her well enough to have seen her without her kit on passed on and passed on those little nuggets. On the other hand, it might be some mental game these nutters like playing. A fucking stupid one, yeah, but still a game – not fucking evidence."

"There is one way to find out, sir."

"Yeah. Do tell?" he replied witheringly

"We could organise a small search team and follow the directions on the map. It shouldn't take that long, and at least we'd know one way or the other."

He pondered this suggestion for quite a while, occasionally referring to the map, as if he was seeking inspiration. "You say this girl – Connie – won't take us to this place on the map?"

"Yes, sir. She says it's too 'scary' – her words, not mine. Her mother says these visions are very traumatic for the child, so she'll do all she can to protect her."

"I think that might be the answer," he said thoughtfully. "If she *is* for real – and I'm not saying she is, mind you – you'll have to talk her into leading the search. That'll call her bluff."

"Sir, I don't that'll work," I protested. "Connie was adamant that nothing on earth would persuade her to visit that place. She says it frightens the life out of her – and I believe her."

"Constable," he said testily, "you are a policewoman, aren't you – not a wet-nurse? So use your training. Make the silly cow join the search."

I was really stuck now. If I asked him for suggestions he would think I was an idiot; if I didn't I would still be an idiot because I had no idea how to go about persuading the girl. "Stuff it!" I thought. "All I've got to lose is my job! Oh yeah, and my career… And my self-respect and…"

"Sorry sir, but it's not like I've got the experience you have. Can you give me any hints how I might persuade her, or her mother?"

He glowered at me for a moment, and then softened.

"You've just answered your own question, Angela."

"Sir?"

"The mother. That's how you get through to the daughter. You tell Mrs Rowden that if her daughter won't cooperate you'll have to arrest her – the mother, not the daughter – for wasting police time. That should focus her fucking mind a bit, don't you think?"

"Are you serious?" I gasped. "You'd actually arrest her?"

"Too bloody right I would! Since that little girl disappeared we've had more than 500 calls from punters, most of them genuine, and all of them out of concern… None of them any fucking use, mind you. But this one – *this one* – has the gall to actually turn up here, waste my time listening to her crazy story, and then gets me to send you off to talk to the kid, only to be told that the most she's prepared to do to prove her story is to draw us a pretty picture. If that ain't wasting police time then I don't know what is. You gonna tell me I'm wrong, eh? What about you, Constable Horton?"

Brian Horton had been sitting there like a deaf mute, saying nothing. "You've got a point, sir."

"And how did she handle herself?" he was asked.

"Well, she handled herself quite well, sir. But as you said, I was only an observer."

I butted in. "Since you put it like that – yes, sir, I do agree with you. Shall I go back on my own or take Constable Horton with me?"

"No. You don't take Horton with you, Angela; you take DS Robbins. I want them to realise we mean business. I'll set it up for you – but you make sure this Connie's going to be at home. She's the one we're putting the pressure on. Okay?"

"Thank you, sir. I'll sort it."

* * * * * * * * *

It took the team the better part of two hours to find the road into Longwood, the site Connie had pinpointed on her map; it was some four or five miles from the city centre. In reality it was nothing more than a dirt track, barely visible from the side road leading in to it. Frankly, if Connie had not been with us, I doubt if we would have found it at all. As it was, we were able to proceed only so far with the vehicles before the undergrowth closed in on us, and we were forced to continue on foot. Even though there were eight of us in all, I still found myself sharing the teenager's description that this was a very scary place. I couldn't imagine anyone wanting to visit this place with anything other than evil intent. The foliage seemed to wrap itself around us the more deeply we penetrated the forest. Once or twice I stumbled, catching my trousers, making me glad I wasn't wearing a skirt, and having to be helped back to my feet by a very disgruntled Detective Sergeant Robbins, who regarded the whole excursion as a bizarre pantomime. From time to time he swore aloud at the continuing discomfort, particularly when the heavens opened and the rain dripped onto us incessantly from the overhanging branches. Also, it was becoming increasingly difficult to see as the rain blurred the light from our torches. And I was becoming incredibly weary – my shift had finished hours ago and I wasn't even sure I now qualified for overtime.

From time to time we stopped while Connie rechecked her bearings. The whole time, since leaving her house, she had not spoken, even though I tried my best to apologise to her for the threats to her mother, which had forced her to accompany us. I had tried to be as gentle as circumstances would allow, but it made little impact on the girl. Unfortunately, our dear Sergeant Robbins, on the other hand, was about as tough as they come. He had positively intimidated poor Sylvia to the point where I thought she was going to pass out. He was still relatively young for a detective sergeant; much more to the point, he was extremely good-looking. He was a little over six foot, with a mop of sandy hair and the sharpest blue eyes I had ever seen. It would be an understatement if I were to admit to fancying him, even in these ludicrous surroundings.

In the event, his tactics certainly did the trick. When Connie saw the state her mother was in she readily agreed to join the search.

Eventually I gave up the attempt at conversation; it was fairly obvious the girl blamed me for her distressing situation, making it clear by her silence that she was here only under extreme duress. I had to admit, secretly, that I had a great deal of sympathy for her, and in a way I was half hoping that the whole episode would turn out to be, as the DCI suspected, some kind of irrational game.

* * * * * * * * *

We must have been travelling for almost an hour, fighting our way through the foliage, before we came across the glade Connie had earlier referred to. Very little light was visible, but what there was was sufficient for us identify the woodman's cottage she had also mentioned. I felt a shiver run up my spine when I spotted it. Either Connie's visions were indeed real, or else she had visited this place a number of times in the past. She couldn't possibly have known about it otherwise.

At the sight of the single-storey building Connie began to shiver, just slightly at first, them almost uncontrollably. When I put my arm around her shoulder she didn't resist, convincing me she was genuinely frightened. She refused to enter the derelict cottage, so I stayed outside with her while Sergeant Robbins and two of the others went in. It seemed to be an age before they came out, the sergeant looking particularly grim.

"What?" I asked. "Found something?"

He nodded but didn't explain. Instead he dialled a number on his mobile, and I heard him asking for a police helicopter and forensic assistance. He gave instructions as to our location, and then instructed us to form a ring with our flashlights pointing upwards.

Standing in the open we were all soaked by the time the helicopter touched down. The DCI and a couple of civilians emerged with various equipment and went into the hut. I was later informed they were SOCO – Scene of Crime Officers.

Connie, holding my hand, said: "They've found the kids' clothes." She started to weep softly. "The bodies are in the pit at the back of the building."

I took her with me inside, and was met with the traditional glower from the DCI. "What you doing in here?" he demanded.

"Connie says the children's bodies are in a pit at the back of this hut."

He rubbed his face wearily with his hand, glancing round at the neatly arranged piles of clothing in a corner of the room, many of the individual items clearly showing bloodstains. "Can you show us, young lady?"

Connie didn't speak; she simply turned, led me by the hand, and took me round to the back of the hut.

"Where?" the DCI said gruffly. "What fucking pit? I can't see anything." He pointed to the area around us; there didn't appear to be anything there.

Connie ignored his abuse, walked a few yards towards a bush, pulled back the foliage and revealed a rusty metallic ring attached to what looked like an iron trapdoor.

It took two of the constables to open the cover. An overpowering, foul stench hit us immediately, causing one of the officers to vomit. Covering his face with a handkerchief Jim Robbins approached the cavity and shone his torch into the black hole. It was obviously an old septic tank that hadn't been emptied for years.

"Oh, sweet Jesus! No!" He stepped away from the pit and visibly buckled at the knees, at the same time pressing the handkerchief hard against his mouth. Beyond him I could make out, from the reflection of his torch, the decaying hand from a child's body, encircled, almost like a halo, with hair, her decomposed face protruding above the surface of the revolting sewage tank. A little further away I was sure I could see the skeletal features of a small girl. I felt my own knees give way at this ghoulish sight. But it was Connie who actually pulled me down with the tightness of her grip as she fell to the ground in a faint. Her whole body was convulsing with an epileptic type of seizure. She was frothing at the mouth and her eyes were open but glazed, as if she had escaped into a different world. Frightened for her I leant down beside her, unsure what to do, but wiping her mouth and covering her with my jacket. Then she began to moan, softly at first, and then louder and louder, like a dog grieving at the feet of its master; more feral than human.

"No!" she then screamed. "Don't hurt me! Please don't hurt me again!"

All I could do was hold her to me tightly, tears coursing down my own cheeks. "Poor girl," I kept thinking, over and over. "What have we done to you?"

"Get that kid out of here!" DCI Templar shouted angrily. "This is a crime scene, not a fucking nursery. Robbins, tape off the area and get another helicopter here; we need more equipment. You – Crossley!" he snapped at me. "Take that child back on the 'copter. Get a doctor to meet you at the hospital. And for Christ's sake shut her up, can't you?"

Fuming, I half carried, half dragged Connie away from the scene and towards the helicopter. I remember distinctly hearing Sergeant Robbins telling the DCI to piss off as he dropped what he was doing and came over to help me. "Ignore him, Ange," he seethed. "The guy's an insensitive arsehole."

Together we lifted poor Connie, still sobbing hysterically, onto the helicopter, and Sergeant Robbins gave the pilot instructions.

"Take her to St Thomas's, Andrew, will you? If you radio ahead they'll let you land on the roof. Ange, why don't you go with her? I'd go myself, but I'm going to be tied up here for quite a while - obviously."

I felt sick and dizzy myself at the horrors I had witnessed, and, frankly, I was relieved to be leaving the nightmarish scene. During the journey I hugged Connie, trying my best to soothe her, but without success. Fifteen minutes later we landed at the hospital and I transferred the weeping and trembling young girl into the care of a doctor and a nurse. All I could think was: "Dear God, what have I done to you?" as I half-collapsed against a wall of the hospital roof.

Hindsight was a wonderful thing; if only we'd believed her story at the beginning all this could have been avoided. I felt terrible: consumed with guilt, and for the first time regretting ever joining the police force. I stayed on the roof for a while, ignoring the heavy rain, unconcerned that I had lost my jacket and torn my trousers, not even worrying whether I should go back to the scene or just go home. In the end I decided to wait at the hospital to see what the diagnosis was on Connie. She was my responsibility and there was no way I could abandon her, although I did drift off to sleep in the waiting room. An hour or so later a nursing sister awakened me to tell me that Connie was heavily sedated. She also said her mother was on the way, so it seemed sensible for me to return to the station for an update.

CHAPTER FOUR

It actually took the best part of three days to complete the picture from the crime scene. Seven bodies were recovered in total: all of them children; all of them girls. Two were still awaiting identification and could have been in that hellish pit for more than three years. The children who were identified, apart from Alice (who was local), were all from different areas of the country and had been missing for varying periods of time. One was from the Stoke-on-Trent area, whilst another was from as far afield as Leeds. Until now, because of the wide geographical spread of the victims and the lack of liaison between the various forces, plus the lack of any hard evidence, it had not been concluded by the authorities that a serial child murderer – a dangerous paedophile – was at large. Consequently, the National Crime Squad was never informed; but even if it had been notified it was still in its infancy and so disparate that the chances of its pulling together a unified strategy were extremely slim.

The results from the forensic examination of the bodies were also disappointing: the decomposition of the victims had removed any DNA evidence that might have been there. Conversely, the blood samples on the clothing offered no clues; it wasn't even possible to determine, other than in the case of Alice, who the blood originated from. Some faint DNA traces were discovered on the body of Alice, however, but again – unfortunately – there was no match in the National Computer Bank. It would, however, remain on file for future reference. The very thought of the terror those poor children must have endured – vicariously passed on to Connie – caused me to have recurring nightmares for months afterwards. I doubted I would ever erase the picture of the crime scene from my mind.

A further sad by-line to these tragedies was informing the parents of the dead children, especially when they wanted to know how their child had died, and we were unable to tell them. It was a task I became involved in as, at my rather impudent request, I had now been transferred to CID, on a temporary basis, and given my own desk and terminal. Thrilled as I was at this mini-promotion, it was still particularly hard for me, because I was taking on board part of the responsibility for their deaths. Common sense told me, of course, that this was quite ridiculous, but then in the question of murder, particularly where children were involved, common sense always seemed to disappear. What hit me the hardest was seeing the haunted look in the parents' eyes as the news of what had happened to their daughter was imparted to them. And it went without saying that life 'would go on', except that – in their case – they would remain forever-tortured spectators as the tide of life swept past them. For them, life was virtually over.

* * * * * * * * *

I went back to the hospital a number of times, but Mrs Rowden had left specific instructions that no one was to see Connie. It was only through a combination of luck and perseverance that I finally made contact with Sylvia. I bumped into her, unexpectedly, one afternoon at the hospital; she knew it was me but she avoided looking at me, averting her eyes as if in the hope that I might disappear. Ever the persistent one, I caught her by the arm, bringing her to a halt.

"Sylvia, please! Why won't you let me see Connie? I've been here nearly every day now for over a week. How is she? No one will tell me anything."

"Leave us alone!" she snapped. "Haven't you done enough damage?"

"Please. I know you must be angry with us. Angry with me, if you like. But I promise you, no one meant to hurt her. We were just trying to find a missing girl - a girl we now know was viciously attacked and murdered... The DCI had to check out Connie's story – and he had to do it the only way he knew..." I maintained a hold on her arm. "I'm really sorry, Sylvia. But I've got to know how Connie is. I've been so worried about her." At the same time I was thinking to myself: "Come on; answer me, woman. I'm not some kind of monster."

"She's being transferred, if you must know."

Puzzled, I repeated her statement. "Transferred? What do you mean?"

"Come on, constable; you're not a complete idiot. Transferred as in children's psychiatric hospital. She's had a complete mental collapse, and the doctors doubt she'll ever fully recover."

She pointed a finger at me angrily. "I hope you lot are proud of yourselves, especially after I warned you what'd happen. Now, piss off and leave me alone! I've got nothing more to say to you. You got that?" She turned to leave, then paused and added: "Oh – one more thing. Before Connie became totally catatonic she told me she'd had a clearer vision of the murderer. She might even have been able to identify him, given more time. Now you'll never know, will you? At least, not from my daughter."

I was speechless. All I could do was to stand there, rendered numb and horrified, as I watched Sylvia walk away.

It was a situation that would haunt me for years to come, and I don't believe the guilt ever did completely leave me. What I was left with was a feeling of immense sadness for those poor children.

And my only companion for many years was the haunting shadow of remorse at the part I had played in the whole episode.

CHAPTER FIVE

Of course, matters didn't just end there. Next came the autopsies on the bodies, all of which – other than the earlier victims, whose cause of death would never be determined – shared the same MO: death by strangulation, following sexual assault including rape. The CID spent many months investigating the murders of the children, involving a great deal of man-hours, interviewing known – or even suspected – paedophiles and investing a tremendous amount of resources. I myself spent hour upon hour, either in the incident room checking lists of known offenders, or out on the streets with many of the other CID officers, interviewing potential witnesses. It was frustrating work, and the pressure was immense and unrelenting.

Despite nationwide involvement, national exposure in all the media, and even appeals for public help on the Crime Watch programme, it seemed as though the trail ended at the crime scene itself. There were simply no clues, other than the possible DNA sample, which might – or might not – have come from the killer; there was no other evidence. Even the clothes found in the woodsman's cottage revealed nothing. Either our man had been extremely lucky or he was very cunning and had some knowledge of forensics. In the event time went by and the killer was never found, although the investigation remained open as an 'unsolved' case, and it would stay on the files indefinitely. Then, increasingly, other crimes took up our time and resources, and the 'paedophile killer' case slipped from the headlines and into the background.

One benefit that did arise from the tragedy was the creation of a computerised National Paedophile List, comprising convicted – and also known, or even suspected – paedophiles. This was followed shortly afterwards by a National Sex Register. Now, any felon with convictions for sex crimes against children – or, later, even adults – went onto a register and was legally required to check in with the police to confirm his whereabouts.

And, from now on, if any child went missing the computer could be searched for possible suspects and cross-matched with the MO for linkage. It was highly unlikely – unless our man was a complete unknown – that there would ever again be a repeat of the terrible crimes that I had been involved in, and which had had such a traumatic effect on Connie.

As I had promised myself, I travelled, almost religiously, the 30 miles or so to Forest Hills, down the A45 to the outskirts of Coventry, to the psychiatric hospital specialising in children's disorders. The hospital was discreetly situated in extensive grounds some way from the main Birmingham to Coventry road. Whilst it was a typically late Victorian building, money had, nevertheless, obviously been allocated for an extensive refurbishing programme to make the institution appear more up to date and less like an old-style mental hospital from the nineteenth century.

Over time my visits to Connie developed into a bi-monthly vigil. I would sit with her for an hour, sometimes two, talking to a young girl who was in reality a completely blank page, and my conversations with her were, in effect, merely writing new chapters.

Connie had slipped back into a world of defensive make-believe, where her mind had totally blocked out the horrors of that night in the woods. She knew her mother, of course, but she had no recollection of who I was. Initially, I'm sure she thought I was in some way connected with the hospital. At first it was a kind of penance, if you like, for my sins, but gradually, for reasons that I didn't fully understand, I drew closer to her. I found myself actually chatting to her as I would a friend, telling her about all my gossip, laughing whenever I thought something I said might seem funny. I shared my excitement with Connie when I received a police sponsorship to attend Warwick University to study for a degree in criminology, assuring her at the same time that I would still be able to visit.

Sometimes it tore at my heart to see this teenage girl, almost unknowingly, transforming over time into a beautiful young woman. And all the time she remained in a world of retreat. For Connie, reality was the here and now. The past no longer had any meaning; perhaps it never would again. She had escaped the horror of her experiences and found sanctuary in the dark recesses of her mind.

I remember on one occasion, after visiting Connie, being invited by Dr Simmons, her psychiatrist, into his office for a discussion. He was a giant of a man, standing well over six feet, but still managing to remain slim. He was in his mid-fifties, with grey silvery hair and a ruddy, cheerful complexion. His eyes seemed to hold a permanent twinkle, as if he had seen everything and was still able to smile at life. I thought he was a lovely man, and so easy to talk to.

"Come in, Angie," he said, warmly, and pointed to the couch for me to take a seat. "So," he went on, after we were seated, "how's our young patient today?"

"She seems well enough in herself, Doctor," I said. "Physically, I mean; but psychologically I can't see any difference. But then, you'd know more about that me... Is that what you wanted to talk to me about?"

"No," he admitted, smiling; "I was just opening the conversation. What I really wanted to say was that I'm a bit worried about you."

"I don't understand."

He rubbed the side of his face for a moment, as if seeking the right words. Then he said, "I suppose what I should really be asking you is: 'Why do you keep blaming yourself for Connie's condition?'"

I sat there for a few moments, mouth wide open in dumb silence. Then I said, "Well, I don't know about blame... But I do feel some sort of responsibility... I mean, her collapse might be down to us. But isn't that pretty normal in the circumstances?"

"Really? You think you're responsible?"

"Yes, really. Have you heard the story, doctor?"

"Not your version of it, no. I know from the newspapers and Connie's mother about the murdered children, of course, and what the whole thing's done to her daughter. And I've had a briefing of sorts from your superintendent – he and I go back quite a way. But your personal role in it hardly came up. So why don't you talk me through it now?"

So I proceeded to do so: about how Connie was a psychic, how she had experienced visions from time to time, and the traumatic effect they had on her – leaving out, of course, any reference in our conversion that her gifts could be the real thing. And then I spoke about her mother visiting us at the police station to tell us her daughter might know where the missing child, Alice, could be found. And finally I talked about the part I had played in coercing her – by threatening her mother – into allowing the child to accompany us on the search through the forest. Then, of course, there was the ghoulish nightmare of the dead children in the pit, Connie's subsequent mental collapse and the guilt I had suffered ever since.

"Tell me, were you brought up in a religious family?"

I felt myself frowning at the question. What had that to do with anything?

"As a matter of fact, yes," I replied eventually. "My mother's a devout Catholic – or so she reckons; not that you'd think so looking at her lifestyle. Not exactly up for a sainthood. But, yeah, I went to a convent. The Sisters of Mercy educated me. Why? What's your point."

"Do you still see your mother?" he asked, ignoring my question.

"Yes. From time to time," I answered. "She remarried a few years back and moved away so I don't get to see her as much as I'd like."

"How about your father. Was he religious?"

"I have no idea. I never met him – apparently he did a runner just after I was born, so I doubt it. Why all the questions, Doctor?"

"Have you never wondered where this disproportionate sense of guilt comes from?" he asked, again ignoring my question.

"Not really, no. But then, I'm not convinced it's out of proportion. You've heard the story now; surely you must agree I was at fault?"

"Actually, no I don't." He ran a hand through his hair, again as if he were trying to find the right words. "It's not uncommon, you know, for people who were raised in the Catholic faith to carry forward the stain of 'original sin' into their daily lives. This is something the Church encourages in the family; it's their way of controlling people all the way through the generations."

"And what d'you suggest we do about it – apart from ensuring that the next generation is protected from this religious 'disease'?"

This brought a smile to his face. "Actually, that's not a bad idea. But I'm being serious, Angie. I believe that if it's passed on through generations there is a danger of it becoming endemic. Worse still, it has been known to cause the more sensitive to become partly dysfunctional.

"In the case of Connie, you were just doing your job. Not a nice job, either, at the best of times. And you were trying to find a missing child; and then you found out the kid had been violated and brutally murdered. Which is fair enough – surely. And you seem to forget that the order to coerce the mother came not from you but from your superiors. And, from what you tell me, it's not as if you did that all on your own! Your detective sergeant was with you – and he's the senior officer after all.

"So, I don't agree with you Angie. You weren't at fault, any more than your Sergeant was. Responsible? All right, yes, partly. To blame? Absolutely not. As I said, you were doing your job. What you've got to ask yourself, though – and please don't take this the wrong way – is whether you can really handle the more, um, *unsavoury* aspects of your job; whether you're psychologically tough enough for a police career." He paused once more, as if he was carefully selecting his words. At least it gave me some time to absorb the import of his little "lecture".

"That nightmarish incident in the forest you told me about," he continued. "It's not going to be the last. There'll be others just as nasty – probably in a different way, but just as vile. I'm sure you must have thought about that, Angie. And you know you'll be expected to absorb the effect it'll have on you – just as you are now. Look, I'm just an observer but all that disaster and human suffering… They come with the territory unless you can find a way to cut yourself off from it. Otherwise every nightmare situation you're involved in is going to make you feel like this. You'll just end up beating yourself up with the victim's pain and distress – and it'll get worse every time. Do you see I'm trying to say, Angie?"

"Christ!" I was thinking. "What's he trying to do to me? I only came in for a friendly chat!" It was all I could do to nod my agreement.

"You certainly wouldn't be the first officer to realise a future in the police is not for them." He held out a hand, apologetically. "I know what you're thinking, and you're right. It's really none of my damned business, because you're not my patient, and you've every right to say so. I really am trying to act in your best interests though."

Best interests? It sounded to me as though he was recommending that I should resign!

"I'm talking to you as a friend here, Angie – not as a shrink. I've watched you for a while now, and you're trying to somehow take on Connie's pain because of this overdeveloped sense of contrition. And

I'm not about to apologise for worrying that you're clothing yourself in some shroud of guilt.

"Jesus! You don't pull your punches, do you?" I said, my mouth agape with astonishment.

"I did say 'forgive me' to start with," he said, smiling. "The question is, though, whether I've struck any chords with you?"

I shook my head, trying to conjure up a balanced response to the good doctor's analysis of my guilt complex. Eventually I replied, "I can't really say whether you're on the nail or not - as you know, Doctor, I'm hardly qualified to give a professional opinion." All the while I was thinking: "What the hell has this got to do with you anyway?"

"Okay, I accept that I've a habit of going over the top," I continued, "but surely that's understandable if you think what we put poor Connie through. She was terrified of going into that woodland – and basically we blackmailed her poor mother into letting her daughter go with us, and sod the little girl's fears. So I'm not too clear what you're saying. Okay, you might have a point. Maybe my guilt feelings a bit much; the question is: how am I supposed to deal with them?"

I think I was actually having two conversations at the same time here. On the one hand I was talking rationally with the doctor, and on the other I was getting really bloody angry because he was treating me like a child.

He looked at me thoughtfully for a moment before continuing. "Well, the first step, Angie, is to recognise that there really is a problem. I'm not altogether sure I've even convinced you of that."

"Bloody right you haven't," I thought.

"All I can suggest for now is that you keep in mind what I've said, and if you ever feel a need to talk I'm here for you. In the meantime, I hope I haven't put you off seeing Connie; I know how much she looks forward to your visits and stopping them will do neither of you any good. Will you do that for me?"

"Of course. And there's no way you could discourage me from visiting my friend –that's what we've become, you know: close friends, even though she hardly knows who I am. And I do appreciate you're only trying to help me.

"Mind if I ask you something, Dr Simmons?"

"No. Go ahead."

"You're not suggesting by any chance, are you, that I might have a psychiatric problem – you know, a potential mental illness?"

He shook his head vigorously as if to make his point. "No! No! No! Not at all, Angie. You misunderstand me. What I'm saying is that a trauma like the one you've just been through is bound to have a fundamental effect on your conscious mind – and maybe even your judgement. In your particular case, given your strong Catholic upbringing, it's perfectly understandable that you'd associate personally with blame – it's a kind of 'sackcloth and ashes' thing. And all I had in mind to help you, Angie, was for us to meet now and then and give you a chance to express yourself; to talk about whatever it is that's bothering you. If you'd be up for that, I really believe it'll help you tremendously to develop a sense of self-awareness."

He held up his hands in a gesture of surrender. "Well, I've said my piece; I'm just glad I apologised in advance! But seriously, I really do think you should recognise there's a specific type of behavioural problem arising from deep traumatic shock that's getting more and more common with personnel who're in the line of fire, so to speak. Your profession's probably at the top of our list of sufferers - and there's a growing consensus in the psychiatric and psychology professions that this phenomenon should be accepted as a very real issue and dealt with accordingly. Especially in your case because – and I do hope you won't mind me saying this – you're still very young and therefore a lot more vulnerable than your older colleagues."

I had to admit he had a point there.

"I don't want to go on about it…"

"But you're going to," I interjected with a wry grin. He nodded sheepishly.

"Um, yes… As I said, having watched you with Connie over a period of time I've concluded that you're not equipped to deal with this on your own. Would you at least grant me that?"

"Well, I can see the sense in what you're saying. And if memory serves, the police service does have some kind of counselling facility… if you really think I need it."

His face took on a cynical expression. "And how many of your fellow officers do you know who've used it?"

"Yeah, right. Point taken. We'd be as embarrassed as hell if we thought anyone knew we were seeing counsellors." The thought came to me that he did talk some sense occasionally!

This brought a smile to his face – a welcome relief from the heavy stuff we had just dealt with.

"So," he said, "shall we leave it open? If you ever feel the need to talk to a professional I'm here for you as a sounding board - and since you nearly always let us know in advance of your visits to Connie, I can usually fit you in if you feel like a chat. And if you don't…well, that's fine too."

"Would you mind if I gave this some thought, Dr Simmons? Frankly, it's all a bit of a shock. I think I need to come to terms with that first. Is that okay?" I was hoping that would be enough to get me off the hook!

He treated me once more to that warm smile of his, and then nodded his agreement. "It's no big deal, Angie, believe me. Whatever you decide's fine with me. Before you go, though, mind if I ask you one or two questions about Connie's background?"

"No, course not. But I don't know that much. I only got to talk with her mother a couple of times."

"Did Connie or her mother ever mention Mr Rowden?"

"There never was a Mr Rowden. Sylvia told me she and Connie's father were never married; apparently she was his housekeeper at the time and Connie was an accident – a one-night stand. She did mention that they left when Connie was about eight and moved into their present house. Other than that there's not much I can tell you, except she did say that she and Connie didn't like to talk about him."

"Did she say why?"

"No. That's all that was said, although they did exchange what I'd describe as a conspiratorial glance. Not that I could read anything into it. Why do you ask, doctor?"

"Because he's become something of a mystery. In all the time his daughter's been a patient here Connie's father's made no attempt to visit her - or even make any kind of contact. I'd have thought the least he could do was phone. But not a word. Must admit I find it a little worrying; it's certainly unnatural in my experience."

"Well, I got the impression that was never a real dad to her; as Sylvia said, she was just an accident - and it certainly isn't as if she was the product of a meaningful relationship."

He got up from his chair and ran his hand through his hair. "Perhaps you're right... But, from what you tell me, she was a part of his world for eight years. Poor kid!" Sadly he shook his head. "She's never known a real family and now she's got this to contend with. I'm glad she's got you as a friend – she certainly needs someone other than doctors and nurses," he said, walking me to the door. "You will let me know what you decide, won't you? And, please," (he flashed me one of his lovely smiles again) "I don't want you worrying about it. Okay?"

It wasn't that easy, though. He had just put me through the wringer, psychologically speaking, and, to put it mildly, I felt exhausted and drained. I suppose I was also suffering from mild shock; it had never occurred to me before speaking with Dr Simmons that my feelings of guilt over Connie's breakdown were not normal, and in fact should be dealt with professionally. I left the hospital feeling decidedly uneasy, for a number of reasons. Aside from the 'counselling' I had received, and its effect on my self-confidence, I was also – for some strange reason – remembering the question I had asked, rhetorically, that night in the woods. Had Connie visited the burial site before? Either that – for some obscure reason – was true, or else her psychic visions were absolutely genuine.

I made a mental note to make some further enquiries.

CHAPTER SIX

A number of times, after my discussion with Dr Simmons, I called on Sylvia during college recesses to see if I could help in any way; and also, to be absolutely truthful, to try and build some bridges that might make me feel better about things. And of course, I did have a hidden agenda; I wanted to find out more about Connie's psychic gift. Was it something she was born with? Did it run in her family? How often did it manifest itself? To be honest, I know I was being nosy, but at the same time I couldn't help but find the subject fascinating. On each occasion she refused to let me in; in itself this was perfectly understandable, but what I found increasingly worrying was her self-evident decline into depression. She had lost a lot of weight since Connie's hospitalisation; her face was terribly drawn and pinched, and her eyes were lifeless, as if she had lost all interest. I tried to talk to her, even with one foot in the doorjamb to prevent her from closing it in my face; urging her to seek medical help. Her final response was to tell me to piss off.

I never went back after that; nor did I hear anything more either from her or about her until, some time later when a report came into the Steelhouse Lane station of a woman discovered dead in her home. Tragically, police investigations had determined it was Sylvia Rowden. It had all the hallmarks of suicide, although no note was found at the scene. Obviously, I took the trouble of reading the investigating CID officer's report into the death. It seemed that when the milk on the doorstep had piled up sufficiently, someone – one of the neighbours, in fact – had become concerned and had called the police. Sylvia's body had been found dangling, a rope around her neck, from the upstairs banister. The autopsy report listed the cause of death as strangulation, and although the crime report said there were no suspicious circumstances attached to the death. I still had difficulties in accepting it was suicide, but then that could simply be an overreaction of the novice detective in me. And she had left no note, which I was informed, is the normal act in cases of suicide. It was a terrible shock, made all the worse because I had been unable to get through to her. For me, it was yet another layer on the already burdening conscience I was struggling to deal with.

The next day I went over to see Dr Simmons, relaying the tragic news. It took me the best part of two hours to make the trip, the heavy rain slowing the traffic almost to a standstill. I had Garth Brooks, the country-music superstar, for company though, to take my mind off the road conditions. It occurred to me that morning that the Midlands' weather could just as easily be included in its list of tourist attractions!

Doctor Simmons was just as shocked as I was, and he asked me if I could be present when he told Connie the tragic news. I agreed, but it was the last thing I wanted to do. How do you tell an already trauma-tised girl that her mother is dead?

When we entered the room, Connie was sitting on the bed silently weeping.

"Connie," I said softly, "can we talk to you?"

"I know," she sobbed. "It's about my mother, isn't it?"

"How did you know, Connie?" Dr Simmons asked.

"I just do. She's dead, isn't she? And it's my fault."

"No, Connie. Please don't say that; it just isn't true." I went to put my arms around her but she pushed me away.

"Please. Leave me alone. I don't want to talk about it. She's dead and there's nothing anyone can do."

She lay back on the bed, her shoulders heaving with her sobs. I sat down on the only chair.

"I'll stay here with her, doctor, if that's alright. I can't leave her alone like this."

As Dr Simmons nodded then left the room, I took out a handker-chief to wipe away my own tears. "This poor child," I thought. Her life seemed to be a catalogue of tragic events. At the time it didn't strike me at all strange that Connie had experienced some psychic communication about her mother's death. Why should I? I was too upset, anyway, at witnessing her terrible grief. She cried for what must have been a good hour before falling asleep. I kissed her gently on the forehead before leaving, and headed for the doctor's office.

"How could she possibly have known?" he asked, somewhat rhetor-ically, after I was seated.

"Oh, that," I said, almost dismissively. "That's just Connie, I s'pose. She doesn't live in the same world as us; she doesn't see things the way we do... Or maybe she does but, more, somehow."

"Remember the story I told you about the children in the woods? Well, that threw me at first. When you think about it rationally, it's pretty bizarre: you know, visions of dead children, the traumatic effect on Connie, then realising it wasn't just fantasy. I think this is the same kind of thing. It still scares the shit out of me though... I don't even know why really. I'm glad you saw it for yourself, though; if it helps you understand why I felt so guilty after that incident."

He shook his head in bewilderment.

"No. It can't be right," he protested. "There's got to be a logical explanation."

"Yeah, right. Maybe she's got a mobile hidden in her room!"

For a moment he thought I was being serious. He sat there considering the matter, and then began to shake his head once more.

"I'm sorry, Angie, I just don't believe in all this psychic stuff. OK, your story about the murdered children and Connie's visions sounds plausible on the face of it. But didn't you say yourself that you wondered whether she'd been to those woods before?"

"I did at the time, yes; and again later, as it goes. But if that's the explanation, it doesn't bear thinking about. It'd mean the murderer actually took her there. And that I don't believe. I really don't. No. *I'm* sorry, doctor, but it looks like you're going to have to face up to the fact that this 'psychic stuff' is for real."

"Yes, well, you might be in a hurry to accept that – but I'm not. And anyway, I think it's Connie we should be worrying about right now, don't you?"

"Of course. Shall I stay with her for a while, d'you think? She was sleeping when I left but..."

"Maybe not... Let's leave her, shall we... Sleep's a natural escape from grief for children so at least she's at peace for a while. I'll get one of the nurses to sit with her so she won't wake up alone. But Angie... I think it would be good for her if you could come and see her again tomorrow. Can you do that? I mean... know you've got a job to do and..."

"No problem – I'll be here. I'm off duty for the next three days anyway so I'll come again in the morning if you like. By the way, I know it's a difficult time, but what you said about my getting some counselling? Do you still think I should after today's events?"

"Definitely, Angie. Even more than before, if anything. You're now in danger of irrevocably convincing yourself that you're right to take responsibility for Connie's condition. And that just can't be right. It's also very unhealthy. Let's have a chat about it tomorrow, shall we?"

"Of course. I look forward to it."

* * * * * * * * *

I spent the next three days with Connie, slipping between her room and Dr Simmons' office, where he talked to me at length about the origins of self-imposed guilt. He also encouraged me to talk about myself, about my childhood, even about how I felt being brought up without a father. Surprisingly, I found the sessions very helpful; I also felt I could relate to Connie more after that, both of us – if you like – having a father who had rejected us. I can't claim to have been cured overnight from these sessions, but I could certainly see the benefit in them, and I was grateful to Dr Simmons for his time and patience.

Connie said very little during my visits; I could only guess at what she was feeling. She cried frequently and for long periods at a time, sobbing for her mummy. All I was able to do was hold her and comfort her as best I could. For a time she was inconsolable, until Dr Simmons relented and allowed her to attend the funeral. We both accompanied her to what was a very sad occasion, but – all credit to Connie – she handled it resolutely. After that she seemed to become stronger, a little at a time, as if it had been a kind of breakthrough. If anything the experience had drawn us closer together and we became good friends, although she still made no mention of the awful events that night in the woods.

When I said goodbye at the close of my brief leave from the station, Connie was considerably improved. She allowed me to give her a parting kiss and a hug, and made me promise I would be back to see her soon. As for myself, it was a salutary experience in a number of ways. I had made a close friend, and, moreover, the sessions I had with Dr Simmons – although not producing anything dramatic – were teaching me to become more circumspect in my daily life.

CHAPTER SEVEN

My story should have ended at that point. There was really nothing else to tell. The murderous paedophile was never caught, despite the intensive efforts of the police and the associated publicity through the media, and although children continued to disappear from time to time there was never a correlated pattern that might have caused the authorities to conclude that the perpetrator was still active. And so the case remained on the files – crimes of this magnitude are never closed – and was allowed simply to lie dormant.

Over the years that followed I ceased altogether to think of Connie as a kind of adjunct to the case of the murdered children, a sort of impersonalised entity over whom I had a responsibility. Instead we seemed to develop a special type of relationship, and we came to regard each other as true friends: fellow soul mates, with each of us needing the other – the difference between us, of course, being the level of awareness. I bought a variety of clothes for her to wear – not exactly designer gear, I couldn't possibly afford that quality, but simple skirts and coloured tops that might help to make her feel more human, and the odd sweater in winter.

Never once though, throughout the years, was she able to recall anything of the horrors she had endured. Dr Simmons never lost hope, patiently continuing with her treatment: a combination of drugs and intensive psychotherapy. I continued to have the occasional session with him, and was pleased at the benefits I was getting. I felt that my sense of self-imposed guilt was slowly beginning to relax its hold on me. I visited Connie on a fairly regular basis, and I know how much she looked forward to our chats. Also, she seemed to have adjusted to the tragic suicide of her mother, and, although I doubted if she would ever completely recover, I liked to think that in some way I was able to help her, if only by repeatedly assuring her she was always in my thoughts.

I quite enjoyed the years at university, partly because of the subject matter, and partly because, during term breaks, I was able to carry on working as a policewoman, spending time in the CID offices at Steelhouse Lane, sometimes on the beat or occasionally with the squad cars;

better still, now I was attached to CID I didn't have to wear that awful police uniform and those ugly and uncomfortable shoes that came with it. By now I was dressing in the latest style of jeans, tank tops, and denim jackets. It was an exciting time, although the work was very demanding. But I did put the effort in at Warwick and it was particularly rewarding when I got a first in criminology.

I was the station's celebrity for a while that summer, the effect of my achievement resulting in an immediate and permanent appointment to the CID – as a detective sergeant, would you believe! As a result of my promotion I was able to afford to rent a one-bedroom flat in the rather unfashionable suburb of Moseley. It was cheap and cheerful but close enough to Steelhouse Lane Station to make it convenient for public transport.

The only one who was predictably ungracious about the development was my old friend, DCI Templar. On the rare occasions he did appear on the scene I tried to keep my distance from him – aside from his rudeness I got the distinct impression he was heavily into the booze.

Other than those idiosyncrasies he had changed very little, and certainly not for the better, although I was no longer the naive 19-year-old shaking with fear at the sound of his voice. Now I was a 23-year-old graduate, confident in my abilities, and quite assertive with it. In short, I was a detective sergeant, and I was determined I would earn the respect of my colleagues in the force, more especially the males who never let me forget I was the only woman amongst them.

One person, besides Connie, who I had kept in close contact with during those years, was Jim Robbins – Detective Sergeant Robbins, now Detective Inspector Robbins.

During the early part of my career Jim was something of a mentor to me. Despite his harsh, professional exterior, there was a caring side to him, which, unknowingly, I must have touched because he went out of his way to help. And there was no ulterior motive, I'm glad to say; not once in all that time did he come on to me, although, I have to admit, there were many instances when I would have welcomed him trying to get into my pants. He was an extremely attractive man, was Jim, as I have mentioned before, but not in any way you would describe as special, but his dark hair and matching eyes drew me to him like the proverbial moth to the flame. He was eight years older than me, and I think it was his dry, almost sarcastic sense of humour that endeared him to me. He made me laugh. He was also always up-front: what you saw was what you got with Jim, and I found him easy to talk to, with no sense of pretentiousness. I found myself growing ever closer to this man.

We started dating shortly after I graduated from Warwick. At first it was more out of friendship; we were good company for each other. At least, that is what he maintained. Then, one night, over the dinner table, he leant across and took my hand in his, and proceeded to tell me how beautiful I was. I had to admit I had gone to a lot of trouble that evening. I was wearing an ankle length black dress with a dangerously low-cut neckline, a choker of pearls that could have been mistaken for the real thing, and my perfume was straight from the Chanel expensive range. But beautiful?

When I realised he was not kidding I felt myself blushing again. My auburn and largely unkempt hair that I was never able to discipline no matter how much I spent at the hairdressers, is a constant source of irritation to me, and despite the compliments I had received in the past about my eyes, I still believed they were unremarkable and would look decidedly better with coloured contact lenses; I also had the shape of nose that only plastic surgery would improve. But I was on the slim side, so I guess that worked in my favour.

Mind you, having denigrated myself, I have to admit I do have very shapely legs, and they have been known to prompt more than the occasional wolf whistle. I'm also told I have beautiful white and even teeth, and, since I do take extra care with them, I am inclined to agree with that. When I tried to protest to Jim about his perception of me, however, he responded by placing a finger over my lips to keep me quiet, insisting that he had always thought me alluring. What had prevented him from approaching me in the past, he said, was the possibility that I might have thought he was taking advantage of a young novice. All that had since changed, and he felt he could now open up to me. He then confirmed his feelings by stretching forward and kissing me softly on the lips. I felt a shiver of anticipation run down my spine.

Needless to say, one thing led to another and we ended up spending the night together. It began slowly, back in Jim's flat in Edgbaston, with

Jim treating me as though I were a china doll. I remember him fumbling, first with the zip on the back of my dress, and when I had let that fall to the ground he struggled with the clasp on my bra. In the end I ran out of patience, undid it myself, slipped out of my panties, and then grabbed him in a deep sensuous kiss as I felt his penis rising against me. We barely made it to the bedroom.

After that night Jim and I became an item, lovers as well as close friends, and I couldn't have been happier. I am still resisting his constant urging to move in with him, though; I quite like my freedom, and it also makes it easier for me when I visit Connie.

As I said, that would have been an appropriate ending to the story. I realise there are still certain aspects left unresolved, such as: what happened eventually to Connie? And did we ever discover who the murderer was? But then, life itself is never as simple as that, is it? So, at this point they remain unresolved, and my story should have reached a natural conclusion.

Except, a few days later, a curious thing happened. I received a telephone call at the station from Dr Simmons asking me if I could find the time to visit. He refused to satisfy my curiosity on the phone, suggesting it would be more appropriate if I could come to the hospital. No doubt, had it been Jim, he would have put it off until it suited his convenience; but then, he wasn't me. I dropped what I was doing, finished my duties at the station early, then – leaving a note for Jim – I set off for the hospital, not knowing if I was heading for some good news or yet another tragedy. It was a beautiful afternoon for a change, with the sun blazing through the windscreen of the car. I drove most of the way with the visor down to keep the sunlight from my eyes. Also, it was one of those days when the A45 Coventry road was practically deserted, so I had a comfortable but still rather tense journey, listening to the latest Elton John CD, and trying to keep my mind off what the problem might be that awaited me.

CHAPTER EIGHT

Dr Simmons was waiting for me in his office. When I went in I was reminded how large such a small space made him appear. With his height he seemed to tower over the desk, and, I found I had to strain my neck to look at him. He was surrounded on three sides of the room by endless shelves of books, all of them – from the covers I saw – medical textbooks. Two of them, I noticed for the first time, had his name on the spine.

He waved me to a seat in front of the desk, which at least stopped me from having to gaze up at him. He ran a hand through his thinning, silvery hair, and then broadened his smile.

"Angie!" he said, welcomingly. "Good to see you again. I'm glad you could get here so quickly."

I nodded, not sure what to say, afraid of what was awaiting me. He obviously noticed my discomfort and attempted to ease my fears by saying: "Sorry if I alarmed you, but it's not the kind of thing I wanted to discuss on the telephone. I think you'll understand why when I put you in the picture."

"It's Connie, isn't it?" I said, stating the obvious. "Is she ill?"

"No…no, of course not. Well, nothing physical anyway. But she's become frightened all of a sudden. Scared out of her wits. We've no idea why or what's happening to her. That's why I called you; I thought you might be able to persuade her to tell us what the problem is."

I was puzzled, to say the least. Last time I had seen Connie – only two weeks ago – she was a bright and cheerful 17-year-old. Still suffering from her fugue state, of course, and still without any recollections of the cause of her trauma; but certainly not frightened.

"I'm not sure I understand, Dr Simmons. When you say scared, how do you mean exactly? I mean, what make you think that?"

Dr Simmons sighed heavily and rubbed his eyes, as if he were fatigued. "I'm not sure I understand myself, Angie. It started a couple of days ago. Just walk in the room and she jumps out of her skin and her eyes glaze over… No focus – as if she's looking right through you. When I went in to see her she actually screamed, like I was some kind of monster." He sighed heavily. "I don't know what the hell's going on; I've never seen anything quite like it. As a psychiatrist I'm totally at a loss; so I was hoping you might be able to help. I should also tell you, we've got another problem."

"Oh marvellous. What's that?"

"She's talking about leaving the hospital. We can't keep her here, of course, if she's adamant about signing out. She's not a child anymore; she's 17 – still terribly dysfunctional, but free to leave whenever she wishes. We can't make anyone stay who's no danger to others or herself… But the idea of her leaving… Well, obviously it's awfully worrying – and I have a feeling it has something to do with this sense of dread that seems that have a grip on her."

"Leaving? How can she leave? Where could she go? She's… I mean, she can't possibly manage on her own. You're right – basically Connie's still a child."

"I know," he said, heavily. "And obviously if she went it would be against my advice. She knows she's got a long way to go before she's anything like normal, and I'm far from convinced could cope on her own in the outside world. But if she wants to go, there's nothing we can do. Will you talk to her?"

"Where is she now, Doctor?"

"Where she's been for the last 24 hours or so: in her room, cowering on the floor in a corner. She's now refusing to eat anything. Will you see her? Please?"

"'Course I will. Probably best if I see her alone first?"

He ran a hand through his mop of hair.

"Good idea. I'll ring the ward sister and let her know you're on your way up. I only hope you can do something."

I nodded and made my way, via the old, creaking lift, up to the third floor, where the ward sister was waiting for me. Margaret was from the old school, middle-aged with her hair tied back in a bun, and what seemed to be a permanent look of concern on her face.

"Do you want me to come in with you?" she asked.

"No, thanks. I'll be fine. I'll call you if I need anything though, if that's alright."

When I entered Connie's room it was exactly as Dr Simmons had described it: Connie was huddled on the floor, trembling in a corner, looking for all the world as if she was possessed by demons. Her eyes were as big as saucers, and her bottom lip was quivering. She had obviously been crying.

I went over to her and sat beside her on the floor, taking her hand in mine.

"So what's my favourite girlfriend been up to?" I asked softly, squeezing her hand in reassurance. "Whatever it is that's scared you, Connie, I'm sure we can sort it out between us."

She didn't answer at first, but I did get a response. She leant over and buried her head in my bosom, still shaking.

"It's alright, sweetheart," I said, comfortingly, as if she was still a small child. "Let's just sit here quietly, shall we? And when you're ready you can tell me what the problem is. There's nothing to be afraid of, Connie; I'm here now."

"You don't understand," she said eventually. Before I could follow it up my damned pager went off with a persistent screech. I checked it, knowing there could only be the one source. It was Steelhouse Lane. Christ! Talk about timing. I turned it off – a cardinal sin for a CID officer; there was no way I could talk to the station with Connie in this state.

"What don't I understand?" I asked. "It's alright Connie, you don't have to be scared any more; I won't let anyone hurt you."

"He's here," she whimpered, enigmatically. "He's real!"

"Who's here? Who's real? I don't understand."

She gazed at me through tearful eyes and stammered: "Him... That horrible man ... the one from my nightmares... The man who's trying to find me. He's here, Angie; I saw him. It wasn't a dream though – it was real! He exists and he's coming after me."

Momentarily I was stunned. All I could think was: "Jesus, is it starting all over again?"

"How do you know, Connie? Is your memory coming back?" I then began to wonder if she remembered anything about the girls in the forest. "Or are you having bad dreams again?"

"No. I told you – this wasn't a bad dream like before. This was real. He's taken a little girl. Yesterday. I had a vision. I *saw* him."

"Who is he, Connie? Do you know him? Is he the man who killed the children from the forest?"

"Forest?" She looked at me puzzled. "I don't know anything about children in the forest. But I do know I've seen him somewhere before – I'm sure about that. I just can't make him out clearly; it's like looking at a picture through a broken mirror. But it's *him*, the same man I dream about. And he's evil, Angie; really evil – and he knows I've seen him."

"There, there," I said, holding her tightly. "No one's going to come after you while I'm around. Try not to be afraid." I spent a moment with her, until she'd recovered a little, then took my mobile from my bag and sat on the bed whilst I rang the station and asked for Inspector Robbins.

"Robbins," a voice, which I immediately recognised, said.

"Jim? Ange here. You paged me." For some strange reason Jim had decided to address me as Ange rather than the common Angie. I didn't try to correct him – in fact I found it rather personal and pleasing.

"Hi, Ange. I got your note. Where are you? Still at the hospital?"

"Yes. What's up? Urgent? Or just personal?"

I heard him sigh, heavily. "No, sorry, not personal. I think you'd better get back here. We have a situation."

"Lemme guess," I said, pre-empting him. "A child's gone missing – a little girl."

There was silence for a moment, then, trying to keep the astonishment out of his voice, he said: "How the hell did you know that? We only found out a couple of hours ago. What the fuck's going on, Ange?"

"I can't explain now; I'm still with Connie and she's pretty upset."

"Did *she* tell you about the kid?"

"Sort of, yeah - but I was only guessing when I mentioned it to you. She's had another vision. She's seen the man, but only vaguely. I don't know yet if it's connected to the last episode. She still doesn't remember anything about those other children."

"But why now? Why, after all these years, should she come up with this? Do you think they're connected? Or is it just a horrible coincidence?"

"Right now, I don't know any more than what I just said. God knows why she's suddenly got this vision after all this time... Only she can tell us that – but I bet she can't. At a guess I'd say it's because she's beginning to get over it, so her mind's a bit clearer. But who knows, really. What I do know is that Connie's scared – I mean really, genuinely, scared. She's convinced that this man, whoever he is, knows she's seen him and that he's coming for her. There's no way I can leave her in this state; she's far too distraught and scared to be left on her own."

"For Christ's sake, Ange; don't they have doctors and nurses there who can look after her? The kid's obviously disturbed. Look, I know you mean well, but I need you here – now. Understand?"

I returned his sigh, more out of exasperation than anything else. Jim Robbins was my favourite man and I loved him to bits; I just wished that at times he could be less of an arsehole and a little more sensitive.

"Don't be ridiculous, Jim; of course they have nurses. But I happen to be the nearest thing she has to family. I'll get back as soon as I can – when Connie's feeling stronger. But I'm not leaving her on her own in this state. I don't think you get how terrified she is – trust me, she's frightened to death."

"God! You can be bloody difficult at times." He paused, then added: "Okay. I suppose that will have to do. But while you're there it wouldn't hurt to question her a bit more. See if you can find out if there's any connection." As an afterthought, he added: "Ask her, by the way, if she knows where this missing child was taken from. Do it now, Ange. I'll hang on."

"Connie," I said, placing the mobile on the floor next to us. "This little girl you've seen; do you know where this man took her from??"

"Solihull," she said tearfully but without hesitation. "Outside her school. Her mum was late picking her up. She's called Josephine - and I think she's about seven or eight."

"Jesus!" I heard Jim exclaim through the phone. "I got all that. And it's dead right in almost every detail. Josephine Marsden. The mother's car wouldn't start, so she had to take a taxi, which made her late."

I could almost hear the thoughts churning around in his head during the ensuing silence. I think I was as stunned as he was; I continued to sit there, on the floor with Connie, our backs to the radiator, holding the phone to my ear as if I expected it to enlighten me.

"Ange," he said, after a couple of minutes, "you're right. You stay there with Connie. But try to use the time productively, if you can. See if you can get her to open up more. Ask her if she knows where the kid is now. Get her to describe this bastard, if she can; anything that might give us a lead."

"I'll see what I can do," I said cursorily. "But I can't promise. Psychic visions aren't like the telly you know. You can't just switch them on. You've got to make the conditions right, create the mood and have some patience – not unlike myself actually!"

"Give me a break, will you! Oh, a couple of things. Don't let her talk to anyone else about this; we've got to keep a lid on this. And, if you feel you still can't disengage after another couple of hours, give me a ring and I'll come over there. But, Ange, please, seriously – we do need more information."

"Disengage?" I repeated, testily. "You make me - and her for that matter - sound like a bloody gearbox!"

"I only meant…"

"I know what you meant, Sweetie. And don't worry; I know where you're coming from. Speak to you soon."

It occurred to me how difficult it must be for him at times to separate his official duties from his private life.

I cut the connection before he could give me any more instructions, and turned my attentions back to Connie. We were still sitting on the floor, but she did seem to be more settled and a little less scared than she had been earlier. I placed my hand under her chin and lifted it slightly, trying to make her smile. It worked. She returned the grin and let me help her up and onto the chair.

"Was that another policeman you were talking to?" she asked guilelessly.

"Yes, and he's promised to help us."

"How? How can he help me?"

"By catching this man who's hurting the children. And stopping him from hurting you."

"Angie, please; don't talk to me like I'm a baby. I know I've got these cognitive problems, and I'm anything but totally together – but that doesn't make me retarded." She looked at me, an expression of undisguised indignation on her face. "It might surprise you to learn this, but I'm actually quite an intelligent 17-year-old. Fairly well-educated as it goes - I sat three A levels last month. That makes me an adult doesn't it? Yeah. So I'd appreciate it if you'd treat me like one. Why not cut to the chase? He's trying to catch this bastard but he can't do it without my help! There. Is that succinct enough for you?"

I laughed. I couldn't help it – she looked so serious.

"I'm sorry, Connie, really I am. It's just we've known each other for so long I forget you've grown up. I'll try to behave from now on, honest!"

"Great. Just don't patronise me any more. Okay?" She took a flannel from the washbasin and wiped the tears from her face.

"So," she continued, "what's he want me to do?"

"Well, just talk about it, really. He wants me to ask you exactly what it was you saw in your vision. Can you do that, Connie, or would you rather leave it a while - till you feel more in control?"

"No. I'm okay now, thanks. But there's nothing more to tell, apart from what you already know. I don't know where the girl is now - if that's what he's after. The bastard took her away in his car, but it's not like I could follow him. It doesn't work like that." She hesitated and looked at me, frowning. "He's cynical, isn't he – this other copper? He thinks this is crap... *You* believe me though, Angie, don't you?"

"Of course I do. And, no, you're wrong about Jim. He *does* believe you. Really. Because he knows everything you told me checks out. He just wants to understand why you get this vision now – so suddenly. What brought it on? And why now?"

"I'd have thought that was obvious," she replied, indignantly. "Till now I'd only been having nightmares about him. You won't get this but I know it meant he hadn't actually snatched a kid – he was just planning it. But he's done it now. So I see him like it's real... Like in real time, if that makes any sense..." She shook her head, almost as if to say *I* was the dummy – not aware of just how adult she sounded.

What was obvious to me was that either she couldn't make a connection, because of her memory loss, between this incident and the horrors of four years ago, or there simply was no connection between the two. And, if that was the case, then it raised the question even more pertinently: why now? There had been a number of child abductions during the last four years, including savage murders, and whilst some of the perpetrators had been apprehended, it had never been concluded that the serial killer from four years ago was still at work. So why had this particular incident triggered off the vision? The more I thought about it the more convinced I became that we were now talking about the same man, and the reason the vision had surfaced at this stage was because Connie was getting better. I decided, however, that the timing was not right to pursue the issue. So I changed the slant of the conversation. "Do you think you could describe the man for us? If you can remember enough we might be able to put together a photofit of him. Maybe we've already got him on file."

"No," she said forcefully. "He's not on your files. No convictions. Never been nicked."

"How can you possibly know that, Connie? You said yourself you couldn't even remember much about him."

"I don't. But I'm dead sure… Don't ask me how - trust me. This monster's never been caught. He hasn't got a record. In fact, he's taking the piss out of the police."

I shook my head in bewilderment; it felt a bit like *Alice in the Looking Glass*. This was so bizarre. I was reminded of what I had said to Dr Simmons after Connie's mother died, about her living in a different dimension from the rest of us.

"Okay," I said slowly. "Could you help us with a photofit, do you think?"

"Yeah; I guess. It's not going to be easy, though. So tell your beloved constable whatever-his-name-is it won't be an exact likeness; like I said, it was like seeing him through a broken mirror, you know – kinda fucked up."

"Okay," I breathed.

"But, Angie, please," she went on. "Can we keep this between ourselves – and your mate I suppose… I don't want anyone else to know about my... My *thing*... It's hard enough trying to convince this lot here I haven't lost the plot let alone people outside…"

"Of course Connie. But what about your dreams? Do you see him clearly then?"

"No. They're so vague. I can't make out his features - but I *do* know it's the same man. I recognise him from his mannerisms, his shape, even his walk and especially his eyes. Oh God, Angie, please… If he finds out I'm helping you…"

"He won't. He can't," I assured her.

"If he did - if it got out – it's all over. He won't just be stalking… Scaring me... He'll come and get me – he'll have to! And nothing'll stop him"

"He'll never know. No one will. You have my word on that, Connie. And while we're making promises, I want you to promise me something."

"Yeah? What?" she asked, an edge of suspicion in her voice.

"Promise you won't sign yourself out of the hospital without telling me first. I know you can do that any time you like and that's your right - and if you decide that's what you want then I'll support you. I just don't want you to be on your own. Will you do that for me, Connie? Please?"

"Sure. I promise. But you'd better give me your mobile number. If this fucker *does* come after me, he's not gonna phone up and let me know in advance… Don't think murdering bastards do that kinda thing. So, call me old fashioned but I might have to just do a runner."

She wasn't kidding, either, and knowing her as I did I'd be a fool not to take her fears seriously. We spent the next half-hour or so compiling details of our assailant. On the whole he seemed to be pretty nondescript. According to Connie he was around five foot ten inches tall, slim build, thin face, with mousy brown hair slightly balding; probably in his late thirties or early forties. He could literally have been anyone he was so anonymously commonplace. Still, if the police artist could put something together from this description – a face that Connie might recognise – it would give us something to go on. It would be a damned sight more than we had now, that was for sure. Needless to say, I ignored Jim's suggestion that I follow up with Connie the possibility of there being a connection with the child murders of four years ago. Right at this moment I think it would have blown her mind.

I spent the next hour or so with Connie, just chatting in general, really just trying to take her mind off the present issue. A little later I rang Jim back and gave him an outline of Connie's description. He asked me to fax it through to him so he could begin briefing the police artist.

Dr Simmons gladly lent me his fax machine, and at the same time I filled him in on my conversation with Connie, and the promise she had given me about signing out from the hospital. In a way he was quite relieved; at first he had considered she might have had another psychotic breakdown, though he continued to reject any suggestion of psychic phenomena. I didn't argue, especially since this ran parallel with Connie's wishes on the matter.

CHAPTER NINE
0000

It was approaching dusk by the time I left Forest Hills. The fading sun was about to slip over the horizon and the sky was filled with a whole variety of gorgeous reds and pinks. It was a beautiful evening, which had the effect of saddening me that Connie was unable to appreciate the normal, everyday magic of nature. I shook off the feeling and headed back towards Birmingham, leaving behind a promise that I would return the next day. I tried the radio for any news on the missing Solihull child, but other than the inevitable headline there was nothing of any import. So I drove back in silence contemplating Connie's latest scary episode and wondering what its origins might be.

Hopefully, by the time I returned to the hospital the police artist would, have something for Connie to examine, although I suspected either he or Jim would have to accompany me to make any changes. If anything I was more puzzled and confused now about my friend than I had been all those years ago. When her mother had told me her daughter was a psychic I must admit I wasn't too clear on the implications. Oh, I had read about those strange people who dabbled in the occult and life after death, but it hadn't had any meaningful impact on me. Perhaps it was because I was very young myself then. Now, after leaving the hospital, I found myself wanting to know more about this phenomenon. It wasn't that I doubted Connie's abilities. She had demonstrated clearly enough that she did indeed possess this esoteric gift; after all, it was she who had led us to the burial pit in the woods, and it was she who had now informed us about the little girl from Solihull. What I wasn't clear about was: how did this insight work. I mean, did she have visions of other happenings? ...Like, for instance, would she know beforehand if a plane were about to crash? Or if someone were destined to die if they undertook a particular journey on a particular day? It crossed my mind that, since I was suddenly becoming so interested in the subject, I could always research it on the Internet. I made a silent promise to myself that I would do that whenever I had a spare moment.

Jim was still at the station when I got back. It was like history repeating itself. An incident room was already set up on the third floor, and Jim had positioned his desk at the front of the room to head up the investigation; he had placed me, together with two other sergeants, at the head of each of the three columns of desks, manned by detectives, stretching the whole length of the expansive rectangular space. Squads of uniformed police had already been dispatched to the Solihull area, together with dozens of volunteers, to search the surrounding country-side for any trace of the missing child. The thought that there might be some connection between this incident and the horrors of four years ago left me with a sickly taste in my mouth. Since that time there had been other cases of missing children in the West Midlands. That was the kind of world we lived in. Two young girls, about the same age as Josephine, were found murdered, brutally strangled after being sexually assaulted. I recall there was a distinct lack of forensic evidence at both crime scenes. That was about a year ago, while I was still at university. In themselves, they were unspeakable crimes, and naturally provoked outrage among the community. But, at the time, no one considered there might be a connection with the earlier crimes. And there was a very good reason for that since no attempt had been made to bury the bodies. Nor would we now, I suspect, had it not been for Connie's vision, and her conviction that he was here. To my mind this expression could well have been her self-protective way of saying that *he* was back!

Connie's paedophile killer, not unlike serial killers, was the most dif-ficult of all criminals to apprehend, unless they had previous convictions where evidence was on file. The distinction between the paedophile and the serial killer, however, was that although their MOs tended to be very similar – that is, the victim was pre-selected, stalked, and then seized, and there were very few unique 'signatures' in the method of slaughter – the paedophile's crimes were motivated entirely by a sick desire for bestial sexual gratification with children, of either sex. The serial killer, on the other hand, was fed – generally – by a compulsive hatred of women and an uncontrollable urge to destroy them. Invariably, his method of slaughter would be repetitive.

Jim was busy on the telephone when I presented myself in front of his desk. He waved me to a seat and carried on talking, evidently to the Superintendent, going by his tone.

"So," he said, after replacing the phone; "any more information from our psychic? We've got nothing new this end - although someone did report seeing the child being driven away in a car."

I shook my head before replying, "No registration, I suppose?"

He nodded. "Too much to ask. Sod all except that it was blue. Oh yeah - and it could have been a Sierra. So that narrows it down! Fuck all's what we've got – apart from the fact that it backs up Connie's story – about the car, I mean. So we have to assume the girl has been abducted. And fear the worst, I guess."

I leant forward across his desk and cupped my chin in my hands, suddenly feeling very weary.

"Poor thing," I reflected, imagining the terror she must now be going through. "What about the artist, Jim? Any luck there yet?"

"He hasn't come back to me yet. I'm still hoping he'll give us some kind of lead. God knows, we've bugger all else. You clocked the mob of media arseholes hanging round the Reception doors like flies on shit? The duty sergeant's going apeshit."

"Yeah – that's why I used the back stairs. What the hell can we tell them, anyway?"

"Fuck all, that's what. That was the Super on the phone earlier; he wants to issue a statement. I don't suppose you fancy doing it, Ange, do you? Would you? This kind of thing comes across better when it's a woman... You know, sensitive stuff. You'll know how to handle it."

"I s'pose so - if I really have to. But in my humble opinion, I'd have thought a case like this warrants someone high up – not a mere detective sergeant. Don't you think?"

He rubbed his eyes, as if he were trying to remove the exhaustion. "Point taken. I'll get the DCI to do it. All he does these days is sit on his arse waiting for his pension to kick in."

"Can you trust him? I hear he's been on the piss in a big way lately."

He sighed, and then shrugged.

"Yeah. Okay. It's me then. Can you get someone in PR to bang out a bit of blurb for me? You know – sensitive and thoughtful and fucking fast! Tell them I need it in half an hour. Oh, and Ange – chase up the artist, will you? We want a likeness not the fucking Mona Lisa!"

"Have you eaten?" I asked.

"I had a sandwich at lunchtime. Wanna get something later? You and me? Unless you're busy, I mean?"

"Nope. I'm clear. You're on! Catch you later."

The main incident room was a hive of activity as I left to make my way to public relations. Every one of the twenty or so computer screens was lit, casting an eerie fluorescent hue over the desks, whilst printers in the room were stuttering out reams of paper. Telephones had never stopped ringing – no doubt from the concerned public – whilst the noise level made thinking very difficult.

It was call-in time; all known paedophiles, and other offenders on the police sex register, in the area were being subject to intense scrutiny, both for their existing whereabouts and for their alibis for the preceding day. It was a lengthy procedure but, as a means of elimination, absolutely vital. One or two of the duty detectives shook their heads at me in disappointment as I went by; frustration hung heavy in the room.

All of us in the force were affected to a similar extent by crimes against children; it was the unspeakable act committed by unmentionable human garbage. Feelings ran high, anger was the principal motivator, and each officer would contribute everything he had, in time and energy, to trace the missing child. The private fear that each of us shared was: would she still be alive when we did find her?

CHAPTER TEN

There was a buzz of excitement in the incident room when I returned with the draft for Jim's press statement. Evidently, two known paedophiles could not be traced. They were both from the West Midlands, although, presumably, not known to each other, and they had been due to check in with their local police station by no later than 5 p.m. the previous day. Each had failed to do so, and there was no trace of them at their registered addresses. In normal circumstances, the event would have followed standard procedures. A car would have been despatched as a matter of routine; failure to provide justifiable reasons could give rise, were one or the other on parole, to a breach, involving, as a consequence, a return to prison. The two men in question were: a Michael Dobson, aged 35, a convicted paedophile released on parole after serving four years of a seven-year sentence for persistent child sex abuse; and a Jeffrey Hart, aged 67, a long term offender whose parole had only recently expired. Dobson, assuming he was innocent of the present offence, was already in serious trouble. He was the one we concentrated our efforts on, by issuing a general alert, although I was mindful of Connie's assertion that 'her man' had no previous convictions. Still, we had to follow the normal lines of enquiry, so I said nothing at the time to Jim.

As Jim and I were discussing the press release the artist, Reg Smith, arrived with his first outline of the identikit picture. We both grimaced when we looked at it; it could, literally, have been any man between the ages of 30 and 50.

"You're not expecting me to circulate this, are you?" Jim grunted. "We'll have thousands of calls, and there's no way we could handle them."

"Well, it *is* the first shot," Reg protested. "And you didn't exactly give me much to go on." He wasn't very old – I put his age somewhere in the early thirties - and he was very serious about his job. He also gave me the impression he couldn't handle any kind of criticism. A typical temperamental artist in other words, but hardly a Van Gogh.

"So what do you suggest we do – arrest every fucker in town? I can't use this – it could be anyone."

Reg, shrugged non-committal.

"If you do release the photofit, what you gonna say? You don't even know she was kidnapped – she'll probably be found safe and well."

I thought, "Christ, that really is leading with your chin."

Jim glowered at the artist.

"Sometimes, Reg, your talent for deduction amazes me. What the hell do you think we're going to say? 'Have you seen this man? He may or may not be wanted for a crime'?" He sighed with the sheer frustration of it all. "Try not to be so bloody obtuse, will you? The child was last seen getting into this man's car. So we have to find him. Simple as that."

"Why don't we take Reg with us to Forest Hills tomorrow?" I suggested, trying to temper the discussion. "Between him and Connie maybe something will gel... I'd have to get her agreement, of course."

Jim nodded in assent. "Alright. See what you can do, Ange, will you? You and Reg here sort it out between you. In the meantime, I have to keep the wolves at bay with this press statement."

* * * * * * * * *

In the incident room information had already come in about Jeffrey Hart, the older of the two unaccounted-for paedophiles. Detective Sergeant Peter Corkhill, who was a little older than myself, informed us that evidently Hart had been admitted into hospital three days ago, as an emergency patient. He had died this very morning, of heart failure. That reduced our suspect list to a solitary figure: Michael Dobson, about whom there was still no further news. The search for his whereabouts was consequently widened.

Dinner that evening for Jim and me consisted of Chinese takeaways, eaten across his desk in the incident room with plastic chopsticks, and continually disturbed by the noise around us from the team, and the incessant questions that were thrown at him from the detectives. Between trying to eat, dealing with the commotion, and answering phone calls, we managed to spill more rice than we consumed. At least it lightened the proceedings a little. Jim spent the night at the station whilst I went back to my dingy flat to catch a few hours' sleep.

The next morning I rang the hospital from home to speak with Dr Simmons to ask him about the artist and me visiting Connie. He promised to get back to me later on the mobile, so I set off for the station, feeling somewhat down. I recalled Dr Simmons' warning about objectivity; it was about the time when Connie was first admitted to Forest Hills. But, no matter how insular we trained ourselves to be, these cases never failed to impact on us all. I just prayed that the child, Josephine, would be found safe and well, though every instinct within me knew this was not going to happen.

Dr Simmons rang me back whilst I was still in the pool car,- Jim had loaned me its use for the duration of the case - confirming that Connie wouldn't mind my bringing along the artist. I said a quick 'good morning' to Jim at the station, was informed above the hubbub of constant noise there was no further news, then grabbed a recalcitrant Reg from his studio on the fifth floor and headed back towards Forest Hills.

We spoke very little on the way. I think Reg was still smarting at the tail lashing he had received from Jim the night before. When I tried to make conversation, the only response I got was a perfunctory grunt. Around forty-five minutes later I pulled the car onto the driveway of the hospital grounds, stopped, and turned to Reg.

"Listen to me, Reg, will you? If you think I'm going to let you near Connie with that attitude, you've got another think coming. When we get to Reception I want you to stay in the car. I'll nip in to say 'hello' to Connie and then we'll go back to the station. I'll leave it to you to explain to the DI why *you* didn't get to speak to Connie. Okay?"

I could have sworn he blushed at the rebuke.

"Alright, Sarge, you've made your point. And I'm sorry."

He did in fact, look duly chastened, I had to admit. "What's your problem, Reg?" I asked him sotto-voce.

He shrugged, in that irritating way he had.

"Just sulking, I guess. I thought the way the DI attacked me last night was unwarranted. I was only trying to be helpful. Anyway, Angie, you're right; I've got an attitude problem and I'll have to learn to deal with it. Can we start again? Please?"

I smiled, thought better of letting him know his contrition was way over the top, and continued towards the main hospital building. Even with the sun glistening on the old Victorian asylum, it looked gloomy and positively forbidding. The ivy creeping up the weather-battered walls gave me the impression of tentacles about to reach out and enfold me in a crushing embrace; it reminded me of one of those 'haunted house' horror films. There was nothing at all welcoming about it, and I saw Reg try to hide a shudder as we entered reception. I could never imagine myself spending years here, as some patients – including Connie – had had to. Dr Simmons came out of his office to welcome us, and he smiled as I introduced him to Reg.

"How's Connie this morning, doctor?" I asked.

"She seems fine. A lot stronger and looking forward to seeing you. Actually, she was quite excited about working with your artist. I just hope it helps."

Connie was waiting for us this time in the patients' lounge; this was quite a cheerful room, with windows (still barred, of course) overlooking the sweeping lawns. It was carpeted, had comfortable easy chairs, and was brightened considerably by the pale green chintz curtains. Prints of popular paintings hung at varying intervals along one wall of the room. A large television, with VCR, stood – solitarily – in the corner, its dark screen peering out at us menacingly. I looked away from it quickly, turning towards a relaxed and smiling Connie. She looked exceptionally pretty this morning. Her hair had been brushed until it shone like silk, down to her shoulders, and, for the first time, she was wearing make-up. She was dressed in a pretty pink blouse, open slightly at the top and revealing a hint of cleavage, and a short, loose skirt, finishing just above the knee. I gave her a warm smile, and then introduced her to Reg, our police artist, when her face immediately coloured. Obviously she wasn't very experienced at flirting.

"Hello," she said, proffering her hand almost formally. "Would you like some coffee?"

"You're kidding me, right?" I said.

"No. We're becoming quite civilised here nowadays. How about you... Reg, isn't it?"

"Yeah. Reg." He was still taciturn. "Thanks. Coffee would be good."

"Angie?"

I nodded, surprised. In all the years I had been coming here I had never been offered refreshments, other than by Doctor Simmons. But then, I hadn't seen this lounge before, either. Nor had I seen Connie dressed up as if she were going on a date. She made me appear positively dowdy in my traditional white blouse and midnight blue trousers, underneath which, I'm ashamed to admit, I was wearing standard police-issue black tights.

"So, Reg, how do you want me to help you?" Connie asked when we were all seated.

Reg. pulled out his laptop from his briefcase, together with various drawing materials and the sketch he had completed from Connie's description. He looked around the room for a socket, unplugged the lamp and replaced it with the plug for his own computer. It crossed my mind that he was too mean to waste his own batteries.

"I thought we'd begin by my showing you this, Connie," he said, presenting her with his drawing.

She studied it for a moment, and then giggled. "Sorry," she apologised, "but this looks like someone out of *The Simpsons*!"

He scowled at her comment. "Well, it isn't easy, you know, trying to create a likeness of someone from flimsy information."

I rolled my eyes at Connie, as if to say: 'Artistic temperament!'

Connie then actually laid a hand on Reg's arm – something, again, I had never seen her do before. "I didn't mean to offend you, Reg; really I didn't. But you have to admit, it does look funny." Then, unexpectedly, she pulled away as if she had been suddenly stung. Her head dropped and she began biting at her bottom lip – something I *had* seen happen beforehand. The colour seemed to have drained from her face.

"Are you alright, Connie?" I asked, concerned at the sudden change.

She nodded. "Yeah, I'm fine. Just a twinge."

Reg didn't notice. He merely grunted an acknowledgement. "Yeah. I suppose it's a bit funny. We could try again, maybe? If you're up to it?"

"Sure."

"Connie," I interjected, "shall I sort the coffee out while you and Reg get started? I've got to ring the station anyway."

She pointed towards the door, a frown on her face.

"Sorry. I forgot. The kitchen's down the corridor on the left. You'll find one of the aides there and they'll sort you out."

Something about retreat and valour prompted me to get the hell out of there; there was no way I could maintain a straight face watching Connie playing her woman's game with our artist. I didn't head for the kitchen at first, but settled myself in the first available chair in the corridor and dialled Jim.

"Hi," I said, when he answered. "Ange. Any news, Jim?"

"Oh, hi, Ange. No, nothing yet on the kid. But we have tracked down that Michael Dobson. He's in the clear."

"Where is he?"

"At his aunt's in Southend. Apparently she collapsed with a stroke two days ago. Dobson's been visiting her in the hospital. Says he forgot to check in with his local police because he was distraught. Can you believe that?"

"Does his alibi check out?" I asked, somewhat unnecessarily.

Jim responded with a typical sigh; his nicer way of letting you know you were being stupid.

"Sorry," I said, before he could have a go at me. "But that does give more credence to Connie's claim that our man has no convictions."

"Yeah, it looks that way. How's it going with the sketch?"

"They've just started. Connie did laugh, though, when Reg showed her his first attempt. I've left them to it."

"You will let me know if they come up with anything that looks like a lead won't you? You can always fax the photofit through, or download it from Reg's laptop."

"I'll get back to you, Jim. Soon as I can."

When I returned to the lounge with the coffee Connie and Reg were deeply involved in a discussion about profiling, with Reg making periodic adjustments to the picture displayed on his laptop according to various instructions from Connie. I sat there in silence watching the two of them work – harmoniously, I'm glad to say.

Finally, Reg stopped what he was doing, looked towards me, and shrugged.

"Well, we've improved the image slightly, but not so you'd really notice."

Connie looked crestfallen, as if somehow she had failed.

"I still can't get a clear picture," she said apologetically. "Like I said, Angie, it's kind of distorted, as if I'm seeing him through a broken mirror. But I've got this feeling I've seen him before somewhere; I just wish I could remember where."

"Don't worry about it, sweetheart; it'll probably come back to you in time. Let's see what you've got, shall we?" I glanced at the drawing. Reg was correct up to a point; there wasn't a great deal of improvement. What we did have now, though, was a clearer outline; sufficient to make identification more of a possibility than previously. I was looking at a portrait of a weasel of a man, with thin, almost pinched features and a distinctive, hawk-like nose – neither of which we had before. His hair seemed to be thinning and receding from his forehead. From his features I would guess his age at early to mid-forties; a little older than we'd previously estimated. His eyes were the problem; they were dead, without any life in them, almost as if Connie had seen into them once, recognised the murderous intent and refused to bring them back into focus. If only she could remember, we might have something really positive to go on.

"I don't suppose you can remember what his eyes were like, can you, Connie?" I asked, with an innocent slant.

She shuddered, and the fear I had seen the other day resurfaced. "No. And I don't want to. When I saw his eyes that time - in my vision I mean - I knew they were looking straight at me. Like we were watching each other, only he was warning me not to get too close."

She started to tremble again, prompting me to put my arm around her.

"It's okay, love; we're going to get him – believe me. Try not to think about him now."

"We finished here?" Reg asked, displaying his usual lack of sensitivity.

I nodded, then said: "Download the picture to Jim's computer, will you. I'll join you in the car in a minute."

God! That man could make me so angry; I have never seen anyone so lacking in empathy.

I stayed with Connie the best part of an hour, just chatting about this and that; anything to take her mind off her ordeal. I did ask her, though, why she had suddenly pulled back from touching Reg.

"Because he's dying," she said solemnly.

"What...?"

"He's got cancer and it's spread into his spine – but he doesn't know yet just how serious it is."

My God! This girl never failed to shock me.

"Does he even know he has cancer?" I enquired.

"Yeah - he's been having radiotherapy. But no one's told him it's terminal. Can we change the subject, Angie, please? I can't handle this."

I found myself shaking my head.

"Of course," I agreed. "Have you thought any more about leaving the hospital?" I noticed I had let my coffee go cold – not that it was very appealing anyway. And I seemed to have gone some way to answering my own questions about the nature of psychics; Connie had just demon-strated that they could, in fact, see events before they happened.

"I've talked with Dr Simmons," she confirmed by way of response. "He said that if I really wanted to leave he'd help me. Talked about something called a halfway house, just outside Birmingham, where patients from here go for a while for what he called 'readjustment'. I'm going to think about it, Angie. But, if I *do* go, we'll still see each other, won't we?"

"Don't be silly, sweetheart," I said, placing my arm around her shoulder. "We're friends. Always will be - no matter what happens. Anyway, if you do decide to move into that place you can always come and spend the weekends with me. I've got loads of room." This, of course, was a lie; the place was horribly cramped, but there was always the sofa! "Would you like that?"

She brightened up considerably at that, almost as if I had given her some hope for the future.

"I do love you, Angie," she said. "You're like a big sister to me. I don't know what I'd do without you now – you're the only family I've got."

"I love you too, Connie. And I promise I'll always be here for you."

It was such a tragedy, I couldn't help thinking. She was still very much the child, a child who had pretty well lost everyone who mattered in her life. I didn't feel altogether comfortable at playing the surrogate sister to a psychic, but I was very fond of her and I realised how much she needed me. So, when I told her I would always be there for her, I meant every word of it.

I left with Reg, after filling in Dr Simmons with the morning's events, and urging him – as if I had to – to keep a watchful eye on Connie. She was still genuinely afraid of what this monster was capable of doing to her; I got the impression from her that it wasn't so much a case of 'if' he found her but 'when'.

CHAPTER ELEVEN

The journey back was equally as silent as the morning trip; and it had
begun to rain. Reg was busy sketching, whilst I tried to avoid thinking
about what Connie had said about his health. Perhaps that would explain
his moods. It must be a terrible thing to have to confront – but then I
remembered Connie saying he didn't yet know just how serious his
condition was. I found myself sighing. In spite of his problem I still
couldn't bring myself to warm to Reg; there was something decidedly
depressing about the man.

I tried to concentrate on the more pressing issue of tracing the missing child during the journey back to Birmingham. And, of course, there
was the question: where do we go from here? I doubted if the photofit
would be all that helpful. What it might have done was frighten the
abductor sufficiently to return Josephine to her parents. It would be
naive to expect he would turn himself in.

The incident room was as frantic as ever that afternoon. Telephones
were still buzzing unceasingly, although the printers from the computers
had gone strangely silent, as if they had exhausted their information bank.
The atmosphere in the room also seemed, somehow, to have changed. It
was subtle rather than pronounced – rather like walking through dense
smog – but in this case the haze was an essence of despair. As I said,
people were still busy and the noise levels hadn't gone down at all, but
there was an air of pointlessness about the proceedings. The room all
but screamed at me: "We're wasting our time!"

At the time I was the only sergeant in the room: virtually everyone
with any seniority was out, either helping in the search or organising the
standard house-to-house enquires. The search for Josephine had been
going on for two full days now, and we knew from experience that every
day that passed almost exponentially reduced the prospects of finding the
child alive. But we mustn't give in, I urged myself.

"Listen up, people!" I shouted across the room. When only one or
two of the detective constables stopped what they were doing I repeated
the demand, this time even more loudly and more firmly. When I finally
had all their attentions I said (*hopefully with authority*), "What's the problem

here? You all look like you won the lottery and lost your ticket! Can I remind you, in case it's slipped your minds, a child's missing and it's down to all of us to find her. Alright, I admit the chances of finding her alive aren't looking good - but that doesn't mean we give up. Got it? If we can't help the victim we do everything in our power to get the bastard who abducted her. DO YOU UNDERSTAND?" I shouted across the room. I insisted that all of the 30 or so people in the incident room nod their assent before I continued: "Then let's get to it, and for Christ's sake give it all you've got - people are relying on you. And so's that little girl... I hope."

"Good speech," Jim commented from the door of his office - he had vacated his desk in the incident room for a meeting with the Superintendent.

"Should have thought of it myself. Come in, Ange. I've been waiting for you to get back. The Super and I have been talking about that photofit. Is the original any better than this fax copy?"

"Afraid not. Think we've gone as far as we can with this – unless, of course, Connie remembers some more detail." I joined him and Superintendent Connors at the table and handed over the original of the drawing. The superintendent was an imposing figure: tall and slim, with dark brown hair and a serious, almost permanent, worried look on his heavily lined face. I would guess he was late forties or, perhaps, early fifties. He was self-evidently a man who found it difficult to smile, although to be fair, the present circumstances made it   difficult for anyone to feel like smiling.

As they studied the photofit I said: "I really don't want to push this. I'm aware Connie knows more than she's telling me, but – I have to tell you – she's frightened to death of this man. Literally."

The superintendent frowned and glared at me.

"Sergeant, please, don't insult my intelligence with this psychic crap."

"Sir?" I questioned, returning his glare.

Jin held out a hand, as if he were separating us from a brawl.

"Please, both of you, we can do without this. What the Super means, Angie, is that anything we say about young Connie and these so-called *powers* of hers remains strictly between the two of us – and, it goes without saying, strictly off the record. Is that clear?"

The superintendent coughed as I nodded.

 "Point taken," I said. "So, what do we do with the photofit?"

"We circulate it," the superintendent said, a little more softly. "But internally only; West Midland area police stations. The last thing we need now is a national publicity campaign on the say-so of a child psychic. We're looking pretty incompetent as it is; that would make us a laughing stock."

"Do you mind if I ask where we go from here, Sir?" I said. "I mean, I thought we were doing everything possible. I don't see how our PR profile's suffered so far."

The superintendent forced a smile – a condescending one, it seemed to me.

"My dear young woman," (*"Oh, Christ; not another sexist!" I thought*) "this is one of those cases where the police cannot win; no matter what we do it will never be enough. I'd have thought by now you'd have sufficient experience to realise that."

'What an arsehole,' I thought. I mean, I realised he was under tremendous pressure because of the publicity surrounding the case, but you'd have thought he would have learned not to take it out on his more junior colleagues.

"Shall we move on?" Jim asked, deliberately changing the subject. He handed back the photofit. "Arrange for this to be circulated, will you, Ange. Also, we need to organise another house-to-house: places close to the school. Show people the picture. If anyone remembers this man, or anyone who bears even the slightest resemblance, we want to know. Then talk to the headmistress again. Ask her if you can speak to any of the kids who were either outside the school that afternoon or who might have seen this character hanging around a few days before the incident."

"Will do. Anything else, inspector?"

"What about intelligence?" the superintendent wanted to know.

"Nothing yet, sir. We'll go back to our informers again, now we have the picture - see if that pushes any buttons. Other than that – well, as Angela said, we're doing everything that can be done. If nothing breaks by tomorrow morning I'm going to ask the army to help with the search - if you agree, that is."

The superintendent nodded.

"What about the parents? Do you want television coverage?"

"Let's wait till tomorrow, shall we? If we've got nothing by then, yes - we use whatever we've got. I'll speak to them myself; see if they're agreeable. Shall we get together again later for an update?"

"Yes. Let's say seven o'clock, shall we? The press will be hounding us to cough up something before their deadlines. I'll handle that, Inspector; it'll show them how seriously we're taking this case." He stood up from the table. "That's all for now. Let's just hope something breaks quickly. And Sergeant, I'm sorry I was snappy – it's a bad time for all of us ..."

Christ! An apology from the Master.

CHAPTER TWELVE

He was wrong. In the event, nothing did break. I carried out the inspector's instructions regarding the renewal of house-to-house interviews, around the area of the school. No luck there. Solihull was a small suburban town, on the outskirts of Birmingham. Very chic, and very upmarket, with fashionable shops displaying all the latest designer clothes. The kind of place I personally would like to live in if ever I could afford it. But I did gain the impression from talking to people that its inhabitants were somewhat insular, to say nothing of superior.

After spending some time with colleagues, including Sergeant Corkhill, on the re-interviews, I then visited the school and spoke with the headmistress to seek permission to show the photofit picture to some of the children. She didn't disagree; she just thought it might be a better idea if I showed it to the parents, who would have been waiting for their children shortly before the incident occurred. It was a good suggestion. I waited outside the school for a while, until the parents started arriving to collect their youngsters, and then spoke with a number of them and showed them the photofit. I struck lucky. One of the ladies waiting for a child to exit the school clearly remembered a man bearing that – or a similar – description asking her, a few days earlier, if she was the mother of the little girl with the blonde hair. He said he was looking for her, so she pointed her out to him, thinking nothing more of it.

She looked at the picture again, then said: "There's something wrong with the eyes. "There's no life in these eyes; the man I remember had staring eyes – grey, staring eyes – like he could see right through you."

"Weren't you suspicious?" I asked.

"Well, no. He was nice enough. I never thought he was after a child. I mean, why should I?"

"And you didn't think to mention this to the police?"

"They never asked me."

"Jesus!" I thought. A child goes missing from the same school as her daughter, a strange man approached her a couple of days earlier – and she didn't think it important enough to inform the police? "Do you think you might recognise him, if you saw him again?" I asked her, patiently.

"Oh. I'm not sure about that. I mean, I'm fairly certain from the picture it was the same man - especially if you get the eyes right. But if you're talking about an identity parade – well, that's a different matter, isn't it?"

"What about his accent? Would you say he was from the Midlands area?"

"Oh, yes. I'm positive about that. He had a very pronounced accent."

Sometimes I despaired! But it had given me an idea, though. After I had taken her details I set off to visit Josephine's mother, hoping to get to her before Jim was scheduled to talk with them about the television interview. The Marsdens lived approximately two miles from the school, in a largish detached house, set back some distance from a tree-shaded road.

Mrs Marsden was far too distressed to get much sense out of; she was virtually on the point of hysteria, continually berating herself for being late at the school that day. It was Mr Marsden who was the calmer of the two. He sat his wife down on the lounge sofa and put his arm around her.

"I'm afraid you're not going to get much sense out of either of us at the moment. But I'll do my best. How can we help you, Sergeant?"

He was a kindly man, rather dull, really, as you'd expect from an accountant – especially one with his own practice. He was showing all the understandable lines of stress on his face. He couldn't have been much older than 30, but today he looked closer to 40. Worry lines were etched down his cheeks and his eyes had a haunted look about them.

"I want to ask your wife about her car," I began by saying.

"Her car? Why? What's that got to do with anything?" His eyes opened wide in an expression of amazement. "Our daughter's missing and you want to talk about Susan's car? I don't believe this."

I gave a helpless shrug. I had very little experience in dealing with the victims of tragedy. "I'm sorry, Mr Marsden. I know it seems a bit weird, but if you'll bear with me it will become clearer. What I want to know, if she can remember, is: did your wife have any trouble with her car before the day in question?"

"Will you please stop talking about me as though I'm not here," his wife said in irritation, her voice shaking. "And the answer is no I didn't. I can tell you that for certain because it's only six months old and it's never given us any problems. Before that day, that is. Why?"

I ignored the question and continued with my interrogation. "And who takes Josephine to school in the mornings?"

"I do," Mr Marsden confirmed.

I looked towards his wife. "And did you have the car checked out later? To find out why it wouldn't start?"

"Yes. I did." Mr Marsden said. "I rang the AA that same afternoon. I came home early, saw the car was still parked in the garage and no sign of Susan. I tried to start it, but nothing. So I assumed my wife had gone with one of the other mothers to pick Josephine up. I just didn't think."

"Did they say what the problem was?"

He pondered the question for a moment before replying. "Funny, now I think of it. They said some wire or other had come loose – don't ask me which one. But I do remember now the mechanic asked me if I thought the car had been vandalised. Which, of course, was silly. We keep it in the garage - and it's got central locking, so I doubt anyone could have tampered with it. It was just one of those things, I suppose. There doesn't have to be an explanation."

"Could anyone have got into the garage?" I asked. "During the night, I mean?"

"Well, I imagine so. It's hardly Fort Knox." He gazed at me, the picture of bewilderment. "But why would anyone want to break in and then steal nothing?"

"To disable your car?" I proffered. "To make certain Mrs Marsden would be late for school that afternoon? To enable whoever it was to persuade your daughter he was a friend of the family – or a taxi service, even – who had come to take her home because Mummy's car had broken down? It's possible isn't it?"

"Jesus! You're saying whoever did this planned the whole thing? It wasn't a chance abduction?"

"No. I'm not saying that, Mr Marsden. I'm just exploring theories; and I'm sorry – I shouldn't have brought them up in front of you and your wife. You've got enough to worry about, without me adding to it. But what I do think is wrong, Mrs Marsden – and, believe me, I know what I'm talking about – is that you're still blaming yourself for the car not starting that day. Believe me, it was no fault of yours."

"Thank you," she sobbed. "Thank you for that. You will let us know as soon as you've any news about Josephine, won't you?"

I breathed a sigh of relief as I left the house. That had been incredibly stupid of me, and I almost blew it. As it was I didn't feel I had done too much damage; or, at least, I'd been able to limit it. I gave the garage a cursory inspection, but it revealed nothing. But then, if our man were as clever as I thought he was, he would hardly leave any trace of entry.

But now, at least, I had a connection. And once again it confirmed – to me, at least – that Connie's vision was authentic. Evidently, just as she had intimated, this appeared to be our man. It went further than that. It also proved that, whoever he was, he wasn't your average impulse paedophile. This man planned things, almost down to the last detail; which in turn prompted the thought that he must have also planned the endgame. I felt myself shudder; the prospect of the Marsdens never seeing their daughter alive again suddenly crossed my mind.

CHAPTER THIRTEEN

On the way back to the station I reflected on how we might use this information. We now had at least an outline of what the man looked like; I made a mental note to get Reg to correct the omission with the eyes. We also knew he was a meticulous planner, which indicated he was coldly calculating. I felt that what we needed now was one of those psychological profilers, who could give us an insight into the man's personality, his behaviour patterns, possibly even the type of occupation he had. And, maybe, what had motivated him to this depraved self-indulgence in the first place. I had covered the subject at university, but I was well short of the experience to take something like this on. The nearest person I could think of who did have that kind of experience was Dr Simmons.

It was then I had another inspiration. What was it Connie had said that day of her vision? "He's here; that horrible man is here!" What if I was right, and subconsciously, she had experienced a flashback, and this was the same man responsible for the murders of those children from the forest that had caused her breakdown? And, if it was, how could we ever tie them together without Connie fully recovering her memory? It was a fascinating postulation, and I decided to give it more thought. It was at that moment I felt something tugging at the back of my mind in this regard, but it was too elusive to pin it down. Perhaps it would come to me later.

When I got back to the station I quickly discovered I was in trouble.

"What the hell did you think you were doing, visiting the Marsdens without clearance?" Jim demanded.

"Oh. Hi," I said nonchalantly. "I thought that's where *you* were supposed to be?"

"Never mind me; that's none of your concern. I want to know what you were doing there?"

I returned his scowl and sat down at the office table. "If you calm down, SIR, I'll explain. And I didn't realise I needed your permission to do my job!"

"Don't come that one with me, Ange; it won't wash. You knew I was due to visit the Marsdens and you also knew the state they're in. What the hell were you hoping to achieve?"

I shrugged, philosophically. There was no point in trying to reason with him when he was in that kind of mood. "Is this case getting to you, Jim? Is that why you're having a go at me? You're beginning to sound like the super."

He shook his head, more in frustration than anger. "Okay. Let's start again, shall we? I didn't go to the Marsdens because something came up here. So I sent Sergeant Kewell …" He was the third sergeant in our team. "He rang me on his mobile a few minutes before you came in to say you'd already been there - and asking me if there had been a duplication. Has there, Angie? Is that why you went? To persuade them to do a television appeal?"

"No! Of course not," I protested. "I went on a completely different matter." I pushed a finger forward, almost in his face. "Just listen for a moment, will you?" I snapped. "I interviewed a woman at the school this afternoon; when I showed her the photofit she remembered speaking with this creep a couple of days before the child was snatched. He wanted to know if she was Josephine's mother."

"So?"

"So he was trying to identify the child's mother, so he could follow her, find out where she lived – everything about her."

"And what would be the point of that? He didn't take her from the house – he got her from the school."

I sighed. God spare me from men!

"Because he was trying to give himself a clear run. I think someone immobilised the Marsdens' car the night before the incident; that's why Mrs Marsden was late. I'm pretty certain it was our man who engineered that. He knew she was going to be late for the school collection – he'd made sure of that. So he was able, somehow, to persuade the little girl her mummy had sent him to pick her up from school. Perhaps he was even wearing a chauffeur's uniform – to make him appear more convincing. *That's* why I went to the Marsdens', to check out my theory about her being late for the school collection. It makes sense, don't you think – *Inspector?*

He rubbed his chin, stubbly from two days' growth, then – reluctantly, I thought – gave me one of his schoolboy grins.

"So, who's a clever girl, then?"

"Piss off, Jim!" I said, laughing.

"And, for your information, young lady, this case is not getting to me! I just don't like surprises. Anyway, your deduction's very plausible. And, as you've no doubt guessed already, it tells us a lot more about him. He is not your typical paedophile; this one's a planner. And you know what else bothers me?"

"He's already planned the endgame."

He took hold of my hand and gave it an affectionate squeeze, grinning all over his face.

"We'll make a detective out of you yet, Sweetheart. Oh, and, as a matter of interest, the reason I didn't go to the Marsdens' was because the superintendent gave me another call. Evidently, DCI Templar's decided to take early retirement – because of ill health, would you believe? So, you're now talking to the new acting Detective Chief Inspector!"

"Jim!" I almost shouted. "That's marvellous news. Congratulations! When will they make it permanent?"

He shrugged and spread his hands ceremoniously.

"Who knows. When and if we catch this bastard, I imagine. Still, I agree, it's good news; it's also flattering. And I'm sure we're all pleased our old DCI has waved goodbye! Anyway," he went on, "Frank Kewell's talked the Marsdens into doing the TV interview. The crew will be here shortly, so we'd better be prepared."

"Where's it happening?"

"Here, in the conference room. And, since you've already met the folks, I'm making you the 'babysitter'. Don't have a problem with that, Ange, do you?"

I smiled; at the same time thinking that I'd better get out of there quickly. Just looking at him today for some reason made me feel incredibly horny; I was tempted to do something about it! Jim must have read my mind, because he suddenly appeared uncomfortable, as if I'd communicated the same feeling to him. I made a hasty exit.

* * * * * * * * *

At the television interview I felt terribly sorry for the Marsdens, especially Mrs Marsden. It was almost impossible for her to maintain any sense of composure in front of the cameras. Most of the time she wept, saying very little; when she did speak, it came out fractured, like a woman breaking under the terrible strain. It was Mr Marsden who did most of the presentation, appealing for the public's help more or less as we had scripted it. On the whole the superintendent thought it had gone extremely well, which, personally, I thought was a strange description. After all, we were dealing here with a potential tragedy; it wasn't a variety show.

The film went out that night on all of the national news stations; all we could do now was wait to see if it provoked any response.

CHAPTER FOURTEEN

It was after nine that evening when Jim and I left the station. We returned to his flat, a two-and-a-half bedroom modern block he owned in the Edgbaston area of the city. Jim lived on the second floor of the building, and from the rear window of the master bedroom it was just possible to make out the structure of the cricket ground. That was the main reason for choosing the flat, he maintained; his rather passionate love of the game.

Whilst Jim went for a shower and an overdue shave I caught the latest news on the lounge television. There was no startling new information to report; the news channels were all full of the story of the missing child, including the interview with the Marsdens; I only hoped it might produce some results, although I wasn't going to hold my breath. There followed background information on the schoolgirl, with interviews from her school friends and her headmaster. It was all very sad, especially to see those youngsters breaking down at the prospect that their friend might have come to serious harm. I switched off the picture of constant misery and started preparing dinner in Jim's rather cramped kitchen. It consisted of a cooker, a fridge, a sink and little else, and – other than the basic crockery and cutlery – the cupboards were well and truly bare. But, as he said, whenever I chided him about the lack of utilities, "What do I need a kitchen for, anyway? I only use it for breakfast and whenever you're here."

He seemed to be absent for an eternity, so I stepped into the bedroom to see if he'd perhaps fallen asleep. He hadn't. He was standing there, completely naked, drying his hair with a large bath towel, and sporting the most enormous erection. Well! What was I supposed to do? I slipped out of my clothes before he could notice – at least, I believe he hadn't noticed – then sidled up to him and made a grab for his penis. His only reaction was to cuddle me, fondle my breasts, sexily, and say: "What took you so long?"

Instead of answering him I gave him a long, lingering kiss, shuddering with anticipation as I felt his tongue almost at my throat. I couldn't wait; I just had to have him, there and then! So I mounted him – a little difficult in that position, but fortune favours the brave – and I let out a gasp when I felt him penetrate me. I don't think I will ever get used to the sheer size of the man. We staggered, still coupled, over to the bed, and then spent what seemed to be eternity making incredible, passionate love. It was probably lust, if the truth was known, but who the hell cared? We drained into each other all the stress and tension we had undergone the last few days. For a while afterwards we lay exhaustedly in each other's arms; then I felt myself drifting gently off to sleep.

After what seemed only a matter of minutes the ring of the telephone awakened me.

"Robbins here," I heard Jim say.

Christ! Will we never have any peace? I turned towards the bedside clock. I couldn't believe it! It was 5.30 in the morning. We had slept all those hours, and we still hadn't eaten.

"Where was this, you say?" Jim asked. "Ward End? Yeah, I know it. Off the 4040."

The morning light was already filtering through the window; I was suddenly wide-awake.

"What is it?"

"That was Frank Kewell. Some child's clothing's just been found. Near Ward End. "Come on, Angie; Frank's picking us up at the station. He can take us to the scene."

We were dressed and ready to leave in a matter of minutes, still on empty stomachs. When we arrived at the station Frank was already waiting for us. We transferred into his car and set off on the five-mile or so journey to Ward End.

"What's new?" Jim asked him.

"Nothing. Only what I told you. It's a bit sketchy at the moment - but they did say there was a pair of child's red shoes with the rest of the clothes. Ring any bells?"

"Oh, no!" I said aloud, from the back of the car. "Please don't let it be Josephine."

Frank half turned from his driving position. "I think we should prepare ourselves," he said.

Frank Kewell was the archetypal career police officer, having been in the force for almost 20 years and moved only so far through the ranks.

He was a quiet, deep-thinking kind of man, in his early forties, with dark hair and matching moustache. He was of average build, with a gentle nature, but always serious and very slow to smile. I liked him (though not all of the time!), and had always found him helpful.

CHAPTER FIFTEEN

The flashing lights of the police vehicles, even in semi-daylight, could be seen at least a half a mile away from the discovery scene; four squad cars and a couple of unmarked vehicles were parked around the site. Some of the other police officers were in a field, at the side of the road, which I saw could be entered via a five-barred gate. The ubiquitous yellow police tape was already spread around the site, passing through the entrance and marking off an area inside the field itself. A lone tractor stood some little distance away, and a man I took to be the farmer was smoking a cigarette and talking to one of the constables.

It was an eerie scene, silent and virtually without air, almost as if it were a sanctuary. One thing I noticed immediately was the absence of birds chirping their early morning chorus. It was probably too bloody early, even for them, I thought, still rubbing the sleep from my eyes. I followed Frank Kewell and Jim into the field, feeling nauseous at the prospect of what awaited us. The child's clothes, far from being scattered in disarray, had been folded neatly in a small pile, just as a mother would do before putting her daughter to bed. The red shoes were set aside from the rest of the clothes; they were patent leather with a buckle-over clasp, and I noticed a single speck of dirt on one of the toes. I was tempted to lean over and wipe it clean, as if it were hallowed ground. I pulled up when Jim grasped my arm, and instead choked back a tear, struggling for control. From the description we already had it was fairly clear that these were Josephine's belongings.

We all stood back and let the SOCOS and the forensic people do their job: photographing and then labelling each item of clothing, then bagging it for further examination. I stood there, sharing the silence, whilst Jim went across to speak with the farmer.

Those clothes, those tiny items, were the only pitiful legacy of a child's life. Strangely, I didn't feel as I had done at the murder scene all those years ago, when I had wondered whether or not I was cut out for the police force. This time I felt only a slow, burning anger, and a determination to do everything in my power to catch this bastard – this sick, bestial monster that could do that to a little girl – because, looking at the evidence, it was fairly obvious that we would never find Josephine alive. But right at that moment I don't think I had ever felt so diminished, so frustratingly helpless.

Jim came over after talking to the farmer.

"The clothes were left here sometime between nine last night and five this morning. The farmer always checks the gate, more or less at those times, so he's pretty confident. Whoever left them had to have come here by car; it's too isolated to get here on foot. But why here, in this particular field? And why did he lay the clothes out so tidily? I can't get my head round that; does it make any sense to you?"

"Because he knew they'd be found quickly. And that's what he wanted. I think he was trying to leave us a message."

"Okay. But why? And, if you're right, what kind of message?"

"Remember what Connie said: that he was laughing at the police. This seems to bear that out. Maybe it's a challenge. You know: a 'catch me if you can' message? Also," I added as an afterthought, "he might be trying to confuse us – you know, make us believe that he lives in this neck of the woods."

"Yeah, well, maybe we'll get lucky. Hopefully he'll have made a mistake and left some evidence. Won't hold my breath though."

"What about the Marsdens, Jim? Are we going to tell them anything?"

"No. Not just yet. We'll check the forensics first; once that's complete we'll ask the Marsdens to come to the station to see if they can identify the clothing – or the shoes."

He rubbed his hand across his eyes, a gesture more of futility than anything. It was as if the pleasures we had shared a few hours ago were now something in the distant past, subordinated by the awful reality of paedophiliac murder. "I'll organise a search of the surrounding area; see if he's left us anything there. Otherwise, there's not much more we can do here. Come on, Angie; let's get back to the station. I think we need some specialist help on this one."

"What kind of help?" I enquired.

"Profiling help." (*Great minds thinking alike!*) "We need to involve a criminal psychologist; someone who might be able to give us an insight into this character. If you're right, and I believe you are, then, whatever message the scene contains, it's much too subtle for us to interpret."

"You mean we're out of our depth?"

He shrugged. "Precisely. And I make no apology for that. In fact, it would be arrogant not to admit it."

I touched his arm before getting into the car.

"I agree with you, Jim. About the profiling. I did quite a bit on it at university, so I do know something about it. Doesn't make me an expert – but I know just the man we need."

He nodded his assent.

"You're thinking of Dr Simmons – right?"

"Yeah. As well as being a psychiatrist, he told me once he'd worked on offender profiling. Apparently, he's done some work in the past with the superintendent. And, as far as I know, he's kept pretty well up to date with scientific developments in that area. So, unless you've got anyone else in mind, I'd say Dr Simmons is as good as anyone in that field."

"Okay. Get hold of him soon as we get back. If he thinks he can crack this and he's up for it, bring him in and I'll brief him."

CHAPTER SIXTEEN

Scores of reporters, standing alongside a number of television cameras, were milling outside the station when we arrived; someone, obviously, had leaked news of the discovery to the media. Jim was absolutely furious. Somehow he managed to hold a tight expression on his face as we made our way through the mob, ignoring the barrage of questions about the child's clothing, until we reached the steps of the station. Then he turned to address them.

"At this stage," he began, "you people know just about as much as we do. Aside from confirming that some clothes belonging to a child have been found, I have nothing to add. And I advise you not to speculate – any of you. We don't yet know who the clothes belong to, and until we're certain we will be making no further comment."

Ignoring the responses this statement triggered we headed towards the incident room, Jim still seething with anger. He stormed into his office whilst I discreetly went over to my desk. There were two messages on my pad, one from the Marsdens, the other – coincidentally – from Dr Simmons. I was curious in both cases, except with the Marsdens I suspected that one of the more insensitive members of the press had contacted them about the discovery of the clothes. Just then, Peter Corkhill came over to talk to me, an obvious expression of curiosity on his face.

"What have we got?" he asked, pulling up a chair..

Sighing heavily, I put him in the picture about this morning's developments, describing the child's clothing we had found and the way they had been so carefully laid out on the ground.

"'Sounds like they're from our missing youngster – Josephine."

"Yeah. But we'll have to wait for forensics to confirm that, Peter. And someone's already leaked it to the media – have you had a look outside the building?"

"We all have," he said, gesturing around the room full of officers. "It seems to me, Angie, it could well be the killer who leaked the information. That would fit with your idea - that the bastard's playing games with us. No doubt he's getting a lot of fun outta this."

I nodded my head.

"I agree. But we'll still have to wait for forensics. If he's left us a message it shouldn't be too difficult to find… What?" I said, as I saw him hesitate.

"Do you fancy joining me one evening … you know … for a drink?"

I didn't know what to say. It was the last thing I expected him to ask me. It wasn't that he was unattractive, I actually quite liked Peter, with his boyish good looks and wicked grin. It was just that… Well, it's all about chemistry I suppose. "Do you mean socially, Peter, or to talk about the case?" was all I said in the end.

"Well … socially, I thought. I'd like to get to you know you better … you know … working together on the case …"

I smiled. "You don't know then … about the DCI and me?"

"Oh. I see." His face now had disappointment written all over it. "No … sorry, Angie … I didn't realise. Hope you didn't mind my asking?"

"It was very sweet of you, Peter. And any other time…"

I stopped him from moving away by picking up the note from the Marsdens.

"Have you seen this?" I enquired, changing the subject to save him.

"The Marsdens – yes. Jeannie Crane took the call from Mr Marsden. She said he sounded upset."

"Yeah. I can guess why. It suggests to me that someone's already told the parents what we've found out – maybe it was him… Or the killer…"

And if I was right and I rang them, I thought, I wouldn't have a clue what to say. Denial was out of the question. I shook my head when Peter asked me if I'd like him to stay. I picked up the phone and dialled the number: there was only one way to deal with this, and that was by telling the truth.

"Mr Marsden?" I said when a voice answered. "Good morning; Sergeant Crossley, West Midlands Crime Squad. I got a message saying you wanted to talk to me. How can I help?"

"Here goes!" I thought.

"Sergeant? Yes, thank you for ringing. It's just that my wife had a very distressing call this morning. One of those anonymous callers."

"Really? You mean as in heavy breathers?"

"No. Anonymous as in he didn't give his name."

"What did he say that distressed your wife so much, Mr Marsden?" I heard him stifle a choke.

"He said he'd left Josephine's clothes in a field for you to find. He then said for you – the police, that is – not to bother searching for her body because you'd never find it. What do you think, Sergeant? Is he some kind of nutter? Or should we take it seriously?"

I hesitated, remembering Jim's words about being out of our depth.

"Mr Marsden, could you try dialling 1471 for me? I'll put the phone down and ring you back in a few moments."

"I've already done that. I got one of those 'the caller did not leave a number' replies."

"What about his accent? Could you identify it?"

"Yes. Definitely a Midlands accent. Quite pronounced, actually."

"What time was the call?"

"A couple of hours ago – he got my wife and me out of bed. I rang you straight away. It's serious, isn't it? Have you found her clothes? Is that it?"

"Please Mr Marsden," I said, as levelly as I could. "Let me check this out. I'll get back to you quickly, I promise."

"You haven't answered my question, Sergeant. Is there something you're not telling me?"

"No, sir. there's not. The truth is, yes, we have found a child's clothing. And, yes, we did find them in a field not far from here. But so far we've no idea who they belong to. It could well be that your caller's just a sick hoaxer who gets his kicks out of upsetting people. So, I can only ask you to try not to worry. And please, Mr Marsden, can I urge you not to tell your wife about this? There's no point in upsetting her more unless we have to. Now, I have to check out where this call came from and, as I said, I'll get back to you as soon as I have anything."

I ended the call and went straight into Jim's office. "I need you to authorise a phone trace. Urgently."

"What's the panic?"

"Someone called the Marsdens' home about two hours ago, claiming to be our man. I want to try and trace the call."

"Okay. Give me the n umber. It'll only take a sec."

I waited anxiously for a result. Jim was already shaking his head as he replaced the phone. "No luck, I'm afraid. It was a public call box in Walsall. So, what did this character say exactly?"

I repeated the conversation, almost word for word, including the part where I was forced to admit we had found some clothing.

"You were right to tell Marsden. The press'll be onto him before long - so at least you've managed to pre-empt them. Do *you* think it's our man?"

"I've got a feeling it is, yeah. Mr Marsden said the caller had a strong Midlands accent, which ties in with the character that turned up at the school. And, if it is him, you're right; we definitely need a profiler on the job. In fact, this telephone call might help him."

"Yeah. I agree. Look, Ange, you ring him back and I'll chase up forensics. I know it's too early for results, but it won't do any harm to push them. And then get on to your Dr Simmons, will you?"

I pacified Mr Marsden as best I could, but I was forced to lie when he asked me if we had found a pair of shoes. Red, patent leather, with a buckle-over strap. I told him I hadn't actually seen the clothes, so I couldn't comment. I don't think I convinced him. Next, I returned Dr Simmons' call. It seemed to take forever to connect with him.

"Angie. Thanks for calling back. It was Connie who wanted to speak with you, actually. She said she'd tried to contact you on your mobile, but apparently you had it switched off."

"Oh, Christ. Yes, I haven't turned it on yet this morning." The truth was I hadn't wanted anyone disturbing me last night at Jim's. "How is she, Dr Simmons? There isn't a problem, is there?"

"No. Only that she told me at breakfast this morning that she definitely wants to leave Forest Hills. I've just got off the phone from talking with Ashworth House – to see if they can accommodate her straight away."

"Straight away?" I said, puzzled. "You mean she wants to go right now, this morning?"

"Yes. Curious, isn't it?"

"What's brought on this sudden urgency? Has something happened"

"Well, if it has, Angie, she's not telling me. The only thing I've noticed about her today is that she is decidedly nervous. D'you want to talk to her? I can put you through to the lounge; I'm sure she'll be – what? Relieved? – To hear from you."

"Have you made the arrangements with Ashworth House?"

"Yes. Not a problem. I'm taking her there myself – about lunchtime."

"Why don't I meet you there, Doctor? If you let Connie know, I can have a chat with her then. There's something I want to discuss with you anyway."

"Hmm. Sounds mysterious."

"Well, it's police business, actually. But I don't want to talk about it on the phone."

"Even more mysterious. All right, Angie. You obviously know the place; I'll tell Connie, and we'll see you there about one-ish, if that's okay?"

"Fine. It'll give me time to sort one or two things out here first. See you later."

I was curious about Connie's sudden decision, although I did have an idea what it was all about. I knew that in some way it was connected with her last vision, and if that were true, and she was in any danger, then I for one would feel happier if she was literally just around the corner where I could keep a close watch on her.

Just then, Jim came out of his office with a fax sheet in his hand. "That bit of dirt you spotted on one of the shoes? It's blood." He stopped me from interrupting. "Before you ask, no, we don't know yet whose it is. We might know that later in the day. It'll take some time, though, for the DNA to come through. For now, we assume nothing. And we say nothing. Okay?"

"Right. You have to admit, it does look ominous."

"I'm admitting nothing at this stage. I've told you before, Ange, we're not in the business of speculation. Now, did you manage to get hold of your Dr Simmons?"

"I'm meeting up with him at lunchtime."

"What? You're going out to the hospital again? Can't he come here?"

"I'm not going to the hospital, Jim, I'm meeting him at Ashworth House. He's taking Connie there; she's leaving Forest Hills."

"Well, that's got to be good news; she's a spooky kid, and, no, I don't mean that unkindly. Isn't Ashworth House a halfway house?"

"Yes. Dr Simmons has arranged for her stay there and sort herself out a bit before she moves back into the community."

"I hope it works out for her; she's suffered a hell of a lot. I take it you're going to keep a sisterly eye on her while she's there?"

I nodded. "It'll be easier for me, anyway. And I've told Connie she can spend the occasional weekend at my place."

"Sounds like a good idea. That should cheer her up - looks like she's going to need you for quite some time yet. Listen, when you speak to Simmons, try and get him to come back here with you, will you? That's assuming he's up for helping us. I'd like the Super to brief him. You know the kind of thing: terms of reference, how long he thinks it might take, how much it's going to cost us, and – more to the point – can we afford it? But we do need to know now – today. One way or the other. Time's against us."

"I appreciate that. Let me talk to him. I'll call you from the residence."

CHAPTER SEVENTEEN

The journey from the station to Ashworth House, in Winson Green, took no longer than 20 minutes, and that was on a busy Monday, with the roads around Birmingham typically choked with lunchtime traffic. I worked it out that, on a quiet day, or in the evening, it should only take me ten minutes or so, which was a hell of an improvement on the 60 minutes or more it used to take to Forest Hills.

Winson Green was quite a pleasant suburb of Birmingham, fairly close to the city centre. It also possessed a modern shopping precinct – nothing compared to the Bull Ring, of course, but it did have a small number of fashionable shops, restaurants, and even a cinema. Ashworth House, situated about a mile from the centre, was nowhere near as imposing a building as Connie's previous home; or as threatening. It was a large but old, and somewhat shabby, detached house, situated on the corner of a busy street, quite close to the local shops. It was bordered by a low, crumbling wall, with a rusty iron gate as its entrance. There was no parking at the home so I left my car on the main road, in front of what I took to be Dr Simmons' car, and pulled down the 'Police' sign. I climbed the steps to the entrance, carefully avoiding the cracks in the concrete slabs, and rang the bell.

It didn't appear to be working, so I gave the door a good thumping until I heard some movement from inside. A middle-aged lady, with a thickening waistline and a cheerful smile, eventually opened the door.

"You must be Angie – right?"

"How do you do," I said formally.

"Come in, come in. I'm Sheila; I'm what they call the house mother around here." The words came tumbling out without any pause for breath.

"Has Dr Simmons arrived yet?" I asked politely. I had a job to keep up with her, she moved so quickly.

"He's just showing Connie her room," she said, over her shoulder, and heading through a door on the left of the hallway. "Would you like to see it? I'm sure they won't mind. It's a nice one, on the first floor overlooking the garden."

"If you're sure it's alright."

She smiled again, more broadly. "Course it is! Connie's told me a bit about you. I know you're close friends. Up the stairs," she pointed vaguely, "down the landing and it's the second door on the right."

Dr Simmons opened the door, shook hands with me and waved me inside. Connie was looking out of the window, obviously pleased, not only with the view but I imagined it also had something to do with having windows without bars, and which actually opened.

"Hi, Angie!" she squealed in delight. "What do you think of it?" she asked, encompassing the room with her arms.

Before I said anything I went across and gave her a big hug. "It's lovely, Connie." And it really was. It was more like a studio apartment than a mere bedroom. It was a large room, which had obviously been a principal bedroom in former days. It was made up of a sitting area with easy chairs and a settee, a coffee table in the centre, decorated with a vase of fresh flowers, and in one corner a television and hi-fi equipment. Opposite was the sleeping area, which sported a queen-size bed. A door led off from here into a private bathroom. I noticed also that the room was centrally heated, which was a good thing because I should think it might be a cold house in the winter. I was more pleased than I could have hoped. This was just what Connie needed to help her readjustment. And the view from the window, compared to what she had been used to for the last four years, was inspirational. It overlooked a lawned garden, well maintained, and surrounded by a variety of colourful flowers. It was evident that a great deal of thought and attention had gone into the refurbishment of this old building, with the emphasis on a friendly, secure environment.

"Do you think you'll be happy here?"

She looked sombre for a moment. "I think so, yes. But more importantly, will I be safe?"

I noticed the puzzled expression on Dr Simmons' face when he heard this remark.

"You're not still afraid, are you Connie?" he asked tentatively.

"Yes, Doctor. 'Course I am. Oh, not crapping myself like last time... Not panicking even, but I'd be stupid not to be scared."

"Last time?" I queried, puzzled by what she meant. "Are you saying something else has happened, since then?"

Dr Simmons frowned as Connie nodded assent.

"If you'll excuse me, ladies," he said hurriedly, "I can see you two have things to discuss, and I do have some paperwork to sort out. I'll be downstairs in the study, Angie. Sheila will show you where it is, when you're ready. I'll wait for you, if you want?"

He left before I had the chance to say anything. Obviously, he had anticipated that Connie was about to divulge another psychic experience – something he very definitely didn't wish to be involved in.

"What happened, Connie?" I asked, taking a seat on one of the comfortable lounge chairs. "Another vision?"

Again she nodded. "Different this time, though. I saw that man again – or, rather, I think he was seeing me. If you get what I mean?"

"Not really," I said, slowly. "Can you explain?"

She hesitated, as if she was struggling to find the words. "Well, I think he came looking for me. It wasn't terribly clear, but he was trying to show me something."

"There was a field – somewhere in the country – and there was a bundle of child's clothes, near one of those five-bar gates. They were piled neatly in a corner, with a pair of children's shoes. At first I didn't understand what he was trying to tell me – but then he took me across a common; I've no idea where – it was dark, and I couldn't see very clearly. He had the body of a little girl with him; she was slung across his shoulders… and someone had taken all her clothes off. I knew she was dead by the way her head was hanging."

At this point she stopped. She was trembling again, and the tears began to run down her cheeks. I went over and placed my arm around her shoulders. "It's alright, Connie. You don't have to go on if it's too much for you."

"No, Angie. I want to tell you…It might make me feel better. Anyway, you're the only one who understands; you're the only one who really believes me." She wiped her eyes with my handkerchief, and then forced a smile. "This is all we seem to do these days, isn't it? I tell you about my horrible visions and you wipe away my tears. Do you think it will ever end, Angie?"

I sighed. "I really don't know, sweetheart. But I do think you're right to tell me; it could make you ill again if you bottle it all up. Do you want to go on? Or shall we leave it for a bit?"

She sniffed and rubbed her eyes. "I'm okay, really. And you have to know the rest of it; I think this part is important. The man took the little girl across this wasteland until he came to some abandoned buildings - old sheds or offices I think. There's a deep shaft in the ground behind them – I think it's a disused mine. All I know is it's very deep, because he threw the body down there and I waited and waited but I never heard it hit the bottom."

"Oh, no!" I found myself thinking. "I don't want to hear this." But I had to, if only for Connie's sake. "Then what?" I asked.

"He looked straight at me and – I can't describe it, really, but it was like he could see me; he wanted me to watch because he loved it, making me look at his perversion – like he was making me part of it. He was sneering at me, the whole time – it's like he was gloating."

"Perhaps he thinks it gives him power over you. Does he, Connie? Have any power over you?"

"No," she said, adamantly. "Not any more. At first he did, when he took Josephine from her school and made me watch him. You remember how scared I was then? I was terrified." (*And that was only three days ago, I reminded myself.*) "But not any more. Like I told Dr Simmons, I'm still shit-scared, but I think that's mainly 'cause I've got a feeling he'll come after me one day. But he he'd got to find me first, hasn't he? And now I've moved it won't be so easy for him. And anyway, Angie, I want to help you to find him first. You've got to – he's not going to stop now."

"Have you any idea where this place might be?"

She shook her head. "No. I was affected more by what I was seeing … the little girl he was carrying … and the fact that now could to 'see' me. I'm just glad I left Forrest Hills. I feel safer here."

"Do you think he's killed before?" I asked.

Connie looked at me thoughtfully for a moment. "You're not play-ing games with me, are you?"

"Sorry? What d'you mean."

"Yes you do, Angie. I know what you're getting at... this is about my 'amnesia', doesn't it? You're testing me."

"Connie! Give me a break! I wouldn't dream of playing games like that with you – or anyone else, come to that. That would be sick - I thought you knew me better than that."

"You're right. And I'm the one who should be sorry," she said con-tritely. "It's just that I've got this image of this bastard in the back of my mind – from somewhere in the past... I don't know when, or where, he's in there all right. Maybe that's what my amnesia's all about; I just don't know. I'm not even sure I want to know. This man's totally evil, Angie, believe me. And I suppose it's possible he's killed before but I don't know anything about that."

"Could I ask you something?"

"Sure."

"Well, it's just that your visions seem to be on the increase lately; what I mean is there was nothing for a few years – and now, suddenly, your psychic powers have come back. It's almost as if you've been sleeping and something's sort of snapped you awake. Am I making any sense, Connie?"

She treated me to one of her enigmatic smiles as she considered my question. Then she said, "I don't even try to make sense of it. I remem-ber the last vision I had was when my mum died..." She shuddered at the memory. "I saw her so clearly, hanging there from the banister..." She peered then as if she was trying to penetrate the darkness, before continuing, "If I look carefully now I'm sure I can still see her. She's..."

She screwed her eyes tight as though she was shutting off the image. "I'm sorry, Angie; I can't do this. It's like another nightmare. Anyway, after that, I suppose I somehow managed to shield myself – stop them from appearing. And when I saw that man pushing Josephine into the car – well," she shrugged. "I can only think it was because I was getting better." She grinned. "Now it's me who's not making any sense."

"Yes you are. It was just nature's way at the time of telling you enough was enough. Tell me, though: when you first saw the man in the field, did he have the child with him?"

"I don't know. I only saw him put the clothes in the corner of the field. Do you think it's Josephine?"

I was pretty sure it was Josephine, even without conclusive evidence. I was also certain the bastard really had murdered her.

I nodded, too choked to say anything, too filled with outrage at the terror and suffering that that evil monster had inflicted on a small child. We had to find this man at all costs, capture him before he had the opportunity to torture and kill any more children. I needed to speak with Dr Simmons – as a matter of some urgency. But there was a final question I had to ask Connie.

"Connie; this common where you think the mine is – d'you think if you went back there, in your mind, you might get an idea where it is? Or at least some clue to point us in the right direction?"

"No. Sorry. Anyway it was so dark I couldn't see a lot."

"Got idea how long it took to get from the field where he left the clothes to the common itself?"

"No. My vision was kinda fragmented. One minute I was with him in the field, the next I was at the mineshaft. I don't know how I got there - except we went over this waste ground."

"Could you think about it some more? Let me know if anything comes back to you – anything that might help?"

"Yeah of course. What you going to do now, Angie?"

"I'm going to speak with Dr Simmons; I've an idea he might be able to help us in our search. He used to be involved in offender profiling - and that's exactly what we need now. Then I have to get back to the station. How about you, Connie? How you planning to spend your time here?"

She grinned and got up from the chair. "I'm going to enjoy my new freedom – and I'm going to have a look round the shops for starters! Do you know how long it is since I went into a shop?"

"Yes. Actually I do. But you're not going out alone, are you? I don't think you're ready for that yet."

"No, Angie; stop worrying. Sheila said she'd take me. Anyway, I've got my own social worker now to look after me."

"Well, if you're going shopping you'll be needing some money." It was my turn to grin. "You do remember what money is?" I said, handing her a few pounds.

"Yeah! I had a briefing at the hospital. And they've already bunged me a few quid, so I don't think I'll need any more. But thanks anyway."

I kissed her on the cheek. "You're going to be fine, Connie. And I'll be back to see you, probably tomorrow. And, this time, I'll remember to keep my mobile switched on, in case you need me."

"Bye, Angie. And thank you."

I gave her a wave, as if to say that her thanks weren't necessary, then went down to meet up with Dr Simmons.

CHAPTER EIGHTEEN

"Do you mind if I take some time to think about this, Angie?" he said after I had laid out our proposal. "I'm not sure I'm the best person to help the police with this. It's been quite a while since I was involved in profiling."

"I'm sorry, Doctor, but there's no time. We need your input now. I'm supposed to bring you back to the station with me as it goes; the Superintendent wants to brief you personally."

"Really? So why hasn't he contacted me direct then? I mentioned, didn't I, that we've locked horns in the past, professionally speaking I mean." He shook his head. "I'm sorry, Angie, but in the circumstances it's probably better if I recommend another psychologist. I know someone who's a specialist in criminal profiling; he's far better qualified than I am."

He took out an address book from his desk and was busily thumbing through it when I said: "We don't want an alternative, Dr Simmons. We're not short people we could go to. It's you we need in this particular case."

He frowned, obviously puzzled. "I don't understand? What's so special about me that makes you turn down someone infinitely more qualified? I fail to see how that can possibly help your case. Unless there's something you're not telling me. Is there, Angie? Something I should know, perhaps?"

"Bite the bullet!" I told myself. "Shit or bust!"

"Alright, yeah…There is something. It's Connie – she's involved."

He frowned again, more deeply this time; evidently my admission had disturbed him.

"You'd better explain," he said caustically. "And it had better be good."

"You won't like it, but, what the hell; here goes anyway. Now, you're not going to like this, and I realise you're not with me on this one, but, accept it or not, I've got evidence that's convinced me Connie's visions are for real. For instance, she's come up with specific information she couldn't possibly have got hold any other way. Psychic phenomena, or however you want to describe it are the only answer." I held out my hand – the only way I could think of to stop him interrupting. "No, please, bear with me a moment. Connie's just described to me, in detail, some articles of clothing we discovered only this morning in a field quite a way from here. She couldn't possibly have known about it. We think the clothing belongs to the missing eight-year-old, Josephine Marsden. The one I mentioned earlier. We now have reason to believe she has been murdered.

"But there's more to it than that. Much more. Connie actually believes this man, whoever he might be, is aware of her - as if he's knows he's in these visions of hers - and she's afraid he will come after her. Now, if you could bring yourself to put your scepticism aside and treat this as the phenomenon it is, I'm convinced you'll be able to help. And you won't just be helping the police – you'll be helping Connie too. Will you try, Doctor? Please? Just try and approach this with an open mind? For Connie's sake if nothing else?"

"What does your Chief Inspector Robbins think of all this? Is he as cynical as I am, or have you managed to convert him?"

"All the evidence Connie's given us has convinced him she's for real. Anyway, you can ask him about it yourself if you'll agree to work with us!"

"And your Superintendent? My old colleague… he subscribed to all thus mumbo jumbo does he?"

"No. To be honest, he won't get involved. I take it you're not interested then?"

"Not at all. Don't anticipate me, Angie. I'm just curious about who else I'll be working with – that's all. Now, don't misunderstand me, I'm not ready yet to join your little club but I can see why you believe in these psychic phenomena so I'm prepared to adopt an open mind. However, my dear, the reason I'm willing to help you is that I think Connie does genuinely believe she's in danger. I don't need any convincing about that. And I'm still of the view that her underlying problem has its source in her early environment. Well, we'll see, shan't we? And, you're right, it's important I maintain a close involvement with her; that way, as you say, I can help her and the police at the same time." He smiled wryly.

"And, by the way, if we're going to be working together, then the name's Paul – not Dr Simmons. Shall we go, then?"

CHAPTER NINETEEN

I rang Jim on the mobile to let him know I was on my way back, accompanied by Dr Simmons. He made no comment other than to ask me to go straight to the main conference room, where he would be waiting with the superintendent and Frank Kewell. When we arrived I made the appropriate introductions; as I already knew, the superintendent and Dr Simmons – I still had to get used to thinking of him as Paul – went back quite a long way, although he hadn't met the others before today. He took a seat at the large, oblong conference table looking relaxed and confident, despite the tension evident in the room.

He made a prayer-like gesture with his fingers, leant forward in his chair and smilingly said: "So, Phil – or do I call you Superintendent Connors, as you're on official duty? – How can I help you?"

"Come on, Paul; we know each well enough to dispense with the formalities." He forced a smile, made his customary clearing of his throat and then continued, "Has Sergeant Crossley here given you an outline of our problem, at all?"

"Only briefly. I know you're looking for a missing child, and you now have reason to believe she may already be dead. And Angie said you'd welcome some help with offender profiling; although I did point out I haven't done that sort of work for some time."

Jim cut in, "Your reputation precedes you, Doctor…"

"Paul. Please."

"Quite. Paul. Anyway, as I was about to say, the superintendent informs us you were instrumental a few years back in helping to bring Stewart, the serial rapist, to justice."

"Yes, but that was a while ago, Jim. I've been out of the loop for some time now."

"I accept that. But I doubt the criminal psychology has changed any. A child murderer's still a murderer – that'll never change – and one of the most effective ways of apprehending them is with the help of experts like yourself…You know, giving us insight into the darkest recesses of his mind.

"So, Paul," the superintendent said; "having heard that, will you help us?"

The doctor nodded. "Yes, I'll do the best I can. But first I need to be fully briefed. Is that something you'll do, Phil?"

"No. The SIO on this case is Detective Chief Inspector Robbins here – Jim Robbins. He'll carry out the briefing, with some help from the three detective sergeants - we also have Peter Corkhill on the team - but I want the two of you to liaise constantly with me. That said, I can give you an initial outline of the case."

He then proceeded to take Dr Simmons through a summary of the incident, from the time we first received notification of the abduction, up to the recent contact we had via the Marsdens. Throughout it all, Paul made copious notes on a foolscap pad, and didn't interrupt until the superintendent had completed his review. Interestingly, no reference was made of the role Connie had played in the proceedings, and – to my relief – neither Jim nor the doctor picked up on it. The latest discussion between Connie and me, I had, so far, kept to myself. I would put Jim in the picture later, when it was appropriate, but I would have to consider the doctor's position. Not so much on a need-to-know basis, but more on how dismissive he might be.

Paul looked thoughtful for a moment as he reread his notes. Finally, he said: "You might think this is a superfluous question, but what makes you so sure the child is dead? Is it because of the discovery of the clothes? Or the telephone call to the Marsdens? Or, perhaps, a combination of the two?"

It was Jim who answered. "First off, Paul, that's just an internal view, in the absence of any hard evidence. We don't want that to get into the public domain – not yet anyway. It's based not only on the issues you've raised but also primarily on the MO. We now have reason to believe this man planned the abduction over a period of time; it wasn't what you psychologists would describe as a disorganised crime…"

Paul smiled at the mistaken reference to his qualification, not bothering to contradict him.

"He very carefully surveyed the site, selected his target, then identified the child's mother and followed her to her home, with the intention of disabling her car so she'd be late picking up her daughter the following afternoon."

"And did he? Disable her car?"

"Yes. We've had forensics check and the car was broken into the night before the child was taken."

"How would he know the mother wouldn't try to use the car the next morning?" Paul asked. "Wouldn't that have backfired on him if she had?"

"Because, obviously, he'd been watching the house for some little while, and he would have learnt that it was Mr Marsden who always dropped Josephine off at school in the mornings. Had she intended to use the car the following morning, earlier than her scheduled timetable, then our man would simply have altered his plans accordingly, then tried again later. He was very meticulous. And he wanted Josephine. He appeared to be very clear about that."

"Yes. I understand that, and I don't disagree with you, Jim. From what you're telling me there is no doubt he planned this abduction very carefully. But you still haven't convinced me he's actually murdered her. How long's it been? Three days? Have you considered he might be holding her as some kind of trophy? Paedophiles have been known to do that – especially if they're involved in a ring."

"What about the clothes? And the telephone call?" Frank asked, speaking for the first time. "We believe it was this man who told the Marsdens their daughter was already dead; it had to be because he knew exactly where we found the clothes. That information has still not been disclosed outside of this police station."

"A leak?" Paul suggested.

"No," Jim said adamantly. "If there'd been a leak it would've been to the press… and we haven't heard a word about it from them. Anyway, whoever phoned the Marsdens is one sick bastard, and I really can't believe it was one of ours." He frowned. "No, doctor – sorry, Paul; the child is dead. We're certain of that. All of our experience tells us she's been murdered. And there's one other thing we haven't mentioned. There was a bloodstain on the child's shoe, and we have reason to believe it's from Josephine; we'll know for certain within the next few hours."

Paul still had that cynical expression on his face; apparently he remained unconvinced.

"What about DNA?" he asked. "Any possibilities there?"

"It's too early yet. That will take a couple of weeks for the complete analysis."

The superintendent reached out and placed a hand on Jim's arm. "So, Paul; I'm not going to ask you what you think – I realise that would be premature. But I want you to know that all of our resources are available to you, and we've set aside an office for you to use. Can you make a start on the information we have so far?"

"Well, I can certainly make some postulations. But if we assume for now the girl's dead, then I'm sure most of you will be aware that we're dealing with the type known as a 'sadistic offender' – the most vicious of all paedophiles. Of the many children each year abducted and never seen again, it's almost certain the archetypal sadistic offender will have murdered them. And it's unlikely their bodies will ever be found."

My mind drifted back to the children in the drainage pit, and the effect it had on me at the time. Sure, it was true that I was stronger now, and that was in no small way down to the patience of the good doctor here. But one thing that nothing would ever eradicate was the reaction of the parents when I told them we had found their daughter's body. I would do anything to avoid having to go through that torment again.

"The only thing I'd ask you to bear in mind if I take this on," the doctor was saying, "is that, I've still got patients in the hospital to care for, and it's out of the question that I neglect them in any way."

The superintendent nodded his agreement. "'Course not. That goes without saying. All I ask is that you give us as much time as you possibly can. We've got to catch this man."

Dr Simmons pursed his lips thoughtfully. "Well, you don't need me to tell you that's not going to be easy. Perhaps it might help if I gave you an outline of the profiler's role in this sort of case, so you're all familiar with how we go about it. Angie, you'll have to excuse me; I know you've already covered this at Warwick, but I don't think your colleagues will object to a bit of a lecture."

I nodded, pleased he at least acknowledged my limited expertise.

"First off, the correct terminology is 'sociopsychology profiling'. There's a good reason for that, and it's essentially because, aside from attempting to analyse the criminal's psychological profile, we also need to understand his social pathology. That is, his background, education and level of intelligence, and, together with that, attempt to establish a social environment – principally his parents – and how they treated him as a child. All of these issues, and more, will help to identify his psychological make-up. These days, of course, we drop the reference to 'socio-', more as a matter of convenience – but it's still vitally important.

"The second aspect of offender profiling deals with what are known as 'treasures', or collectors' items. These are either paraphernalia he will collect, such as pornographic photos he'll have taken or items that belonged to his victims. These could be pieces of jewellery, or even small body parts, such as fingers. So, if you do find a body, you have to watch out for mutilation because it's bound to tell us something about the criminal.

"The third element of profiling, in case some of you aren't familiar with it, is the interviewing technique. Having established the offender's social pathology and psychological framework, we can then use it to create an effective programme for persuasive interviewing - once he's been apprehended, that is. The interviewing technique is mainly de-signed to encourage the suspect to admit to his crimes. That's what happened with the serial rapist the chief inspector mentioned earlier.

"I'm sorry to bore you with all this, but I think it's important for you all to have at least some understanding of how this works. And, of course, you've got to understand that profiling's not an exact science; it's part science and part art form. Now, our particular offender, as I've said, is not going to be easy to apprehend; and I wouldn't want you to think that profiling will catch him. At best, it's a tool. But there is no substi-tute for intelligent investigative police work.

"Okay, having said all that, I do believe he's inadvertently opened the door a fraction."

"How do you mean?" Jim asked.

"For starters he left the clothes where you were bound to find them. That tells us he's challenging the police. Secondly, the phone call to the Marsdens; what was it he said? 'You'll never find the body.' That confirms his invincibility in his own mind; that is: 'You won't find the body, you won't find me.' I believe we can use that against him."

"How?" I was the first to ask.

"By letting him believe we're playing *his* game. When actually, we're making it *our* game." Again, he held out a hand. "Don't ask me yet exactly how we're going to achieve that; I need time to think about it. But one thing I'm sure of: this man's supremely confident, and undoubtedly intelligent – and that too can be used to our advantage."

The superintendent got up from his chair and reached across the table to shake Paul's hand.

"Welcome aboard, Paul. Now, if you'll excuse me, I'm needed elsewhere. I'll leave Jim here to show you your office. Just tell him what you need and we'll make it available. Oh, and good luck."

CHAPTER TWENTY

As Jim and Paul made their way to one of the offices set back from the incident room, Frank and I returned to our desks, Frank to follow up his earlier enquires, me to check if there were any messages. There was one from forensics. I returned the call, and eventually was put through to one of the scientists, a woman called Emma, whom I had met on previous occasions. Emma was in her late thirties, had been with the department a number of years, and was very good at her job.

"Hi, Emma. What you got?"

"Angie? Hi. We've got a match on the bloodstains on the shoe."

"Bloodstains? I thought there was only the one?"

"To the naked eye yeah; different story under the old microscope. They're the same blood type as Josephine's, and we reckon they're three days old. "Whoa…let me finish," she went on as I tried to interrupt. "We've also had the initial DNA results back from the lab. The blood *definitely* came from Josephine."

"Oh, Christ, no!" I gasped. "But how can you know for sure? We haven't been able to test her."

"We didn't have to. Frank Kewell got a sample from her parents; they let him have her hairbrush. That's all we needed. You might also be interested to know the lab found traces of saliva on the child's underpants – enough for DNA testing. But you're going to have to wait a while for definite results."

"The poor kid," was all I could think of to say. "Will you ring me as soon as you have something?"

"Sure. And, Angie, I'm really sorry – okay?"

"Thanks, Emma. Speak to you later."

Jim wasn't surprised when I passed on the information. "Let's hope we get a break with the DNA," he commented angrily. "The bastard might have left us something."

"Has Dr Simmons left?" I asked.

"Yes. He's taken copies of all the files with him. He's going to study them overnight and get back to us tomorrow. So, how did you get on with Connie? Did she have anything more to say?"

I felt myself sighing heavily. "She told me she thought Josephine was dead. Evidently she had another vision last night. She already knew about the clothes in the field – no, I sure as hell didn't tell her," I snapped, reacting to his challenging scowl.

He shrugged by way of apology. "Sorry. Did she say anything else?"

"Yes. It seems, whoever this monster is, he's not only playing games with us... Now he's got Connie joining in. She said it was as if he was actually causing her to have the visions, and he was sneering at her."

"Christ!" Jim said, shaking his head. "This gets more and more bizarre. Have you mentioned any of this to Paul Simmons?"

"Yes. But not in any detail. He's not exactly a believer."

"Well, I'm only glad he didn't say anything in front of the superintendent; he'd have my balls in a sling! Anything more, Ange?"

"She says she saw a man carrying a body through some woods – a small girl's body. Eventually, they crossed a common and then went over some waste ground and came to what Connie thinks is a disused mineshaft. Trouble is she's got no idea where it is. The man then threw the body down the shaft. Connie said she felt he knew she was watching, but that only seemed to excite him. She's still convinced, by the way, that he will come after her. That's the main reason she left the hospital."

He leant back in his chair contemplatively. "Do you think this could be the same man she had the visions about before?"

"You think there might be a link with those murders in the past?"

He shrugged non-committal. "I don't know. There's no real evidence yet, but I've had a funny feeling about this case for a while now."

I grinned, mischievously. "You're not admitting to having intuitions, Jim, are you?"

"Don't be so bloody cheeky!" he said, returning the grin. "There's something weird about the whole business is all I'm saying. Perhaps it's because your Connie's clouding the issue. Look," he continued, "say she hadn't had these visions – the recent ones, I mean – what would we have? Rhetorical question," he added, again before I could say anything. "I'll tell you what we'd have: a relatively simple case of child abduction, where we'd have to rely on old-fashioned police work to get a result. In other words, it would be a bloody hard slog. Isn't that what Paul Simmons was saying, basically?"

"Yes," I said quickly, "but she *has* had these visions. And we both know they're not just fantasies – never mind what the super or the doctor might say. So, what is it you're trying to say, Jim? You're in danger of losing me."

He shook his head, slowly and deliberately, as if somehow that might convince me of his argument.

"All I'm trying to say, Ange, is that if we're not careful we'll stop being detectives – postpone doing our jobs, if you like – because we'll be waiting for the next psychic occurrence and hoping that'll make our jobs easier. In other words, we may come to depend on it. Does that make any sense?"

I nodded. "I see what you mean; but I happen not to agree with you. It seems to me, personally, that there are two interconnected strands to this case: one, we have a paedophile and probable murderer to apprehend; and, two, we have a young teenage girl who's unwittingly involved and frightened for her safety. What I'm really saying, Jim, is that if we ignore Connie we could well have another victim on our hands."

"Yeah, okay," he grunted, conceding the point. "So, what's your suggestion? You don't think we should go back and search those woods again, do you? Like we did four years or so ago, hoping we might stumble across the child's body."

"No. 'Course not. I'm saying we should keep a watchful eye on Connie, partly because I'm concerned for her safety, and partly because I'm sure our paedophile is gonna try and contact her eventually. Trust me, the bastard's going to find her again and that's our chance to get the fucker!"

"You're not suggesting round-the-clock surveillance, are you? You know damned well we don't have the resources for that."

I leant forward across the table, as if to emphasise my point. "No, Jim, I'm not suggesting that either. What I do think is we should put the staff at Ashworth House in the picture. Put them on notice that this *could* happen. And perhaps arrange for a direct alarm link to the station here, coupled to regular bypass patrols. Is that too much to ask?" I said pointedly.

"I guess not," he agreed. "Especially if you're proved right. That would make us appear unforgivably incompetent." He nodded again. "Okay, Ange; I'll leave it to you to organise. Now, how about dinner? You hungry?"

"Oh no you don't!" I said, grinning. "If we're going to eat then it has to be at a restaurant, otherwise you'll want a repeat of the last time, and if I remember rightly we ate nothing that night!"

CHAPTER TWENTY-ONE

And that's what we did. We spent the evening at a very pleasant Italian not far from Jim's flat, had a few glasses of Chianti with the pasta, and followed this up with an early night – a restful one too, I might add.

When I woke up the next morning Jim had already left. There was a note on the pillow: "Didn't want to disturb you, thought you needed the rest – catch you later. J."

"Christ," I said aloud. It was still only six-thirty; he was becoming an insomniac. Or, it occurred to me before I turned over again, perhaps this case – in parallel with his promotion – was making him obsessive.

It was eight o'clock before I finally decided to get up. I had a laze in the bath, a light breakfast with two cups of coffee, resisted the urge to have a cigarette – I had stopped three months earlier – and then gave Connie a ring to see how she was settling in. She was still asleep, which had to be a good sign, so I left a message to say I'd ring her later, and then set off on foot for the station; I had left my car in the pound the previous evening, and I guessed Jim must have forgotten. Not that I minded, really. I could have caught a bus from Edgbaston but it was such a lovely day, with blue skies, freckled with occasional wispy, cotton clouds, and a warm sun that prompted me to put on my shades, it would have been a waste to miss out on it. It was one of those 'good to be alive' days, even though there was nothing to feel good about. I strode out purposefully, enjoying the morning. The streets were fresh and shining, as if they had just been spring-cleaned. I smiled at one or two people in passing, even though my mind was elsewhere.

My eye suddenly caught a news bulletin, featured on a billboard outside a newsagent's shop. The headline seemed to scream at me: "Missing girl believed dead."

A feeling of dread welled up inside me, as I went inside the shop to buy a paper. According to the article, forensic evidence, recently "uncovered", had identified bloodstains from an item of Josephine Marsden's clothing as originating from the missing child. It then went on to speculate that, after speaking with the Marsdens, it had been established that the killer had contacted them by telephone, informing them about the clothing left in a field outside Birmingham, and also advising the parents that their child was dead and her body would never be found.

As a journalistic piece it was, without doubt, the most insensitive and cruel example I had ever come across. It was also evident from the phraseology that the Marsdens, in their distress, had been taken advantage of and 'conned' into making these comments. What I found even more disturbing was the reference to the DNA testing of the blood sample. I was reminded again of the recent references to a 'leak' from somewhere inside the force. How else could the paper possibly have obtained that kind of privileged information?

I grabbed a passing taxi and headed for the Steelhouse Lane station, knowing that Jim would be going 'ape shit' about this development. Christ almighty! It was like fighting a battle with our hands tied behind our backs! I gave it some more thought during the taxi ride; for example, how many people apart from forensics knew about the blood test? It certainly wasn't common knowledge inside the incident room. So, discounting the superintendent and the DCI, for obvious reasons, that only left Frank Kewell and me – and it sure as hell wasn't me!

But that just didn't make any sense. Aside from being a career copper for many years, Frank would certainly know that, even under the media's confidentiality screen, he was bound to be the prime suspect. And for what? Thirty lousy pieces of silver? No; I couldn't buy that. It had to be someone else. And whoever that someone was, he, or she, had to have an entrée into either the forensic department or the incident room itself.

I was still shaking my head, puzzled, as I went into Jim's office. He already had the paper on his desk. He tossed it over to me, his expression, predictably, one of furious rage. "You'd better read this," he said, an angry furrow creasing his brow.

"I've already read it. Sickening, isn't it? But I still don't believe the leak came from inside here."

"No. I agree with you. But I'm damned if I know where else it could have come from. How about that friend of yours in forensics? What's her name?

"Emma?" I exclaimed sceptically. "No, Jim. You've got the wrong one there. Emma wouldn't tell you the time of day unless you had a warrant! She's about the most security-conscious person I know." I shook my head, more in frustration than anything. "And if you're thinking there might have been a leak from forensics, you can forget it. Their admin procedures are as tight as a drum; pretty well everything's on a need-to-know basis."

"Well, the super's meeting with the paper's editor-in-chief at the moment, although I doubt he'll discover anything there – you know what those people are like. I can't see them disclosing their source, can you?"

"Hardly. But if we're discounting the possibility of an internal leak then there's only one other source it can be."

"How do you mean, Ange?"

"The killer! It has to be the killer. Who else would know about the bloodspots on the shoes? Who else would know they came from the body of the little girl? Paul Simmons warned us he wanted to play games; this is just another example. Just like leaving the clothes in the field and then phoning the Marsdens. It's a bloody game, Jim; he's doing his best to make us appear stupid."

"If you're right," he growled, "then he's bloody well winning." He leant forward, placing his chin into the cup of his hands and pondering the suggestion. "It's a good point, though. I should've thought of that myself. The only problem now is: how do we check it out?"

"We don't," I asserted. "We assume I'm right and we ask Dr Simmons – Paul – to help us devise a strategy for dealing with it. Offhand, I'd say we somehow get the newspapers to play ball; see if we can tempt him out into the open."

"Yeah, well, the doc's due back sometime this afternoon, so we'll raise it with him. In the meantime, we say nothing of this to anyone. Agreed?"

"Totally." I said, but only after a hesitation.

"Go on, Ange. What else is on your mind? It's not going to cost us money, is it?"

I smiled. It was extremely difficult to maintain any sense of humour under circumstances such as these. There was very little, if any, escape from the relentless pressure. When you could, I found it helped lighten things a little, and that had to be welcome.

"It's nothing dramatic," I assured him; "it's only that I'm expecting to hear something later today about the primary results from the DNA sample. Do we keep that between ourselves as well?"

He sighed. "Let's not go overboard on this. We'll wait to see what, if anything, the analysis shows; then we'll decide. But I doubt it'll reveal very much – it's too early. Okay?"

CHAPTER TWENTY-TWO

We left it at that, and I went off to make arrangements regarding the added security procedures we planned to introduce at Ashworth House. During the course of the morning Jim caught hold of me for a brief word.

"It look as though you were right about our leak," he informed me. "I've just had the super onto me, reporting on his meeting with the editor. Evidently the informant wasn't a protected source. The story came from an anonymous phone call – to the crime desk. They were going to ignore it at first, then someone had the idea of contacting the Marsdens to see what they could be induced to disclose. They confirmed the part about discovering the children's clothes, and the telephone telling them their daughter was dead; so, the paper merely put all the pieces together and ran with the story.

"So, yes; it seems the killer is playing cynical games with us. And, as you speculated, outside of a restricted few, only he would know about the bloodstains matching. I only hope Paul Simmons can come up with some idea how to beat him at his own sick game. Otherwise we have to wait until he makes a serious mistake." He shrugged. "Unless either you or Frank can think of anything we might have overlooked?"

I shook my head. "We've covered all the bases, Jim. And I agree with you, all we can do now is wait until he screws up. And we know that will happen at some time; I just pray it's before he has the chance to murder some other little girl."

"Yeah. You and me both. Let me know as soon as you have something on the DNA, won't you? Who knows, that might produce a result."

* * * * * * * * *

I took Arthur Talbot with me to Ashworth House. Arthur, a middle-aged uniformed- sergeant, was in charge of the Crime Prevention Unit. He was a big man, probably six feet three or four, with thick forearms and hands and a spreading girth to match. His hair was thick and almost white. His face was a deep brown and heavily lined after years of exposure to the sun. Everyone responded to Arthur; despite his size he was a gentle giant, with a cheerful disposition and a ready smile.

"A bit strange, Angie, isn't it?" he commented during the journey.

"How's that?" I said, swerving to miss a wandering cyclist.

"Giving a halfway house advice on crime prevention. I wouldn't have thought they had anything worth stealing!"

"They haven't. It isn't potential thieves they need protection from."

"No? So, enlighten me, my dear. What sinister crime innovation am I about to be introduced to?"

"'Sinister' is the right word, Arthur. There is a young teenager living there at present; we think she could be in danger from a prowler."

He sighed heavily, prompted no doubt by his considerable experience in the field. "Angie, please. If you want me to help, I have to know the *true* story – not the *fictitious* one. So, why don't we try again, and I'll pretend I didn't hear the first explanation?"

I waved a hand in the air by way of apology. "Yeah. Sorry. But this is something we're trying to keep the lid on; you'll understand why if I tell you."

"And are you? Going to tell me?"

I laughed. "Only if you're sure you want to hear it, and you give me your word you won't let it slip."

"You have my word; and my undivided attention."

I gave him a brief outline of the case, and tried to avoid cringing when I got to the part about Connie being a psychic and how she had experienced a vision of the killer.

"And you believe this guy will come after her?" he said, without a trace of scepticism in his voice.

"Yeah. I'm convinced of it."

"Does he know where to find her?"

"Not yet he doesn't, no. Connie only moved in yesterday; she's spent the last four years in Forest Hills with a cognitive disorder."

"She's not the kid who was involved in those child murders about that time? Was she?" he asked quietly.

I nodded, searching for a parking space in the road outside Ashworth House.

"But you believe he'll find her?"

Again I nodded. "I'm convinced he will." I managed to find a spot, but before getting out of the car I said: "There's something going on here, Arthur – and it's beyond my comprehension. All I can ask is that you trust me when I tell you these visions of Connie's are not make-believe. They're very real."

"Oh, I believe you alright, Angie. It might interest you to know I have an aunt who's psychic; she's a well-known medium, apparently – people virtually queue up for a session with her. And some of the stuff she predicts would blow your mind. So I don't need converting."

"Connie isn't that kind of a psychic … well, I say that but then I'm not altogether sure whether there are different types. It's just that she doesn't see the future, is what I'm saying … she has visions in what she describes as real-time." Whilst I was talking to him an idea was crossing my mind. I had promised myself that, given the chance, I would investigate this issue of psychic phenomena with a specialist of some kind. It sounded to me, from what Arthur was saying, that his aunt could well be the right person to talk to.

He was shaking his head. "It's no good trying to explain it to me, Angie. If that particular gift runs in families then it's passed me by …"

* * * * * * * * *

Whilst Sheila took Arthur on a tour of the premises, I went to find Connie. She was in the kitchen having a sandwich. Today she was wearing a sloppy T-shirt and jeans, and the ubiquitous pair of dog-eared trainers. On the whole I thought she looked rather cool.

"Hi, Angie." She pointed to a loaf of bread. "Want to join me? We have some ham, or cheese, or if you like I could make you a bacon sandwich."

I grinned and said, "Ham would be fine thanks. So, how did your first night go? I rang this morning but they said you were still sleeping."

"Great," she said enthusiastically. "I think I'm going to like it here. And the staff are really nice. Would you like tea or coffee with that?" she asked, handing me a plate for the sandwich.

"Oh; tea would be nice. Has anything been suggested yet about further education? Or is it too early?"

"Yeah. I had a chat this morning with Sheila. She tells me they have an arrangement with a college close by; I'll be able to enrol when my A level results come through – as long as they're good enough."

"Hey! That's great. What are you thinking of taking? Or are you still making up your mind?"

I found it hard to generate any enthusiasm at this news. Part of me was having this normal friend-to-friend conversation with Connie, as if it was all perfectly natural, whilst the policewoman side of me was filled with a sense of apprehension at the thought of her travelling to and from college every day, walking precisely in the killer's territory.

She obviously either read my thoughts or, more likely, anticipated me, because she suddenly said: "Don't worry, Angie; I know what you're thinking, but I won't be walking. There'll be someone to take me and collect me every day. And I don't know if you'll be pleased or not, but I want to take a degree in psychology."

I was pleased, very pleased, and I told her so. "And you'll have your own private tutor here in Dr Simmons," I added.

"Well, I'll be able to pick his brains from time to time, that's true. But I don't know yet how long I'll be able to stay here. Or even how long I'll want to. It can't be forever, though, can it? The time will come, I hope, when I'll want to make a separate life for myself."

I gave her hand a squeeze. "And when it does, Connie, I'll be around to help you. You won't be on your own, I promise. But it won't be for a while yet."

"How's the case going?" she asked, again reading my thoughts.

"Slowly," I admitted. "But these cases invariably do. I've brought a colleague along with me today; he's something of an expert in crime prevention. He's going to give you all a lecture a bit later on, after he's finished surveying the premises. Also," I said, before she could intervene, "I'm sending a technician this afternoon to install some security technology, so you'll have 'state-of-the-art' protection. Add to that a substantially increased night-time car patrols from the Winson Green station, and you should be able to sleep easy."

"You're very good to me, Angie. And I do appreciate it – believe me. But we have to face it; if this man's determined to contact me, for whatever purpose, I don't think anything we do will stop him."

"Perhaps not; but that doesn't mean we have to make it easy for him. Does that thought scare you?"

"Too right it does. But I have to tell you that there's a part of me that recognises this is inevitable." She looked at me intently. "I'm not suggesting we open the front door for him, or hang out the welcome mat; I'm just being realistic here when I say he *will* find a way to contact me."

It seemed to be my day again for sighing. She was right, of course. No building in the world could be made entry-proof against a professional; I suppose the same could be said of a compulsive child murderer. Except, in the case of the latter, it was common knowledge they avoided risk at all costs, and it was that more than anything I was relying on.

"We'll catch him, Connie; don't worry," I said, with not too much conviction.

Fortunately, Arthur came in at that moment, unwittingly lightening the atmosphere. Before introducing him to Connie I took him to one side and asked, "Arthur, if I wanted to meet your aunt – the psychic – could you ... well, would it be possible to arrange something?"

He chuckled knowingly. "I had a feeling you were going to ask me that ... you want to understand more about how your girl's gift works. Is that it?"

"Yes, spot on. I don't like not knowing enough about this ... well, this mystery."

"Leave it with me, Angie. You may have to wait a little while – as I said, she's very busy. But I'm sure she'll see you. I'll give you a ring later."

I then went off to find Dr Simmons. He was just about ready to leave for Birmingham, so I gave my car keys to Arthur, said a quick goodbye to Connie and a thank-you for lunch, with an invite for her to spend the weekend at my place, and joined the doctor to share a ride back to the station.

CHAPTER TWENTY-THREE

"You saw the paper, no doubt?" Paul stated, after we had been driving for a while.

"Yes," I acknowledged. "We've followed it up and we believe it was the killer. Everything points to it."

He nodded his head in agreement. "Yeah. I thought the same. I'm still working on an appropriate response to his games. I guess he's really enjoying himself at the moment."

"At our expense, you mean?"

"Whatever you do, Angie," he said emphatically, "you mustn't take this personally. You'll be playing right into his hands if you do. Remember what we talked about? So try to stay focused and detached - I promise you it'll give you a decisive edge."

I knew what he meant, and – after all those sessions we had held – I was definitely more prepared to be objective, but where Connie was involved it wasn't going to be that easy.

I had also given a lot of thought to something else that had come up in one of our sessions, and that was his views on absent fathers having a reflective effect on a daughter's character and her self-imposed guilt trip. It was all very well to analyse people on a kind of theoretical basis, but the fact is that we're all human, and something else I was remembering was what had been said to me once by a friend: "We are all victims of our environment."

"Did you spend the night at Ashworth?" I asked, changing the subject.

He grinned, letting me know he wasn't the slightest deceived. "No. I went back to the hospital after leaving the station. I did some work there with patients, then spent a couple of hours reading the crime reports."

"Did you find anything we might have missed?"

"Well, I'd have liked to visit the scene where he left the clothes. Invariably that tells us something."

"Forensics went over the ground pretty thoroughly. I'm sure they won't have missed anything there."

"I wasn't thinking of forensics, Angie. It was *extrinsic* evidence I had more in mind. All profilers will tell you that at every crime scene involving violence, even allowing for the fact that the violence may have been committed elsewhere, the perpetrator interacts in some way with both the site and the victim, and leaves something of himself behind. In this case it could have been the way he arranged the clothes; or how he ingresses and egresses the site; how long did he linger there? Perhaps the scene helped him to relive his excitement. I don't know for sure, obviously, but there is always something that might help us."

"Is it too late now?" I asked somewhat anxiously.

"Not totally. I believe it's still important to visit the site; there may still be some intangible clue he left. And if forensics took photos of the scene, especially of the clothes before they were moved, that would be a help."

I took out my mobile and began dialling. "Would you like to go now, Paul? I can ask Frank Kewell to meet us there with the photos."

"Yes. It'd be a good idea to get a feel for the site before meeting up with Jim Robbins. Is it far from here?"

"About an hour if *you* drive," I said, with a wicked grin. "Twenty minutes if *I* do!"

He laughed and pulled over. "Never let it be said…"

CHAPTER TWENTY-FOUR

Frank was waiting for us when we arrived. The area was still cordoned off with the traditional yellow tape of a crime scene. But there was something different about the site: something I couldn't quite put my finger on. Then it occurred to me – the silence was missing from when we were last here. On that morning there had been an eerie stillness about the place; not a sound could be heard, not even the chatter of an occasional bird. Now, it was as if nature had reasserted itself and everything had returned to normal.

We reopened the five-barred gate and entered the field, careful to avoid any contact with the area marked out by forensics. There was nothing special about it – at least, nothing I could identify with anyway. It was merely a corner of a field, quite dry – almost dusty, in fact – due to the lack of rain over the last couple of days. There were no discernible footprints, as far as I could see; it puzzled me what, if anything, Paul was hoping to discover.

"Can you show me where the clothes were placed?" he asked, scanning the photographs.

Frank drew a line in the dusty soil, and then made an oblong shape. "More or less here," he said.

"Can you remember what order they placed in? ...The photos don't show that."

"Yes. I made a note." He took out his notebook and searched for the page. "Here we are," he continued. "Cardigan, pink, on the top; dress, also pink, underneath that; child's slip, white, next; finally child's underpants, white, with small, pink handkerchief, tucked in a pocket."

"What about the shoes – and the socks?"

"The shoes, with the socks inside, were placed at the side of the clothes."

"Was everything arranged neatly? You describe the order of the clothes, Frank, but it's important to know how they were laid-out."

"Very neatly," he confirmed. "Almost as if her mother had undressed her; or, at least, her mother had taught her to be neat and tidy when she undressed."

"And where the clothes clean?"

"Yes. Remarkably so. In fact, I had the impression they'd recently been washed. The only stain of any kind was the blood found on the shoes." He frowned, as if he were questioning what he had just said. "No. hang on, that isn't true, Paul. Evidently there are traces of DNA on the child's underpants – we're still waiting for results on that."

"Hmm," he said thoughtfully. "That's interesting. Would you know if forensics checked whether or not the clothes had recently been washed?"

The question was directed towards me and I felt myself blushing. "No. I don't think anyone thought to ask them. Is it important, Paul?"

"It could be – if only to confirm my supposition."

"Which is what?"

"That we're dealing here with an 'organised offender'. Everything he does has a particular meaning. It's almost a compulsion with him. Everything must be clean and tidy. And I do mean everything. He will be fastidious in the way he dresses, the choice of his clothes – even the specific designer and where he buys them from; he's quite the snob, is our killer. You'll also find his car will be meticulously clean and shiny; he wouldn't be able to cope with untidiness or dirt. And undoubtedly it will be one of the more upmarket brands."

"So you're saying he's loaded?"

He nodded.

"How come he missed the bloodspots?" Frank asked.

"He didn't, Frank. They were put there deliberately, to furnish us with the forensic evidence that she was dead. He wanted us to know that without having to leave the body on show."

"Jesus!" Frank exclaimed. "He *is* a calculating bastard!"

"He has to have left us another clue, though," Paul said, frustrating-ly. "The bloodstains will only give us so much information."

"Do you think he left the saliva stains deliberately too?" I asked.

"Yes. Without question. As I said, everything he does has a pur-pose. In that instance, I have to confess I don't understand his intention, except that – clearly – he's trying to tell you something. I think we'll have a better idea when the DNA results are in; but whatever it is, he wants you to know about it."

He bent down and shuffled some of the soil between his fingers. "Frank, have you got a sample bag with you?"

"Sure. In the car. I'll get it."

"What have you found, Paul?"

"Somebody's pissed here. We'll take a sample back with us, but don't be surprised if it matches the saliva test. This is his way of demonstrating his complete sociopathology."

He took the bag from Frank and partly filled it with soil. Then he got to his feet, rubbing his back and groaning.

"Old age, Paul?" I joked.

"You should never mock the afflicted, young lady. One day, if you're lucky…" He didn't have to complete the sentence. Instead, he moved back to the entrance to the field and scanned the surrounding area carefully.

"I don't suppose there were any tyre tracks, were there?"

"No; nothing," Frank confirmed. "We went over the area very carefully."

"I didn't think so. So, there must be another entrance to the field."

"How do you work that out?" I asked, puzzled.

"Well, if you think about what I said earlier, about his fastidiousness, then it stands to reason he isn't going to park his vehicle here. And it isn't because he'd leave tracks; it's because he'd get his precious car dirty."

Frank and I followed him further up the lane, probable for about a quarter of a mile, until we came to a slight gap in the hedgerow with a strip of hard standing on the lane opposite.

"Here," Paul said, pointing. "This is where he entered the field."

Frank and I examined the strip of asphalt for tyre marks, but there was nothing. Paul ignored us; he was busily inspecting the point of entry to the field.

"Here!" he exclaimed eventually. "Frank, bring me another sample bag, will you?" He then took a small pair of tweezers from his medical bag and proceeded to remove from one of the branches a single strand of material.

"His first mistake. And he's certain to notice it later and worry about it. Come on – we'll check the field for footprints."

We followed him as he squeezed through the narrow entrance and headed back slowly towards the site of the clothing, closely inspecting the ground. Part of the way there we spotted what was obviously cow dung, and there, to our surprise, was a partial footprint embedded at the side.

"He'd clean his shoe," Paul informed us, "but nothing would persuade him to go near the cow pat."

Frank was already on his mobile alerting forensics. "I'll wait for them," he said. "If you've finished, doctor, I suggest you and Angie head on back."

I nodded, whilst Paul handed over the sample bags to Frank with instructions for forensics. Other than the single footprint the rest of the field was clear, so we returned to the car and headed towards the station. It had been a very productive afternoon's work, thanks to Paul.

We spoke very little during the journey. Paul was busy making copious notes in his folder, muttering the occasional comment to himself. Once or twice I asked him a question; either he hadn't heard me or he chose to ignore me.

I pulled up in front of the station, and before he got out I said, "Have you found out any more about this monster, Paul?"

He shrugged, non-committal. "Have you ever come across the term 'Mysoped' in your studies?"

I shook my head. "I don't think so. Why? Is it relevant?"

"Yes. Very much so. It's a word the FBI adopted some years back to describe the very worst kind of paedophile: the 'sadistic offender'. This type of paedophile is unique amongst all of the rest. He not only sexually brutalises children, his ultimate objective is to kill them. It's an uncompromising part of his ritual, and it's that as much as the sexual degradation he inflicts on the victim that gives him the most pleasure. And, in the light of our discoveries, I would have to conclude this is a 'mysoped' who we are dealing with.

"Be under no illusions, Angie; this man will bring your worst nightmares to a chilling reality. He is vicious – brutally vicious. He is also unpredictable, insofar as both timing and location are concerned. And, more importantly, he *enjoys* killing. You must also bear in mind, as I pointed out before, this will not be the first time he has killed; his compulsion will have evolved over quite a period of time. That tends to be the pattern."

"So, how do we catch him, Paul?"

"With professional, investigative police work – something you're good at – and a hell of a lot of luck." He opened the car door. "The good news, though, is that he's already made a couple of mistakes that will help us. Let's hope he keeps being as generous."

CHAPTER TWENTY-FIVE

Paul made his way across the incident room towards Jim's office, whilst I went to check my desk for messages. The incident room was still a hive of activity, only now, following the press and photofit release, the detectives were mostly dealing with the volume of calls from the public.

There was one message for me from the Birmingham newspaper wanting to know if I would agree to an interview – which I promptly ignored; the second was from Emma at forensics. I called her back straightaway.

"Hi, Angie. How's things?"

"You have some news?" I said, almost breathlessly.

"Yes," she said hesitantly. "Can you come over to the office?"

"Can't you tell me now, Emma?"

"I'd rather not; not on the phone. It's too sensitive."

"I'll be right over," I said, thinking to myself: "God, I hate mysteries!" I rang down to the desk to order a car, grabbed my handbag and hotfooted it downstairs. The forensics office was situated quite close to the Bullring, probably within walking distance, but I was in a hurry, And with the driver dropping me off at the front entrance, I didn't have to worry about parking. It was a fairly modern building, although you wouldn't think so from its current appearance. Already it was looking shabby, with cracks showing down two of its walls, and some of the tiles were missing from the entrance canopy. It also could do with a fresh coat of paint.

"So?" I said, after being shown into Emma's small and cramped office on the second floor. "What have we got?"

Emma looked at me, rather gravely, I thought. "Take a seat Angie," she offered, pointing to the only vacant chair. "You'll need to be sitting down to hear this."

I complied, trying to contain myself, as Emma handed across a sheet of fax paper covered with what seemed to me, at least, meaningless hieroglyphics.

"How am I supposed to read this, Emma?" I demanded. "Its just mumbo-jumbo."

"Sorry. I was forgetting. Those figures represent the preliminary results of the saliva swab from the child's clothing. And we have a provisional match!"

"Provisional? What does that mean?"

"It means that, until it's confirmed forensically, you won't be able to use it in a court of law. But other than that it's pretty conclusive."

I held out a hand. "Emma, please; stop keeping me in suspense. Who the hell is it? And why couldn't you tell me this on the phone?"

"I couldn't tell you, Angie, because I want to make absolutely certain before this information is publicised, that the result is definitive and not merely provisional. I'm telling you because I know you and I trust you to keep it confidential for the time being. And the answer to your question is that the DNA matches with the sample we took over four years ago from one of those seven murdered children. At least, we're almost certain it does; but, as I said, to be 100% positive we still need to make more tests. Obviously, we can't give you a name; whoever this character is, he hasn't had any run-ins with the police. But there's very little doubt: it's the same man."

"Jesus!" I exclaimed, letting out a breath. A thousand thoughts raced through my mind at the implications of this news.

One thing, though, stood out more clearly than anything else: it was Connie's remarks that day I was called to the hospital because she was so terrified. "He's here," she had said; "that horrible man is here." In my own mind I was convinced that what she was really saying then was: "He is *back*." And I was right!

I sat in the chair for a while, too stunned to say anything. Somehow, I had to get my head around this development.

"Are you okay, Angie?" I heard her ask.

"I don't know. I don't know that I'll ever be okay again." All I could think of was what Connie must have gone through, her very real fear, her terror, that this creature might be pursuing her, even closing in on her. And I shuddered.

Emma ran me back to the station in her car; I was till too dazed to think clearly, and I think she was afraid I might wander off somewhere. It had crossed my mind that day at the hospital that we could be dealing with the same man. But that was all it had been: a fleeting moment cultured from Connie's oblique comments that she had seen the killer somewhere before. Now we had the evidence, I wasn't sure just how we would be able to use it – except that my instincts about Connie's safety were well founded. The security we had placed around her now seemed grossly inadequate; my young friend, self-evidently, was in grave danger.

CHAPTER TWENTY-SIX

Paul and Jim still had their heads together when I went into the office to report. When they saw me they stopped what they were doing; Jim shot me a puzzled look.

"Are you alright?" he asked, concerned. "You look like you've seen a ghost."

"I have," I conceded. "At least, the nearest I'll get to seeing one. I've just come back from the forensic office – Emma had some preliminary results through on the saliva sample."

"And?"

"They match with the DNA sample from Alice's body all those years ago. It's the same man. You were right, Paul, when you said he was trying to tell us something. But I doubt even you could've guessed the real nature of his message. This isn't merely a – what was it you called him, Paul? – a mysoped? Someone who you also said had probably killed before. We're chasing a mass murderer here; some kind of ghoul!"

Paul took hold of my arm gently. "Why don't you sit down, Angie. Your news doesn't altogether surprise me; it was more or less what I expected when I said he was trying to leave us a message. But we do need to discuss this calmly."

Jim was shaking his head. "Are you suggesting, Paul, that he left that saliva deliberately? Knowing we were bound to make a match?"

"Yes. That's exactly what I'm saying."

"But why? What was he hoping to gain? Apart from a massive publicity campaign, which he's now bound to get." He continued shaking his head in disbelief. "Do you think he's losing it?"

"Losing it? What does that mean, Jim? He's certainly not mentally ill, if that's what you're implying. This man is a cold, calculating killer, who gets his kicks from sexually brutalising children, and then murdering them. When did you say those last murders occurred?"

"Just over four years ago," I confirmed.

"Remind me again; how many children were involved?"

"We found the bodies of seven children. He'd dumped their bodies to rot in an old septic tank in the woods. We'd never have found them if it hadn't been for Connie. Jim and I were both there. I don't think either of us will ever forget the scene. He'd abandoned those poor children as if they were nothing more than animal carcasses. Some of them had been there for over three years. Can you imagine how the parents must have felt? Denied even the rights to a decent burial? Unable to grieve until the bodies were recovered?"

"Whoa. Slow down, Ange," Jim said. "I understand how you feel, I was there too, remember. But we can't let this monster get to us."

"I think that's one of his objectives," Paul added. "It's a rhetorical question, if you like, but where do you imagine he has been these past four years or so? And why suddenly resurface now after all this time? He certainly hasn't been in prison – and that's usually the reason why their activities cease."

"You tell us, Paul. You're the expert in these things." Jim said cryptically.

"I don't know for sure. But if you consider the characteristics of this type of paedophile, then he'll be what is called 'geographically mobile'. In other words, unlike some types of child molesters, he doesn't have to hunt close to home. Usually he'll kill in one district and then move on to fresh territory. Invariably, he'll also hide the body." He rose to refill his coffee cup from the jug.

"Tell me," he continued: "what was the geographical profile of those seven children? Where they all from or around the West Midlands?"

"No," Jim said. "They were from as far afield as Newcastle – upon Tyne, that is. One, if I remember, was from Leeds. Another child was from Manchester. Three of them were from this area. What's your point, Paul?"

"My point is that, following the uncovering of his last burial site, four years ago, he has found a new tomb for the bodies – and the worry I have is that he may have found it shortly after the uncovering of his first graveyard. I know you've been checking police forces around this area in your search for other recent missing children, but I suggest you now check back, during the past four years, for missing children who haven't been found, regardless of their domicile; you'll be able to make an intelligent guess as to just what he's been doing in that time. To put it bluntly, people, it's my view that he's carried on mutilating and murdering little children on a regular basis.

"Sweet Jesus!" Jim exploded. "We could have the monster straight out of hell on our patch. Ange, let's take up Paul's suggestion. Get the team to change their search pattern; let's look up the records for missing children from that period. We need to know exactly what we're up against. Paul," he said, turning to the psychiatrist; "you still haven't answered my question. Why's he suddenly leaving us with these telltale clues? It's *that* I'm having difficulty with."

Paul remained standing, calmly drinking his coffee, as if this were some academic presentation. "Well, to understand that, Jim, you'll have to allow me to complete the profile on this man. I believe we now have sufficient information to enable me to do that, especially in the light of the DNA match. But you'll have to give me a couple of days. The one thing I can tell you for the moment is that these sadistic offenders have monumental egos. It seems to me that our man's ego is expanding, almost exponentially; what I originally described as a game has now become much more than that. This offender's deliberately challenging us."

I couldn't help but notice that, for the first time, Paul had actually joined himself into the action; 'you' had now become 'us'.

"Jim, before I go, there's something I want to raise with you," I said.

He sighed heavily. "Yeah. You're about to ask me about Connie. Right?"

"Well, yes; I was, actually. How did you guess?"

"Because I was having the same thoughts myself. Don't worry, Ange; I'll arrange something more appropriate. Maybe we can place one of the new graduates in Ashworth House. Leave it with me, will you?"

"Yeah, sure. And, Jim – thanks."

"Am I missing something here?" Paul asked. "Or is it something you'd rather I didn't know about? Do you think this character is likely to come after Connie? Is that it?"

Jim shuffled uncomfortably in his seat, trying to avoid meeting Paul's eyes.

"Jim; I promised Angie I'd keep an open mind. And that's precisely what I'm doing. So, you needn't feel embarrassed about broaching the subject of Connie's psychic powers; I've been well briefed, believe me."

"Yes. Well, I believe we have to reconsider the whole question of her safety, in the light of what you've told us." He shrugged his shoulders, perplexed. "There's still something about this whole case that I seem to be missing. Tell me, Paul: why would a paedophile be interested in a teenage girl? ...It doesn't make sense."

Paul returned to his seat, shaking his head. "I can't answer that, Jim, except to say I doubt it's sex related. All I can tell you is that this offender's unique in more ways than one. For instance, it's commonly accepted that 'sadistic offenders' prefer young boys to females. Oh, they'll snatch a girl if the opportunity presents itself; but that tends to be the exception. This character always goes for young girls, though. We've no evidence so far of males being involved." He continued to shake his head. "As far as I can tell we're dealing here with an enigma; perhaps we'll never know the answer. But, in the circumstances, more protection for Connie would definitely make sense."

CHAPTER TWENTY-SEVEN

For the next few days the incident room once again took on an atmosphere of frenzied activity. I could hardly get a word out of Peter Corkhill – I just hoped he wasn't sulking after my rejection. All available computer databases were combed for information on children who had gone missing, without trace, during the period in question, but the problem here was that – unless a crime had taken place – the names were unlikely to have gone onto the National Register. In turn, that meant contacting the various county police headquarters for the information; it was readily available, but retrieving it also took up an enormous amount of time.

We were still working on the problem when Paul returned a few days later for a conference. In attendance, apart from myself, was the superintendent, the now confirmed detective chief inspector, Jim Robbins, Frank Kewell (recently promoted to the rank of inspector, and now my immediate boss), Peter Corkhill, Emma, from forensics, and – of course – Paul.

The session began by the superintendent asking Emma to update us on the results of the evidence found in and around the field.

"Well, sir," she began, reading from her notes. "There isn't a great deal we can tell you about the partial footprint. But it has provided us with some information that may be helpful. We've managed to ascertain that it belongs to a man's right foot; his approximate height is five feet ten inches; we estimate his weight, within two or three pounds, at 12 stone; from the partial pattern on the sole of the shoe we were able to establish it was a Church's make, size eight and a half, obviously expensive; and, from the slight indentation on one side of the sole, we believe at some time this man has had surgery on his right knee."

"Christ!" Paul commented. "All of that from an indent in cow shit!"

This seemed to break the sombre atmosphere, and we broke out laughing. Even our humourless superintendent had a smile on his face.

"Good work, Emma. What about the fibre? What does that tell us about him?"

"What it tells us for certain, sir, is that this man is a snazzy dresser. The fibre's a mixture of cashmere and silk, and it came from an Armani suit. There may be an outside chance of tracing the garment, because it's a very exclusive product – you don't get these down the high street. And the suit was bought quite recently; this type of cloth only came on the market in the last three months – and only the really posh shops in the upmarket areas of the major cities. I'll leave it to your officers to work out how many shops and stores that would involve; but you'll have to bear in mind that Armani's well represented throughout Europe. He could have bought it in any European city. Also, if we add the information about the fibre to what we got from the shoe print, we can assume that he's not exactly skint: either he's someone of independent means, or a businessman with his own set-up. But, he's also squeamish – I know that's weird..."

"How d'you mean, Emma?" Jim asked.

"Well, he must've realised he'd left that footprint in the cow dung; he's far too meticulous not to have. But he made no attempt to remove it; nor did he even try to erase it; he would have had to use his foot, or perhaps a stick, had there been one available, and there was no way he was prepared to do that."

"Interesting," the superintendent commented. "Paul, how d'you think he'll react when he discovers his jacket is torn?"

"I don't think he will. Oh, he'll worry about it momentarily, but then he'll rationalise it by convincing himself that the police are unlikely to find it. And, even if we did (and, remember, he's made that more likely by leaving the footprint), he'll reason that it's virtually untraceable, so there's no real damage done."

"Hmm. Not very helpful, is it?"

"No. I'm afraid not."

"What about the profile? Any progress with that?"

Paul shuffled his papers on the desk, giving the impression he wasn't sure where to begin. No one spoke; we just sat there in expectation. I wondered if perhaps we weren't waiting for a miracle of some kind.

"I'd like to remind you all what I said about profiling," Paul began. "It's not a panacea for all your problems; at best, it's another tool to help you catch particular types of offenders – mainly sexual deviants."

"Paul," the superintendent interrupted, irritation clearly in his voice, "you really don't have to be defensive. No one's going to judge you; all we ask is you do your best."

"Sorry, Phil. Yes, of course. The question is where to begin. We already have a photofit of the suspect, so that's a good start. Before I go on, I'm aware you've already made the picture available to the press, but may I suggest that you distribute it on as wide a basis as you can? If necessary, place the picture in a prominent position – outside schools, in playgrounds, anywhere children gather and might be vulnerable, warning them not to let this man near them. Circulate it to the media – I mean national papers and TV, not just simply the local press. At the same time, don't hesitate to warn the general public that we're looking for a mass murderer."

"Won't that just panic people?" Jim asked.

"It may frighten them," Paul said. "And that has to be for the good. It'll make them more vigilant, more protective towards their children. And, until this man's caught, our safeguard. As I've said already, I really don't think this man's suspended his indulgences for the past four years. I'm convinced you're going to find more victims. And he'll go on killing until he's caught. He's extremely dangerous, so we have little choice but to alert the public."

"I agree," said the superintendent. "We'll get on to it right away. Please – carry on, Paul. What sort of man are we looking for?"

"Well, when you eventually meet him, as you will, he'll appear on the surface to be the last type you'd suspect. Superficially, he'll seem gentle, charming even. He'll be sophisticated, well spoken; you'd do well to bear in mind that the voice he uses on the phone may not be his natural accent. He'll be educated, extremely well dressed – in fact, meticulously so; he'll be wealthy, certainly of independent means, possibly because he owns his own business or has inherited wealth. If I were asked what type of car he drives I'd go for one of the prestige marques: a BMW, or a Mercedes – possibly a Jaguar. It's unlikely it will turn out to be a Ford as one potential witness thought. That'd be demeaning for this chap. Having said that, it's possible he'll have a 4-wheel drive car too – remember, he has to access his burial site, and he's hardly likely to use his pride and joy for that.

"Now," he went on, " as for where he might live – well, I'm sorry say it could almost be anywhere. He's obviously geographically mobile; so, he either doesn't mind how far he travels in search of victims, and he can afford to do it, or his business activities require him to travel, thus widening his net for potential prey.

"What makes this man unique is that he has no previous history with the police. You see, invariably this kind of offender develops his sexual compulsions in a fairly well-set pattern over an extended period of time. During that evolutionary phase it's almost inevitable they'll make some mistake or other, commit a relatively minor misdemeanour, and come to the attention of the police. That doesn't seem to have happened in this case – unless he was apprehended as a minor – otherwise, as a known sexual offender, you'd have his DNA on file. He knows that, so you can assume he also has some knowledge of police procedures, even if it's only basic stuff.

But it's worth considering that he might have a record of mental disturbance, and consequential treatment, if only on an outpatient basis. It's also likely that he's married – or was once. And an apparently respected member of his community, possibly even a regular churchgoer...

"To sum up this aspect of his sociopathology: outwardly, in almost every way, he's a perfectly normal citizen. But that's just a veneer. The real person, the one the world never sees, is a sadistic, merciless killer. He's depraved in the very worst sense of the word; he inflicts the most horrifying atrocities on helpless children, then murders them without any compunction."

Paul shook his head in sorrow at the thought. No one spoke for a little while; I think we were all shocked at the clinical description of this psychopathic monster. Finally, the superintendent said, "Have you finished, Paul?"

"No. There are other characteristics you should know about that could be helpful. Generally speaking, this category of paedophile has an aggressive personality; he may be able to hide or disguise this for long periods, but it's bound to have displayed itself at some point. And I relate this to his social life rather than his paedophilia, where his anger finds – by his standards, at least – a natural theatre. Also, he'll always *abduct* the children he molests; I mean they'll always be strangers - unlike

- 135 -

the other three main categories of paedophile, where the child's usually either be a relative or is at least be known to the offender; and, more often than not, coercion takes place.

"Finally, because of his careful planning, coupled with his innate cunning, he's not likely to be caught early on. Sadly, there'll be quite a number of victims before that; hence my suggestion you comb the records over the last four years for missing children – little girls, I'm talking about. This character won't have the slightest interest in young boys."

He held out a hand to stop Jim from interrupting him. "Please; bear with me for a few minutes more. As I said earlier, I also want to say is we need to formulate a response to these games he's playing. I'm still working on that, but I am not unhopeful. In the meantime, one of the common traits of this type is the use of internet bulletin boards, where information on potential victims is freely exchanged anonymously and confidentially. I believe this could, potentially be a way of entrapping him, but – again – I'd ask you to leave it with me for a little while."

He paused, as if to clear his mind, then said, "So there you have it: the profile of the archetypal sadistic paedophile: the mysoped. Some of the information you are familiar with; some of it will be new to you. It remains only for me to say, however superfluously, that this man must be caught, regardless of the cost. As I have repeatedly said, he'll continue killing girls until you do. I can only hope this will help you catch him."

"Fascinating," the superintendent said. "Thank you, Paul. Tell me," he said, pointing to the papers in front of the doctor: "do you have all that laid out on paper, or is it something you prefer we do ourselves?"

Paul handed across the papers to the superintendent. "It's more or less in the format I presented to you. You're welcome to a copy of it, but I need the original; I haven't finished with this character yet."

"Okay, everyone. We've got something to work on. Frank – follow up on the missing children enquiries, will you? And Angie – why don't you work with Paul here? See if there's some way he can help us look into the mental health history of this guy. I know it's a long shot, but all we've got now are long shots, so we have to follow them up. Jim – can I leave you to widen the circulation of the photofit pictures? ...And talk to the media? When news that we're pursuing the same monster from four years ago gets out, we can expect a full frontal assault from the press and television boys. And be under no illusions; word will get out. We all know what happened last time."

He stood, leant across the table and shook Paul's hand. "Paul, we're all very grateful to you. Jim and Angie will go on liaising with you, and we'll let you know when we have more information on those soil samples.

"That's all for now, people, but I suggest we get together again in 48 hours - or sooner if anything breaks."

CHAPTER TWENTY-EIGHT

Two days later we were hit with a tidal wave of publicity. As the superintendent had predicted, the press were soon in the picture, and, along with the television crews, they were camping once again on our doorstep – Steelhouse Lane was a Police Station virtually under siege. Peter had a slight altercation with one of the national press boys who persisted in trying to take his photo. It took Frank Kewell to rescue the situation. As for me, I preferred to use the back entrance to the station, but even that was soon discovered, leaving us with no clear entrances. It wasn't long before complaints started to arrive 'upstairs' from the uniform boys – the main one being that they were unable to pop out of the station for a sneaky smoke.

Jim quietened things down somewhat by giving a press conference, confirming that the offender was the same man responsible for the murders of the seven girls four years ago, and saying that, although Josephine's body had not been found, we now had every reason to believe that she was dead – murdered. Frank had already revisited the Marsdens the previous day to break the bad news about their daughter, strongly advising them not to attend a further television interview.

Mr Marsden maintained a tight grip on his emotions during Frank's visit. Mrs Marsden wasn't so resilient; she was overcome with grief at the news of her daughter. I felt almost as sorry for poor Frank. How do you tell a family there is no longer any hope?

So far, our enquiries into missing children were incomplete, although the police files from the districts that had responded had reported six possible victims – again, all of them girls. We were still awaiting a response from other forces throughout the country.

The time I was spending with Paul, looking into the question of whether or not the felon had ever spent time in psychiatric treatment, I undertook partly at Ashworth House and partly at Forest Hills, to enable Paul to carry out his other duties. It also allowed me to maintain a cursory eye on Connie, who was by now receiving the full-time attentions of a young probationary police constable by the name of Steve Harrison. He was only a couple of years older than Connie – quite good-looking, in fact – and, from what I could determine, even from my first introduction, he was well smitten. He was also something of a fitness fanatic, probably even a weight lifter, so his presence at the half-way house was very reassuring.

The results of our enquiries so far didn't appear promising; this was not entirely unexpected, since Paul was pretty well convinced our man was not mentally ill. We were following a procedure of searching computer records, some of them going back over 20 years. The problem, really, was knowing where to look geographically. On a national basis it was like looking for the proverbial single needle in a field of haystacks.

So far we had identified about a dozen people who, more or less, fell into Paul's category, but for one reason or another we had to disqualify them all. For instance, there was a patient who, at the age of 15, had sexually assaulted then murdered his sister. A possible profile, I thought; until I checked further and discovered he was still hospitalised, some 20 years later. Another had tried to rape a young girl in the school lavatories. He had managed to avoid the attentions of the police only because social workers had recommended psychiatric treatment. For a short while this one held out some real promise; but, as the timeframe would make him about 30 by now, his age ruled him out. Also, he had – unfortunately – attempted to murder a fellow patient and had been committed to Broadmoor. And so it went on, this authorised voyeurism into the minds of very sick people. It was beginning to make me feel distinctly queasy.

"Do you think we're wasting our time?" I questioned, after we had exhausted the records from the Northwest area. "If, as you say, he isn't mentally ill, how will these psychiatric institutions possibly have a record of him? The possible suspects I've singled out so far have all got specific mental illnesses."

"Because the 'symptoms' he might have exhibited at the time could easily have led

psychiatrists and other mental health doctors to assume he *was* mentally ill. It's a fairly common assumption, Angie, particularly when you consider how unpalatable the alternative diagnosis is: that they might be treating a potentially dangerous psychopath who's not so much sick as truly evil."

"Yeah, I can see that," I agreed. "But my problem is: how will we know if it's our man or not – if they've misdiagnosed him?"

He sighed and treated me to one of his patronising smiles. Actually, and I wouldn't dream of telling him this, that bloody smile of his was beginning to get on my nerves.

"We'll know for a number of reasons," he said. "First off, as a youngster, he'll either have committed some relatively minor sexual offence, or he could have been seen by his own doctor – perhaps at the insistence of his parents – after displaying sexual deviances. You see, Angie, as I tried to explain before, these people don't suddenly become paedophiles. The compulsions develop over time, almost to a predetermined pattern. Usually they start with a sexual fantasy about children – a picture they create in their minds, over which they can masturbate. In today's world we see a lot of it coming from the Internet, where these miscreants can buy and download pornographic pictures of children with very little effort. That might sustain them for some considerable time, but eventually it's not enough and they are forced to find other, more fulfilling avenues. More than likely this would consist of more pornographic pictures at first, followed by actual films of children in various sexual situations. Shall I go on?" he asked, spotting the look of disgust on my face.

"I don't want to hear it," I admitted. "But I don't think I have any choice if I want to learn about these creatures."

"Okay. When this kind of depravity eventually fails to satisfy their lust, as it must, they then begin watching little girls: in playgrounds, or parks, paddling pools especially, where the children are in a state of undress – anywhere they can observe without attracting attention. It has to be private enough for them to be able to masturbate otherwise the exercise is pointless. This is possibly where they first come to the attention of the medical authorities; remember, Angie, they're still relatively young at this stage. So they're passed from doctor to doctor, until finally a psychiatrist, or clinical psychologist, subjects them to longer-term treatment. That's where we'll find him if he has followed the usual pattern."

"How old would he be in that stage of the progression?"

"Mid- to late teens typically."

"How does he progress after that?" I asked.

"Well, with the help of professionals, and possibly some form of longer-term medication, he'll probably be able to keep his urges at bay for quite some time; at least, till he can no longer be treated as a juvenile. Then he'll make a quantum leap. His depravity, fuelled by his aggression, will expand and force him to abduct his first child. I won't describe what's bound to happen then, Angie. I doubt either of our stomachs is strong enough. All I will say is that he enjoys the experience; it exhilarates him, beyond anything he has ever felt before; it excites him far beyond even his wildest imaginings and expectations.

"And he learns from it. He soon realises that, to continue indulging his compulsions, he must take precautions. So he learns to hide the bodies. Of course, he may keep them for a while; this type is certainly not averse to necrophilia and other post-mortem sexual mutilations. At the same time he realises he has to control those elements of his character that could expose him: his anger, his aggression and his sexual desires must also be kept private from everyone. And, the longer he goes on without detection, the cleverer he becomes in disguising his compulsions, and the more children he will violate; and the more difficult it becomes to apprehend him."

"And you believe we will find him in here?" I asked, pointing to one of the computer terminals.

He shrugged. "I can't know that for certain. I do think it's worth checking out though, if only to close down another avenue."

"Paul, we could be here for ever, at this rate. So far, we've spent something like ten hours searching this thing, with no luck. When do we call it a day?"

This time he gave me a wry smile. "Yeah, I know. And you're right. Do you want to stop?"

"It might be a sensible idea. And, when we continue, why don't we narrow down the search? We know, for instance, that he has a predilection for the West Midlands, despite your comments about his mobility and his possibly phoney accent. If you think about it, Paul, three of the girls we found in the cesspit were from this area, and the last one was from Solihull. Now, I realise that, to you, it may not in itself be very significant; sure, he could possibly visit this part of the world regularly on his business travels. But I'd say he's drawn here for some reason; maybe he lives here now or maybe he keeps returning to where he was born and raised." I looked at him quizzically. "So, what do you think? Am I making any sense?"

"Yes. You're making a lot of sense, Angie. Even if you're wrong, I still agree we should concentrate on the West Midlands as a priority, for all the reasons you've spelled out. After that, if nothing comes up, we can always widen our search progressively over time. Let's get back to it, shall we?"

I groaned aloud and leant forward on the desktop, placing my head in my arms. "Jesus, Paul, don't you ever stop? I'm whacked – I've got computeritis!"

He chuckled, then said, "Okay, young lady. We'll call it a day, then. Can you allocate some time tomorrow?"

"No. Sorry, Paul. I've invited Connie to spend a couple of nights at my place, and I don't want to let her down – especially since we're only dealing in long shots here. Can we pick it up on Monday, at Ashworth House?" I suggested, still holding my prostrate position on the desk.

"If you like. But it will have to be around lunchtime. I have a conference here in the morning. Does that suit you?"

I struggled to my feet, yawning. "Great! Gives me a chance of a lie-in at least. See you Monday; I'll be having a sandwich with Connie. Goodnight, Paul."

Then I got the hell out of there fast, before he could think of anything else for me to do.

CHAPTER TWENTY-NINE

I collected Connie from Ashworth House mid-morning on the Saturday and we drove to Stratford-upon-Avon; she couldn't remember ever visiting there before. We had lunch at a country pub by the river, on the outskirts of the town, then spent the afternoon wandering around the Bard's home town – which, of course, had to include a visit to his house at the top of the town's main street. From there we took in an excursion to Anne Hathaway's cottage, followed by a tour of the Shakespeare Theatre and an early evening performance of *As You Like It*. Not really my scene, but Connie seemed to enjoy it.

It was something unbelievable to be able to spend a day with Connie without a single mention of monsters and paedophiles, and all the other nightmarish incidents associated with them. For once, I allowed Connie to be a normal teenage girl, whilst I did my best to behave like a big sister. We talked about all the things that we girls like to talk about when we're together: clothes and men, and sex, then men and clothes, and sex. It didn't take long before we were both giggling like a couple of school-girls. It was a perfectly ordinary day; the weather was a little overcast, but that didn't bother us in the slightest.

On the way home we stopped for a late supper at an Italian restaurant I knew on the outskirts of the city. After pasta and a glass of wine Connie was beginning to nod off; in fact, she was dozing in the car by the time we got back to the flat. It was a shame to wake her, but she didn't seem to mind. A cup of my favourite hot chocolate, then we both had an early night. My dingy flat was nowhere up to the standard of Jim's; his was more like an apartment. And it only had the one bed-room– although there was a small room off the lounge, that I believed used to be some kind of storeroom – and as I didn't have the heart to place her in there (or the courage, come to it), I let her have the main bedroom, so she was able to crash out in relative comfort. I squeezed myself on to the tiny camp bed in the storeroom.

The day had given me a feeling of immense satisfaction, especially spending time with my ward – as I had come to think of her – away from a hospital environment.

The next morning, after a late breakfast, Connie said, when I asked her, that she would like to visit the countryside. So we headed out towards Worcestershire and the Malvern Hills, stopping for a coffee at Bewdley, a small, touristy village on the edge of the river Severn, then on through Stourport and Droitwich, finally arriving – at lunchtime – at Malvern itself. It was truly a beautiful part of the country, with the Malvern Hills rising steeply, virtually from the town centre: a perfect setting for a peaceful day out, and a good spot for a pub lunch. It wasn't a day for talking much; it was one of those tranquil occasions that lent itself to a golden type of silence. It had been a wonderful couple of days, and I was convinced Connie would feel the benefit of relative normality.

It was on the way home that she experienced a kind of seizure. Her head suddenly fell back in the car seat, and her eyes began to roll over as I saw her pupils dilate. She was breathing, heavily and unnaturally. The next thing, she started to tremble, more or less the same as I remembered from that time in the woods. Frightened, I pulled the car from the road and parked in a lay-by.

I found I too was shaking by now with the shock of the sudden transformation. I felt helpless, uncertain what, if anything, I should do. I was so scared for her I did the only thing I could think of; I switched on my mobile and called for an ambulance. It could be anything, I thought; an epileptic fit, or possibly some kind of brain seizure.

It seemed to take an eternity for the ambulance to arrive. All I could do was to leave the car door open, wet my handkerchief from the bottle of water I kept in the car, and douse her forehead.

Coincidentally, we were quite close to Solihull, having tracked our way back via Warwick so I could show Connie my old university. It was to that hospital the ambulance took Connie whilst I followed fearfully in the car. On the way I used my mobile again and tried to contact Paul Simmons, without success. All I got was his answer phone, so I left a message telling him what had happened and where we would be.

We were in the hospital's A&E department before Connie started to come round. She was continually vomiting and terribly confused, and she still couldn't stop shaking. The doctor ushered me out of the resuscitation room, and a sympathetic, middle-aged nurse led me to the relatives' waiting room. She literally oozed compassion, so much so that I felt my hackles go up.

She was about to say something when I saw my hand involuntarily rise in protest. "Please," I heard myself saying, "don't tell me she's in good hands. I couldn't stand it."

She smiled reactively. "I don't blame you," she said. "Anyway, we've been reprogrammed not to say that any more! What I was actually going to ask is if you might know how to contact her parents."

"No. Her mother's dead, and we've no idea where her father is. I'm the nearest she has to a relative. It's probably a silly question, nurse, but does the doctor have any idea what's wrong?"

"It's not a silly question, and I wish I could give you an answer, but I'm afraid I can't. Would you like me to stay with you? I can if you like. Or perhaps a cup of tea? That might help."

"Thank you, nurse; you're very kind, but I'll be alright, really."

"I'll be getting back, then. As soon as we have any news I'll let you know." She touched my arm sympathetically. "I know it sounds glib, but – please – try not to worry."

She was about to leave when my mobile went off at that moment; it was Paul. The nurse gave me an apologetic look. "Sorry, but can you turn that off? We don't allow them in the hospital."

I went to the entrance to the A&E and rang Paul back.

"Are you at the hospital?" he asked

"Yes. Solihull General. Where are you?"

"I'm on my way. Should be with you in about ten minutes. What happened, Angie?"

"I'm not sure," I said, choking back the tears. "We were in the car, on our way home. One minute she was fine, the next it was as if she was having some kind of seizure."

"Take it easy, Angie. Stay calm. Have they told you anything yet?"

"No. They don't seem to know what it is. I'm worried sick, Paul. She looks terrible. Please – hurry, won't you?"

"Is she conscious?"

"Yes, but barely. I think she fainted in the car. She's come round now but she still isn't *compos mentis*."

"I'll be there shortly. Hang on, Angie; she'll be all right, I'm sure. I can't think it's anything too serious."

He broke the connection and left me with my worries about Connie. For some inexplicable reason the circle of my mind always seemed to return to that ghoulish scene in the woods when the children's bodies were exposed, and I couldn't help but wonder if this latest episode had its origins in that experience. But, when it came to understanding the workings of Connie's mind, I had given up some years ago. She was definitely an enigma, and, as I once commented to Paul, "It's as if at times she functions in an altogether different dimension from normal people." But if I fail to totally understand her that didn't mean it would lessen my support for her. She needed me, and my promise that I would always be there for her would remain unceasingly steadfast.

I wandered back into the hospital and bumped into the nurse from resuscitation; she was looking for me.

"How is she?" I asked, trying to keep the concern out of my voice.

"Well, she's come round, and she is feeling much better. But we're still not sure what the problem is, so the doctor wants to keep her in overnight and do a scan in the morning."

"A scan? What kind of scan?"

"An MRI scan – on her brain. It's just a precaution, but we need to be certain there's nothing untoward going on."

"Does the doctor have an opinion as to what it might be?"

The nurse shrugged, one of those irritating non-committal gestures that gives nothing away. "I don't think he's really qualified to diagnose at this level; we'll have to wait for the consultant in the morning. But I shouldn't worry; this type of seizure's not uncommon in teenagers, and they're usually only temporary. Would you like to see her before she goes up to the ward?"

"Yes. Thank you."

Connie was lying back in the bed when I went into the cubicle. The colour had returned to her cheeks, and her eyes were back to normal. But she looked absolutely exhausted, as if she had just run the marathon. She smiled, tentatively, when she saw me, and held out a hand.

"What would I do without you, Angie? I'm pretty hopeless, aren't I?"

"Well, you do have this natural talent for frightening me," I said, returning the smile. "How are you feeling, Connie?"

"Wiped out," she said.

"Any idea what happened back there?"

She nodded. "Can I tell you about it later? Now isn't a good time. I'm really whacked, Angie."

"Sure." I leant over and eased her back in the bed. "You just rest. They're going to keep you in overnight and Dr Simmons is on his way here. I hope you don't mind but I called him."

She groaned. "Oh, Christ! He'll think I've had a relapse. There's no way I can be straight with him; he'll never understand."

I took hold of her hand in mine and squeezed it gently. "You'd be surprised at just how understanding your doctor's become lately. I think we're converting him!"

Connie sighed and closed her eyes. A few moments later she had drifted off, so I left her and went to see if Paul had arrived. He was talking to the hospital doctor in the lobby, and waved when he saw me.

"It doesn't sound too serious," he assured me, after finishing his discussion. "The young doctor seems to think it's nothing more than a slight adolescent seizure, not…"

"…Uncommon with teenagers," I interrupted. "Yeah, I was told. But what do *you* think, Paul? It was pretty bloody scary, I don't mind telling you."

"He's probably right. These episodes are invariably less serious than they appear at the time. But I think the MRI scan's a good idea, as a precaution. It's a good job they have a scanner here, otherwise it would have meant moving her to Birmingham in the morning. Anyway, I'm sure Connie'll be feeling much better by then. Are you going to stay with her for a while?"

"Right now she's sleeping. Whatever it was it took a hell of a lot out of her. I'll stay till she goes up to the ward and then come back in the morning. And, Paul, thanks for coming so promptly. I'm sorry if I alarmed you."

"I'm just glad she wasn't on her own when it happened. As you said, Angie, these things can be pretty frightening." He turned to leave, then hesitated. "Will you give me a ring in the morning? Let me know how she is, and if they're discharging her."

"Of course. And I should know then if I can keep our computer date!"

* * * * * * * * *

A little later, I went up to the ward where Connie had been transferred. She barely woke when they had to move her, and as soon as she was settled into a different bed she crashed out again. I realised how weary I was myself then, so I left the hospital intent on an early night. One way or another, it had been a hell of a day.

CHAPTER THIRTY

Unfortunately, Jim had other ideas. I had only been at home for a little while, running the bath and pouring myself a stiff Scotch, when the phone rang.

"Ange, would you mind if I came over?"

"No. Of course not," I lied, thinking: "Shit! There goes my early night!" I turned off the bath taps, and decided on a shower instead. If Jim insisted on coming over I might as well make myself smell sexy.

It was a waste of time, really, because when he arrived he had only police business on his mind.

He settled himself in one of the easy chairs (that was a euphemism!) and put his feet up on the coffee table. "I want to run through this profile with you," he said. "See if there's anything we can use."

"Yes, I had a nice weekend with Connie, thank you," I said dryly. "Apart from the fact that she was taken suddenly ill in the car on the way home and she's now an overnight guest in Solihull General Hospital."

"Christ! I'm sorry, Ange. What the hell happened?"

I told him, in rather terse, shorthand sentences. He was quiet after I'd finished, then he said, "She's quite something, that girl, isn't she? I mean, she doesn't do anything by halves. Is she going to be okay?"

I sighed. Men! They were incorrigible.

"I think so. We'll know better in the morning. But I hope you're not expecting anything remarkably intellectual from me tonight; I'm drained."

"Yeah. I can understand that. Would you rather I went?"

I got up from the sofa and crossed over to his chair, taking him by the hand. "No. I don't want you to go. What I want is an early night and a nice, warm, sexy male body to relax me. Interested?"

He grinned and pointed to his papers. "I suppose they'll keep until tomorrow. Got to get our priorities right, haven't we!"

I kissed him, if only to shut him up, and then led him into the bedroom; I don't know what I would have done if Connie had still been occupying it!

* * * * * * * * *

Connie was in the X-ray room having her scan when I rang the next morning. The ward sister assured me she had spent a restful night – more than you could say for me! – and she was feeling much better this morning. She could be discharged within the hour, so, this time, it was my turn to leave Jim a cryptic note on his pillow. I dressed quickly in blouse and jeans, and ankle socks (as opposed to those horrible police tights), checked that I had everything, and then quietly left the flat to the sound of Jim's gentle snores.

It was a bloody awful day – a typical English Monday morning. The rain was positively sheeting it down and visibility on the roads was minimal.

I rang Paul from my mobile, en route to the hospital, to let him know they were discharging Connie and that I would meet up with him at lunchtime as arranged.

Connie was already waiting for me when I arrived; she still looked pale and drawn from the aftermath of her experience, but she managed to squeeze my hand and give me a wan smile. Then it took forever to complete the discharge procedures, principally because the consultant insisted we wait until the results of the MRI scan came through. Fortunately they were clear: no aneurisms or embolisms, or any other -isms; and no signs of brain damage. What he did comment on, however, was that there was evidence of intense electrical brain activity recently, but, to be fair to him, he did concede he wasn't sure what, if anything, that signified.

Finally, we were on our way back to Ashworth House. It was the first opportunity I had to ask Connie if she could tell me what yesterday was all about.

She lay back in the seat resting her head, saying nothing for a while. When she did begin to speak her voice was flat and very matter-of-fact, as if these kind of experiences were now becoming commonplace.

"Do you remember when I had that awful vision about Josephine? And how much it took out of me?"

"Of course. And I also remember that the experience terrified you at the time." I hesitated for a moment, and then asked, "Are you saying that yesterday was like that?"

"Sort of. And yet different; I'm not sure how to explain it, Angie."

I stopped for traffic lights, which gave me the chance to reach across and squeeze her arm. "You don't have to talk, Connie, if you don't feel up to it. The main thing is that you're alright physically, and, whatever it was, I'm just glad it hasn't got to you like last time."

"No," she protested. "Really, I'm fine. It's just that I don't know how to describe what happened. It was all kinda weird. You know – more like a revelation than a vision."

"Why don't you tell it in your own way?" I said quietly. "Then, between us, we'll try and make some sense out of it."

"Okay. Well, I remember, one minute it was cloudy and spitting with rain, and the next it was a lovely sunny day. Only I wasn't in the car."

"Where were you, Connie?"

"In a park. And then in a playground in the park. There were lots of children, little boys and girls, laughing and shouting and having a good time. There were swings, a lot of them, and a roundabout and a slide; oh yeah, there was also a seesaw and a sandpit. It was very busy and very noisy. And I saw a number of women with the children; most of them were sitting on benches, talking, not really paying attention to the children.

"There was a man there as well – outside the playground, walking around the fencing. He was some kind of attendant, I think, because he was wearing a uniform – you know, like a policeman – but I couldn't make out his face; it was hidden behind these big sunglasses."

"Did something happen there, Connie?"

"No. Well, yes. But it hasn't happened yet. I think I was seeing something that's *going to happen*. That's why it was different."

"Want to tell me the rest?"

"Yes." She closed her eyes for a moment as if to recreate the vision. "The man came into the playground and started talking to a little girl playing with her friend on some swings near to the entrance. He was smiling and pointing towards something outside the playground. Then the girl went off with him. Then – oh Christ, Angie!" she exclaimed, as if she was seeing it for the first time. "It was a set-up! The bastard snatched her. He had a kind of Range-Rover parked near to the playground - and he bundled her in and drove off."

"Didn't any of the mothers see or hear anything?"

"No. When the little girl tried to scream he clamped his hand over her mouth. It all happened so quickly. One minute it was a peaceful, innocent scene; the next, he'd grabbed her and disappeared. I don't think there was time for anyone to notice – until it was too late."

I didn't know what to say. Jesus! How do you get your head round something like that? One day, I thought to myself, this girl is going to blow my mind.

I managed to find a parking spot close to Ashworth House. After I had pulled in I turned to Connie. She still had her eyes closed, reliving the experience.

"Are you okay?" I asked. She nodded, saying nothing.

"Yeah, thanks. I'm fine. I think it's because it hasn't happened yet." She opened her eyes and turned to me. "That's what's so different about it, Angie. That's what I meant when I said it was more like a revelation than a vision. Can you make any sense of it? 'Cos I sure as hell can't"

I sighed. "I don't know about you, Connie, but these weird experiences of yours are wearing me out as well. And, no, I don't really know what the revelation means. Unless..." I paused, filtering it through my mind.

"Unless what?"

"Unless it's somehow connected to everything else that is going on, and someone is giving you a warning of future events." I shook my head, puzzled. "But if that's the case, they aren't being terribly helpful."

"How do you mean, Angie?"

"Well, if it is some kind of – shall we say? – mystical revelation, then you would expect whoever's responsible to be a bit more forthcoming on detail. We don't know, for instance, exactly where it is, do we? We don't know who it is who snatches the child. And we don't know when it's gonna happen either. It's all a bit vague, Connie, don't you think?"

"I guess – but it's not like tuning into the weather forecast you know! Perhaps I should go back and ask the perpetrator for his name, and the date and location? Maybe he'll do it at a time to suit us… Do you think that might be helpful?"

We both started to laugh at that it was so ludicrous. "Let's give it some more thought, shall we?" I suggested. "See if there's any way we can make it work for us. Now," I added, getting out of the car, "what about some lunch? I fancy one of your sandwiches."

It wasn't the least bit funny, though, I cautioned myself. And it certainly would be irresponsible to take Connie's experience lightly. But, having said that, there really wasn't an awful lot I – or anyone else – could do about it; other than to give it some serious thought and, in the meantime, file it away until I could talk to Jim about it.

CHAPTER THIRTY-ONE

Constable Steve Harrison had already pre-empted our arrival: the sandwiches were on the table. And when he began fussing over Connie, I grabbed a plate and retreated to join Paul in his study. He had a second computer terminal up and running, obviously anticipating a long session. I was right. We worked through solidly until seven, and if Sheila hadn't brought us in a coffee I doubt if we would have stopped at all. Paul even grimaced when I excused myself to go to the loo!

At the end of the day we had three possible candidates from the West Midlands area.

1. Peter Driscoll, a Caucasian, from West Bromwich. At the age of 13 he had sexually attacked and attempted to rape two young girls from his school; they were both aged nine. Evidently, he had lain in wait for them on separate occasions whilst they were on their way home from school. The first time he was given the benefit of the doubt – a nine-year-olds word against his. The second time he wasn't so lucky; an independent witness saw him whilst in the course of the attack. Had his mother not pleaded for him at Juvenile Court he would certainly have received a youth custody sentence. In the event, however, he was referred to the local psychiatric hospital, where he spent six months as an inpatient and received a further two years of therapy as a day patient. At 16 he left school and nothing more was heard of him. He would now be 40 or 41. Other than the above, the police computer confirmed he had no criminal record. Present whereabouts unknown.

2. Brian Ennisford, also Caucasian, from Wolverhampton. At the age of 14 he sexually attacked his sister in a vicious assault, which resulted in her hospitalisation and his being charged in Juvenile Court with attempted rape and grievous bodily harm. Because of his age he could not be named. Before sentencing, psychiatric reports were called for, which diagnosed possible paranoid schizophrenia and recommended an extended period of psychiatric treatment as an inpatient in a suitable institution. He was released into a halfway house after seven years, and told he had to remain on appropriate medication indefinitely, and report

to the hospital as an outpatient on a monthly basis. He adhered to the routine for approximately three years, since when he has disappeared from the scene. He does have a corresponding record as a juvenile offender, but the police confirm there is no DNA record attached to his file. His age now would be 44. Present whereabouts unknown.

3. Arnold Brownlaw, Caucasian, from Edgbaston, Birmingham. A prolific offender throughout his teenage years, who first came to the attention of social workers following a sexual attack on a neighbour's eight-year-old daughter when he was 13. As a result of this, and the corresponding reaction from the family involved, the Brownlaws moved to the West Bromwich area. Two years later Arnold, then 15, was again brought before the court, this time for the alleged rape and battery of a nine-year-old girl. He was accused of abducting the child from a care home, dragging her into some nearby woods and then viciously attacking and raping her. He denied the allegations, and the charges were eventually dropped because the girl's supervisors at the home refused to allow her to give evidence, on the grounds that she was too traumatised. At that time DNA testing was not available, but there was little doubt, from other available police evidence, that it was Arnold who had carried out the attack. At 17 he was placed in youth custody, for an indefinite period, for the rape of a ten-year-old girl. On this occasion the child's parents did allow the victim to give evidence, and as a result Arnold was convicted. During his confinement he was referred for psychiatric treatment to the Birmingham Psychiatric Hospital, where he was assessed as sexually dysfunctional and admitted as an inpatient. Records of his hospitalisation period indicate that he was responding to therapy over a time-span of three years. He was eventually discharged, shortly before his 21st birthday. I accessed the police computer files, which showed that there is no record of further court appearances. His age now would be 39. Present whereabouts unknown.

I leant back in my chair and stretched wearily. It had been a long and exhausting day, and, although we had identified three possible suspects, I wasn't sure where that took us – or in fact, where we went from here. I had no doubts that we would be able to trace these three men, eventually, but we could hardly level accusations at them because of their past transgressions; nor could I really justify asking Jim to place them on an official suspects lists.

"So, Paul, we've achieved what we set out to do; but where do we go from here?"

He yawned, obviously as tired as I was. "The first thing to do, Angie, is to find them. That's your job. Then we investigate their present lifestyles; you know the sort of thing better than I do. Are they, or have they been, married? Do they have children? What sort of job do they do? Are they wealthy? And all the other aspects that will help us build a profile. Then, we see if they match, or come anywhere near, the one we've already mapped out.

"Essentially, it means a great deal of police work, and it's up to you and your superiors to decide whether or not it's likely to be productive. I'm happy to give Jim some input if you think it'll help. I can only add that this way does work, based on my previous experience. It's also consistent, if you recall, with the typical pattern of the 'sadistic offender', insofar as, almost invariably, they'll have committed similar offences in the past. And these three candidates have done.

"Anyway, I'll leave it with you, and I suggest we call it a day. If you agree, I think we'll postpone any further examination of mental health records for other parts of the country until we have approval for our recommendations."

"Yeah," I nodded. "I agree. I'll discuss it with Jim in the morning. Where will you be if I need to call you?"

"At Forest Hills. I have a medical conference there at ten, so I won't be free till the afternoon."

Connie had gone out with her police 'guardian' when I checked; there was a note from her apologising for not thanking me for a 'lovely weekend'. She was going to have her ears pierced, she said – and maybe her navel as well! There was no mention of yesterday's vision, so obviously it hadn't fazed her too much. But it wasn't something that would simply go away, like a bad dream. If it were intended as a prophetic image of a yet-to-unfold event then it would be wrong to dismiss it. As yet I hadn't had the chance to give it much thought – my head was still spinning from the hours spent on the bloody computer – but I did make a mental note to mention it to Jim. I scribbled a quick reply, letting her know I would call her tomorrow.

I was absolutely beat, so rather than return to the station I headed for home. Perhaps tonight I really would manage an early night. I stopped briefly on the way home for tampons and toothpaste. Then I bolted the door, disconnected the phone and placed a frozen pizza in the microwave. When I had eaten I took a cup of hot chocolate into the bathroom and soaked luxuriously for a good 20 minutes, completely undisturbed. It was lovely. I was so tired I put off shampooing my hair until the morning, climbed into bed and almost immediately crashed out.

CHAPTER THIRTY-TWO

It was 7.30 when I woke up, still feeling drained; it was that time of the month again, so it was just as well Jim hadn't turned up last night. But ten minutes in the shower, with the hot water spraying my body whilst I washed my hair brought me almost back to normality.

I felt like a new woman as I set off for the station, completely reinvigorated, especially as the weather was fine, for a change; not exactly summery but not raining. Jim wasn't in his office when I arrived, so I decided to take the initiative and open the various enquiry channels into our three candidates. Driving licences, social security records, voting registers, passport office, income tax, credit cards: a whole raft of recorded information that would pinpoint their addresses.

"What you up to, Angie?" I heard Frank ask, as I was feeding the required instructions into the computer. I smiled a 'good morning' but didn't answer him until I had completed the task.

"Paul and I came up with some names from the mental health records. They're just possibilities who might fit the evolutionary pattern of a homicidal sociopath. I'm following them up to see if we can find these characters."

He took a seat and began checking the list. I instinctively turned my head away; Frank had always had something of a body odour problem, but it seemed to be getting stronger. "Bit of a long shot, isn't it? These cases are ancient history."

"Yes," I agreed. "But that's exactly what Paul suggested we search the records for, based on his experience that the type of paedophile we're pursuing will have some kind of history."

He shook his head, puzzled. "But why mental health? I thought he said our guy wasn't mentally ill?"

"Patience!" I told myself, feeling the exasperation.

"He did, Frank. But he also reckons our killer's activities could have been misdiagnosed as psychiatric in the early stages, when he was young. These three names fit that analysis."

"Hmm. Interesting. It's still a long shot, though... I don't think we should be wasting our resources on it."

"Frank, why don't you get Jim to speak to Paul about this? He thought someone might say that - but he firmly believes it's a valid line to follow. In the meantime, at least allow me to enquire superficially into these men – find out where they're living and what they're up to now."

"I'll do just that," he responded irritably. "But let me remind you, Sergeant; we've had over 300 calls from the public – and they've all got to be followed up." He waved a hand around the busy incident room. "Which is what these guys are doing. And, if you want to play with the computers, why don't you ask if that list of missing children is complete; it's taking a hell of a time."

"I understand, Inspector," I said caustically. "I'll get right on to it."

"Fuck me!" I thought, angrily. "It hasn't taken him long to pull rank" – although, in fairness, we were all under a strain with this case, and we were virtually under permanent siege by the media, which didn't help. I didn't bother to correct Frank about the list of missing children; that it wasn't something the computer could handle, and that we had a specially allocated team of four in the room looking into it.

The identity search for my three candidates, through the computers, was likely to take forever, so I joined the rest of the team in dealing with the public response, helping myself to one of the many lists on Peter Corkhill's desk. He was still acting a bit strange towards me but there wasn't a lot I could do about that. More than half the calls were from well-meaning people horrified at the bestiality of the previous crimes the newspapers referred to and anxious to help, but without having any positive information. A lot of the calls were from the inevitable cranks who were more intent on telling the police what we should do with 'these bastards' than helping us to apprehend them. And it all took up so much time; as quickly as we were dealing with the calls new ones were coming in, and it was hell just trying to keep up with them all. But no one complained; on the contrary, we needed the full support of the public on this one. All it would take would be the one telephone call: someone who had seen something, either up to the time of Josephine's abduction or afterwards. In cases like these it very often depended on eyewitnesses for a successful conclusion, so we were particularly sensitive about discouraging the public from contacting us. Unfortunately, thus far, nothing of any substance had come through.

Later that morning one of the WPCs brought a computer printout across to me.

"I thought you might be waiting for this, Serge," she said, placing it on my desk.

"Thanks, Sandra." I replaced the receiver, after finishing yet another abortive call, and began to read the detail. It was the first response from my search enquires and it concerned Peter Driscoll, originally from West Bromwich. He was the playground rapist, I remembered. The report was very comprehensive, listing driving licence with current address, mortgage details, social security number, tax coding and an assembly of other meaningless information. There was no record of credit cards, so it was logical to assume he didn't possess any. At the present time he was living in an end-terrace house in Handsworth, a suburb of West Bromwich. He was married with three children, and was employed as a bricklayer for a local building company; he drove a ten-year-old white van.

Obviously, Peter Driscoll was not our man. It appeared from his background details that he had reformed since his psychiatric treatment and had become a model citizen. "Good for him," I thought, as I put a cross against his name. Two names to go.

The remainder of the day was spent largely on the telephone, dealing with the public response; needless to say nothing emerged, and I found it terribly frustrating. I looked over to where Sandra, the WPC was working, to check if she had had any further communications from my enquires. She shook her head to let me know nothing more had come in.

I gave Connie a ring shortly before I left the station. She was still out with PC Steve Harrison, but had called in to say they were staying out for supper. In a way I was relieved that she had found someone else in her life; it wasn't healthy to be totally dependent on one person – as my mother had constantly told me.

So, it was back to the flat, another frozen meal in the microwave and a night in front of the telly. I was rather hoping Jim might have called, but I was disappointed. I did think of ringing him but then dismissed the idea. Still, a second early night wouldn't do me any harm.

The next morning there was a further computer printout waiting on my desk. This one concerned Brian Ennisford, the Wolverhampton suspect who had attacked his sister, and had been diagnosed with probable schizophrenia. Evidently, after having attacked and raped another young girl four years ago, he had been committed to Broadmoor for an indefinite period. It had not come up on criminal records because it was determined, at the time, that he was unfit to plead, and he had therefore been declared criminally insane.

"Another one gone," I thought, crossing his name off. That left only one possible remaining, and so far nothing had come through on him. I checked my list again. Arnold Brownlaw from Edgbaston, Birmingham. Three rapes against young girls, youth custodial sentence, followed by three years in psychiatric hospital. "Where are you now, Arnold?" I wondered. At the same time I realised that, if he came through blank, it would be back to the computer for Paul and me; more burning the midnight oil and searching medical records in other parts of the country. I shuddered. Most of the time, I had come to realise, detective work was just plain, bloody hard graft, with little or nothing to show for it at the end.

"Ange!" Jim shouted from the door of his office. "Got a minute?"

I was glad of the interruption, dreading having to go back on the phone to Mr and Mrs General Public; I didn't think my nerves were up to it.

"You didn't ring me," I glared at him.

"What? Oh, yeah; sorry, Ange. I didn't leave here till gone eleven." He grinned sheepishly, putting a hand to my face. "I'll make it up to you, I promise."

He glanced down at his desk, then picked up a handwritten sheet of paper. "The results are in from the remaining county forces." I must have had a puzzled look on my face. "The missing children Paul asked us to investigate – remember?"

"Sorry. I wasn't with you. What's the total?"

"In all, during the last four years, 16 young girls have gone missing between the ages of seven and ten. And that's after we drew a line north of Leeds."

"Jesus! You mean they simply went missing without a trace? And no one has connected them?"

"There's no evidence to connect them. Even now we don't know for certain that they are connected. All we know for sure is that they're listed as missing. We're looking into the details of each child now to establish the individual circumstances and see if there's a common denominator." He sighed. "Ange, we can't get carried away with this. For all we know these children could have been snatched by one or other of their parents. Right now, we don't even know for certain if foul play's suspected. All I can tell you is that the usual procedures were followed in each case. No signs of violence – at least visible violence – and so we have no suspects, other than estranged fathers who can't be traced."

He passed the list on to me with the comment: "As you can see, quite a number of the missing children were the subject of extensive searches – as you'd expect. But they were never found. So, 'Let's be patient,' is what I'm saying. What I'd like you to do is to contact the relevant police force and speak to whoever was handling the case. Get as much information as you can. You'll need some help, so I've assigned two constables to work with you. And, whatever you do, Angie, please don't let whoever you speak to know we're trying to tie all these cases together."

"Of course not. I don't want to be responsible for starting an even bigger national panic. I'll get on to it."

"Any luck with your medical suspect list?" he asked innocently, knowing damned well I would realise Frank had been talking to him.

"Piss off, Jim!" I grinned. "But there is something I need to chat to you about; I wanted to yesterday but you were conspicuous by your absence, as they say."

He pointed towards a chair. "Sounds serious. You'd better take a seat."

I gave him an outline of Connie's story about the vision she had related to me after her discharge from the hospital, including her own explanation that this was an event that had yet to happen. I then added my own concerns that, although I hadn't a clue what – if anything – we could do about it, it wasn't something we could dismiss. Connie's visions were never to be treated lightly.

Jim pondered the information for a while, saying nothing. I was glad that he wasn't rejecting the story as something from the mind of a disturbed child. I must admit that had occurred to me.

"And she says she has no details of where or when this event is likely to take place?" he asked eventually. "Or even if it's definitely going to happen?"

I shook my head.

"Well, I think you were right to mention it to me, but I'm a bit like yourself; I haven't a clue what we do about it..." He raised a hand. "And, no, I'm not dismissing it; we know the young lady too well for that. I just don't see what positive action we can take that we aren't already taking, other, perhaps, than stepping up our warnings to parents to be ever vigilant, especially in or around children's playgrounds. Do you?"

"No, of course not. I just think it would be terrible if we did nothing and it happened. Connie would never forgive us."

It was Jim's turn to shake his head. "I doubt the parents would, either. But if it really is some kind of portent then I don't see we can do anything to stop it happening in any case. I doubt even Connie can change destiny – that's if you believe in that sort of thing. Look, Ange; let's keep a watchful eye on it, shall we? We've been alerted to the possibility; now we'll just have to be ready to move fast if it happens."

I sighed. He was right, of course. The best we could do in the circumstances was preparation.

* * * * * * * * *

Back at my desk I checked the list he had given me. Of the 16 children, nine were from a circumference around the West Midlands, as far as north Staffordshire to Warwickshire in the south. Of the remaining seven, two were from Shropshire, three from Worcestershire; one was from Northampton and one from Nottinghamshire. Each of the last two had involved the army in massive searches on land and water, but with no sign of the children. All of them fell within the proximity of Birmingham. I sighed and tried to follow Jim's suggestion not to get carried away. It was very difficult. It was going to be another long day, I thought, as I began listing the various police telephone numbers. I passed Worcester and Northampton on to PC Rodney Blake, a 20-year-old rookie, and WPC Sandra Fletcher, a patrol officer who was trying to make it into CID. They were both keen to be involved.

I took Stafford, which was the earliest of the cases, dating back a little over four years, and managed to speak with a DS Peterson, who had been involved in the case. There was no information of any consequence – at least nothing that could definitively link the child's disappearance to our paedophile. The little girl, a Pamela Stretford, aged nine, had simply gone missing from her home one afternoon. Her mother had been upstairs, taking a bath. She had heard nothing, but when she came down Pamela had gone. There were no witnesses, it was broad daylight, and no one was seen loitering around the house at any time up to the incident. It was a complete mystery. The mother was convinced her estranged husband had snatched the child, however. An all points bulletin, or APB, had immediately been issued, but to no avail. The husband was never found, and it was presumed he had gone abroad with his daughter. Given the circumstances, the case was only ever designated under 'missing persons'; foul play was not suspected. It could have been our man, but then, on the other hand, it could just as easily be a case of parental abduction. Unless we apprehended our killer and he confessed, I doubted if we would ever know.

I scribbled the appropriate notes in the file, then tried Nottingham. Three years ago Laura Sinton, aged eight, was abducted from a public swimming baths. She was a member of a supervised children's swimming group; the session had finished and Laura, a little early in dressing, was waiting outside the main entrance for her mother to collect her. She disappeared.

This incident did bring forward a witness, however. Evidently there was a car park opposite the baths, and the attendant had observed a man acting suspiciously. He was seen entering the baths partway through the session, which the attendant thought was odd because parents never showed up that early. Unfortunately, he was mistaken; the man came forward and verified that he was, in fact, the father of one of the children. "So much for that," I thought. Apart from that, there were no other witnesses; no clues of any description. It was as if little Laura had vanished into thin air without trace. The detective inspector I spoke to took me through the police investigation in some detail. All the usual avenues were explored, including questioning locally registered paedophiles, and the case – as expected – received a tremendous amount of publicity, none of which produced any results. Eventually, as happens, the case fell off the front pages, and although the file remained open no further information was obtained.

As I expected, the DI asked me what our interest was in this case. I decided to ignore Jim's suggestion, and I more or less told him the truth: that we had a missing child and we had reason to suspect that other abductions might be involved. He sympathised and wished me luck; he also asked if I would keep in touch, and I promised I would.

So, once again, the case paralleled that of Josephine; but there was no firm evidence to definitively link them.

In the meantime, my two helpers were also drawing blanks, with similar stories from the areas they had contacted. If I were looking to connect the disappearances of all these children, I wondered if it was enough that the commonality was they had all disappeared without trace? As far as I was concerned that was definitely a common denominator – children vanishing into thin air without trace, when the standard pattern with missing children was for the body to eventually turn up. But I could hardly act on that assumption.

I took a break and went out for some air to clear my head. It was the case, not the atmosphere in the incident room that was suffocating me. It was so bloody frustrating, and I told myself that if I weren't careful it would freak me out. All those missing children, presumed dead, probably murdered, and parents trying to grieve over them with no bodies, no proper funerals, no graves to lay flowers. It choked me to think about it, and in a way it strengthened my resolve to catch this evil bastard.

When I returned to my desk the final printout on our third possible suspect was awaiting me: Arnold Brownlaw, from Edgbaston. He was my hot favourite: accused of three rapes and violent attacks on children; convicted of two of the charges; youth custody sentence for an indefinite period; and then three years spent as a secure inpatient at Smethwick Psychiatric Hospital.

Curiously, the report on Brownlaw was a complete blank. I read it twice to make sure I wasn't hallucinating. This cannot be right, I told myself. No address, no driving licence, no social security, no tax details or credit cards or employment records. Absolutely nothing, and since there were no passport details either it was logical to assume he hadn't gone to live abroad. I shook my head, puzzled; I had never come across a complete blank before. Like the children, it was as if Arnold Brownlaw had disappeared into the mist.

I took it into Jim for his advice. He too shook his head.

"This doesn't make any sense," he concurred. "In this technological age it's just not possible for someone to completely vanish. There has to be some record of him somewhere. Have you checked the deceased files? Even people of this character's age do die prematurely, you know."

"Oh, Christ. That never occurred to me. Sorry, Jim; I'll get on to it right away." There were times in this job when I had the strong feeling I wasn't going to make it. This was one of them.

"Let me know, will you, Ange? Also, why not check if he's changed his name by deed poll? There's also another possibility to consider: he could have 'borrowed' the birth certificate of someone around his own age who died some time ago, as an infant maybe."

I shook my head impatiently. "You mean like the *Day of the Jackal* film?" When he nodded, I quickly went on to enlighten him. "That's old hat now, Jim. They've blocked that particular avenue."

"I know. But he could have done it – say – ten or twelve years ago, before the loophole was closed...." Then he added, cryptically and – I thought – unnecessarily: "Don't you think?"

I felt my face colouring at my stupidity. "So, I'll stop trying to be clever, and check if there's any way we can find that out."

"Don't expect miracles," he warned me, more kindly. "That kind of deception's almost impossible to trace. Remember I told you I had a funny feeling about this case? Well, it hasn't gone away."

CHAPTER THIRTY-THREE

But there was no record of the demise of one Arnold Brownlaw. Nor was there any evidence he had changed his name. I checked back in the records up to the time he was released from Smethwick. Nothing. Then it occurred to me that this man must have chosen to disappear, in which case that made him not only very clever but also very wealthy. It also made him my number one suspect. It would be almost impossible to trace someone who simply didn't exist. And no one without considerable resources could pull this off successfully. And, if he had taken the route Jim suggested, then the only way it was possible to trace him would be to go over the records of all males who had died who would today be the same age as Brownlaw, and somehow check if there was evidence that their name was currently still on the records. An almost impossible task. The question also had to be asked, though: "Why?"

Purely on a hunch I rang Smethwick Psychiatric Hospital and asked to be put through to the secure unit. I was first placed on hold, then transferred around a number of unconnected departments, and finally found myself speaking to a Dr Margaret Simpson, the senior psychiatric doctor in charge of the unit. Initially, when I informed her I was seeking information regarding one of the past patients, she was only just short of hostile and managed to avoid answering a single question. It wasn't until I threatened to refer the matter to her seniors, and also involve the superintendent, that she softened a little and invited me to come over to the hospital.

I let Jim know that the results of my search on Arnold Brownlaw were negative, and that I was on my way to Smethwick, leaving Blake and WPC Fletcher to contact the remaining forces involved in the missing children cases. I'd had another idea on the Brownlaw problem, which I passed on to the two constables to look into when time permitted, and that was an enquiry into any bank accounts that might be held in his name.

As was normal, the weather was atrocious; it was pouring with rain and I found myself stuck in traffic on the M5. It took me the best part of an hour to reach Smethwick, frustrated and short on temper.

* * * * * * * * *

Dr Simpson was a stern-looking woman in her late fifties. Her greying hair was tied back in a bun, as if she had made a deliberate attempt to
neutralise her sex. She peered at me over thick glasses, her face expres-
sionless, her lips pressed tightly as if they had been stitched together. She
made it very clear she did not intend to be friendly. Her office and its
furnishings seemed to match the woman's personality in every way: dull
curtains hanging alongside an old, worn blind; a desk that at best would
be described as utility; and two matching chairs covered with a material
that was so worn it was hard to identify.

"I asked you to come over, Sergeant...?"

"...Crossley."

"Yes; quite. Sergeant Crossley. As I was saying, I asked you to
come here because I wanted to avoid the embarrassment of a public
inquisition into our patients' records. But I must make it clear, we don't
reveal information, as a matter of policy, on individuals and their treatment at this hospital."

"I understand that, Dr Simpson, but I do need to have some information on Arnold Brownlaw, the patient I mentioned on the phone.
We're talking about a potential killer here, and I must make it clear to you
that we'll obtain whatever authority is required to access the records of
the patient in question." I stood up from my dilapidated chair. "Now, if
that's all you have to say on the matter, I'll report back to my superiors
and we'll go through the official channels. I'm only sorry you've wasted
police time."

She coughed nervously and held out a hand as if by way of apology.
"Don't be so hasty, young lady," she said. "I had to say what I did for
the purposes of the official record. Now, if you can give me more
information on what this ex-patient is suspected of, perhaps we can make
some progress."

I could cheerfully have hit her, the patronising bitch! Instead, I
forced a conciliatory smile and said, "The patient concerned was treated
here some years ago after being referred from youth custody. Evidently,
the hospital diagnosed him as sexually dysfunctional and he stayed here

for about three years. The record I have shows his treatment consisted of a cocktail of various drugs linked to counselling. Shortly after his discharge, on or about his 21st birthday, he simply disappeared. There are no records whatsoever of his whereabouts. As no doubt you'll have read, we're investigating the disappearance of a number of children, young girls, some of them going back more than four years (one of them quite recently), and we have reason to believe that your ex-patient may be involved in their abduction. At the very least, we need to find him and interview him, if only to eliminate him from our enquiries. Can you understand that, Doctor?"

She pursed her lips even more tightly, then pressed her hands together as if she was giving the matter her deepest thoughts. "Yes. I can relate to that," she conceded reluctantly. She pulled a file from the drawer of her desk. "Arnold Brownlaw, 1979 to 1982 – the patient you referred to?"

I nodded. Let her do the talking!

"Hmm. Can we speak off the record?"

Again I nodded, smiling inwardly. There was no such thing as 'off the record' when the police were involved.

"Well," she continued, "it might interest you to learn, Sergeant, that I was the doctor responsible for this particular patient, and, although it was a long time ago, there are certain aspects of his behaviour I do remember very clearly."

"What can you tell me, doctor?" I pressed.

"One thing I can you tell you, unequivocally, is that he was one mean son of a bitch! I wouldn't have wanted him anywhere near *my* children. When he transferred to us from youth custody we were given no choice but to accept him. It wasn't that we were asked to diagnose him and then give our recommendations. In fact, we all had the impression they were simply trying to dump him. So we treated him; for three years we kept him partly sedated on drugs, but even that didn't entirely suppress his violent tendencies. He still gave us problems."

"What kind of problems?" I asked

She studied the file for a moment. "Shortly after his arrival, in '79, he attacked one of the junior nurses and indecently assaulted her. She was lucky we were close at hand, otherwise it could have been a lot worse. Then, a year or so later – and bear in mind by this time we had him on heavy doses of tranquillisers – he tried to rape one of the children of a ward sister; it was a little girl who was spending the day here with her mother. Again, he was stopped, but he damaged the child psychological-ly. And that wasn't the end of it: there were two more attacks while he was in our care."

"Why was he released then?" I wanted to know. "If he was so dangerous, why was he allowed back into the community?"

"Because, during the last 12 months of his incarceration (and that is what it was), he changed. He became more subdued, much more placid; he even developed a sort of charm, which he used to good effect on the senior doctors. But, in my professional view, he was just being devious; it had finally dawned on him that the only way he was ever going to get remission was by assuming a veneer of normality. And of course it worked. Finally, he managed to convince the board that he was no longer a risk to society, so he was given a clean bill of health and released under a supervision order in the care of his mother."

"His mother? You wouldn't have an address by any chance, would you, doctor?"

"It won't do you any good, Sergeant. She's dead. She was killed, by all accounts, in an accidental fall at her home, shortly after Arnold's release. It was a tragedy, in more ways than one."

"How's that?"

"Well, she absolutely worshipped Arnold. At first I put it down to her being a widow; you know the sort: a lonely, middle-aged woman who was lost without the attention of her only child. For instance, she never missed a visit to the hospital, and – to tell you the truth – I came to regard it as downright unhealthy."

"Could you elaborate on that a little?"

"She was … How shall I put it? … Too tactile. She never had her hands off him; in fact, it was becoming so obvious that I eventually had to insist that her visits were always supervised. And Arnold didn't seem able to do anything about it."

"Perhaps he didn't want to," I suggested.

"It's a point of view, I suppose. Anyway, as I said, shortly after his release she slipped one evening and fell down the stairs; broke her neck, unfortunately. And the tragic part about that was that her son inherited her not inconsiderable wealth – her late husband was a very successful industrialist. Arnold was only twenty-one, suddenly incredibly wealthy and totally unequipped to deal with it."

I made a note to look into the circumstances of the 'accident', if that's truly what it was. To my suspicious mind it was a very fortuitous coincidence. "And then he disappeared," I added.

"So, you tell me. I do know he didn't comply with his supervision order, but as to whether it was followed up seriously by the authorities, I wouldn't know. That was beyond my remit."

"I don't know whether or not this is a fair question, doctor, but I'm going to ask it anyway. Is it your professional opinion that this man's still capable of the crimes I outlined?"

She looked at me over the top of her glasses, as if she was trying to read my mind. "Very definitely! As I've already said, as his psychiatrist, in contact with him on an almost daily basis, I was in a better position than any board member to assess his mental health. And I was not deceived by his so-called metamorphosis; he was playing a game and he won.

"If you asked me to sum him up in a word, I'd say he is a psycho-path. And going by the way he behaved in his first two years in Smethwick I'd have to go further and suggest that this man would enjoy killing."

"Did you consider reporting your fears to the police?"

"I didn't have to. A copy of the appropriate files, which gave a de-tailed record of his stay at Smethwick, was passed on to the authorities. That was as far as I could go."

"I understand, doctor. And thank you for your time – you've been very helpful."

"Jesus!" I thought. "She certainly doesn't pull any punches." But she had given me far more than I had expected; without doubt, Arnold Brownlaw fitted Paul's profile almost to a tee. All we had to do now was find him, and that was a different matter altogether.

I said goodbye to the uncharismatic Dr Simpson, and as I walked out of the hospital door I realised I had left my brolly in the car, so, for my sins, I received another soaking.

CHAPTER THIRTY-FOUR

Back in the incident room the two rookies reported they had made better progress in following up the remainder of the missing children's list. As I glanced down at their notes it became evident that in each separate case it could be argued, however inconclusively, that our man could well have been involved. As we had been informed, none of the children had been found, but, nevertheless, the circumstances surrounding their disappearance seemed to possess the hallmarks of our paedophile. I shook my head at the sheer scale of the horror, at the same time aware that, unless we were able to recover the bodies, not only would we never establish the actual fate of the children, we would also be unable to level any charges.

I redirected them both onto the Brownlaw problem and went into Jim's office to report the details of my meeting with the good doctor, for good measure adding her 'off-the-record' personal comments regarding Arnold Brownlaw.

"So – we have a match," he concurred. "The mystery remains, though, how the hell he managed to disappear; and, more importantly, how we go about tracing him?"

"I've got an idea, Jim. Why don't I enquire into the family background? Trace his father, find out how he died. Did he have any other living relatives – either on his father's side or even his mother's? Somewhere, there's got to be at least one surviving member of his family. Don't you agree?"

He shrugged by way of acceptance. "Why not? We seem to have exhausted the other routes. How are the youngsters coping with the missing children list, by the way?"

"It's virtually finished."

"Any conclusions?"

"Not really. It's pretty much as we expected. Each case *could* be attributed to our paedophile, but there's no hard evidence to link them to him. If Paul's right, though, and this maniac's found another burial site, I dread to think what horrors we'll uncover if we ever trace it."

"Well, that in itself will provide the link, won't it? Meantime, we continue with old-fashioned police work, and we try to find this Brown-law character. We just have to hope our offender will make a mistake; God knows, we desperately need a break – the media are slaughtering us on this one."

I nodded. "Yeah, I caught the news last night on telly; they're giving us a rough ride alright, but I don't know what the hell they expect us to do."

He gave me a wry smile. "That one's easy to work out, Angie. They expect us to perform a fucking miracle and apprehend a killer who's been on the loose for Christ knows how many years; and we may never find out just how many children he's brutalised and murdered."

I shuddered at the thought. "I'm not sure I want to know," I said.

"Fancy dinner tonight?"

This time I grinned. "I thought you'd never ask!" Then I looked at him meaningfully. "I'm afraid that's all it can be, though."

He looked at me blank faced. "Why don't I pick you up about eight? We can go to that Italian you like."

"Look forward to it, lover boy!"

CHAPTER THIRTY-FIVE

And so I put into motion the appropriate procedural mechanisms for the investigation into Arnold Brownlaw's family background, whilst the two constables worked on the question of possible bank accounts. The staff in the incident room continued, patiently and sympathetically, to handle the public response calls. The CID followed up on the missing children's list with personal interviews in police stations across the Midlands and the North. The amount invested in resources and energy to bring this tragic episode to a satisfactory conclusion was tremendous. And, still, we were left with frustration, as positive leads failed to materialise. I discovered, for instance, that Brownlaw's father, himself an inheritor of substantial wealth, died of lung cancer when Arnold was only four years of age; his upbringing was left entirely to his mother, who never married again. That fact, coupled to what Margaret Simpson had told me of her unhealthy possessiveness with her son, gave me cause to wonder if perhaps Arnold had himself been a childhood victim of sexual abuse. Again, this would be consistent with the profile of the sadistic offender.

His father, in fact, did have a brother, but enquires revealed that he had lived in Australia for the last 30 years, and no contact had been maintained with his brother's family. On the other hand, I ascertained that Mrs Brownlaw was herself an only child, leaving the trail as cold as it was when I began my enquires.

I also followed up the personal promise I had made to myself by looking into the circumstances associated with the 'accidental' death of Mrs Brownlaw. If I were suspecting a crime, as opposed to an accident, I would have to say the circumstances were definitely suspicious. The woman was, apparently, in the house alone; she was known (by the son!) to have something of a drink problem.

When Arnold returned home that night he is said to have found his mother unconscious at the foot of the stairs; he also claims she smelt strongly of alcohol. Arnold 'immediately' telephoned for an ambulance, which arrived some 20 minutes later. She was declared dead on arrival at the hospital. There were no other witnesses, and foul play was not suspected. "Why would a son want to murder his own mother?" I wondered to myself. An autopsy was carried out, and the cause of death was found to be a fracture of the second and third cervical vertebrae – or, simply, a broken neck. On the face of it, nothing really suspicious except no traces of alcohol was found in her bloodstream.

As I commented, however, there were two very good reasons for a motive to murder: one, he wanted revenge on a mother who, most of his life, had sexually abused him; and two, he stood to inherit a great deal of money. Proving it, though, was an entirely different matter, so I filed the case in my memory, classifying it 'subject to further examination at a later date'.

On the matter of his bank accounts, there was good news and bad. The good news was that they found him; an account was registered in his name at the main branch of the Midland Bank. It was also in credit by a considerable sum. The bad news, however, was that this was 18 years ago, since when the balances had all been transferred offshore to a trust account in an unrelated name, in the Cayman Islands, and nothing further had been heard of him. So, another dead-end. Yet, somehow, even though I had never met the man, I couldn't envisage him spending the rest of his life sunning around on some Caribbean island.

The follow-up with the missing children alas produced no additional information that might have tied the cases to the present one. The signals seemed to be clear that our man was likely to be involved, but to prove it we would have to establish material evidence; regrettably, that meant finding bodies, the very thought of which brought bile to my throat. In this respect, I had the horrible feeling that another ghoulish nightmare awaited us.

A few days later I received a call from Arthur Talbot – the sergeant I had taken to Ashworth House to check the security. In truth I had forgotten all about my conversation with him concerning his psychic aunt. She had cleared a space in her busy diary, he informed me, and she could see me that evening at her home in Stourbridge. I took a note of the address together with some directions, thanked Arthur for his help, and went back to the computer.

Stourbridge was a busy dormitory town some 15 miles or so from Birmingham. It had a population of around fifty thousand, many of who commuted into the city to work. It was fairly typical of many similar towns in the West Midlands, with good road access to the M42 and M5 motorways, and it wasn't far from Birmingham Airport.

My appointment with Arthur's aunt wasn't until seven, so I had time to go home and change and get a bite to eat before setting off. The roads were quiet and with the help of Arthur's instructions I completed the journey in less than half –an-hour.

Edna Morrison, as she was called, lived a short distance from the town centre of Stourbridge in a tree-shaded avenue of detached houses, causing me to think there must be a lot of money in clairvoyance – or perhaps I should stop being the policewoman! I was a little early, and as I presumed she would already have a client with her, I waited, down the street in the car, a little way from her house, until my appointed time. I just hoped Arthur had properly briefed his aunt and she wasn't expecting me for a 'psychic session'.

Mrs. Morrison, or Edith, as she insisted I call her, was a truly delightful lady. Despite her age – I would have guessed she was in her mid-seventies – she was sprightly and very alert, with what seemed to be a permanent twinkle in her eyes. She was also dressed quite elegantly in a beige tailored suit, and her greying auburn hair was nicely coiffure; I had the impression she was dressed for business.

Before she would discuss anything with me she insisted on my having coffee with her, which she served in a silver pot and a china coffee service. I wondered if this were standard procedure for her clients, who, no doubt, would be somewhat apprehensive about meeting the 'great lady'. But instead of sitting me at the round table at one end of the room, she beckoned me over to the comfortable sofa; Edith took a seat opposite me in a large armchair. I had looked a round the room whilst she was getting the coffee and, contrary to my expectations, it was furnished very simply with the settee at one end by the fireplace, and the visiting table at the other. I assumed from the size of the house that this room was set-aside purely for her psychic work. The colours throughout the room were also friendly with long green drape curtains and a fitted carpet of gold and burgundy.

"Now, my dear. Arthur said you wanted me to help you …" she held up a hand and smilingly said, "No, you don't have to worry, Angie,

Arthur *has* told me you are seeking information rather than deceased ones." She gave a little titter at her attempted joke. "So, where do you want to start?"

"Well, I'm grateful for you agreeing to see me at such short notice – one of the things Arthur told me was how busy you are. Actually, Edith, I'm after information. You see I have this young psychic friend and I would like to know more about how her gift works ..."

"But surely, you could find that in any of the many books on the subject?"

"Yes, but Connie, that's my young friend, doesn't fall into what you might describe as the usual category of clairvoyants. Maybe if I tell you the story it might help you understand."

Edith nodded and treated me to another of her warm smiles. I noticed the lines on her face crinkled when she smiled – laughter lines I would call them. So I went over the background of my relationship with Connie, condensing it as much as I could. I began with the discovery of the bodies in the woods four years ago, and how it was Connie who reluctantly guided us to the burial site and the terrible psychological effect it had on her. I then covered her long period in Forrest Hills psychiatric hospital, including the vision she had of her mother's death, followed by the 'preternatural' image she had received a few days ago of the little girl from Solihull who was abducted from outside her school. And finally up to the present, where Connie is staying in Ashworth House, the halfway house, and when, last weekend when we were on our day's excursion, she had what appeared to be her first prophetic vision of a child who may or may not be snatched from a playground in an unknown park. I ended with Connie's repeated expressions of terror that this man knew she was watching him and was trying to trace her to do her physical harm.

When I'd finished I leaned back in my seat on the settee and rubbed my eyes. I had never found it easy talking about psychic phenomena.

"You seem to be as worried as your young friend is," Edith observed. "Are you?"

"Yes. I'm concerned because I've seen the terrible things this man's capable of doing to children ... I've seen the bodies, Edith. And, although I don't profess to understand Connie's gift, or how it works, I do believe it's completely genuine; if Connie tells me that the killer is hunting her, I believe her. I just thought that by talking to someone who's an expert in the subject I might be able to help her ... And it might help us catch this monster. So, I'd appreciate anything you can do to enlighten me on psychic phenomena ... anything you think might help me protect Connie."

The psychic pursed her lips thoughtfully before saying anything. It was as though she was trying to communicate somehow with Connie – at least that was the impression she gave me. Finally she said, in a slow measured voice, " You do understand, do you, that there is no commonality amongst psychics? What I mean by that is that we do not fall into one little box with identical labels on it." She paused as if gathering her thoughts again. "You see, my dear, there are different characteristics that define our gifts. For instance, I communicate with the departed ones – the deceased. Others see ghosts, whilst some have visions, either prophetic or in real time. I agree from what you're telling me that your friend's gift doesn't fall into any one of these categories, but that doesn't necessarily mean anything. It could well be Connie's abilities sub-divide – I mean, sometimes her visions are in real time, while others are prophetic. But it seems to me from the way you describe her experiences, that the real problem's the fact that she doesn't understand her gift herself... She's not familiar with it..."

"I'm sorry. I don't understand."

"No. Of course you don't, my dear. Let me explain ... Psychic gifts don't arrive gift- wrapped and ready to use. We don't, any of us, wake up one morning to discover we have the psychic gift presented to us, ready to use, if you like. It is an evolving blessing that takes many years to reach ... shall we call it maturity? I remember when I had my first experience ... I'd have been eleven at the time ... I had a terrible vision of Sandy, our Labrador, being run over. It broke my heart, even though the dog was lying in front of the fire at the time. When my mother asked me what the problem was I daren't tell her in case she thought I was losing my mind. Three days later, Sandy chased after a car in the road and was knocked down and killed ..." she paused as though the telling of the story brought back unhappy memories for her. "I remember I was very angry at the time – I hadn't asked for this vision, nor could I control it.

But that became the pattern of my life for years afterwards. It wasn't until after my grandmother died that I realised my true vocation was communicating with the dead – it was she who visited me and told me I was to help people in their grief.

"It was the scariest period of my life, made worse because I had no one to talk to about it."

"So how did you learn to cope?"

She shook her head, as if to say I had asked the wrong question. "I don't believe you ever learn to cope with this special kind of gift. What happens is that you learn come to terms with it, and from there you nurture it as you would a child, allow it to develop and mature over time. And you accept that it will never be something you can control, no matter how much you want to or how hard you try." Edith shrugged at the memory of her learning curve. "It can be both a blessing and a curse, my dear – and I don't really know how I can help your young friend, except to say she has to be patient. And above all she mustn't be afraid of her visions … they can't harm her – and they don't mean to. It's simply that part of her psyche lives on a different plane to other people; she experiences happenings that fall outside the realms of normal laws, and she'll involuntarily shift into that dimension when something - or someone - wants to make contact or convey a message either verbally or visually."

"What about this paedophile killer she's afraid of, Edith. Is he going to be able to find her?"

"Not by any supernatural means, no. Any more than … Connie? …can find *him*. They undoubtedly share a common prescience, but you can be certain it's frightening him just as much as her. But that's not to say he won't find her. He obviously knows she exists somewhere in the ether, and his constant fear now is that she'll find him. That, I suspect is his overriding concern at present – that she'll find him before he finds her. So he'll have to hunt her down to stop her. So you see, Angie, they share the same fear for the same reason. "I'm sorry if that scares you," she added, after seeing my reaction to this news. "I know it isn't easy to digest, and I certainly wouldn't pass it on to your friend. But I do believe you should be aware of its possibility."

I couldn't help but smile at the seriousness of her comments. "You sound more like a policewoman than I do," I told her. "But I am very grateful for your help and advice, Edith, and I'll try to keep a closer watch on Connie's safety. And thanks for finding the time to talk to me."

We talked for about an hour on the subject of the supernatural; it was hard for me to get my head round some of the things Edith told me, and I suspected that at the end of our discussion I was very little the wiser about the preternatural talents of psychics - principally the origin of their gift and its application. I suppose what really threw me was the almost casual way she treated the kinds of phenomena she had experienced in her life. But then, isn't that precisely what she had advocated Connie would have to learn to do? Come to terms with her gift and accept it for what it was to a psychic – the most natural thing in the world.

As we said goodbye and I made my way back to the car it occurred to me that I hadn't made very much progress. It was true I was a lot more knowledgeable about the mysteries of psychics and the strange world they spent part of their lives in, but it wasn't something I could pass on to Connie. I mean, I can imagine her face if I were to tell her she will have to learn to come to terms with her gift and nurture it over time. She would probably think it was me who had gone round the bend. But at least I had gone someway to satisfying my curiosity about the phenomena as well as fulfilling my promise to myself to learn more about it..

I was still shaking my head though as I made my way back to Birmingham.

The public response to our requests for information slowly began to abate, and to a large extent it was becoming repetitive as well. Unfortunately, there was no fresh information that might be helpful to the police, and we were now dealing with the tail end of the calls. We did discuss the question of issuing a further appeal, but, on reflection, decided against it, at least for the time being.

The publicity the case had attracted began to subside, as these things do with the passage of time, until eventually it was relegated to the 'lower case', and finally it fell off the front pages.

As the days and then weeks went by our investigation lost none of its importance, as far as the police were concerned, but other cases started to command our attention … a fatal shooting in Birmingham's club area, suspected to be linked to a gangland killing … an armed robbery of a building society involving the shooting of a cashier … a serial rapist attacking elderly women in daylight hours around the sub-urbs of the city-centre. As they say: life goes on: it was as if we had been shunted into a cul-de-sac with the missing child case and there was nowhere else we could go. So, we got on with our lives.

I saw Connie regularly, and once a month I had her stay with me for the weekend, which we both thoroughly enjoyed. By now, she and constable Harrison had become something of an item, and, although she was still very young, I did nothing either to lecture her or to discourage her from her first romance. Tongue in cheek, I did suggest she would be well advised to take precautions!

Jim and I remained close, although I was rather glad I hadn't agreed to move in with him; I didn't feel yet that we were close enough for that kind of commitment. I still had no idea where the relationship was headed. I loved the sex but I also knew I appreciated the freedom that living alone gave me, and I was very reluctant to surrender that.

Weeks went by with no further developments in the case, but we in-sisted on trying to maintain a high profile as far as public awareness was concerned. The posters and photofit pictures remained on display as an ongoing warning that this evil predator was still at large. I did notice, though, in passing a kiddies' park one afternoon that the poster on display looked rather sad and worn.

I sat my inspector's exam, and was relieved to pass with flying col-ours. Gradually life reverted to something like normality, and I concen-trated more and more on trying to advance my career. Secretly I harboured ambitions to one day making it as high as Jim – if not all the way up to Superintendent.

CHAPTER THIRTY-SIX

The playground that morning was filled with the sounds of children: laughing, shouting, occasionally screaming with delight – all the sounds youngsters make when they're enjoying themselves. It was a lovely sunny day, perfect for spending a morning in the park; where the children, under supervision, could freely go wild, and the mothers could find a little peace, sitting on the various benches, chatting to each other and exchanging the daily gossip, knowing their children were safe and protected.

The playground was in an enclosed part of the park, surrounded by a wire mesh fence that was childproof, in case any of them were tempted to wander. The floor area was filled with loose sand – another safety precaution in the event of spills from the various slides and swings.

At the perimeter of the playground a vigilant park attendant, suitably attired in council uniform and wearing sporty custom-made sunglasses, wandered slowly around the circumference, keeping a lookout for mishaps of any kind. It was a day for relaxing, for unwinding in the sunshine and allowing the children to expend their abundant energy.

The recent media publicity concerning the abduction and probable murder of the child from Solihull, and – more particularly – the link with the other murders of four years earlier, had made the mothers extra cautious, although the message had waned somewhat. The posters, warning parents to be on the lookout, were displayed prominently. The extra security, a surprising and welcome innovation from the local council, gave added comfort, however; it was largely because of this development the children could be left unattended.

"Well, it's been very nice, but I suppose I should be getting back," Marion, an attractive brunette in her late twenties, said to her friend sitting next to her on the bench. "Geoff'll be home from the pub shortly, and you know what they're like if there's no Sunday lunch on the table!"

"Tell me about it!" Audrey, her friend, replied. "If you don't mind, Marion, I won't come with you. My old man's away for the weekend, so I've got the day to myself." She stretched her arms and yawned with pleasure. "I'm going to make the most of it. You can leave Lisa here, if you like. Give you a bit of peace; I can drop her off later."

Marion gave her an envious grin. "No. Thanks, anyway – her dad'll be asking after her if she's not home. Enjoy your day, Audrey. Some people have all the luck! Where's Lisa? She was with your Josie a minute ago!"

"She can't be far away. There's nowhere for her to go. LISA!" she shouted; then again: "LISA!"

"Josie's over there, playing on the swings. I'll go and ask her where Lisa's got to."

By now Marion was beginning to panic a little. As Audrey had said, there was nowhere for the little girl to go; the playground was completely enclosed, and if she had tried to wander away the security guard would have stopped her. But where was he? He seemed to have disappeared now as well. Both she and Audrey ran across to the swings to ask Josie where her friend had gone. She looked at them bemused. "The man said she had to go with him."

"What man?" Marion almost screamed. "Go where? Where did he take her, Josie? Do you know?"

The little girl shook her head. "No. But he said it was okay 'cos her dad was waiting outside."

Audrey gasped in horror. "The security guard, Marion! He's not here! Dear God – you don't think he could have taken her, do you?"

Marion burst into tears, and then, panicking, she ran towards the gate of the playground in a state of near-hysteria. "Audrey," she shouted behind her, "call the police; there's something not right here. LISA!" she screamed. LISA! Where are you?"

* * * * * * * * *

The man dragged the child roughly, her feet scuffling along the ground, towards the door of the Land Rover, one hand clamped tightly across her mouth to prevent her from screaming. He cursed loudly when she bit into his hand, causing some drops of blood to appear and fall onto the grass by the side of his vehicle, and he had to restrain himself from punching her. So far it had gone well; his surveillance of the playground before the start of the school holidays had paid dividends, and his plan to masquerade as a security guard had worked perfectly. Now all he had to do was to bundle this obstinate little brat into the car and they'd be off, free and clear.

He did exactly that, after first punching her in the mouth, then virtually throwing her into the front passenger seat, whilst with his free hand he grabbed the piece of material from the dashboard that would serve as a gag. At the same time he quickly tied her hands to the restraining strap on the car seat to prevent her jumping out of the vehicle. Then he was set. He started the engine and was about to pull away when suddenly he felt a cold mist descending on him. He shuddered, recalling that he had experienced something similar all those years ago in the woods. The mist seemed to cloak him, interfering with his breathing and starting a panic attack. Someone, or something, was definitely watching him, observing him with a kind of detached interest, as though the incident was being recorded for some future reprisal. As he had done the last time, he peered through the icy cold of the mist, trying to make out a face; but not only was it was too obscure, he distinctly felt a pressure on his face pushing him away, as if the apparition was determined to remain undetected.

He let out a shriek at the realisation that whatever it was was alive and aware. In a panic he punched the gears into drive and hit the accelerator as hard as he could, causing the tyres to skid as he pulled away from the park. Beside him, the little girl was still struggling against her bonds, tears, mingling with blood, pouring down her cheeks; he had almost forgotten about her in his anxiety, and he was somewhat relieved to find she was still there. He reached across to the passenger seat and gently stroked the inside of her thigh.

"Oh, we're going to have such a lovely time together," he said, smiling now. The mist was gone, almost as quickly as it had appeared, but he was left with the resolve that he had to do everything in his power to discover who it was who was haunting him...

* * * * * * * * *

I was on the point of making coffee at Jim's when the mobile went off. I groaned in exasperation; we had enjoyed a long lie-in this Sunday morning, and I was quite looking forward to a pub lunch. I quickly changed my mind when the station informed me of that morning's incident in the park.

"Oh, dear God, no!" I said aloud, just as Jim came out of the bathroom. I held up a hand to stop him interrupting the rest of the message. I repeated it for clarification, making a note of the address, then put him in the picture as I grabbed my jacket. It wasn't until we had gone some distance in the car, heading towards the scene at Castle Bromwich, that I remembered Connie's vision of some weeks ago. I also remembered I had said nothing to Paul, at the time, partly because I had not been convinced by his assertion then that the episode was nothing more than an adolescent peculiarity that some youngsters experienced, but mainly because I was becoming tired of his inherent cynicism. I was only glad I had mentioned it to Jim.

The details the station had given me over the phone matched virtually word for word what Connie had described to me at the time, even down to the designer sunglasses the attendant was wearing.

"This sounds like Connie's nightmare come true," Jim commented. "And before you say anything, Angie, let me remind you what I said when you told me about it: even Connie can't change fate, and there isn't a thing you could have done about it. You do realise where we're headed, don't you?" he asked, by way of changing the subject.

"Castle Bromwich," I grunted, distracted by my conscience. At the same time, I was thinking: "Damn that doctor. He told me I'd learn how to deal with guilt; well, he was wrong."

"I know the way, Jim," I added as an afterthought.

"I wasn't talking about the directions, Angie. I was trying to point out that we pass Ward End on the way; you know – the place where Josephine Marsden's clothes were found."

"I hadn't realised," I admitted. "It all seems so long ago."

"You mean you were hoping he'd silently slipped away. It doesn't work like that, and, anyway, nine weeks is not a long time for these psychopaths. All I know about them is what Paul told us: they satisfy their bloodlust for a while, but there's no predetermined timetable they stick to.   Apparently, the inactivity only lasts as long as their feeling sated."

"Jesus. I feel sick," I admitted. "You make him sound like some jungle predator that kills whenever it's hungry."

"Isn't that more or less what he is? An animal, constantly on the prowl – only worse? The only real difference is that he prefers young children – little girls." He sighed. "I share your nausea, Angie, but I can only remind you what I warned you a while back: you've got to stay focused."

Out of the corner of a tear-stained eye I caught his finger, pointing a warning at me. It didn't help very much; I wasn't kidding when I said I was feeling sickly. I also had a feeling of terrible sadness creeping over me. All I could think of was that poor child and how completely helpless we were to protect her.

We were eating up the miles on the Sunday lunchtime roads, but I lengthened the journey by deliberately bypassing Ward End; the current situation was hard enough to cope with without the additional burden of painful memories. I went onto the ring road around Castle Bromwich and followed the directions I had been given to the park and the children's playground.

Two squad cars were already on the scene when we arrived, and I noticed a WPC comforting a young woman who was sobbing hysterically. My heart went out to her – she was obviously the mother of the abducted child – and I knew there was no way we could offer her any reassurance. Jim went to speak with a uniformed inspector, whilst I joined one of the constables, who were interviewing a second mother.

"Morning, Sarge," he greeted me. "This is Mrs Thornton; Audrey Thornton. She's a friend of the missing girl's mother." He was a tall, bespectacled young man with dark, thinning hair and pale blue eyes. I already knew of him, as our PC Connelly was beginning to make quite a name for himself at the station – evidently for his astute deductions and quick grasp of detail.

"Marion," she said. "Her name's Marion; Marion Carter. Her daughter's Lisa."

She was visibly upset, and her hands, I noticed, were shaking. Probably from shock, I thought.

"Can you tell us what happened, Audrey?" I asked.

"There's nothing to tell, really," she said, wiping away a tear. One minute Marion and I were chatting - we felt safe because there was an attendant there - and the next Lisa was missing, and so was the park keeper. It was Josie, my little girl, who told us the man had taken her outside to meet her daddy. Dear God," she choked; "we only took our eyes off her for a moment."

I made a note of her full name and address, and then asked her if I could speak with Josie.

"You can, of course, but she's only six. I'm not sure she can tell you any more than I have."

"Let me speak with her anyway, can I?"

As she went to collect her daughter from inside the playground I asked Bob Connelly what he thought had happened. "It's pretty much like she said," he said. "Except I've looked around the perimeter and you can see the indents where the 'park keeper' had left a vehicle.

"I didn't go too close in case I disturbed the scene. The SOCOS are on the way with Forensics so they may be able to tell us more in a while. The only other comment I'd make, Sarge, is that this character obviously had the abduction carefully planned; it took a hell of a nerve to masquerade as an attendant. He'd have had to reconnoitre the site at least a couple of times to be sure no one would be here to expose him. And he'd have had to either buy or hire the uniform. I'm not sure you can do either with council uniforms."

"Yeah," I agreed. "Which mean he must have stolen it. Let's check with the local council, shall we, Bob. See if they've reported anything. He's also one clever bastard to carry off something like this. He encouraged the parents to feel secure in his presence and then pounced." I let out a heavy breath; I was feeling far less confident today about catching him than I did when we first started on this case.

"Sergeant, this is Josie," Marion said, holding her daughter by the hand.

"Hello, Josie." I smiled, hoping to make her feel at ease, but she returned the smile with a serious facial expression. "Has your mummy told you I'd like to talk to you."

"Yes. You want to know what happened to Lisa. The man took her away. He said her daddy wanted to meet her outside."

"Did you see which way they went?" I asked.

She pointed with her finger in the direction where PC Connelly had found the tyre tracks. "That way. But I didn't look real careful 'cos it was my turn on the see-saw."

I thought for a moment how to ask a child a question about accents, and then said, "Did his voice sound like anyone you know?"

"Yes. Like daddy."

"Is your husband from around these parts?"

"Yes. He's from Walsall originally."

"And does he have a West Midland accent?"

"Very much so, although it's softened a bit in the past few years."

"But it's still distinctly West Midland?"

She nodded.

"Thank you," I said. "And thank you, Josie, for helping us."

"Will you find her?" the little girl asked.

"I hope so, Josie. I really hope so."

Well, at least we had now confirmed what we previously suspected: our offender was definitely from this area. I thought again of Arnold Brownlaw. "There must be some way of tracing him," I told myself. I wandered over to speak with Jim, who by now was engrossed with the forensic team.

"He was using a four-wheel drive vehicle," he confirmed. "And his front offside tyre is almost bald." He shook his head. "It's not much to go on, but it's something, I suppose."

"He's definitely from this part of the world," I informed him, then went on to describe what Josie had said.

"Are you thinking the same as me?"

I nodded. "Arnold Brownlaw. Yes. He fits the bill almost perfectly. The question still is, though: how the hell do we find him?"

"We apply more resources," he said vehemently. Then he shook his fist angrily. "If we have to we'll commandeer every fucking detective in the West Midlands to help us! Whatever it takes, Angie, we have to catch this monster."

"Focused," I said teasingly.

"Yeah, I know I said that, but even I'm finding it hard to stay objective now." He shrugged. "Is young Connelly taking statements from the mother and her friend?"

I nodded. "Do you think I should give Paul a ring? He may have some insights on today's abduction."

"Why not. We need all the help we can get. Just don't mention anything about Connie's vision. Oh, and while you're at it why not give Connie a call; ask her if she can tell us anything more."

I took my mobile from my bag, promising myself that I would speak to her to see if she could throw any further light on the matter. I managed to get hold of Paul at Forest Hills and arranged to meet him at the station later in the day. As I was leaving the scene a bevy of media were beginning to arrive. I squeezed Jim's arm supportively. "Do you want me to stay?"

"No. You get off, Ange. I can deal with this lot. I'll see you back at the station."

CHAPTER THIRTY-SEVEN

I joined Connie and Steve Harrison in the lounge at Ashworth House. She had an all too familiar look about her today; her face was very pale, her eyes clouded by dark shadows, and she was trembling. I recognised the symptoms from previous experiences.

"I'm glad you came, Sarge," Steve said, a worried look on his face. "She's been like this most of the morning, and I can't persuade her to tell me what the problem is. Maybe she'll talk to you."

"Do you think you can leave us alone for a while, Steve?"

After he had left the room I turned and held Connie in a sympathetic embrace. "It's okay, sweetheart," I said, comfortingly; "I do understand. You don't have to talk about it if you're not up to it."

"Have you come from the crime scene?" she asked, almost as if we were exchanging telepathic messages. I wasn't at all surprised; it was obvious, to me at least, what had happened.

"Yes. Just now. I'm only sorry there was nothing we could do about your vision."

"What could you have done, Angie? I wasn't totally convinced myself at the time it was a prophesy. How could I? It had never happened before."

"Are you okay to talk about it, or would you rather leave it till later?"

"I don't mind talking to you, Angie, but I couldn't discuss it with Steve. And it's become very important, hasn't it?"

"Yes. Very. But I'll have to ask you to try and relive the whole thing, if you can. And if you don't mind, I'd like to tape our conversation. Will you be comfortable with that?"

She nodded, and then said, "As long as it's understood that you don't make it public – I really couldn't handle that."

"How about if I let Paul – Dr Simmons – listen to it?"

"Well, I guess that's okay, if you feel you have to; but if he gives me one more of his cynical smirks, I swear I'm going to hit him." Laughing now, she went on, "Where do you want to start?"

I placed the tiny recorder on the table and pressed the start button. "Well, let me take you back to that day in the car. It was Sunday afternoon, if you remember, and we were on our way home from Malvern when you suddenly 'disappeared'; you literally went off into a world of your own. At first I didn't really notice your reactions, I was tired and we'd had a long day, and I suppose I just wanted to get us home. Then, the next thing I was aware of you were moaning, and your eyes had rolled over as if you were having some kind of a seizure. You looked so terrible it frightened the life out of me. I thought it might be some kind of epileptic fit. So I pulled off the road and called for an ambulance. Thinking about it, I would have to say you were out of it completely for about 20 minutes, and then it was another half an hour before you were fully back with us. Do you remember having any awareness of time at all?"

"No. None. I recall being in the car one minute – it was a cloudy day; I remember that – and the next minute I was in a public park, on a sunny morning, heading towards a children's playground. It was as if I was seeing everything through some kind of veil."

"Can you explain that, Connie? I'm not sure I understand."

She sat back in the chair and closed her eyes in deep concentration, saying nothing for quite a time. Then, with her eyes still shut, she said, "Whoever was showing me the picture didn't want anyone to see me; I think I was being protected by a screen of some kind. I could see out but no one could see in. I saw the playground, with all the children enjoying themselves; I saw the mothers on the benches; then someone turned my vision towards a man in uniform – I believe it was a ranger's uniform, but I'm not certain. He was walking around the outside of the playground, just watching the children."

"Did you get a look at his face...?"

Her eyes still closed, she held a hand up as if to tell me not to break her concentration. "I saw he was watching one little girl very closely; she was tiny and had blonde hair, and she was playing with her friend on the swings. Then I noticed he had moved closer to the entrance; he was beckoning to the little girl with his finger, wanting her to go over to him. She did, with her friend; then he leant down to talk to her. All the time he was smiling and being friendly." I watched her face screw up tightly with anxiety before she was able to continue. "He took the little girl's hand in his – she was smiling too – and they went out of the playground.

No one noticed, except her friend, and she headed towards the seesaw. No one seemed to be bothered at all, apart from me; I shouted a warning but no one could hear me."

Connie was obviously suffering by now, her features showing a mixture of fear and anger. I thought of bringing her round, but decided that might be dangerous. She said nothing for at least five minutes, just sitting there with her eyes closed and her hands clenched into fists.

Then, at last, she spoke again. "I followed them to his car; it was one of those Range Rovers, I think. The girl began to struggle, so he clamped his hand over her mouth while he tried to open the car door. The child was kicking him now and trying to scream. His hand slipped from her mouth and she bit him – hard, very hard; I noticed his finger was bleeding and spots fell onto the ground beside the car. Then he punched her – hard – with his fist. He was furious with her, but I can tell he was also frightened. She was barely conscious when he threw her into the car; then his sunglasses fell off and I saw his face."

She opened her eyes suddenly, very alert but extremely distressed. She took hold of my hand and gripped it tightly; I noticed tears were trickling down her cheeks. "Dear God, Angie," she stuttered. "It's the same man! The one who killed Josephine."

I put her hand in both of mine and squeezed it gently. "It's alright, Connie. He can't reach you here. Could you see the number of his car?"

"Some of it. I know it began with a 'T', and it had the number '2' in the middle, but the rest is just a blur. I'm sorry." She shrugged her shoulders in frustration.

"Do you remember the colour?"

"Black. Or dark blue."

"And this time you got a good look at him?"

"Yes. It was very clear. Almost like a photograph. And he's younger than I thought – he can't be any older than 40 at the most. And he's smaller, and thinner."

"Does he resemble the photofit you did of him?"

"Not quite. I'm sure I can do a better one now." She frowned. "I'm positive I've seen him somewhere before, Angie. I just can't remember where."

Déjà vu, I thought. "Don't worry about it, Connie. I'm sure your memory will recover in its own time if you don't try to force it. But you've done brilliantly," I said, punching Jim's mobile number.

"DCI Robbins."

"Jim. Where are you?"

"Hi, Ange. I'm still at the crime scene. How about you?"

"I'm with Connie. I'll fill you in later on all the details, but you have to get forensics to check the area around the car. They should find some bloodstains on the ground."

There was silence for a moment, whilst his mind adjusted to this latest esoteric phenomenon, but he didn't question the source of the information. "Good. I'll get them on to it. Anything else?"

"Yes. As you said, his car was a type of Range Rover – a four-wheel drive. It's either black or dark blue. Also, we have a partial Reg: it's a 'T' registration, and it has the number '2' in it. And, Connie informs me that he punched the child with his fist, because she bit him, so it's likely he'll have blood on his clothes."

I heard a sigh. "Yeah, okay. We knew about the type of vehicle from the tyre tracks. But the colour and the partial will help. We've put out an APB and roadblocks, but the problem with that kind of motor is he doesn't have to stick to the roads; he can go cross-country. Anyway, at least we can broaden the description. And, Angie, when you get back to the station, set up the procedures for a mass vehicle check, will you? Let's see how many T-Reg four-wheel drives we'll be talking about. Got to go. I'll see you later."

I checked my watch. It was time I was going; Paul would be at the station shortly.

"Will you be alright, Connie, if I leave you with Steve?"

She smiled and wiped her cheek with a handkerchief. "Go and catch him, Angie. I'll be fine."

CHAPTER THIRTY-EIGHT

Paul was already waiting for me in one of the interview rooms when I returned. I handed the tape over to him and left him to listen to it whilst I organised the vehicle search.

"What do you think?" I asked, after he had shut the machine off.

He gave me one of his non-committal shrugs. "Well, I'm doing my best to keep an open mind, as I promised. But this – this is really something. If I didn't have the details from the chief inspector I'd have to say this was some kind of 'Alice in Wonderland'. Is this exactly how she saw her vision?"

"Yes. In almost every detail, except Connie's added one or two things we didn't know about."

"I'll listen to it again in a bit, if you don't mind. But, accepting for a moment that what Connie says is true, and from what I've heard, it does sound as though our man's getting more and more desperate."

"How do you make that out, Paul?"

"He's beginning to expose himself, for a start. He abducted that girl almost in front of her mother – that was a hell of a risk to take. Anyone could have seen him, in which case I doubt he would have got very far. As a matter of procedure, generally, our man is very, very careful. He'll research his quarry with almost painstaking detail; and he won't act till he's absolutely sure of his security. And now he's made his first mistake; today's incident has all the appearances of an almost impulsive snatch – there was very little planning involved other than his disguise as a park ranger.

"His second mistake was leaving his car in the park. We've only got a partial number from Connie, but I'll bet someone in that park saw it and will be able to give you a better description. If you think about it, Angie, it had to have been there for quite some time, and it certainly wouldn't have gone unnoticed. And now, of course, you've got the bloodstains. No doubt the DNA will match him with Josephine Marsden's abductor. That was another mistake; and unlike the clothes in the field, it wasn't intentional. It was outside his control, and he really won't like that. What you have to do now is to keep up the pressure on him." He shrugged. "I realise it doesn't help this latest victim, but it might stop him getting another one.

"Let me think about it some more, Angie. I'll play the tape again and see if there's anything I've missed. Where will you be?"

I pointed towards the incident room. "I'll be out there, helping with a vehicle search. But I'm not banking on getting anywhere. This is going to be some trawl."

And I was correct. In the West Midland area alone there were over 6,000 four-wheel drives with a 'T' registration, ranging from Toyotas to Jeeps to Range Rovers, and a host of other smaller manufacturers.

"Where the hell do we start, Frank?" I asked Frank Kewell. I was damned if I was going to address him as 'inspector'!

"Well, let's see if we can narrow it down somewhat, shall we? First off, we'll eliminate all the women owners." One of the WPCs keyed the information and the search question into the computer, and a matter of seconds later the list was reduced to a little over 4,000.

"Now," Frank said, "let's print out a list of the dealers in this area who sold this type of car in that year, together with their e-mail addresses."

That process took the best part of half an hour, and at the finish we had more than 200 e-mail addresses. Whilst the computer was carrying out the search, Frank was drafting an e-mail communication to all the dealers, asking them for the following information:

1. The names and addresses of all males who had purchased T-Reg four-wheel drive vehicles, new, in that year together with the full registration number of the vehicle concerned.

2. How they paid for the vehicle.

3. Did they do a trade-in? And, if so, please supply the details.

4. Are any of the customers known to you personally? If 'yes', again supply details.

5. Please try to exclude all purchasers over the age of 50 and under the age of 25.

Please note, this information is required urgently to assist our en-quires into the recent child abductions. We would be very grateful for your immediate cooperation. All replies to:

Detective Inspector Kewell, etc., etc.

"Well that should grab their attention," I told him. Then I took the printout and a pair of scissors and began cutting the list into a number of much smaller lists; Peter Corkhill then handed them out to the teams of staff in the incident room.

"You've only got about six or seven each to send," I informed them. "So, come on gang; let's get to it. But listen up: give each of them an hour to respond, and any that haven't by then – chase them up again. And keep chasing them, on the phone if necessary; and if that fails we'll arrange a visit. This is number one priority. In the meantime, the inspector and I will set up a database for the replies. Go straight into Access and type in the information; I can do a sort when we have all the details to hand."

Frank Kewell actually grinned at my call to the troops. Perhaps his earlier irritation with me was just frustration and not rank pulling. I decided to give him the benefit of the doubt by returning his grin.

When I went to rejoin Paul in the interview room he also handed me a draft communication. I was no wiser after I had read it.

"What on earth is this, Paul?"

"It's a computer bulletin, for the notice board. The phraseology is just the kind of stuff paedophiles use on the Net."

"Fine. But what does it say?"

He looked at me, with embarrassment, I thought. "Effectively it says that I know where there's a girl available – a child of eight – in the Manchester area, and that I'm willing to trade."

"Jesus!" I gasped. "Is that how they do things? Like a kind of white slavery, only with children?"

He nodded. "Remember I mentioned that the sadistic offender is likely to use computer bulletin boards or coded chat lines to seek out victims? Well that's exactly what we're going to do to try and trap him. I'm banking on him becoming that desperate, particularly if we keep up the pressure on him, that he'll go for something like this – that's if he hasn't already. And, bear in mind, this system is supposedly totally anonymous and fail-safe; it has to be for it to have any value to these people."

I treated him to one of my naive, puzzled glances. "But if it's so secure, Paul, how do we use it to trap him? Won't it simply be a case of one anonymous advertiser dealing with another anonymous customer?"

"In theory, yes. But eventually, once each party is satisfied about the *bona fides* of the other, they can't stay anonymous."

"They have to show their hand, you mean?"

"Precisely."

"Well, it sounds reasonable on the surface, but how do we go about it? Who accesses the computer and how do we get to place it on an appropriate website? I don't think any of us in this police station has any experience with this kind of thing."

"No. Of course you don't. But you must know people who do."

"You're talking about other paedophiles, aren't you?"

He just nodded, almost conspiratorially. "What you do is find one in the Manchester area who's a persistent offender, who has a record for this type of trade – obviously – and who's well known to the local police. And you recruit him, by any means you consider necessary. He'll know all the procedures we have to go through, and the coding I'm sure these people adopt for secrecy." He held up the draft document. "Like this website notice I've drafted. I've been taking lessons from one of our patients."

"So, why can't we use him?"

"Wrong area; these people aren't stupid, you know. It has to be someone actually based in or around Manchester. If we enter a chat room from this part of the country it might throw up suspicions of a trap. Also, it contravenes the Mental Health Act."

"Right. I'm with you. Anything else on the tape?"

"No. I think I've covered everything. But there are a couple of things I'd suggest to keep the pressure on him. One, update the photofit with Connie's latest input and circulate it over an even wider area. And two, enquire if it's possible to have CCTV cameras installed outside the principal schools and children's playgrounds in the area; then publicise the fact."

"Well, the photofit isn't a problem, Paul, but I don't know about the cameras. You're talking a lot of money here."

"Then ask if it's possible to rent the system for a short period. And if you can't do that then lie about it, let him *think* that's what we've done. Believe me, Angie, it'll push him into a corner and that might produce dividends." He paused thoughtfully. "One other thing. If I accept that Connie's vision *is* genuine – and I'm coming more and more round to that view – then I'm even more concerned now about her safety than I was before. Talk to Jim about that, will you? I believe it's essential to increase her cover." He glanced at me, puzzled, when I didn't acknowledge him. "Do you have a problem with that, Angie?"

I shook my head. "Not at all. It's just that I have something nagging me at the back of my brain; I'm damned if I can put a finger on it."

"Don't worry; it'll come back to you. It always does with me. Look, I have to dash now. I have a patient review this evening. If Jim wants to speak with me he can catch me later at Forest Hills. Keep me in touch, won't you?"

"Absolutely. Take care, Paul."

* * * * * * * * *

The database was almost complete when I returned to my desk; very evidently Inspector Kewell knew his stuff when it came to computers.

"Finish this off, Angie, will you? Jim's on his way back and he wants me to set up a meeting with the superintendent."

"Sure."

"Oh, and then you'll need to save it on floppy disks."

"I realise that, Frank. Then we'll have to network it – right?"

He grinned. The second time today; he was definitely softening! I finished off the database just as the first replies to Frank's e-mail started to filter in. I left the team to deal with it, and then joined the others in the conference room. It was a very gloomy atmosphere.

"Any news?" I asked.

Jim just shook his head. "This guy has more lives than a cat," he grunted. "Nothing on the APB; nothing on the roadblocks. But for him to disappear so quickly must suggest that he lives somewhere in the vicinity of the abduction. I recommend that's where we should concentrate our efforts. Did you talk to Paul, by the way?"

"Yes. He made some good suggestions." I went through my discussion with Paul; they listened in silence until I had finished.

"I like the idea of the CCTVs," the superintendent said, "even if we have to install phoney systems then lie about it. I'm buggered if I understand the suggestion about computer bulletin boards, though; it's a bit out of my league, I'm afraid. Can anyone explain it to me?"

"Yes, I can," Frank said, then proceeded to give a detailed and simplified explanation of how the plan might work, including the logic of a Manchester base.

"Well, I'll be damned," the superintendent said. "These bastards not only have their own communication network they also have their own language! How do we implement that, Jim?"

"We'll have to send someone to Manchester to work with the local CID. Fancy volunteering, Frank?"

"I'll go if I have to. But wouldn't we be better off with a computer boffin?"

"No; I need someone with senior rank. We don't want any ego clashes with the locals. And you're better with computers. So, we'll pencil that one in. I'll get on to the DCI at Manchester and make the arrangements. When can you go?"

Frank shrugged. "Today, if necessary, providing Angie takes over the vehicle investigation from me."

"Angie?"

I nodded my head in agreement. "Sure, I think I can organise the legwork."

"I'll contact the various school governors if you provide me with a list," the superintendent offered. "Persuade them to go along with the CCTV suggestion."

"And I'll try to stave off the press," Jim said, tight-lipped. "They're screaming for blood out there. Christ knows what else I can say that might pacify them. Any ideas, anyone?"

"Why not tell them we've got a witness who's given us a good description, and we'll be issuing an updated photofit later today?" That was my input, but it was very tongue in cheek in case it exposed Connie's position even more.

Jim pondered over it for a few moments. "Yeah. I think I know what you're getting at, Angie, and I'm sure you're aware of the risks to that friend of yours."

The superintendent got up from his chair. "This is where I leave you people," he snapped. "I thought I'd made it clear I have no wish to be involved in that airy fairy nonsense."

Jim let out a sigh of exasperation. "You did, Phil. You made it abundantly clear. But I have to tell you that I'm keeping an open mind, rather like Dr Simmons, and I'm not going to reject any avenue that might lead to an arrest. And I'd remind you that a completely closed mind is a completely unreceptive mind." He then stood and glared at the superintendent. "And if you find that offensive, *sir*, then you had better take me off the case and replace me with someone with less imagination."

The superintendent raised his hands defensively. Jim was glowering at him in real fury. I didn't think I had ever seen him so angry.

"Alright, alright," he stammered, trying to contain his own irritation. "Let's try to compromise on this one, shall we? I won't interfere with your running of the case if you don't involve me directly in this so-called psychic stuff. Is that fair?"

Jim softened at that. "Yeah, Phil. Okay. Sorry about the outburst, but this case has got us all uptight."

"I understand. Let me know if you need any help with the media." He turned to leave. "Oh, and, Angie, I believe you're right to arrange additional protection for that young friend of yours."

"Okay, team," Jim said, after the superintendent had left. "Let's get to it, shall we? We've got a hell of a lot to do. Frank; start making your arrangements, will you. I'll try to get you up to Manchester later today. Ange; see if you can arrange for a team of two to give Connie extra cover. And ask PR to come up again; I really do need some help with this media thing."

The meeting broke up and we went back to our appointed tasks. The response from the car dealers was coming in thick and fast now. It seemed everyone wanted to help us catch this vicious psychopath.

CHAPTER THIRTY-NINE

I noticed a number of new faces in the incident room; it appeared that our DCI was as good as his word and was drafting in all the help he could summon. One of them was actually sitting at my desk.

"Excuse me."

"What? Oh, sorry," the newcomer said. "You must be Sergeant Crossley."

"That's correct. And you are?"

He rose and held out a hand. "Peter Conway; Sergeant Peter Conway, Wolverhampton CID." He wasn't very much older than I was. Tall, slim – quite an athletic build. In fact, he wasn't at all bad looking, with his dark wavy hair and hazel eyes. I shook his hand, noticing that he held onto mine longer than was normal. He had a distinct twinkle in his eye. It told me a lot about him – especially to watch myself with him. "My DI instructed me to report to you for allocation of duties."

"To me?" I said surprised. "He doesn't know me."

"No, but it was arranged between him and your DCI, Jim Robbins. Evidently you have been appointed as liaison officer between the various forces helping out."

I scowled fiercely. "I wish someone had bothered to tell me." God! That Jim could be really infuriating at times. "Anyway, welcome aboard. I'm sure you realise by now we need all the help we can get."

"What would you like me to do, Sarge?"

"Angie; my name is Angie. Alright if I call you Peter?"

"Fine…Angie. I hear your current serious crime cases have been handed across to other West Midland forces. So, how can I help?"

"Let me introduce you first to Peter Corkhill –Sergeant Peter Corkhill. We've been working together on this case."

"Glad to meet you," Peter said warmly. "We really could do with all the help we can get on this case."

I filled him in on the current state of the investigation, emphasising the need to follow up on the dealers' lists, which were fast approaching completion.

"Any good with computers, Peter?"

"Not bad, actually. They're a bit of a hobby of mine. Would you like me to merge the list when it's finished?"

"Thanks. That would be a big help. After that you can help me to organise the house calls."

"How many are we talking about?"

I hesitated. When I gave it some thought it sounded quite ridiculous. But it still had to be done. "It could be as high as 4,000. Hopefully fewer. Do you think we're taking on too much?"

He shrugged philosophically. "You're trying to catch a vicious killer. If that's what it takes, then that's what we'll do."

I think I was going to like Peter Conway. We set to work assimilating all of the responses after the incident room team had inputted the information into the computer. I left Peter to handle it whilst I got on to PR for Jim's media problem. Next I dealt with the question of extra security for Connie, and then I telephoned her to put her in the picture. She wasn't at all fazed by the news.

"Have there been any developments?" she wanted to know.

"No. Not yet, Connie. We're still chasing up the leads on the vehicles. After that it's going to be a lot of legwork, I'm afraid. Will you be okay for the next couple of days if I can't get across to see you?"

"I'll be fine, Angie; honest. You just do what you have to. Maybe Steve and I could meet up with you in town for a sandwich or something."

'Steve and I', indeed – as if they had always been an item. Or, was I becoming possessive? Also, I was forgetting that Connie would be 18 in a few weeks; then she was free to do whatever she wanted. Still, I couldn't help but feel a little put out at the news.

"Good idea," I said, managing to inject some enthusiasm in my voice. "I'll ring you tomorrow. Bye, Connie."

By the evening all the information from the car dealers was complete, the staff had fed it into the computers, and Peter Durning began the mail merge. The number of vehicles wasn't as high as I first estimated; of the 4,000 or so on the original list more than 2,500 had been eliminated because of the various constraints we had introduced. Even so, 1,500 were still a hell of a lot and would more than stretch our resources. I had asked Peter Conway to begin the merge in alphabetical order; the other Peter was assisting him and they seemed to be getting along well together. This gave me the chance to scan the list quickly for my Arnold Brownlaw – not that I really expected to find him. I was right: my suspect did not appear. Next, we sorted in areas closest to the abduction site, as Jim had suggested. There were 35 in this category. I fed them out to the other officers in the room with instructions to check each purchaser's name for any criminal background, following which we would broaden the scope to include the remaining names on the list. In doing this, however, I was mindful of Paul's earlier comments when he claimed it was unlikely our paedophile would have a criminal record. I also recalled it was something Connie was adamant about. Nevertheless, it had to be done as part of normal police procedure, and you never knew what it might throw up.

It was getting quite late by now, so I decided to call it a night. More and more these days I seemed to be affected by an intense weariness. I shrugged it off by putting it down to the pressure of the case.

"Fancy a bite to eat?" Peter Conway asked, a smile on his face.

"No. Thanks anyway, but I'm whacked. I'm off home; see you to-morrow."

"Sure. I'll be here bright and early. I'll make a start on the rest of the list, shall I?"

"If you would. Thanks."

CHAPTER FORTY

I tossed and turned for most of the night. We were currently experiencing a high-pressure front, causing the weather to become hot and sticky; at least, that was the excuse I gave myself for not being able to turn off my mind. It was worse when I opened the windows: it was so damned humid I could feel the perspiration literally dripping from me; I couldn't believe I was seriously longing for it to rain!

My mind kept going back to forensics and the clues the perpetrator had accidentally left us. That something at the back of my brain that had been nagging me for some time just wouldn't go away. I got up and made myself a hot chocolate, then thought of a cigarette. I even went as far as searching the flat for an old packet, but there was nothing. Then I thought of an all-night garage; they would have some ciggies. My craving had become so desperate that I was just about to get dressed when a flash of lightening lit up the kitchen window, followed by a loud crack of thunder. I felt like bursting into tears. Everything was going wrong. Once again I tried to sleep, but my mind still refused to switch off.

"Oh, fuck it!" I shouted out loud, deciding I would get dressed anyway. I would be more useful at the station than moping around here trying to cope with my frustration.

I left the flat in a heavy downpour, thinking: "So much for the high pressure!" and followed my customary route to the station. I don't know what it was but something instinctive made me change direction and head towards Ashworth House. I hadn't even been thinking of Connie at the time.

I pulled up outside the residence and asked myself: "Now what?" Other than a small porch light the house was in complete darkness and shrouded in torrential rain; it was actually bouncing off the paving stones. I checked my watch; it was 2.45 in the morning. They would think I was crazy if I knocked on the door at this hour. Sighing, and regretting my impulsiveness, I decided to leave. It was then that I saw – or, at least, I thought I saw – a flashlight going on and off by the side garden. Ever the policewoman, I got out of the car, let myself in through the front gate and made my way silently to the side of the house. I couldn't see a damned thing it was so dark; the rain was beginning to ease a little but I could still feel it trickling down my neck. I was uncomfortable and beginning to think I had made a mistake when I felt a blow to my head. I fell against the wall of the house, dizzy and in pain, when the second blow came. I felt myself losing consciousness, at the same time as I slid down the wall and onto the ground. Just before I passed out completely someone kicked me viciously in the ribs.

When I came round it was still dark. My head was throbbing, my ribs hurt, and I seemed to be lying in a pool of water. At least, I thought it was water until I placed my hand in it and discovered it was blood. I groaned aloud; it was my blood. What the hell had happened? I crawled round to the front of the house and fell against the doorbell. It rang for ages before the lights came on and the door opened. It was Steve; I thought he looked very silly in his pyjamas and dressing gown.

He put the porch light on and gasped, "Angie? What the bloody hell's going on?" Then he must have seen the blood. "Jesus! You're hurt."

"You'll go far in the police," I thought, as he took hold of my arm and helped me into the house. I was on the point of laughing at my own joke when I collapsed again. In the distance I heard him calling for Sheila. That was the last I remember. I came round briefly in an ambulance strapped to a gurney, and I recall both Steve and Connie were there; one of them was holding my hand, and I remember hoping it wasn't Steve!

When I eventually came to I was in a hospital bed, a swathe of bandages around my throbbing head and ribs, which felt as if they were on fire. Connie was sitting at the side of the bed. She looked as if she had been crying half the night. I tried to reach out and take her hand, but almost screamed with the pain in my side where I had been kicked.

"What the hell happened?" I managed to croak.

"We don't know for sure," she said tearfully. "Steve opened the door for you and you collapsed in a pool of blood. Someone hit you on the back of the head, and then must have kicked you while you were on the ground. Steve found some footprints in the side garden. After he called Inspector Kewell he rang forensics – they're sending someone down this morning. What were you doing there, Angie? It was the middle of the night."

I groaned again. "Get me a glass of water and I'll tell you." There was a pitcher on the bedside table. It was all I could do to lean my head against the side of the bed and take a sip.

"How long have I been here?"

"About four hours. It's just gone seven. If you feel up to talking I'd like to know what happened. Why would a burglar hit you like that? He could have killed you. And why would he want to break into this place? There's nothing worth nicking anyway."

"I don't honestly know. I couldn't sleep, so I decided to get dressed and go into work, when some instinct made me change direction and go to Ashworth House. Don't ask me why, Connie, because I haven't a clue; in fact, I suspected you might have something to do with it. Did you? ...Have anything to do with it?"

Her eyes opened wide in shock. "Me? How could I be involved?"

I tried to smile, but gave it up as a bad job. "Forever the innocent! Anyway, I was sitting outside, feeling very foolish, when I saw a light at the side of the house. I'm sure it was a torch. I went to investigate, but whoever it was must have heard me because he – I suppose it could have been a 'she', but I doubt it – whacked me round the head. That's pretty well it, really." I managed to lift my head a fraction to see Connie's face. "Are you sure you had nothing to do with bringing me to Ashworth House?"

She hesitated, looking at me thoughtfully for a moment before she answered. "All I can say, Angie, is that if I did then it was another of those subconscious things. I do know I was dreaming I was in danger." She laughed nervously. "So no change there then! And, if you came into the dream – well, I don't remember if you did. Who do you think it was? A burglar?"

"I honestly don't know, Connie," I said wearily. God, I felt really drained; my head throbbed like hell, and my eyes were beginning to turn over. "Could we talk later? Do you mind, sweetheart?"

I didn't catch her reply – I was already drifting off again.

When I awoke there was a less welcome figure sitting by the bed: none other than Inspector Kewell.

"Oh. You're awake," he said. When it came to stating the obvious he was a class act.

"Hi, Frank."

"How are you feeling?"

"Shitty. How do you think?"

He leant forward in his chair. "Angie, what the hell were you doing alone at Ashworth House at that time in the morning? And why didn't you call for back-up before checking out a burglary in progress?"

I sighed. The questions were reasonable enough, and I supposed that, with hindsight, I had been pretty stupid. But by now I had some well-rehearsed answers.

"I went over to check out the additional security arrangements. And I didn't realise it was a potential burglary; I assumed it was one of our lads wandering round the gardens. So I just went in to make contact."

"Really?"

"Yes, Frank. Really. I'm not altogether stupid, you know. And, now I've had time to think about it, I'm not convinced either that it was your average burglar. From my experience, those people tend not to be violent. Certainly not to the extent this guy was. Besides, he'd have to be pretty thick not to know there's nothing worth nicking in a halfway house."

He tightened his lips in disapproval. "So, what do you think he was after?"

"I honestly don't know. He could have been a burglar; on the other hand he could have been after Connie. Anyway, it's as well I was there; the security was almost non-existent."

He grunted in reply, then said, "I think that's a bit far-fetched; how could anyone possibly know she was there?" He held up his hands defensively. "Okay, okay – I'll have someone look into it; but if you ask me it's a waste of time. I'll pass it on to your Sergeant Durning – he seems a competent chap."

"I can handle it, Frank."

"Not from where I'm sitting you can't. I've spoken to the doctor and you've got pretty bad concussion, aside from a fractured rib and severe bruising. They want you stay here for the next two or three days."

"What about you? Can't you look after it?"

"Afraid not. I'm on my way to Manchester, remember. I was due to go there yesterday but Jim couldn't arrange it." He checked his watch. "I don't have a lot of time."

"Did forensics find anything?"

"Yes; a smudged footprint, which must have been a result of your disturbing whoever it was. I doubt it will tell us much - but we should have some more details later today. If there's anything positive I'll get Conway to call and see you. Oh, and Jim sends his best. He says to tell you he'll be across later. Now, I really have to go, Angie; I've got a train to catch. Take care, you hear?"

"Bye, Frank. And thanks for coming. Enjoy Manchester."

A whole procession of people came in and out following Frank's departure: nurses easing my pillows; a maid nearly blasting my head off with a vacuum cleaner; someone asking me about lunch, which I thought was a bloody silly question given the state I was in; and finally a doctor, except that he looked far too young to be a doctor. He took hold of my hand and checked my pulse, followed by the routine of a blood pressure machine. Finally, he got around to asking me how I felt.

I managed to bite back the sarcasm. "Christ!" I thought. "What an insane question."

"I have a very bad headache and my ribs are throbbing."

"Yes, well, that's understandable after what you've been through. You were lucky, in one sense, not to have suffered a skull fracture given the force of the blow you received. As it is you have severe concussion, and one of your ribs has a crack fracture."

He leant forward and shone a torch into my eyes. Next, he held out a finger in front of me. "Try to follow this, will you?"

He moved it from side to side. I followed it okay; the only problem was there were two of them instead of the one. I told him the truth.

"We'll give you something for the headache, but there isn't a lot we can do about the concussion, other than rest and observation."

"Can I leave now? I have a lot to do."

He frowned, as if he were talking to a moron. "You're not going anywhere for the next three days, young lady..."

"Not so much of the 'young'; you're no older than I am."

"Concussion can be very dangerous," he said, ignoring my interruption. "Sometimes the patient can develop blood clots in the brain, especially if they don't rest. Is that what you want, Miss Crossley?"

I seriously thought of telling him to fuck off, but quickly decided it wouldn't be in my best interests. So I merely said, meekly, "No; of course not, doctor. I'll be a good girl – I promise."

At least that made him smile. He almost looked human.

CHAPTER FORTY-ONE

After he left I laid back into the pillows and found I was already drifting off again. Something told me that, by rights, I should be angry; after all, I had been coshed on the head with Christ knows what instrument, and then viciously kicked whilst I lay on the ground. Except – I was quite unable to take it personally. I was much more concerned for Connie's safety, still afraid it could be she the assailant was after and not me. I was just a bloody nuisance who happened to have got in his way. But what was even more frightening was the confirmation of what Paul had said, which was just how desperate this character was becoming – that's if it was our perpetrator.

Before I slipped into that semi-conscious state, somewhere between a black hole and sleep, the thought occurred to me that I could not simply leave Connie at Ashworth House as bait. If I was right and he now knew where she was, he wouldn't stop until his objective was achieved; except that next time he would be a lot more careful. I decided, for her own protection, that I would have to move her out of there. The problem was: where to?

I had no idea how long I was out this time, but I awoke feeling much better, with a clearer head. It didn't stop me groaning when I saw Jim standing in front of me, looking decidedly irritated.

"Are you here to give me a telling off too?" I asked.

He shook his head, with disappointment, I suspected. "I'm here because you frightened the life out of me, and because I'm worried about you. How you feeling now?"

"Better...thanks, Jim. And thanks for coming."

"So. Want to tell me about it?" He held out a hand. "Not the Frank Kewell version. The real one."

"Why? Don't you believe me, sweetie?" I said innocently.

He bent down to kiss me and then said, "Come on, Ange; this is not the least bit humorous. And I know you too well to buy that crap about checking out security." He took a seat and then grasped my hand. "You do realise you could have been killed, don't you? What on earth were you up to?"

"I don't honestly know, Jim. I couldn't sleep last night…"

"The night before. You've been out of it for almost 24 hours. I called in last night but they wouldn't let me see you. I brought some things for you: toothbrush, nightie, one or two bits and pieces."

"Good God! Have I?" I lay there for some time – I think 'gob smacked' is the word.

When Jim leant over and kissed me again, softly on the forehead I felt the tears spring to my eyes.

"And you don't have to play the tough guy with me, either. Just tell me what happened, Ange."

"Yeah…well, as I was saying, I couldn't sleep," I began tearfully. "So I decided I'd go to the station – you know, make myself useful. Anyhow, there I was, on my way, when something made me change direction, and the next thing I knew I was outside Ashworth House and wondering just what the hell I was doing there. Can you believe that?"

"I can believe anything where our Connie is concerned. By the way, Frank told me you were worried about her, so, just to ease your mind, Peter Conway's now put her under 24-hour protection. Although I have to tell you I agree with him about this being a botched attempt at a burglary."

"Well, I suppose that's something; I'd rather be patronised and keep Connie safe than take a risk."

He shrugged again as if to say he was indulging me. "What happened then?" he continued.

"Right. Well, I was about to leave when I saw what I thought was a flashlight flicking on and off; as if whoever it was realised someone was watching." I squeezed his hand as hard as I dare. "I know; you don't have to tell me, Jim. I shouldn't have gone in there on my own. I just didn't think; I mean, I certainly didn't think it was our man. Anyway, the next thing was I got a crack on the head. I remember trying to turn to see who it was when he hit me again; I went down and the bastard put the boot in. Pity I didn't get a look at his face. Don't suppose we've got any clue who it really was?"

He shook his head. "'Fraid not. Whoever it was got lucky; the footprint was too smudged to tell us anything."

Then I suddenly remembered: the footprint in the cow shit. There was something about it I had intended to investigate, but had overlooked it. "Jim, do you mind doing me a favour?"

He looked at me suspiciously. "If it's anything to do with work – yes, I do mind. Look, Ange, apparently they're doing another scan this afternoon, to make sure there are no blood clots. If you're clear they might let you go home tomorrow, but you'll need another week, maybe even longer, before you'll be fit enough to return to work. As a matter of fact, I was going to suggest you stay at my place; at least I can look after you at night."

I grinned. "I know your idea of looking after me, especially at night; except this time I really will have a headache! Besides, I'm not asking for a lot; I just want to have another read of that forensic report on the earlier footprint. Something's nagging at me and I think it could be connected. Surely you can do that little thing for me, can't you?"

He leant over and gave me another kiss, this time on the cheek, choosing to ignore my request. "I'll see how you are this evening, sweetie-pie. I'll be in about eight – all being well."

"Jim. How are the enquires into the vehicle checks getting on?"

He put a finger to his lips to silence me. "Bye, Ange. See you later."

"Bastard!" I managed to say, but I think he'd already left.

CHAPTER FORTY-TWO

I would have spent a boring day if someone had remembered to confiscate my mobile. I thought about ringing my mother, but on reflection I realised she would only panic then drop everything and dash halfway across the country to see me, by which time I would probably have been discharged. As it was, I got straight to work instead and rang Emma at forensics.

"Where are you? I heard you were in hospital, badly injured."

"Well, you know how people exaggerate, Emma. I'm in hospital but I'm all right, really. Listen; could you do me a small favour?"

"Go on. I'm listening."

"The forensic report on the evidence we found in the field - the Josephine Marsden case. You remember?"

"Sure. What do you want to know?"

"Would you mind reading it to me again."

"Couldn't someone from the station read it out to you?"

I let her hear my dramatic sigh. "Emma. Come on; you know what they're like. If you listen to them I'm lying here on my deathbed. Please – I'm begging you."

"Okay. But you didn't get it from me. Do you want to hang on, or shall I ring you back?"

"I'll hold, if you don't mind. I ain't going anywhere."

After what seemed to take an age Emma said, "Here we go." She then proceeded to read out the section on the fibre, which I asked her to skip over.

"What is it you're after, Angie?"

"I don't know precisely. But I'm sure it has something to do with that footprint."

"Well, it doesn't tell us much, other than his approximate height and weight. Oh, yes. It also appears he must have had surgery on his right knee; we could establish that from the weight distribution of the print itself."

"That's it!" I exclaimed excitedly, remembering what it was that was nagging me.

"What is? The surgery?"

"Exactly. If he had surgery then there must a record of it some-where. That's what we should look for."

"But, Angie, how on earth are you going to trace a knee operation? There must be hundreds of hospitals doing them every day. I wouldn't know where to begin."

"No; *but I would*. Emma, thank you – thank you very much; you've been a big help."

Peter Conway was the next on my list.

"Sergeant Conway, CID."

"Peter. Hi, it's Angie. How are the vehicle checks going?"

"Angie! You're supposed to be laid up in hospital. Have they re-leased you?"

"Not yet. But I'm fine now. Listen…"

"That isn't what the chief tells us. Last I heard you were taking it easy, and we hadn't to expect you back for at least a week. What are you up to, Angie?"

"Peter, for fuck's sake, stop rambling and answer the damned ques-tion, will you?"

"It'll take more than a crack on the head to sweeten your disposi-tion, won't it? Anyway, the answer to your question is: they're not. …Going, that is. Quite a number of owners have sold their vehicles on for cash, and the registration documents haven't been returned to DVLC at Swansea. But when you think about it that isn't unusual; sometimes they don't bother till they want to sell the car on again. Also, a lot of the owners seem to be away – at least, we haven't been able to contact them. And we can hardly put out APBs on them, can we? So, we're running into dead ends. Does that answer your question?"

"Yeah. Sorry, Peter. I'm a bit light on patience at the moment."

"Oh, shit!" I thought, feeling the tears starting to flow again. I was behaving more like a silly schoolgirl than a mature police officer.

"Angie? Are you still there?"

"Ye…yes, Peter."

"Why don't you just give in to it? By all accounts you've had one hell of a shock, and you don't get over these things that easily. I know; it happened to me not too long ago. I was laid up for over two weeks."

"Can't afford to; we're trying to catch a very dangerous psychopath in case you'd forgotten. And I think he's somehow found out where Connie's staying, and he's bound to go after her again."

"Look, Angie; I don't know what it is with this friend of yours – no one's bothered to put me in the picture – but I'll tell you one thing. Right now she's got more security than the bloody Prime Minister."

"Peter. There's something I want to ask you. Do you mind coming over…to the hospital?"

"Course not. I'll try and come by this evening. Are you sure you're up to it?"

"No. I don't mean later. Can you come now?"

"Now! You've gotta be kidding. We're as busy as hell here. The place is a bloody mad house. It can't be that important, surely? Won't it keep until later? Or you can ask me now, if you like – I've got a minute. No, sorry, cancel that; the DCI is calling me. Look, I'll come by later, Angie – promise. As soon as I can."

I let out one of my customary sighs. I suppose it was too much to ask him just to drop everything and dash over here. And, of course, he was right; it wasn't that urgent. Anyway, I thought, closing my eyes yet again, it would give me more time to plan what I had in mind.

I found my thoughts drifting back to my own life, to my mother and older sister, who had married and moved to America when I was still a teenager. I hadn't seen her since then, although we still kept in touch from time to time. Marie lived in Seattle, had two children of her own now and would love it if I visited the States to meet them.

I'd already dismissed the idea of ringing mother; I would have loved to see her but she was much too far away, and, anyway, I wasn't sure I was up to her lecturing me at the present. I decided I would contact her when I was out of hospital. Still, it would have been nice to have some-one to comfort me in my distress, someone to love me and make me feel wanted.

I found myself sinking into a deep well of self-pity – something I hadn't experienced for some time. Poor Angie, lying on her own in a small clinical room in the general hospital, badly injured, and not a relative in sight. I forced myself out of it by switching my thoughts to Connie and what a terrible childhood she had suffered. In truth, she hadn't had a childhood. When other children were experiencing the joys of school holidays and Christmases with the family, Connie was having nightmarish visions of murdered children and helping the police to uncover dead bodies. I shuddered at the thought of what fate had done to an innocent young girl, imposing this terrible gift on her. Instead of playing hide and seek with her friends, Connie was forced to play the vision game, even now, with a murderer. All her teenage years to date had been spent in a psychiatric hospital, apparently abandoned by a mother who, for reasons we will never know, felt compelled to take her own life. No doubt she too was sick, but I found it hard to sympathise with a woman who left her own daughter in hospital, then committed suicide without any communication whatsoever.

I remembered, too, that time I was visiting Connie, not long after her mother had killed herself. She was sitting on her bed in the hospital, alone, crying her eyes out. When I asked her what the trouble was she sobbingly told me that something inside her had burst and she was bleeding to death. Sadly, no one had forewarned her about menstruation or the biological facts of life. I recall absolutely exploding with fury at the nursing staff because of their negligence, and spent the rest of the day explaining to Connie how her body functioned. She smiled when I convinced her she was about to become a woman. But what I found terribly sad about the whole episode was that it was something every mother should do for her daughter. "Where the bloody hell are you, Sylvia?" I remember almost screaming aloud.

A further near-tragedy that occurred with Connie was when she contracted a particularly nasty infection of the ovaries. She was dreadfully ill, and I took three days away from Warwick to be with her; three days I couldn't really afford, since I was in my final year, but it was out of the question to leave her on her own. One of the repercussions of this awful illness, the seriousness of which to this day Connie was not aware of, was the improbability of her ever being able to have children. It was decided by Dr Simmons and the rest of the medical team – a decision with which I concurred – that nothing would be gained by adding to her suffering. Poor kid. She had endured the most appalling childhood; she had yet to reach 18; and, even today, she was frightened for her very life because some psychopath was probably hunting her.   And here was I feeling sorry for myself.

CHAPTER FORTY-THREE

A soft knocking at the bedroom door interrupted my thoughts. A porter came in pushing a trolley, followed by a young nurse.

"Miss Crossley; we've come to take you down for an MRI scan. Did they tell you about it?"

"They did, yes. Will it take long?"

She giggled. "I don't know really. They'll let you know in the scan room."

I was helped onto the trolley, and then pushed along a typical hospital corridor to the lift area. It seemed to take an age but eventually we arrived at the MRI unit, where I spent the next hour encased in a tomb-like shell, bombarded by a noise that penetrated my head like a pneumatic drill. Even the earmuffs they had given me did little to help. I was tempted once or twice to press the panic button they'd placed in my hand, but the thought of the embarrassment I would suffer if it ever got out restrained me. I tried thinking about sex but that didn't help much, and, anyway, my thoughts were frequently disrupted by someone asking me: "Are you alright in there?" Bloody silly question; of course I wasn't alright. Who would be in this coffin?

Then it was over and I was back in my room, to be greeted by the cheerful, and very welcome, face of Connie.

She lent a hand in helping me back into the bed, and then drew up a chair.

"It's good to see you, Connie. How did you get here?"

She smiled and took my hand. "Steve gave me a lift. Are you feeling any better, Angie? You scared the life out of us the other night. Have they come up with any answers yet? Any idea who it could have been? No one will talk to me about it."

I thought, seriously for a moment, about lying to her – in her own interests, of course. But Connie and I didn't have that kind of relationship. We had promised each other a long time ago that we would always be honest with each other; now would not be a good time to break that pledge.

So I told her the truth; about my feeling that it could well be the same man we were pursuing, and how particularly concerned I was that, if he had been able to find her so easily, it was highly dangerous for her to remain at Ashworth House. I also told her that the idea had crossed my mind that we should consider moving her to a safe house.

"If you're right, Angie, and he found me here, then I don't think there's such a thing as a safe house, do you?"

I shook my head. "Probably not, no. But I'm still worried about how the hell he found you."

"If you think about it, there's no great mystery. For instance, he could have phoned Forest Hills asking for me, saying he was a relative or something, and they could have told him I'd moved to Ashworth House. Or, if they'd just told him I wasn't at the hospital any more, it wouldn't take much to work out that I would go to Ashworth House."

"That's perfectly logical, Connie. But how would he know *who* you were? He doesn't know your name. And, even if somehow he did, how would he know you were in the hospital in the first place?"

"He would know that in exactly the same way he knows who I am. I've told you, Angie; just as I've seen him, he's seen me. That's what's so scary about him. Besides, I'm less worried than I was now Ashworth House has been turned into Fort Knox - and he'll know that as well. So I can't see him trying that one again, can you? Honestly?"

I sighed and squeezed her hand. "He also knows now that if he wants to get you he's got to go through me first! And I'd actually quite like him to try that again. He won't be so lucky next time."

"When do you think they'll let you out of here?" she asked, changing the subject.

"Hopefully, in the morning. Providing the scan is clear and there are no monsters lurking inside my head. And then, young lady, I'm told I've got to spend at least a week convalescing, so I've decided I'm going to ask Paul if he can find me a room at your place."

"Hey! That's great. Then I get to look after you for a change."

"And I get to keep an eye on you – and that boyfriend of yours."

She actually blushed. "Yes, well – I'd better be going, Angie; the 'boyfriend' is waiting downstairs." She leant over and gave me a kiss on the cheek. "Hopefully, I'll see you tomorrow sometime. Will you give me a ring?"

"Connie?"

"What?"

"I hate to remind you again, but you will be careful, won't you?"

Her blush deepened. "Not big on subtlety, are you? And I'm not a child, you know."

"I'm only thinking of you. The last thing you need right now is a pregnancy."

"Don't worry; I'll be fine."

I nodded and waved her goodbye, just as the evening meal arrived – a veritable feast of inedible rubbish. But when you're hungry, then, as they say, you will literally eat anything! After a few mouthfuls of God knows what I pushed the plate aside; no one could be that hungry, I decided.

CHAPTER FORTY-FOUR

Peter Conway didn't show; Jim came in his place, almost snorting with anger.

"Come on; hand it over," he demanded.

"Hey. Calm down. You're talking to an invalid here. You're supposed to be oozing compassion and concern. Anyway, I don't know what you're talking about."

He held his hand out and looked menacingly at me. "The phone, Ange; the bloody mobile. Hand it over. I'm not leaving here until you do – and I'll search you if I have to."

I shot him a wicked grin. "Now you *are* trying to make me feel better." I slid the covers back tantalisingly. "Go ahead, lover boy; I promise not to try and stop you."

"Ange! I'm being serious. Give me that bloody phone. Now!"

I handed it over, scowling. "What's the big deal, Jim? It's not as if I'm exerting myself, is it? Besides, it's boring in here; what harm can the odd phone call do?"

"You're breaching doctor's orders, and mine." It was only after he had taken possession of my phone that he took a seat at the side of the bed.

"I don't suppose you brought any food, did you? I can't eat that crap." I pushed the portable table to one side. "Look, Jim – stop fussing, will you? I've got concussion, not paralysis…"

"…And you've been advised to rest and do nothing," he interrupted. "And getting involved in the case – and that's exactly what you were trying to do by using your mobile – is about as far from relaxation as you can get. So knock it off, Ange. You stay here and behave until the doctors give you the all clear. And then you convalesce – understand? That means you keep away from the station for at least a week, you stay away from telephones, and you put your feet up. Is that clear enough for you?"

"God! I love it when you're being masterful!" I gripped his hand tightly. "I promise I'll do what the doctors advise, Jim. Providing it's not altogether unreasonable. Is that fair? Oh, and am I right in thinking Peter Conway won't be coming to see me now?"

That, at least, made him laugh. "Give him a bit of credit. He was worried about you, said you sounded terrible on the phone. And if you want to know anything about the case, ask me, and if I think you're up to it, then I'll discuss it with you." He held out his free hand. "And if I don't, I'll tell you so. Agreed?"

I nodded. "So, what's happening?" I asked in my most innocent voice.

Jim shook his head. "I'm wasting my time here, aren't I? Okay. Nothing much has happened since you spoke to Peter, except that we might have a lead on the four-wheeler. Evidently, one of the customers with a T-Reg dark blue Toyota – also with the figure '2' in it – sold it on for cash about a year ago, to a man he reckoned might fit our suspect's description. The problem is, as I think Peter's already told you, we don't know yet whether he's registered it with Swansea. Some people don't bother until they come to sell it on."

"How do you know this bloke's telling the truth?"

"Because he bought it for his wife – one of those 'keeping up with the Jones's' things – and then she found she couldn't drive it because it was too big for her. And she's confirmed that, by the way. OKAY?"

"Yeah. I guess. Listen, Jim; I had an idea about this guy and his knee problem…"

"You're doing it again, aren't you?" He took my hand in both of his. "Ange, you've got to switch off; even if it's only for a few days. Until you get the all clear. Please, will you try to do that for me? I'll be speaking with the doctors later, after they've given you the results of the MRI scan. They said they'd ring me about your coming out tomorrow. But don't get too optimistic. That's a dangerous injury you know, and if you're not careful it could backfire on you; seriously backfire."

"Okay, Jim. I've got the message, and I promise I'll be sensible about it. If they do let me out tomorrow I thought about spending some convalescing time with Connie at the halfway house. I sure as hell don't want to be in that flat on my own for week; either mine or yours."

"Good idea. Just as long as you stay away from the case." He leant over and gave me a full kiss on the lips. "Got to go, sweetheart. Take care. And if you are allowed out in the morning I'll send a car to collect you; that's if I can't come."

"Bye, Jim."

* * * * * * * * *

The consultant came in to see me later that evening, holding the scans in his hand.

"Miss Crossley. Angie, isn't it?"

I just nodded.

"Well, your scan look pretty good, you'll be pleased to hear. Nothing sinister, although it does show some bruising to the brain round the area that got thumped. That, I'm afraid, is a matter of time – and rest – before it'll go down. You've got quite serious concussion, Angie, and you'd do well not to treat it lightly. Do you have someone to stay with for a few days if we release you in the morning?"

"Yes. I can stay with a friend of mine."

"You won't be on your own? Otherwise, we'd rather you stayed here."

"No, doctor. There'll be someone with me all the time."

"Good. Then you can leave in the morning. I'd like to see you again in about four weeks though – we'll send you an appointment card with the details." He placed the scans back in the folder. "Now, remember what I said, won't you? Rest. No stresses. And no work for at least a week. And the first sign of a violent headache, or any double vision, you come straight back here. Understand?"

I managed a smile. "Thank you, doctor. I'm very grateful."

As soon as he was gone I reached for my mobile. Damn! I'd forgotten; that bully Jim Robbins had taken it from me. I slipped out of bed and made my way into the general ward, where I was intercepted by one of the nurses.

"Can I help you?"

"Yes. I'm trying to find a telephone. Is there one on the ward?"

She smiled. "There is, yes. A payphone. But you don't look as if you're carrying any money with you."

"Oh, Christ. I couldn't – I mean, you wouldn't…?"

She pulled a purse from the pocket of her uniform. "I could stretch to a local call. Is that okay?" she said, handing me a 20p piece.

"Bless you, yes. And thanks, nurse; I'll see you get it back."

I managed to get hold of Paul, explained my circumstances and asked him if I could stay at Ashworth House for a few days. It was only after some hesitation that he confirmed that, because I could officially be classified as part of the security team looking after Connie, it would be acceptable; otherwise, he told me, it was highly irregular.

"And I suppose you'll be needing a bit of nursing during this convalescing?" he said, fortunately with that lilt of humour in his voice. When I tried to reassure him that would not be the case he went on to say they would be happy to take care of me for a week. "Angie, believe me, it's the least we can do after what you've been through. How about a lift? Do you want one of us to collect you from the hospital?"

I was just able to thank him and tell him that, no, I was fine, when my money ran out. Reluctantly, I returned to my room and another early night. Life was becoming the absolute bloody pits.

CHAPTER FORTY-FIVE

I was picked up by a patrol car at nine the next morning and whisked to Ashworth House as if we were in pursuit of some joy riders. I didn't like to admit it but I was still feeling decidedly queasy, and was rather relieved when Sheila showed me to a ground floor room at the back of the house. It was comfortable, with a couple of easy chairs, a coffee table supporting a vase filled with fresh flowers, a small television and a single bed against the wall. And, would you believe, a telephone.

"It isn't plugged in yet," Sheila said when she returned with a coffee and spotted me trying it. "It'll only take a sec. But do you think you're being wise, Angie? Paul gave me strict instructions you were to have peace and quiet, and I don't really think he included telephones in that, do you?"

I sat on the bed, suddenly feeling weary. "No. I guess you're right, Sheila. It might be useful later on, though; you know, when I'm feeling up to it."

"So, when you're feeling up to it then I'll connect it for you. But, for now, you put your feet up, drink your coffee, and rest. Right?"

She left me alone resting quietly on the bed. The next thing I knew someone was asking me if I would fancy some lunch. When I opened my eyes I realised it was Connie. She was holding a tray with a plate of hot and what smelt like delicious food on it. It felt as if I hadn't eaten for a week; in fact, it had been two days, and I was famished.

"Hi, Connie. Is it that time? I must have slept all morning. God, that smells good," I said, pulling myself up in the bed.

"It's two o'clock, Angie. We weren't sure about waking you, but Sheila reckons the stomach's just as important as sleep." She set the tray down on the coffee table and then helped me from the bed.

"You've had a lot of phone calls today," she informed me. "Let's see..." and she began ticking them off on her fingers. "DCI Robbins – he said he would visit you later; a Detective Sergeant Conway – just checking in, he said; oh, and someone called Emma rang, asking after you. Sheila said someone also rang you from Manchester, but she didn't catch his name."

"That would be Frank," I said; "DI Kewell. Did he leave a message?"

"Only to say something about wasting his time up there, but you'll have to ask Sheila, Angie; she took the message. Now," she went on, unfurling a napkin, "lunch is served, Madam. I'll leave you in peace for now."

"Hey," I said as she was leaving, "shouldn't you be in college today?"

"No, Angela dear. No lectures today. Besides, it's Friday, if you remember, and we always finish early anyway. Catch you later."

She shot off before I could question her further, leaving me to enjoy the meal, followed by yet another nap. All my objections at the hospital about taking it easy were pretty redundant when I thought about it; I really did not have the strength to begin involving myself in work at the moment. In fact, I was positively debilitated: all I wanted to do was sleep.

Connie told me later that I had been sleeping when Jim called round that same evening, and it was the middle of the following day before I started to feel something like normal again. The good thing, though, was that my head was clearer, and although my vision was a little fuzzy I didn't think it was much to worry about. Sheila had very kindly left me a dressing gown to wear, which reminded me I had to arrange for someone to collect some clothes from my flat. I couldn't remain in a state of undress all week.

That afternoon I was able to treat myself to a long soak in the bath – something I'd been looking forward to for days. When I eventually returned to my room I found my clothes laid out on the bed; it occurred to me then that Jim, bless him, must have left them for me the previous night. I chuckled to myself at the thoughts of the sniggers that priceless gem would have raised had it got out at the station – although we would be naïve if we really thought our relationship was still a secret. Finally, feeling more civilised, I made my way to Paul's office. It was empty, but that didn't stop me from settling myself down at the spare computer console and using his password to access it.

I was still preoccupied with Arnold Brownlaw and knee surgery. So I started at the place I had recently stayed as a guest, Birmingham

General Hospital, and began the process of accessing their records department. They didn't have one. But, better still, they routed me through to the West Midlands Health Department of Records, where records of all the hospitals in the area were held centrally.

I decided to follow the same procedure that Frank had with the vehicle check. Omit the age groups, the wrong sex, the wrong knee (i.e. it had to be the right knee), and search all orthopaedic records from 1982, the year when Brownlaw was discharged from Smethwick. Emma was right; there were hundreds of them, even with the modified criteria. I sat at the computer for ages, waiting for some divine inspiration. Nothing came, so I wandered into the kitchen to make myself a coffee.

Sheila was busily preparing the evening meal. She turned when she heard me come in. "Well, you're looking much better than the last time I saw you. How you feeling, Angie?"

"I'm fine thanks. And I wasn't really in any condition to thank you before for all you've done for me. I truly am grateful."

She shrugged her shoulders, somewhat embarrassed. "It's my pleasure, especially after what you've done for young Connie. I think you've brought her alive. Now, can I get you something? Coffee, tea, some biscuits? I'm doing a goulash for tea – you need building up after your ordeal." She put the kettle on automatically, then placed a large casserole dish in the oven.

"Yes," I admitted, "I was very lucky."

She smiled knowingly. "Well, they got you to the hospital quick enough, didn't they? And they're very good at Solihull General. My mother was in there last year for varicose veins. Not major surgery, I know, but she had to wait nearly 18 months for her operation. It's like they told her at the time: 'You have to be almost dying to get treated urgently these days.' Not that *you* were, Angie – dying, I mean. But it was pretty serious, wasn't it?"

"Yeah. I guess," I said, not really hearing her. She had set my mind racing. Of course: waiting lists. That would knock a couple of years off the dates I had inputted into the computer. And if I could narrow it down even more by limiting the search to men between the ages of, say, 23 and 30, that should help considerably. It was only then that I realised my stupidity; why didn't I simply ask the records department for any patient details they had on an Arnold Brownlaw from Edgbaston? I had his old address and date of birth, so it should be a relatively straightforward enquiry. So I got on with it, blaming my stupidity on the knock on the head.

And there it was! Arnold Brownlaw, etc.; correct address and DOB, but unfortunately no record of knee surgery. He had had his tonsils removed when he was seven – pity, I thought, they hadn't removed his dick at the same time! Appendicitis when he was 12 – and then nothing. "Oh, shit! Don't tell me I've got it wrong again." I so desperately wanted him to be our man I had almost blocked out any other possibility. I sat there once again, trying to will the computer to surrender up the information I wanted. It wasn't at all cooperative.

Then, in one of those flashes of inspiration, the question of hospital waiting lists came into my head again. What if...? Yes; what if he had gone privately? Surely, if he was suffering from a painful knee that required surgery, then – with his mother's money available to him – why wait? The question then was: where would he have had it done? So, applying logic again, I obtained a list of the private hospitals in or around Birmingham, and from the 20 or so that came up I selected two that were situated either near or in Edgbaston itself.

So I contacted the first hospital in that area. No record of Arnold Brownlaw. The next one on the list was a BUPA hospital – a much larger hospital than the first one I had tried. And – bingo! There he was: Arnold Brownlaw, surgery on right knee for the repair of cruciate ligament damage, January 1983. He spent three days as an inpatient, after which he was discharged with crutches, accompanied with the recommendation that he should have intensive physiotherapy for a period of four weeks. There was a footnote to his records which, if I needed it, clinched it for me: "The extent of his injury is serious enough to suggest that he will not achieve a complete recovery, and that it is likely his mobility will be permanently impaired." Exactly as the footprint indicated.

"Gotcha!" I said aloud, hardly able to contain my excitement. It was the final piece of the jigsaw we needed. Put that with Paul's profile and we had now identified the prime suspect. I felt a tremendous sense of elation that I'd been right all along about Brownlaw being our man. But, in a way, that was the easy part; finding him was something altogether different, given that he had literally disappeared off the face of the earth. I ran off the medical record on the printer and then rang Jim on his mobile.

"If that's Angela Crossley, I do *not* want to talk to you!"

"Hi," I said in my meekest voice. "Jim, listen – no, don't cut me off; this is important."

"You're supposed to be resting, not working. And you promised me, remember?"

"I *am* resting, honest. I've only been up an hour, and I'm feeling so much better. And all I've done is spend a bit of time on the computer following up one of my crazy ideas. You can't blame me for that, Jim, surely? Besides, I'd go out of my mind with boredom if I did absolutely nothing. And if you were honest you'd admit you would do the same. Am I right?"

I heard a typical release of breath, which usually meant he had given up the argument.

"So, what have you phoned to tell me? And it had better not take long or I *will* cut you off."

"Arnold Brownlaw. You remember him?"

"From Edgbaston – my part of the world? Yes, I remember him. Go on."

"Well, I told you I had an idea about Emma's forensic test showing our man had had surgery on his right knee. So, I did some checking through the computer a little while ago" – *it was only a white lie!* – "and I discovered that Brownlaw had surgery on *his* right knee in January of '83. I pulled his medical records from the BUPA hospital in Edgbaston, and listen to this: 'His mobility is likely to be impaired in the future.' In other words, Jim, he walks with a slight limp – as Emma suggested. I'm *convinced* he's our man."

There was silence for a while. No doubt Jim was digesting this latest development. Finally, he said, "You're a damned good copper, Angie. Not many of us would have thought of that. Can you fax me his medical records from there?"

"Sure. I've already printed them off. And then, I promise, I'm going back to bed. Just one thing, though, before I do go. How do we pierce the veil of his anonymity?"

"Bloody hell, love; there's no need to get carried away! We can talk about that later when we've had more time to think it through. I can tell you one thing though - it's not going to be easy. With computers these days, apparently you can become virtually anyone you like - completely reinvent yourself if you wanted, even to the extent of creating and registering a new valid birth certificate, driving licence, the works. In other words, Ange, we now know everything we need to know about him except his current identity; and that's something we all need to apply our minds to.

"Look, you've done remarkably well, my darling" – it was the first time he had called me that –"and at least you've now provided us with a meaningful label to pursue. But we mustn't get carried away with this one. We've still got a lot of solid police work to put in before we catch him. And, talking of work, you've done more than enough of that today, young lady. So, back to bed like you promised. I'll give this some more thought and I'll call round to see you early this evening. And – well done!"

With that he broke the connection, leaving me somewhat deflated after my moment of euphoria. He was also right: I was feeling quite exhausted; so I followed his instructions and took myself off to bed, deciding I would give lunch a miss.

CHAPTER FORTY-SIX

Dinner was delicious. I could really get used to Sheila's cooking, especially after my regular diet of frozen pizzas and microwave dinners for one. On the whole, I was beginning to improve, although my head still hadn't entirely cleared. The consultant did warn me that it would take six to eight weeks before I fully recovered. I knew what he meant, although I was determined I wouldn't allow it to turn me into an invalid.

It was an enjoyable hour or so around the kitchen table; Connie was in good form, telling us about her day. She was becoming increasingly confident as the days passed, and the vision of her tormentor was fading. She was also becoming more and more taken – if that's the right word – with young Steve Harrison. He never seemed to be away from the place, even when, I noticed, he was supposed to be off duty. Still, I didn't see any harm in it, just so long as he remembered that his primary task was protecting her and not courting her.

Jim arrived just after seven, accompanied by Paul. When we went into Paul's office he made a comment, jokingly, about my using his password to access the computer.

"You're the one that gave it me, if I remember rightly!" I countered.

He shrugged philosophically. "Help yourself, Angie. Just don't overdo things, will you?"

"Paul and I have been discussing how we might persuade Brownlaw to come out of hiding. He's come up with an interesting idea that could possibly work. At the very least, he'll be tempted. Tell her, Paul."

"Well, you may remember, I predicted on the profile of this type of paedophile that he'll more than likely have extremely extravagant tastes, in clothes, cars... all the luxuries. Now, I know we assumed he's probably wealthy in his own right, but the standard profile also suggests that he tends to be innately avaricious. In other words, he can't help himself when it comes down to sheer greed. So, Angie, my idea is to try and lure him into a trap."

"Interesting," I commented. "But just how do we go about that?"

"One way is to place an advert, prominently, in a number of local papers, purporting to come from a firm of solicitors, to the effect that they are seeking to find a Mr Arnold Brownlaw because they have information that would benefit him. You know the kind of thing: the implied suggestion will be that he has come into an inheritance and they need to contact him."

I looked at him with only veiled astonishment. "You don't really believe he's going to respond to something as obvious as that, do you? Paul, this man's not stupid; he'll spot that a mile off… If anything it'll do us more harm than good by alerting him to the fact that we're on to him."

"Why do you think he won't respond?" Jim asked.

I shook my head in exasperation. "Firstly, because he has no known relatives, other than a distant uncle in Australia who's had no contact with his nephew for more than 30 years, and who, by the way, made it abundantly clear he wanted nothing to do with Arnold. Secondly, 'cause this Australian bloke's got kids of his own, so they'd obviously be the primary beneficiaries. And, thirdly, his uncle's still alive, and if I know that it won't take our dear Arnold long to find it out either.

"So, all we'll be doing is sending him a message that we now know his original identity, and that we're hunting him. All this'll do is warn him that we know his real name – whereas right now he has no idea what we know. Personally, Jim, I'd rather keep it that way; I think it would be wrong to alert him. If he thinks his cover's blown I bet he'll either go into hiding or just change his identity again."

There was a prolonged silence after my minor outburst, until Paul said, cryptically, "You won't help your recovery very much getting all worked up like that, Angie. But you obviously feel very strongly about it. What do you think, Jim?"

"I don't know, to be honest. Ange has made some very good points, especially about his relatives – or lack of them – and I agree we shouldn't send him a direct signal. Perhaps we should think about it some more; I still like the idea of laying a trap, but maybe we need something a bit more subtle. How about you, Ange? Do you think it's worth progressing?"

"I'm not opposed to it," I said. "But it's going to have to be incredibly devious to trap Brownlaw. And remember: as Paul has told us frequently, this character is a control freak; he would somehow have to be convinced that *he* was calling the shots, not us."

"Maybe that's what we should concentrate on," Paul added. "His compulsion to be in control all the time. Let me work on it some more, will you? I'll see if I can come up with something more creative. Anyway, young lady, how are *you* feeling? By the sound of it, you're in danger of overdoing it."

"If I am, Paul, then – believe me – it's only marginally. Most of the time I'm too knackered to do much, and my head's still a long way from clearing. I'm told it could take up to six weeks before I'm back to normal."

"It can do, yes, depending on the extent of the damage. It hasn't stopped you identifying Arnold Brownlaw though; and, if you feel up to it tomorrow, help yourself to the computer – and my password, if you need it." He grinned at that, as if he had just cracked a funny joke.

"Some joke!" I thought. Still, the computer was very helpful, and I wouldn't have the same privacy at the station.

"Thanks, Paul," I merely said. "Now, if both of you don't mind, I really need to rest."

And I wasn't kidding, either. Another wave of exhaustion had come over me, and I was too tired even to think. I said my goodnights and retreated to my bedroom, grateful I didn't have far to go. I didn't even bother trying to read; I simply undressed, crawled into bed, and then turned the light off in relief.

Once again, I didn't come round until mid-morning the next day, feeling like shit. "What the hell's the matter with me?" I asked myself. I dragged myself out of bed and went off to the bathroom for a long, powerful shower, switching between hot and then cold until I felt a semblance of normality. Then it was off to the kitchen for a strong, black coffee, and two Panadol. I was tempted to go into Paul's office and start again on the computer, but I really wasn't up to it. Instead, I collared Connie, who was in her room studying, and persuaded her to join me for some fresh air.

"I don't normally do this, you know," she informed me when we were out of the house. "I mean, go out without my personal policeman!"

"So where is he today, then?"

"Day off. He's a 'she' today – a Pauline Wilkins; she's patrolling the grounds. Do you know her?"

"Don't think so. What's she like?"

"She's nice, actually. But very serious. Someone should teach her about smiling – it's good for you!"

"At the moment I prefer serious, Connie. Especially when she's responsible for your safety." I stopped to look at her. "You did tell her you were going out with me, didn't you?"

She laughed, rather like a giggling schoolgirl. "I was tempted not to, purely out of mischief. But I didn't have the nerve. "'Sides, it wouldn't have been fair, would it?"

"No," I agreed, "it wouldn't. Apart from the fact you'd have dropped me in the shit."

We were heading towards the town centre; it was a lovely day, with blue, cloudless skies, and there was a nice warming sun on my face. I was already enjoying the benefits of being outside, apart from which it was definitely helping my return to civilisation. Even my head was beginning to clear – for the first time in days. I felt a spring return to my step.

Connie tugged my arm as we were passing a coffee shop. "Fancy a coffee, Angie?"

"You mean you do," I said, following her inside.

When we were seated she turned to me and said, "Did you notice him?"

"Notice who?" I asked, puzzled.

"The man in the car that's been following us since we left Ashworth House. It was parked over the road when we came out. Don't look now… but he's parked on the other side of the road now. Hell, Angie; you're the policeman, not me."

"Police*woman*, if you don't mind. And, no, I haven't noticed anyone following us. Are you sure you're not imagining it?"

"Possibly. It's just that a dark blue four-wheel drive's been crawling along behind us since we left - and you know me and my paranoia."

"Why didn't you say something earlier?"

"Because I wasn't sure. I'm still not… but …look, there he goes. He's driving away."

She was right. There was a vehicle of that description pulling away from the opposite side of the road. I shot out of the café and into the road in an attempt to read his licence plate. It was covered in mud, completely concealing the registration – other than the letter 'T'. I reached in my handbag for my mobile. Shit! I still hadn't recovered it from Jim. I ran back into the café, breaking a heel on my shoe on the way, and asked for a phone, at the same time realising I had no coins with me either. I called 999, gave the police answering service my identity number, and asked for a pursuit vehicle to cover the area. But, by the time I was able to convince them this wasn't a hoax our tracker was long gone. So I rang Jim, reversing the charges and giving the operator my name.

"What's going on, Ange? Where's your mobile? And where the hell are you calling from?"

"I'm in a café with Connie. And *you've* still got my bloody mobile! A blue four-wheel drive job just followed us here from Ashworth House. I'm pretty sure it was our man, Jim, but I couldn't get any sense out of the emergency operator." I went on to describe the circumstances, and also how his number plate had been deliberately covered with mud.

"He was heading towards the Robin Hood roundabout," I informed him.

"Well, I didn't expect him to go away. But either Brownlaw's becoming increasingly bold or he's getting terribly desperate. Look, I'll put out an APB again on the vehicle; it may be easier to spot him if he keeps his number plate concealed."

"'Again'? How do you mean, 'again'?"

"Well, we're assuming it's the same vehicle I told you about the other day. Remember, the guy sold it for cash and it's yet to be registered with Swansea? We already have an alert out for that one. Leave it with me, Ange; I'll call you later. But I have to tell you - that funny feeling I've had about this case still hasn't gone. If anything, it's getting stronger ."

"Any luck?" Connie asked as I returned to my by now cold coffee.

"All the luck seems to be going the wrong way at the moment." I sighed heavily, feeling terribly disappointed.

"It won't last for ever," Connie assured me.

"No? I wish I had your confidence. Just one break, one mistake, is all we need. I only hope Jim's right and the fucker's getting more desperate."

I glanced at Connie with what must have been puzzlement, because she was prompted to ask: "What? What have I done?"

I squeezed her arm in reassurance. "You haven't done anything, my darling. It's just that I wish we had some idea, some clue, why he's so obsessed with you."

"'Cause he's afraid I'll get my memory back and identify him. Can't you see that?"

"I can, yes. But that raises a whole load of other questions. Like, how does he know you've lost your memory? And why's he worried *now* that it might come back? I spend a lot of time with you, Connie, and I haven't seen any sign of it. Oh, I know you're much better than you were, but that isn't quite the same as your memory returning."

CHAPTER FORTY-SEVEN

With that we left the café and slowly made our way back to Ashworth House – I emphasise the word 'slowly' because I was having to hobble on half a heel, aside from which I still wasn't feeling 100%. Connie must have picked up my discomfort because she led me to a nearby wooden bench, urging me to take a seat. I gladly leant back on the bench, removed the offending shoe and began rubbing my painful heel. Gradually the soreness disappeared and I was able to continue our conversation from the café.

"So tell me, Connie – I don't want to sound insensitive - but what exactly is this shit intending to do to you if he does find you?"

"I'd have thought that was obvious," she said, disarmingly. "Kill me, of course!"

"Bloody hell, Connie! I'm sorry. I didn't want to put that thought in your mind. It's just that he always seems to be ahead of the game – not that I know exactly what his game is."

She was quiet for a moment before commenting, calmly, in that small but determined voice, "I don't think you understand, Angie, do you? At the moment he hasn't got a game. He's been forced to call a time-out because his game's been interrupted by my unintentional vision. He knows now that I *see* him – and at first he thought he could control that. Only it's even worse than that now; now he's realised I can see him even before does anything. And he can't have that, because it means he's totally lost control; it also means, to him, that the next stage has to be that my memory *will* return and then I *will* know him. And since he can't allow that to happen it stands to reason he's got to get rid of me.

"What do you think he was trying to do the other night at Ashworth House? And, I agree with you, it was him alright." She went on, again in that matter-of-fact voice that sounded totally surreal to me. "He certainly wasn't paying me a social call, was he? And I think there's something sort of symbolic about him attacking you like that. Oversimplifying it, if I may:" *("Fucking hell! Where did she get all these fancy words from?" I thought to myself)* "he was after me; you were in the way, frustrating him; and so *you* became a substitute target. Surely, you've worked that one out, *Officer*?" she said, laughingly.

"Not as coldly or as calculatingly as that – no. I hadn't realised, for instance, the extent of the rapport you have with him. It's a kind of empathy that goes beyond anything I've ever known. And it's almost as if, at the beginning, it was something you shared with him, but now you're the one who is starting to dominate this – what shall I call it? – this fucked-up relationship. Does that make any sense to you?"

She laughed. "Perfect sense. You've described it far better than I could."

The conversation paused there – principally because I was trying to sort out my thoughts. The more I tried the fuzzier my head became.

"Are you okay, Angie? Do you think we should go back and let you rest?"

"No. It isn't that – mind you I don't think it's a bad idea. It's just that I'm trying to get my head round this bastard, but I'm not thinking clearly yet. Let's just rest here a while, shall we?

"I was going to ask you, though, if you remember, more or less, when you had your first psychic insight into the children?" *Oh, Christ! I'd completely forgotten she'd erased the incident of the forest from her consciousness.* "No, don't mind me, Connie," I said, attempting to make a hasty recovery.

She gazed at me for what seemed to be an even longer interval before responding. Then she said, hesitantly, "Angie; I've got a confession to make..."

I found myself giggling, for some unknown reason. "You know what they say about confessions, don't you? If you're planning to make one to the police, be sure to have your solicitor present."

She glowered at me, obviously not finding it the least bit funny. "I'm trying to be serious here," she snapped.

"Sorry. Poor taste. Please, Connie, go on; I'm listening."

"Well, I've been afraid to tell you this before now because I thought you'd expect me to give you information I don't have. But I *do* remember something about the children in the woods; I remember leading you there that night, for instance. But everything else is hazy. I have no memory of the actual events, although instinct *does* tell me that this man was involved. So, please, don't ask me for any details, will you? Because I don't think I'll ever recapture a clear picture of that night, except, perhaps, when I'm able to convince myself that I'm completely in the light. Maybe, when I'm really better, then I'll find the answer. Then I'll know him; but all I sensed when the vision came was that he'd come after me. It was that that finally made up my mind to get out of Forest Hills."

Then she raised a hand in the customary manner to stop me from interrupting. I was about to ask her how long she had been remembering the journey through the woods. "Please, Angie. I haven't finished. I just think it would help me if I were to tell you about myself…" She gave a shake of her head, as though she was clearing her thoughts. Then she went on, "What I mean is, we've had lots of discussions while I was in Forest Hills, but I've never really told you how I feel – you know, what's really been happening inside me."

I took hold of her hand and squeezed it gently. "I've never asked you before, sweetheart, because the last thing I wanted was to pry – intrude on a part of your life that I realise must be very painful for you. If you feel you're ready to talk about it now, you'll find I'm a very willing listener. And, if you think it'll help you I'll do everything I can to support you."

She looked away, evidently not sure where to start, which prompted me to say: "Why don't you say whatever comes into your head? …Don't try to think about it; let it flow naturally." I really had no idea what it was she wanted to unload, but if it could act as a kind of catharsis then it had to be beneficial.

Connie followed my example and leant back on the seat, closing her eyes as she did so. "I've never talked to anyone about how I felt – not even to Dr Simmons. Oh, he was always asking me, and I know it was because he was trying to help me, but something stopped me." She turned to look at me. "You see, Angie, for years I lived inside a dark room; there was no light, only this kind of… deep blackness. And there were no distinguishable sounds. Sure, I could hear voices and I could make out the odd visual image, but I never knew what they meant."

"You must have found that very scary," I commented.

"No. You're wrong. I didn't find it all frightening. Quite the opposite, in fact; I welcomed it. I know you can't possibly understand, Angie; no one can. But I was safe in that dark room; the blackness wrapped itself around me and protected me from all intruders. I never wanted to come out, and I wouldn't allow anyone to come in. It was my shelter from reality. Am I making any sense?" she asked with an innocence that touched my heartstrings; there was a part of this young woman that would forever remain a child. It was all I could do to nod, even though I only partly understood what she was saying. It didn't seem to matter, because she continued with her story. "The only time I had a visitor was when my mother died, and I had no control over that. She just sorta let herself in. All she said was that she was sorry she'd died but I wasn't to worry because there'd always be someone to look out for me now she was leaving…"

"Did she say why she'd chosen to die, Connie?"

"No. That's all she said, except that she was on her way somewhere, going on a journey, and she'd be waiting for me. It was all kinda weird, but, at the time, even though I was very sad at losing her, it felt like the most natural thing in the world. But it was a long time after that before I could bring myself to let the light come in; I was far too scared."

"What was it you were afraid of? Did you know?"

She shook her head. "Not at the time, no. It was only when you helped me find the courage to come out slowly, and I managed to get almost fully back to reality, that I realised what it was that frightened me so much." She turned to me, an earnest expression on her face. "It didn't happen suddenly or anything, Angie. I remember it was a slow process and it took many years before I felt I was getting better. That's partly what swayed me into deciding to leave Forest Hills and try to make a life for myself.

"And that decision coincided with the terrible vision of the man – the one in my nightmares. You see, as long as I stayed in my dark room that's all he was, a nightmare, and he couldn't harm me because the darkness protected me from him. That was why I was so afraid. And then, in the light, he became a real person, not just an image from a scary dream. That was when I saw him, clearly, snatching Josephine from her school…

"And please don't ask me to explain how it works, Angie, because I've got absolutely no idea. In a way, it's a bit like asking me why I'm a psychic: the answer is I don't know and I doubt I ever will. Sometimes I have visions where I 'see' things; I don't look for them – they just happen. And other times, like when I touched Reg, the artist, I can 'feel' things. I felt his death that day, and if you gave me a million years I couldn't explain it."

She leant her head against my shoulder, and simply said, "Sorry I can't be clearer, but I'm so glad you listened. Thank you, Angie, for being you."

I kissed her forehead, quite astonished at her admission, and yet at the same time I was heartened by her decision to open up to me the way she had. It was also tremendously encouraging that, somehow, I had played a part in her recovery – especially since for so long I had blamed myself for causing her breakdown. "Did the talking help you, Connie?" It was all I could think of to say.

She smiled. "Yeah; you've been a big help. But I guess I'll always be a bit strange, won't I?"

It was my turn to smile. "Sure you will; that's why I like you so much. But you *are* getting there, believe me. We couldn't have had this conversation before now – you really weren't well enough. But now" -it was my turn to shrug- " well, look at you; you're so much better, and I'm convinced you're going to come through all the bad times. Now, are you up to making a move? The rest has helped me, and I'm beginning to feel quite hungry.

CHAPTER FORTY-EIGHT

We were approaching the entrance to the halfway house when Connie said, "I've been thinking about this paedophile, Angie, and there's one thing I think we should try."

"Oh, right. And what's that, Connie?"

"We should try and find his current burial site. If we can uncover that then I think he'll suffer a severe psychological blow, it'll knock him for six. That's when he'll make a major mistake. Do you agree?"

I nodded thoughtfully. "Yes. Of course. But you make it sound terribly simple. How do we go about it, though – in a practical sense, I mean?"

"We go back on the computer," she said as we walked through the gate. "We get a list of all the disused coal mines in this area and the East Midlands, and then we go and check them out one by one. Trust me: one of them will be the burial site."

I closed the door behind us, turning the lock instinctively as I did so. "It shouldn't be all that difficult to get hold of the list, but I've no idea how many there are. It could be hundreds, so inspecting them could literally take for ever."

Connie took hold of my arm and nudged me into Paul's office. She took off her coat and sat herself down at the console before switching it on.

"We don't have to physically inspect them all; only the ones that seem familiar to me. So you've only got to get some... what are they called, Angie?"

"Aerial survey maps?" I proffered.

"Yeah; that's right. Is that likely to be difficult?"

I sat down beside her. "Let's give it a try, shall we? But, before we start, answer me this, will you? How come you've only just come up with this idea now? Why not before, when you realised that the vision wasn't some adolescent thing but was actually authentic?"

"I suppose it's because, when I was trying to explain to you earlier what was happening between me and this man, well – in a way – it was coming to me at the same time as I was telling you. Does that make any sense?"

I shook my head and grinned. "You keep asking me that. But does anything make any bloody sense in this case any more? Anyway, sweetheart, if you're sure you're up to it, let's make a start, shall we?"

We spent the next few hours accessing various databases on the computer; the problem was that, in parts of the Midlands area, a number of the coalmines had been split off from the National Coal Board some years before. Others had been the subject of privatisation. So, there no longer was a central information bank, which meant we had to split the territory into sections, each covering a radius of 50 miles – which turned out to be an alarming 7,000 square miles.

"Why don't we do what you told me you did with Brownlaw – and work from the centre outwards?" Connie suggested.

"It's as good a way as any, I suppose."

And that's what we did. But, before we could pull off any aerial maps, we first had to identify just how many disused mines we were talking about. Three hours or so later, we had counted up to 280. It was mind-blowing. Even if we limited the search to only the West Midlands, it still amounted to more than 100 closed mines.

"Jesus, Connie. How do we sort this lot out? It'll take forever. Look at this." I handed over to her the volume of survey maps I had printed off from the computer.

"No necessarily," she argued. "Not if we print off the actual aerial photos. I'll have some idea when I see them which mines are worth a second look."

"Okay. It's your call."

It took the best part of an hour to complete that part of the exercise – it wasn't exactly a laser printer – and at the end of it we had a pile of photos a mile deep lying all over the floor.

"Where do you want to start?" I asked her.

"Look, Angie; there isn't a lot more you can do here, so why don't you leave it to me, and you go have a rest. You look wiped out."

She was right, although I hated to admit it. So I simply nodded, wished her good hunting and then headed for my bed. I crashed out almost immediately.

When I awoke, it was time for supper – another of Sheila's specialities. Connie introduced me to WPC Pauline Wilkins, a rather mousy brunette, with dark, sad eyes and pinched features. I thought she was a bit on the old side to be a rookie, but, then, who was I to say? She was also self-evidently nervous, so I tried my best to make her feel relaxed. It was heavy work, and Connie was proved right when she said it was hard to get a smile out of her.

"How long have you been in the force, Pauline?" I asked her, more out of politeness than genuine interest.

"Six months, Sarge. Well, six months since I graduated from police training college."

"And are you enjoying it?"

"Yes. Thank you, sarge."

"The name's Angie," I pointed out. "We don't have to be formal around this table." God, I thought; this was bloody hard work. "Connie," I said, more to save her any further embarrassment than anything else; "how did you get on with the aerial maps? Any luck?"

She hid behind a smile that told me exactly what she was thinking. Little sod!

"I ploughed through them all – all 120 of them. And I've split them into three lots: the ones that definitely don't fit the bill; the ones that are possible but not probable; and the ones that look promising. I thought we could go through them together later, if that's okay."

"Sure. How many of the possibles are there?"

"Eighteen, perhaps nineteen, if you count the one I'm not too sure about."

"How about geographical spread? How far would we have to travel?"

"Well, luckily most of them are in either the West or East Midlands; that's if you include Staffordshire in this area. One's in Leicestershire, and another's in Derbyshire. When do you want to make a start?"

"I'm not sure. I think we should clear it with Jim Robbins first. Apart from which, we'll need some help. I'll talk to him later, but, I can tell you, he won't be at all happy about it."

Connie scowled angrily. "Why not?" she demanded. "We're doing his fucking job for him, aren't we?"

"Connie!" Sheila shouted. "I will not have that kind of language at my table. Is that clear?"

Pauline couldn't have looked more shocked if a male stripper had suddenly sat on her lap. Me, I had a job not to burst out laughing. It wasn't what she had said so much that I found amusing as the way she said it. It came out more like a ten-year old who knew she was being naughty but wasn't really sure why.

"Alright, alright," she said in a surly voice. "But it isn't your precious DCI who's being hunted by that bastard – it's me."

I grabbed her by the arm and pulled her out of her chair.

"Come on, reprobate. If you've finished let's get out of here. We can at least have a look at the maps."

We were still examining them when Jim arrived. He looked completely exhausted.

He gave me a peck on the cheek, and then smiled at Connie.

"What are you two up to?"

"We're looking at aerial maps; of disused coal mines."

He looked puzzled. "What are they going to tell you?"

"It was Connie's idea, Jim. She'd been thinking again of the vision she had, of the man dumping a girl's body down an old pit shaft. Remember?"

"Oh, yeah. I remember."

"Well, she has the idea that it might be possible to identify the place from aerial maps. So, that's what we're doing: examining the maps of those sites Connie believes could match her memory."

"Hmm. Good idea – in principle," he said, with a distinct lack of enthusiasm.

Connie gave me one of those 'I told you so' looks; I raised my eyes towards the ceiling.

"What?" Jim said. "Did I say something funny?"

"Private joke," Connie told him, grinning.

"So. Any luck so far?"

Connie handed him 12 of the maps. "These are the best prospects. It's a bit difficult, because it looks different from the air, but see:" (she pointed to one of the maps) "they each have the right combination of trees edging on to wasteland, which then leads up to an old mine. You can't make out all of the detail from the map, but you can see the old mine buildings here," (she pointed again to the picture) "and, here, this looks to me like the original shaft."

"Interesting," Jim commented. "Are all of them similar?"

"Yeah. Pretty much. But, then, I guess a lot of mines had the same features. We won't know for sure till we check them from the ground. But they look promising."

Jim pulled a chair up to the desk and sat down, still examining the maps.

"Well, it's going to take a lot of time and effort to explore this lot – and resources. I see two of the three are just a few miles from here. One's over the boundary into Staffordshire, and the other is near to Wolverhampton. What about this one in Derbyshire, Connie? It's very remote, isn't it? And I can hardly make out any detail on this map, much less see precisely where it is. What's attracted you to this one?"

Connie shrugged, as if to say she didn't know. "I have a feeling about it; that's all. Don't ask me to explain it, 'cos I can't."

"No. That's okay. But I suggest this is as far as we go. As Ange'll tell you, I'm into intuition these days, but what I don't have is t he time and the financial or human resources to spend the next few weeks flying around the countryside on what might turn out to be a wild goose chase."

I sniggered at the admission – it was so out of character.

"When do we start, then?" I asked.

"You don't, Ange. By the look of the map I think we'll have to approach this site from the air, by helicopter. There's no way you'll get medical clearance to fly – at least, not for the next few days."

"Then we'll wait," Connie said adamantly. "I'm not going near any of those places without Angie." She shuddered fearfully. "It could be a burial site, *for children*, for God's sake. No thank you. If Angie doesn't go, then neither do I."

Jim studied us both thoughtfully. It must have been crossing his mind, as it was mine, what had happened to Connie all those years ago when we found the children's bodies. And, more worryingly, the effect it had had on Connie. None of us wanted a repeat of that experience.

Eventually, Jim said, "I can understand your anxiety, Connie, and of course we'll go along with your wishes. Let me talk to the consultant, can I? See what he has to say first, before we decide. Is that alright?"

She nodded her agreement. I decided to change the subject.

"I got a message that Frank's back from Manchester. Is that true?"

"Yes. He said it was a waste of time. Oh, they managed to recruit a candidate to help with the website, all right but apparently the whole system's been shut down."

"I don't understand," I said.

"Frank says there's so much publicity about this case that the paedophiles have closed off all communication on the site. They're all blank pages. Even the chat rooms are empty. Seems our mutual friend has caused such a stir that his fellow perverts are scared shitless that they might be pulled in with our dragnet." He shrugged. "So, if we've achieved nothing else, at least, for the time being, we've made the streets safer for the children."

"Well, that's something, I suppose. What about the vehicle, Jim? Any news?"

"Nothing definite. But I did get a call on the way over here. Evidently a report came in about a car on fire in the airport car park; they seem to think it could be ours. I'm still awaiting confirmation. But, if it is, that will confirm my own belief that he is panicking. He's trying to destroy any evidence."

"Will a fire do that?" I asked. "I realise it can wipe out most of the evidence, but can it erase it completely?"

"I don't know, Ange. That's a matter for forensics. But I'm beginning to get more and more optimistic about this villain; the noose is starting to tighten around his neck – I can feel it."

"Do you think he might have done a runner? You know, from the airport?"

He shook his head vigorously. "No way. He might want us to believe that, but I think it's more likely he's jumped on a train from the airport into the city centre. We're checking all the flights as a matter of routine anyway." He pointed to the aerial maps. "And, if we can uncover his current burial ground, then I'm convinced we'll have dealt him a blow he'll struggle to recover from. He'll have nowhere left to go. Also, his ego will be shattered."

"That's what Connie believes. So, where does he go from here?"

"Let's see if we strike lucky and find the site first, shall we? ...Before we consider that scenario." He checked his watch, then went on to say, "It's probably too late to contact your consultant tonight, but I'll get on to it first thing in the morning. If he gives you the all clear, Ange, I'll organise the police helicopter. You happy with that, Connie?"

She nodded again, looking pleased with the decision. Jim was about to leave when his mobile went off. He answered the call, made a couple of undistinguishable comments, and then closed the connection.

"That was Peter Conway. They've confirmed the car at the airport is a four-wheel drive, but there's little or nothing left of it to identify either the make or the registration. Forensics are on the way, so we'll have to wait a while longer, but – in my opinion – it's far too coincidental to belong to anyone else. So, like I said, he's getting desperate. I'll ring you in the morning, just as soon as I have any news. Oh – and, Ange, in case I forget, here's your mobile; keep it your in your purse, will you?"

"Yeah. Up you too, Jim! Goodnight."

CHAPTER FORTY-NINE

He was as good as his word. He was on the phone to me just after nine the following morning, to confirm he had made contact with Dr Sutcliffe, the consultant in charge of my case. His assessment was that, providing the helicopter stayed below a ceiling of about 2,000 feet, then I shouldn't be affected by the height. Jim did add, of course, that Dr Sutcliffe had insisted it also depended on how I felt, and if my head had cleared, so I was prompted to tell Jim one of my little white lies and assure him that I was fine and ready again for work. He seemed satisfied with that, and suggested that Connie and I meet him at Birmingham Airport in about an hour; he was already there having discussions with forensics.

I breathed a sigh of relief, and then went off to let Connie know the arrangements. She was quite excited and hardly stopped talking on the way to the airport. She couldn't remember ever having flown before, much less in a helicopter.

We took off almost immediately and headed north towards the Wolverhampton area; we had decided to work outwards, starting with those old mines that were the closest, and then, if we had no luck, finishing up with the Derbyshire pit. Peter Conway had joined the group, leaving Frank Kewell and Peter Corkhill to liaise with the forensics team.

It turned out to be a very frustrating and disappointing day. The pilot, a flight sergeant with the police flying corps, had already pre-programmed his headings before departure. It was a bumpy flight and much too noisy to talk, but I was grateful when Peter poured me a coffee from the flask he had brought. My head was starting to give me hell, and it was more than my life was worth to say anything. We must have been flying for about 25 minutes, during which time we circled a couple of sites, before the sergeant pointed downwards, towards a group of buildings. It didn't mean anything to me, except that when we approached the ground I could clearly make out it was, indeed, an old coalmine. Whether it was the one we were seeking remained to be seen.

We touched down gently on what appeared to be wasteland, bringing up thick clouds of dust that instantly covered the windows, temporarily obscuring our vision. The flight sergeant made us wait until the blades were switched off and the dust had settled before opening the doors and allowing us to alight.

Jim stretched his arms, glad to be out of what he called a 'flying coffin'. He looked around him, studying the landscape, as if he were searching for something familiar.

"Recognise any of this?" he said to Connie.

She shook her head in disappointment. "It doesn't mean anything to me. It looked kinda different from the air, but I'm pretty sure this isn't what we're looking for."

So off we went again. At the end of the day we had either flown over or landed at six of the 11 sites Connie had pre-selected as matching her vision; but no luck. Jim was on the point of calling a halt when Connie said, "Do you think we could have another look at that site in Derbyshire?"

"Which one?" Jim said, somewhat irritably.

"The third one we visited."

"Right. And then we call it a day – okay?"

We all agreed as the pilot once more turned his heading towards the northeast. Fifteen minutes later the pilot began his descent towards the same spot we had landed at the first time.

"Any luck?" Jim asked after the rotors had come to a halt.

Connie was shaking her head. "I was pretty sure about this site," she said, "but it's not right; I mean, there's something missing."

"How do you, mean, Connie?" I asked her.

"I don't know. I think it's the wrong way round."

What she meant by that I couldn't imagine. The wrong way round? How could a place be the wrong way round? Just when I started to believe we were on a wild goose chase, Peter said, addressing the pilot, "Sergeant, can you land on the other side of the site?"

"I don't see why not, sir. It looks pretty flat from here. Do you want me to fly over it, for a look?"

"Yeah. Try it, will you? If it seems okay, come back for us."

We stood well back from the helicopter as the pilot started up the engines again, and the dust cloud immediately enveloped it. He lifted off slowly and cruised over to the far side of the site.

"What's the idea, Peter?"

"I don't really know, to be honest. Connie gave me an idea when she said it was the wrong way round. We could be looking at the site from the wrong angle. It's worth checking while we're here." Then he shrugged. "It would help, though, if someone briefed me on what it is we're looking for here. I don't understand why it should be such a bloody mystery."

"All in good time, Sergeant," Jim said.

We watched the helicopter hover over the ground on the far side, make a couple of tight turns and then head back towards us.

Again, he waited for the dust to settle before opening the doors and waving us across. We climbed in, as the pilot said: "No problem. If anything, it's easier; there isn't as much dust over there."

"What about access? Any roads?"

"Yeah. There's an old entrance road, but it's chained off. Looks as if it hasn't been used for years."

"Right. Let's go," Jim said.

In less than a minute we had crossed over the dilapidated buildings of the old mine and were settling onto a level piece of ground, just beyond some thickish woods.

"How does this feel, Connie?" Jim asked.

She was grinning now. "Totally different. I think this could be it. Look!" She pointed excitedly towards what appeared to be some kind of hut at the side of one of the buildings. "There's the lift shaft I was talking about."

I felt myself go cold all over. "Dear God, please let her be wrong," I thought, knowing instinctively that she wasn't. It was obvious from her demeanour that in some manner she had been here before. She was about to set off towards the shaft when Jim pulled her back by the arm.

"No, Connie, "he insisted; "this is as far as you go."

"What are you talking about? I have to go – I have to be sure."

"The only way we're going to be sure you're right is by actually descending to the bottom of that shaft. It could be up to a mile deep, and you can be damned sure the lift won't be working. So, how do you think we're going to get down there?"

Connie hesitated, unsure how to react. "I... I don't know. I guess I hadn't thought about it."

"Well, I can tell you. We'll need to organise the air rescue services, *and* the mountain rescue experts, if we're to have any chance of searching that shaft. Connie, we're talking about a hell of a lot of resources here; it's not going to be easy and it's certainly not going to be quick. Can you understand that?"

"I guess. But why can't I stay anyway?"

He sighed – the patience of a saint, I thought – then he placed his hands on her shoulders.

"Because I don't want you around when we find what I believe we will find in that hell-hole. We're not just talking about Josephine here – you do realise that, don't you? God knows how many children he's dumped in that shaft. And it's not an experience I want to share with civilians. Now, sweetheart, please; don't argue with me. I want you back in the helicopter and out of here before I get things organised. Will you do that for me?"

Connie had suddenly gone very pale, as if the enormity of what was down there had just hit her. Her lips trembled and a tear came into her eyes. It was all she could do to nod her assent.

I put my arm around her shoulders. "Jim's right, Connie. It's not something you should see."

Peter was studying us, a puzzled look on his face. "Would someone mind putting me in the picture here?" he repeated. "I haven't a clue what's going on. In fact, so far, no one's bothered to explain to me just what *she's* doing here." He pointed towards Connie, almost accusingly.

"Knock it off, Peter," Jim snapped. "I'll brief you later. But, in the meantime, you say nothing about this," (he waved a hand over the scene) "or Connie's presence here, to anyone. Is that clear?" He repeated it when Peter failed to respond. "I said, is that clear, Sergeant?"

"Yes, sir," Peter mumbled. "But it all sounds like mumbo-jumbo if you ask me."

"I'm not asking, I'm ordering you. And if you value your career, you'll do as I say."

I walked away with Connie, leaving Jim to contact the various emergency services. Her job here was finished, and the sooner she got away the better.

I gave her a warm hug and assured her I would see her later. Then I helped her into the helicopter. In a couple minutes they were airborne once again. Jim had given the sergeant instructions that, when they landed at Birmingham Airport, he was to have a car waiting to return Connie to Ashworth House. As I watched them disappear over the horizon I rang Steve Harrison to ensure that he would be on duty when Connie arrived back.

CHAPTER FIFTY

As soon as the helicopter had risen from the ground and the sound of the engines receded, Jim got on his mobile. An hour later a helicopter from the air rescue service landed. I stood there watching it, my mouth agape.

"Where are the rest of the emergency services?" I asked Jim.

"They'll be mobilised once we know we're in the right place."

Oh, of course. There was me being stupid again. It simply hadn't occurred to me that Connie might be wrong. Imagine calling out all those different services and then discovering the pit was empty. So I remained quiet and let Jim do his job.

Two rather young and athletic men from the air rescue service, carrying some equipment, joined us. We exchanged greetings and then went over to the edge of the pit, where I watched them unravel what appeared to be an extensive wire cable, fitted to the end of which was what looked like a small camera. The other end of the apparatus was still plugged into the helicopter's power supply. Neither of them spoke; obviously, they had already been briefed.

They began lowering the cable down the shaft for what seemed to me to be an interminable length of time. I was impatient to discover whether or not Connie was to be proved right.

Eventually, one of the men, addressing Jim, said, "Have a look at this, Chief Inspector." He was holding a miniature TV set in his hands, which in turn was showing what I thought was distorted picture of the ground far below.

"What?" I demanded. "What can you see?"

Jim said nothing; he just stood there for a while examining the picture on the tiny screen.

"Yeah," he said, tension on his face. "We're at the right place." He turned to me, pointing at the screen. "Look carefully," he advised. Then with his finger he traced what appeared to be indentations in the ground. It was rather like looking at a series of humps and bumps, and I had to admit that, in all honesty, I was unable to make what they might be. So I told Jim so.

"They're bodies, Ange. God only knows how many there are – it's impossible to make out with this limited equipment. But there's a hell of a lot more than one, and they're all children."

"Are you sure, Jim?" I asked.

He turned towards the officer holding the screen. "Do you agree?" he enquired.

"Yep; they're bodies alright." He stood, silently, whilst his colleague began withdrawing the cable from the shaft.

I was dumbstruck; not only by the horror of the news I'd been given, but also by the confirmation of Connie's immense and immeasurable talent. She was right! By God, she was right! We had found his burial ground.

Jim was already back on his mobile; when he had finished his calls we went across to the helicopter, where he insisted I take one of the two seats. "You look done in," he said.

It took over two hours for the first emergency vehicle to arrive. It was a caterpillar type of machine I had never seen before, and was obviously designed to climb the most severe of inclines. It was followed shortly afterwards by a whole convoy of police Range Rovers and air ambulance helicopters, together with vehicles with heavy lifting gear. Evidently, the chains blocking the access road had been severed, which in turn allowed the Crime Scene Unit to enter the site.

Very quickly it started to take on the appearance of a film set, with huge, freestanding arc lights set up around the perimeter of the shaft, attached to thick cables running from a generator. Next, a kind of harness was hung over the shaft, with a safety seat attached. I noticed that this too was mechanised, making for a much faster descent into the bowels of the mine.

By now there must have been in the region of 30 police and service people on the site; it gave me the impression of degenerating into chaos, although when I managed to have a word with Jim he assured me it was all well organised. After checking that I was okay to remain on-site, he went off to speak with the assistant chief constable of Derbyshire, whose force had been alerted to our planned incursion into their territory. I wandered across to talk to a very subdued Peter Conway.

"You're not sulking, are you?" I asked innocently.

"Piss off, Angie."

"Oh, come on, Peter. Surely you didn't expect the DCI to brief you when we first set off, did you? There was every chance Connie could have been wrong, and then he would have looked pretty silly in your eyes."

"Who exactly is this Connie? I still don't pretend to understand. And why all the mystery?"

"Because, my dear Peter, Connie is a very special kind of psychic – and, before you snigger, let me tell you she's the one who helped us find the bodies of all those murdered kids four years or so ago." Before he could say anything, I continued: "Connie has visions; not like your ordinary psychic – she actually sees things in 'real time'. And they affect her, badly. Recently she experienced a vision of our paedophile dumping a body into an old mineshaft. There was no way we could be certain which one of over 200 it might be, so this, if you like, is a process of elimination."

He looked stunned and was unable to say anything for quite a time. I could imagine the thoughts whirling around in his mind, like the dust from the helicopter. Eventually he was able to express himself, although, I must confess, it was hardly enlightening.

"I thought that was something that only happened in fiction, or in the films. Now I I've heard it all! You're telling me that we're here" (he spread his arms open) "not as because of police work, as I thought, but because some kid – a highly disturbed one at that – has convinced you and the chief that somehow she can 'divine' her way into the supernatural world and lead us into the mind of a killer? Well – I'm not having that. The very idea that we'd actually use a psychic in serious police work is beyond fucking belief. I can only think you two are off your bleedin' nuts; you've lost it, Angie. And, while you're being so forthcoming, why don't you explain to me why your precious psychic gets all this security. She's not being chased by evil spirits, is she?"

"You're acting like a dickhead, Peter. And you're going to feel pretty damned stupid when she's proved to right again." I held him away with my hand. "Before you say anything else you might regret, let's wait and see, shall we? It shouldn't be too long now."

I walked away from him before my temper really exploded. It wasn't that I objected to cynics so much; it was the utterly wasteful expenditure of energy in trying to convince them they were wrong that I couldn't handle – especially where Connie was concerned.

I went over to talk to the engineers who were assembled at the head of the pit shaft. They were deep in discussion, and, although I didn't like to interrupt, my natural nosiness compelled me.

"Any chance of an update?" I asked. "I'm DS Crossley, by the way."

A heavily built man, who I guessed was in his early fifties and who appeared to be the chief engineer on the site, looked towards me, frowning heavily. "The problem we have here, Sergeant Crossley, is access. As far as we can tell this shaft goes down almost a mile – that's some 5,000 feet. We're just debating whether to drop a fully optimised TV recording system down there, or wait until the cable extensions arrive so we can send a man down on the winch." He continued frowning. "I mean – we are clear on this, aren't we? There's no doubt what we're gonna find down there, is there?"

"You'll have to speak to the chief inspector about that. My information is that the site's already been camera tested and there's enough evidence to justify all you guys being here. I'm sorry, Chief; I thought you'd been fully briefed. We do have reason to believe there are bodies down there – children's bodies – but we've no way of actually confirming exactly how many without getting a proper look. Would you prefer to talk to my DCI about it? ...He's in charge of the scene."

He exchanged glances with his colleagues before answering the question, and then said, thoughtfully, "Well, as you say, sergeant, we don't really lose anything by lowering a television system. Except, of course, it don't come cheap - specially if we lose the fucker! Come on, fellas; let's get it set up."

I left them to it and wandered into the crime vehicle for a coffee and a chat with the SOCOS and the forensic people. There wasn't a lot for them to do at that time, although they had looked over the whole site and were able to confirm they had found a couple footprints. They had also checked out the access to the mine from the area of the trees. Apparently, there was a path of sorts through the woods, and beyond that was a single-track country lane, sufficiently wide to accommodate a vehicle; but that didn't really prove anything. I spent the next hour or so chatting to the scientists before we heard a shout from the engineers at the head of the shaft.

When I got over there I noticed the grim faces. They were examining the pictures coming live from the video camera.

"Sweet Jesus!" I heard one of them say, just before he vomited on the ground.

The chief engineer was doing his best to retain a degree of composure, but I could see that even he was having difficulty hanging on. Finally, I glanced at the screen displaying the pictures. "Oh, no. No … No" I gasped, as I saw my worst fears realised. This really was my worst nightmare come true. It was like watching one of those horror films from a Nazi extermination camp. Bodies could be seen everywhere, jumbled together randomly in a grotesque parody of a death dance. It was macabre; there was no other word I could think of to describe the scene, other than cynically insensitive. They were all children, and, from what I could see, all girls. And each one was unclothed. God only knew at this stage just how many bodies there were – it was impossible to count.

A couple of the women from the forensic team began weeping. All I could do was to stand there, virtually paralysed with shock at this outrageous horror. Then I began to tremble, and I felt my hands shaking. A feeling of rage swept through me as I tried to envisage the kind of evil monster who could visit such atrocities on innocent little children.

There was an eerie silence around the shaft entrance, as if there were no appropriate words to describe our feelings. I felt a hand touch my shoulder and I turned to see Peter there, his face drained of colour and expressing what was obviously remorse. He didn't need to say anything, but I squeezed his hand to let him know I understood. Jim came and stood beside me, joining in the silent memorial. Eventually he said to the engineers, "Turn it off, will you? We've all seen enough to last us a lifetime."

As the visual display went dark people began to move again. Jim and I got involved in conversation with the assistant chief constable as to the best way to organise our resources. Self-evidently, we were facing a long and difficult job. Getting one man down that shaft was challenging enough; now we would need a team of people to enable us to extract the bodies.

I couldn't stop thinking of the children and how they must have suffered. My thoughts also turned to the parents, just as they had done all those years ago. Their grief would be unbearable; how would we tell them, after we had identified the bodies? And who would break the tragic news to them? And even more disturbing was the reality that we couldn't possibly keep this lamentable story off the front pages of the newspapers, which in turn would add to the suffering of the parents, wondering if their child was one of the victims. For the first time in years, as tears trickled down my cheeks, I prayed for God to give me the strength and fortitude to bear up to this tragedy. And, not for the first time, I genuinely regretted ever joining the police force.

I felt Jim's grip on my arm. "Come on, Ange," he whispered softly. "I need you. Please, don't go to pieces on me now."

I almost smiled at his petition; it sounded very much like a lover about to be deserted. In the event, I was able to smile at him, more in gratitude than anything. I wiped the tears away and then followed him in the direction of the crime vehicle, resolved that I would get a grip on things again. The heavens opened as we were crossing the waste ground, quickly turning the area into channels of streaming mud and soaking us to the skin. This sure as hell wasn't going to make the job any easier.

CHAPTER FIFTY-ONE

We were on site for a total of three days and three nights, the weather continuing to work against us. By now there was a total of approximately 70 police officers and emergency personnel actively involved in the operation. Huge arc lights were strung out all across the site, and there was almost as much equipment and lines of cabling as there were people. Overhead, we were constantly bombarded with the incessant noise of helicopters, landing and taking off as they ferried the bodies of the murdered children to the temporary morgue the superintendent had set up in a portioned-off area of the NEC building close to Birmingham Airport.

Extracting the victims was a slow and painful operation, and, in some instances, positively dangerous. During one retrieval the seat on the winch flipped up, tipping its occupant, together with his cargo, partway back down the shaft. In turn that created a further difficulty; the rescue worker concerned, unfortunately, had broken his back in the fall, and the paramedics, together with a stretcher, had to be lowered all that way down the shaft in order to rescue him. That incident added hours to the recovery process.

And in all that time the rain never relented. It was as if the dark, heavy clouds had gathered at the scene of death and were pouring out their contents from the sky in an effort to obliterate the obscenity of the little girls' bodies. It was a distressing, even sickening experience, and more than a few of the duty officers from the emergency services had to be relieved due to the stress. The site by now was a quagmire and it was more like trudging through a swamp than the dustbowl it was when we first arrived.

To compound the difficulties, we were under permanent siege from a vast army of reporters and television cameras from the world's media. Some of their helicopters had attempted to land on the site, and it wasn't until Jim threatened to arrest them that they retreated to the nearby field. Eventually, even he had to give way to the barrage of questions hurled at us from the edge of the waste ground, through electronic speakers, by agreeing to be interviewed.

His statement was short but succinct: "My name is Detective Chief Inspector Robbins and I am the officer in charge of this operation. So far, all I am able to tell you is that a number of bodies of children – young girls - have been recovered from the bottom of the lift shaft. As to the final count, I am unable to give you that, as the work is still ongoing.

"We have evidence to suggest the children were murdered, and we are connecting them to the recent disappearance of two other children in the West Midlands area. But, so far, none of the victims has been identified.

"I will talk to you again just as soon as we have any further information, but, in the meantime, can I ask you please not to obstruct the police or emergency services in the performance of their duties. I have no further comment for now. Thank you."

"Chief Inspector," a reporter with one of the TV stations shouted. "Are you able to tell us how you knew where to look for the bodies?"

"I have no further comments to make at this stage," Jim repeated.

This appeared to quieten them for a little while, but, as the rain persisted and the work carried on in atrocious conditions throughout the night, the press became more and more hungry for information, and the noise began to erupt once more. The TV Company from which the interviewer had asked Jim the question regarding our information about the burial site was the most persistent, practically demanding that he divulge his source. He continued to dodge the question by refusing any further comment.

Finally, by dawn on the third day, the rescue team was able to confirm that all of the bodies had been recovered. The scale of the numbers left us all dumbstruck and in a state of severe shock. There were 11 in total. It was mass murder on an almost genocidal scale, which I had never before witnessed – nor ever wanted to again as long as I lived. The horrors of the children in the woods four years ago almost paled into insignificance by comparison.

Jim prepared a further statement for the media, whilst I, together with one or two of the forensic team, retreated in an exhausted and traumatised state to the crime unit vehicle. At least my head was clearer – I think I was far too stunned to worry about the state of my health.

We had just spent three of the most awful days imaginable at that site; I hadn't even managed a change of underwear! True, we had portable toilet facilities, but there was literally nowhere to wash, and I hadn't brushed my teeth for three days.

Whilst we had been all that time on-site Jim had been in constant communication with the superintendent at the National Exhibition Centre. One piece of news that did encourage us was that the vehicle set on fire in the airport car park was confirmed as that belonging to the offender from the child's playground; the offside front tyre, still undamaged, was a match to the tread taken from the vehicle tracks in the park. Furthermore, various samples of fibres had been recovered from the areas left untouched by the fire, and forensics were optimistic they would reveal more confirmatory evidence.

As Jim had said: "We are tightening the noose." Now the killer was without suitable transport, other than his own upmarket vehicle, and he had also just been deprived of his burial ground. My only concern was that, with the almost intolerable pressure of international press and television exposure, he would go to ground without a trace. That didn't seem to worry Jim too much, as he quite rightly had commented: "Remember what I said, Ange: It will be solid police work that will catch him in the end. He certainly isn't going to walk into the police station and give himself up. But, trust me, he *will* make another serious mistake."

And so we carried on with standard police procedures. After finishing at the mine, the group of us, smelling as though we'd just come off a pig farm, flew back to Birmingham Airport, where Jim immediately went into discussion with the superintendent and the pathologists who had been drafted in to the temporary morgue.

I scrounged a lift in one of the squad cars and returned to Ashworth House. One of the only good things to have come out of that nightmarish experience was that my concussion seemed to have gone, although I was desperately in need of sleep after three days of catnapping. I let myself into an empty house. Connie had gone off to college, accompanied by her escort, whilst Sheila, no doubt, was out shopping; but she had forgotten to turn on the alarm system, and, since the other boarders had all been transferred following my altercation with the intruder, I was alone. So I made myself a cup of coffee and took it into my room, telling myself that after a long sleep – followed by a long-overdue bath – I would arrange to move back into my flat. I felt I needed my own space again, to say nothing of a man's warm body next to me in my bed. I was asleep long before I thought of drinking my coffee.

* * * * * * * * * *

I was awakened from a deep drug-like sleep by the persistent ringing of the telephone. For what seemed an age I tried to ignore it, hoping either that it would cease, or that perhaps someone else would answer it. The problem for me was that it was the phone in the hall, almost immediately outside my bedroom. I groaned and stuck my head under the pillow, urging it to stop. It didn't oblige, and in the end the incessant noise forced me to look at my watch; it was still only two o'clock – I had been asleep for only an hour. Cursing aloud, I dragged myself from the bed, put on my dressing gown and went to answer it.

"Yes?" I snapped.

"Did I wake you, bitch?" I heard a voice say – a man's voice with a slight Midlands accent.

"Who is this?" I demanded angrily. "What do you want?"

By now I had resurfaced into something like normality. But, after the nightmare of the last few days, this was one shock I was really in no condition to handle. I heard myself saying, virtually on automatic pilot, "Is that who I think it is?"

He sniggered – contemptuously, I felt. "I just wanted to let you know, you and that other little bitch, that I'm coming for you next. I'm going to make you both suffer for your interference.

"And, in case you think you're protected in that place, why not have a look round; you'll soon see how easy it is for me to get at you both."

That arrogant claim triggered off in me a pent-up rage that I'd forced myself to control for a long time now. I totally freaked out, not really aware of what I was saying to him. All I could think was, how dare that monster ring here and threaten Connie and me!

"Is that so? You sick bastard!" I retorted. "Well, you just remember this, psycho; we're no more than a day away from arresting you! You've lost your transport, and you'll know now we've uncovered your vile burial ground. You've got nowhere left to go, so you're not gonna get the chance to touch me or Connie you... Scum!

"I've got a better idea for you, pervert. Why not call it a day and give yourself up. Because *I'm* coming for *you*, Arnold Brownlaw; and you have no place left to hide!"

He didn't respond. Not a word. All I could hear was heavy breathing down the phone, as if he were gasping for air. I really believe my revelation had left him dumbstruck; I don't think he was capable of speaking. He simply cut the call, leaving me to curse my indiscretions.

"You stupid, stupid bitch!" I reprimanded myself. How could I have been so moronic? I had completely lost it, in a moment of intense rage, when, as an experienced police officer, I should have been prepared for this kind of eventuality.

I tried to calm myself by getting dressed and going into the kitchen to make a coffee. I sat at the kitchen table, trying to collect my thoughts and wondering if there was anything I could to rescue the situation. I couldn't think straight. Connie and I had just been threatened with our lives, and, instead of being shocked, or even frightened, I was still shaking with anger at his outrageous violation.

Deciding I was quite incapable at present of behaving like a professional, I did the only thing that came to me: I rang Jim on his mobile. He had to know of the damage I had caused, regardless of the personal consequences.

"Ange? I thought you said you were going to sleep until tomorrow? What's up?"

I was hesitant, unsure of how to phrase my confession of stupidity.

"Ange...? What is it?"

"Jim. I don't know how to tell you this but I've just had our psychopath on the phone."

"What! At Ashworth House?"

"Yes. He woke me."

"Christ! What the hell did he want?"

"He threatened me; Connie and me. He said he was coming after us - coming to kill us."

"I don't suppose you thought to trace the call, did you?"

"It's the public phone in the hall. I don't think it's traceable. But, Jim – that isn't really why I'm ringing you. I'm afraid I've fucked up, big time. I called him by his original name: Arnold Brownlaw. Jesus! I'm sorry, really sorry. He'd woken me up, I was feeling groggy and he was coming out with all sorts of vile threats about what he would do to us both – and I just went ape shit."

"Well, you can stop blaming yourself for a start. Clearly, you were wrong to do what you did, Ange; but after what we've just been through I doubt either of us could have kept a cool head. So, knock it off, will you, and let's think how we might turn this to our advantage."

Good old Jim, I thought. I'd never known anyone who could impart reassurance so easily and so genuinely.

"Listen. Let me have the number of your public phone, will you? I reckon his call might still be traceable."

"Okay. Give me a sec." I went into the hall with my mobile in my hand, checked the number and passed it on to him.

"Fine. Let me get something moving on this – hang on..." I heard him giving instructions, and then he said, "Ange, is Connie there with you?"

"No. She's at college. Don't worry, Jim; Steve Harrison is with her."

"Right; what I want you to do, if you're feeling okay, is go and check out her bedroom. See if she's had an intruder; I'm puzzled as to where he got that telephone number. Can you do that?"

"I'm alright, honestly. A bit shaken, and still knackered, but other than that I think I can cope. I'll get back to you shortly."

* * * * * * * * *

I climbed the stairs to Connie's room with some trepidation. The thought that that monster might have gained entry into the house disturbed me considerably. But when I looked at it logically I realised it would not have proved that difficult. I remembered that when I arrived back from the airport the burglar alarm was off; I was too tired then to give it much attention, but I do recall now reminding myself to have a word with Sheila about it. And, to make sure I wasn't completely off the wall, I checked to ensure I had turned it on when I closed the front door. I was relieved to note that in fact I had – so part of the policewoman in me was still functioning.

Connie's door was unlocked: something I also found worrying – except that, when I went in, everything appeared to be in order. Her bed was made up neatly, and there were no unwashed clothes visible. Her bathroom, at least from the door, seemed to be orderly and tidy – most unlike a teenager, I thought. But when I went inside I saw a message scrawled on the bathroom mirror, probably written with a lipstick the colour of blood. The message, threateningly, spelt out a warning to Connie:

'YOU'RE NEXT, BITCH'

"Oh, shit!" I said to myself. Jim was right. The bastard had gained entry. I rang him back from the bedroom and quickly put him in the picture.

"Where's Sheila?" he said, quickly.

"I...I don't know, Jim. I thought she'd gone shopping. When I came back I more or less went straight to bed."

"Were the alarms switched on?"

"Well, no; as a matter of fact they weren't. Do you think something might have happened to her?"

"Oh, fuck!" he yelled. "Ange, listen to me: I want you out of the house. Understand? Don't touch anything. Just leave. Now. I'm on my way."

The connection broke and I found myself instinctively following his instructions. I ran down the stairs and out into the street. I didn't even stop to close the door. All I could think was: "No, please; don't let anything have happened to Sheila." And then I wondered if Jim thought the psychopath might still be in the house. He could easily have used a mobile from one of the other rooms to ring the hall phone. I shuddered at the prospect.

A whole train of thoughts raced through my head. How had he got in? Why was the alarm system turned off? And where was Sheila? Then it suddenly hit me. He hadn't broken into the house. He had simply rung the doorbell and Sheila had let him in. But why? She was under the strictest instruction not to open the door to anyone she didn't know personally.

And where was she now?

"Oh, my God!" I said out loud as I realised the truth. Sheila was still in the house. She was dead! That, and the message he had left for Connie, was what he was telling me on the phone. I was still reeling from the shock as I heard the police sirens. A few moments later Jim arrived, accompanied by Frank Kewell and Peter Conway. A second squad car pulled in shortly afterwards, followed by an ambulance. The four officers exiting from the second vehicle were, I noticed, from the armed response unit. Their automatics were already at the ready.

"Have you touched anything, Ange?" Jim asked.

I shook my head in a daze. "No. I got out when you said to. I think he's killed Sheila. That's what he was trying to tell me on the phone, wasn't it?"

Jim nodded and then turned to the paramedics. "Take care of her, will you. She's had a hell of a shock."

"No, Jim," I insisted forcefully. "Stop treating me like an invalid. Sheila's my friend; I'm going back in with you."

"Okay. If you're sure that's what you want." He then signalled to the officers from the ARU vehicle. "Go ahead of us," Jim ordered. "Let us know when it's clear."

The officers didn't speak. They nodded a silent communication to each other, then, in military fashion, they softly opened the front door and moved in. Some minutes elapsed before they emerged. One of them, presumably the senior officer, said to Jim, "Clear to enter, sir. No intruders. One body; female; first floor rear bedroom. Badly mutilated."

"Thank you, officer. You can stand down." He turned to me. "Are you sure about this, Ange? You heard what the officer said. This is going to be pretty sickening."

"I want to see her," I said. "I want to witness first-hand what this monster's capable of. And she looked after me when I needed her; the least I can do, now she's dead, is to look after her. I'm coming in with you, Jim."

"Okay, guys. Tread carefully; I don't want anything disturbed before forensics get here. Ange;" (he gripped my arm tightly) "you stay at the back."

* * * * * * * * *

It took only a glance at the scene in the bedroom for me almost to lose my grip. It was one of the most appalling sights I believe I had ever witnessed – worse even than the bodies in the mine shaft - Sheila's body was spread eagled across the bed, naked and covered in blood from slash wounds. The bedspread, part of the floor, and even one of the walls were all spattered with blotches of her blood. Her legs had been deliberately left wide open, bent at the knees at an obscene angle, too clearly visible, and a knife wound extended from her genital area up to her abdomen. Her eyes were wide open, an expression of terror still evident, and a secondary stain covered the blankets where she had urinated. Sheila had died a violent and agonising death at the hands of the most depraved of psychopaths. I couldn't stop my thoughts from straying back to the children he had also done this to, and for a moment I actually felt the fear and the madness inside this room; it was so tangible I could virtually touch it.

I shook my head, more in sadness than revulsion. To do this to any human being, to deprive her of even a modest degree of dignity in death, to strip her of all traces of humanity, and – above all – to do this to my friend defied any attempt at description. I took in the scene once more, allowing the tears to run freely down my face. I was quite unable to speak, but, despite this, one thought, which I felt growing deep inside me, was a resolve to catch the rabid animal capable of such monstrosity.

Peter was busily taking photos of the scene, from just inside the doorway. Around the bed itself, up to a radius of some three feet, Frank Kewell had laid out a yellow crime scene tape for forensics. I wasn't allowed into the room, as I was the only one not wearing protective gloves. We were at the scene for no more than a few minutes, but during that time no one spoke. We were each of us too shaken for conversation. We left the room to give the SOCOS (who by now had arrived) access to the crime scene. Emma, who normally spent her time in the laboratory, glanced at me in sympathy. Her presence confirmed that recent events had caused acute staff pressures in her department. Jim and the others went up to Connie's room to view the message on the bathroom mirror, whilst I gladly retreated from the scene.

CHAPTER FIFTY-TWO

Outside, I took huge gulps of the fresh air, and then rang Steve Harrison on the mobile. Connie wasn't due out of college for another hour or so and I wanted to ensure she didn't have to witness yet another horror scene. I heard him gasp when I broke the news about Sheila. Then he asked me what they should do and how long I wanted them to stay away. The truth was I was damned if I knew, except it didn't seem right that anyone should be asked to stay in that house for even one more night. So I told him to stay where he was with Connie, and said I would come and collect them presently – my car was still in the street from almost a week ago.

Next I rang Paul Simmons. He remained silent as I relayed the details of the tragedy to him. Like all of us, I don't think he knew what to say. What can you say when you hear that someone you're very close to has just been murdered?

Finally, Paul said, "I'm sorry, Angie; I'm too stunned to take it in. All I can think of right now is that her family's got to be told. I once met her mother… and I believe she has a younger brother."

"I'll tell them, if you like, Paul."

"No. Thanks. It's better coming from me. I was the closest to her." He was quiet for a moment; then he continued: "Where will Connie go now? She can't possibly stay in that house again. I'll have to give it some thought, won't I?"

"I thought I'd take her home with me, Paul – if that's alright with you?"

"Yes; of course. Good idea - if you're sure you don't mind. At least till I can sort out some alternative arrangements for her." He paused again. "I'm sorry, Angie, I'm too distraught to deal with anything just now. It's such a shock. Is it okay if I ring you later?"

I assured him it would be and then broke the connection.

I was numb. I felt I had suffered a week of successive shocks, each one impacting with greater ferocity than the previous one. I wasn't sure I could take any further traumas. And yet, I told myself, here was I being totally selfish, having departed from a burial site containing the bodies of

11 little girls and having seen the results of the same monster at work on my friend. It was not a time for self-pity. There were debts to be repaid. Justice was essential if I was to wipe out the memory of these atrocities, and find any kind of peace for the poor victims.

I shook myself out of it and went to find Jim to let him know what I was planning to do about Connie's accommodation. He was following the paramedics out from the house; they were carrying Sheila's body on a stretcher.

"How did he gain entry?" I asked.

"She let him in. Whether she knew him, or whether he was wearing some convincing disguise, as he did that day at the playground, we'll probably never know. One thing I am sure of, he didn't have to break-in; Sheila opened the door for him. My guess is she was taken in by his disguise; otherwise she wouldn't even have opened the door, much less let him in. And he must have got rid of whatever outfit he was wearing before leaving the house, otherwise his clothing would be covered in blood."

I couldn't believe it. "You're saying she invited him in to murder her?"

He shrugged angrily. "Yes. You could put it that way. Let's hope forensics can tell us more."

I went on to put him in the picture about Connie, but he was short with me and insisted on interrupting.

"Ange; listen to me. Your flat won't be any safer than this place – less so, if you think about it seriously for a moment. Look what we did here. We installed a state-of-the-art alarm unit, coupled to a 24-hour personal protection arrangement for Connie, as well as through the night regular patrols. And it was all useless. He still gained access and murdered Sheila.

"You don't even have a functional alarm system at your place, and the security in the building is nothing short of woeful. No, I'm sorry. I'm not having you expose yourselves any further."

"So what do you suggest, Jim? A cosy cell for us both?" I said sarcastically. Then I quickly rethought what he had said: and of course he was right. Any petty burglar could gain entry to my flat with probably just a piece of wire. What I was suggesting was unacceptably risky.

"Sorry," I added quickly. "That was uncalled for. So, you must a better idea, yeah? Want to tell me about it?"

He glared at me initially and then softened at my apology. He let out one of his deep sighs that seemed to start in his stomach. "As a matter of fact I do. We have two alternatives. One, we have a couple of safe houses; they're secure and very well protected – they have to be. The only problem is that they're outside our immediate jurisdiction; they come under the National Crime Squad, so we'd lose any personal involvement in Connie's future situation. I don't know whether we are prepared to accept that – aside from which, they're quite a distance away."

"What's the second alternative, Jim?" I asked cryptically.

He looked at me, pure innocence shining from his hazel eyes. "My apartment." He quickly held out a hand before I could say anything. "Just listen to my reasoning, will you? For a start, I have got an alarm system that's way better than the one at yours. The flat's on the third floor, making access extremely difficult, and the building already has 24-hour security, with CCTV and a direct link to the station. Anyone who comes near the building is immediately caught on camera. We didn't have that here remember? ...The Super said we couldn't afford it.

"Also, it's a large apartment; as you know, I've got three bedrooms – well, two and a half anyway. My idea is that we install the young WPC – the one who's on duty here – for night supervision; she can share one of the bedrooms with Connie. Then, you can take the master bedroom while I move into the box room." He grinned. "There; how does that sound?"

"I'm not altogether sure just who we need protection from: the psychopath or you! Anyway, I can't think of a better alternative, and you're right about my flat; even I could break into that. So," (I held my hands out in surrender) "I agree. But, of course, I'll have to ask Connie; I can't make the decision for her. And Jim – thank you."

And I meant it. He might well have some personal and ulterior motive, but he would be giving up his privacy, and I was grateful. I knew also that Connie would agree, providing I was with her; she would, in addition, be comforted by Steve Harrison's presence during daylight hours. I did remember one thing, though, that I had overlooked.

"What about Connie's college arrangements, Jim? It's a hell of a way from your place."

He studied the problem for a few moments, scratching his chin for inspiration. "No," he said finally. "Definitely no college. Connie's effectively under 'house arrest' for the duration – a kind of protective custody, if you like. That means all present routines are cancelled until this business is over. Not just college – everything you and she usually do on a day-to-day basis: shopping – change your supermarket; hair-dressers –do your own; paper shop –change your habit. Anything – and I do mean anything – you would do regularly, think before you do it."

"That's a bit harsh, isn't it? And, surely, you're not suggesting I'm under house arrest too, are you?"

He laughed at that. "No, but it wouldn't half give me a lot of pleas-ure. And it's only harsh if you want to carry on underestimating this arsehole. After today" (he pointed towards the house) "we *do not* give him another opportunity to establish a consistent pattern of behaviour for either of you. Whenever you're outdoors you both become unpre-dictable. We have to frustrate him into committing an impulsive act – a serious mistake. And it has to be something he can't plan. I still believe that's how we're going to catch him. Understood, Ange?"

I nodded, still sick to my stomach at what had happened. "Yes. Acknowledged. Now, if it's okay with you, Jim, I have to contact young Harrison; he'll be at the college waiting to hear from me. What do I tell Connie about… you know... Sheila?"

"As little as possible for now Does Harrison know where my apartment is?"

"Well, if he doesn't I can soon tell him."

"Good." He handed me some keys. "Arrange for a copy of these to be made on your way back. And tell Harrison he's to meet you at the flat with Connie. Tell him to suggest it's because I want to talk to her. I've got one or two things to clear up here first, but I'm putting Frank in charge of the local enquires, so I'll join you shortly."

Frank was doing his best to persuade a TV company to leave the scene as I departed. I wondered just how the hell they had got onto it so quickly, until I realised they were obviously monitoring the police wavebands. That was another little nugget that I stored at the back of my mind.

CHAPTER FIFTY-THREE

It was with a heavy heart that I set off to meet up with Connie. It seemed to me that most of her life had been filled with tragedy. As a young child, it had been made clear to her, by both her mother and her father, that she was not wanted; following that she had to endure the painful empathy of her visions, and then her mother had committed suicide whilst she herself was interned in the psychiatric hospital. And so it went on. Now, somehow, I had to tell her of the death of Sheila, our friend. God only knew how she would take it; she was nothing if not resilient, but perhaps this might prove one loss too many.

When I arrived at the college Steve was still waiting for Connie to emerge; I was early. I warned him not to say anything to Connie about Sheila's murder, (other than what Jim had instructed her to be told) gave him directions to Jim's apartment and said I would go up there with them.

I pulled into the parking area outside Jim's apartment block, furnished, as he had suggested, with spare keys. I nodded 'good afternoon' to the rather suspicious porter, took the lift up to the third floor and let myself in to wait for Connie and her police escort. As was normal with Jim's flat, the place was a mess, with clothes thrown anywhere and everywhere.

It occurred to me that Connie and I would need to do some shopping, more especially Connie. At least I could transfer most of my things from my own flat; she would literally have nothing but the clothes she was wearing.

I went into the kitchen and did the very 'British' thing and put the kettle on for tea. A few minutes later the doorbell went and I let a very sombre Connie into the flat. Steve Harrison, she informed me, was waiting downstairs in the car.

Once again she pre-empted me. "It's Sheila, isn't it?" she said. "I just felt something was wrong so I made Steve drive me past Ashworth House and there were lots of police cars outside. At first I thought it was you, but Steve assured me you had just been on the phone. So I put two and two together: it had to be Sheila. Oh, Angie!" she said, bursting into tears and putting her arms around me. "Why? Sheila was such a lovely person; she wouldn't harm anyone. Why did he have to do this to her?"

"I don't know, Connie," I said softly; "I really don't know. We're dealing with a maniac – a complete evil, twisted, sadistic nutter. Poor, poor Sheila..."

We stood there in the hallway for quite a while, holding each other protectively, sharing our common grief. Then I took her hand and led her into the apartment. She wiped her eyes, then took off her coat.

"Does Jim Robbins really want to speak with me, Angie? Or were you just trying to soften the blow?"

"A bit of both, I suppose. Jim doesn't want either of us to stay at Ashworth House any longer – for obvious reasons."

"Is he suggesting we stay here then?" she asked, glancing around the room.

"Yes. He reckons it'll be safer for us both. There's better security here than we had at Ashworth, and that's his main concern really."

"Why you, Angie? Me I can understand, but why do you need security?"

"Oh he phoned me up with a charming little message... A warning, Connie. He's after both of us. So we're in this together. Can you handle that, sweetheart?"

She nodded tearfully. "It gets worse, doesn't it? How are we going to stop him? Steve told me they found 11 bodies at the mine. Jesus! Think of the horror of it, Angie. Eleven little children. And now Sheila, who wouldn't hurt a fly. He won't think twice about killing us, will he? We're just a bloody nuisance to him."

I didn't know what else to say. But I couldn't help thinking it was insensitive of Steve to tell her about the number of bodies; it was also unnecessary, even though she would have read about it in the papers soon enough, I guessed.

We were both drinking tea when Jim arrived. He said 'hello' to Connie, before asking me if I had said anything to her. I gestured that I had.

"We are all of us terribly sorry, Connie. And I know what a good friend Sheila was to you both." He took her hand. "We're going to catch him, sooner rather than later. Has Ange explained why I want you both to stay here for the time being?"

She nodded. "Yes."

"And are you alright with that? We'll try to make you as comfortable as we can, and hopefully it won't be for long. But you do realise, don't you, that until this is over there can be no college? We think it's an unnecessary risk in the circumstances. But that doesn't mean you can't do some work while you're here, young lady!" He pointed towards the computer on his desk against the far wall. "That machine's got a modem, so you'll be able to hook up directly with the college. And if we have a word with them I'm sure they'll be able to keep you up to scratch with your studies. Okay?"

"Yeah, fine. Has Doctor Simmons been told yet?"

I confirmed that I had contacted him, and that, in turn, he would be getting in touch with Sheila's family. "He'll let us know eventually about the funeral arrangements," I informed them.

"Do we know how she died?" Connie asked.

Jim shook his head. "It's too early to say. We'll have to wait for the autopsy result – that won't be until tomorrow. But we have found an eyewitness; a lady in the flower shop opposite the house says she saw a priest at the door, just before lunchtime." He shrugged. "She didn't think anything of it, but, then, why should she? Also, she says she didn't see him leave the house, which must mean, as I suspected, he shed his disguise and let himself out the back way.

"So," he went on, "we now know how he gained entry. He seems to like disguises: the last time he was dressed as a park ranger; now a priest. I've got people checking out the local costume hire shops – you never know, maybe we'll get lucky. Oh," he said, almost as an afterthought; "you were right about the phone. The call *was* untraceable." He checked his watch. "I have to go - want to come with me, Angie?"

I held my hands out, as if to say: "Just look at me."

"I badly need a bath, Jim. Where can I meet you?"

"I'm going back to the NEC. I want to speak to the pathologists." He looked at me, frowning. "Come on, Ange; you can bathe later."

"Is that where the children are?" Connie asked. "The exhibition centre?"

He nodded, saying nothing. "I'll tell Harrison to stay here with Connie until Pauline Whatever-her-name-is comes on duty."

"Wilkins," I said, grinning; "her name is Wilkins."

Jim and I left after he had given young Steve strict instructions about opening the door. I was still feeling shattered, so God only knew what Jim must have been feeling like; at least I had had an hour's sleep.

We had driven some distance when Jim said, "The medical examiner thinks Sheila died either by strangulation or loss of blood from the knife wounds; it has to be confirmed but he's pretty sure that he must have grabbed her by the throat almost as soon as he got inside the door. Then he half carried, half dragged her upstairs, to finish off his work. The doc also tells me that the knife wounds are not post-mortem – that explains all the blood – which means they could have been concurrent with death." He shook his head – a gesture of disbelief or dismay at this insight.

"So, we know he was in a hell of a rage," I commented. "It will be interesting to hear what Paul has to say about that, but it does seem as though he's rapidly losing control – if he hasn't already lost it."

"Yeah," he agreed. "And I reckon your telling him we know who he is – or, rather, who he was – will have given him another push towards the edge. That's what I'm banking on."

"How so?"

"Well, I reckon he's going to get more and more desperate, and I've given some further thought to that in the context of the security arrangements for you and Connie. You see, we want him to take a kind of quantum leap in terms of risk – something totally outrageous, where he's bound to expose himself. Now, I've figured that he's less likely to chance something like that if he sees we have the apartment surrounded with a tight ring of security. So we slacken it a little. Sure, we maintain a visible level of security – this guy isn't stupid – sufficient to convince him it isn't a trap, but not tight enough to discourage him from trying something."

"Wait a sec, Jim. You're losing me here. Surely you're not saying you will deliberately let him know where Connie is ensconced, and then reduce the level of security in order to entice him? Are you?"

I watched his face and saw his mouth tighten, the way it does when he is resolved to do something. "Christ! You are, aren't you? I don't believe this, Jim. What the fuck gives you the right to play with someone's life like that? We've already had one murder today, and you're suggesting we invite him to commit a second one." I felt my hands clenching in anger. "How will you justify it? In the cause of duty? Or have you something more ingenious in mind?"

"Knock it off, Ange. No one's talking about putting Connie at serious risk. The security'll be in place, don't you worry about that. He just won't see it – that's all. Not until it's too late."

"And just how do you achieve that? Are you going to fill the apartment with armed response officers?"

"Something like that," he confirmed. "Look – give me a break, will you. I haven't worked out the detail yet, when I have I'll let you know. But it'll be safe. Trust me. Now, can we give it a rest? It's been a very bad few days for all of us, and you're not making it any easier."

"Well, pardon me!" I exclaimed, and then lapsed into silence. There wasn't a lot more I could say at the moment, but I was damned if I was going to allow him to use Connie's safety in some kind of enticement trap – especially where this monster was concerned. For the present, I thought, I would keep my counsel. But – trust him? Like hell I would!

Our heated debate was quickly put to one side after we arrived at the temporary morgue and engaged ourselves in discussion with the pathologists. There were four of them carrying out the macabre task of establishing the cause of death of the 11 children, and also determining those characteristics that would help in identification.

The senior pathologist, a woman in her mid-fifties who I knew (from attending post-mortems at the Birmingham morgue), was able to tell us that one of the bodies was already identified as that of Josephine Marsden; but, so far, she was unable to tell us if the body of Lisa, the child taken from the park, was amongst the others. She also informed us that a team of experienced counsellors were on hand to help the parents, who would be contacted progressively to corroborate identification of the children.

So far, five of the eleven autopsies were complete; the cause of death was identical in each case. Each of the children had been sexually violated, either concurrently with, or consecutive to, death by strangulation. A police officer, in accord with the law, was in attendance at every one of the autopsies. From the grim looks on their faces I would have suggested they were also in need of counselling.

Forensics had finished at the site, but I noticed a couple of the team were present in the temporary morgue, no doubt examining the remains of the children for any further forensic evidence. It was an unenviable task; in some cases the bodies were in an advanced state of decomposition. And I thought my job was difficult enough; I positively shuddered at what they had to be going through.

Just then, Jim called me over.

"We're wanted back at the station," he said curtly. "The superintendent wants us in conference. Evidently he's already contacted Paul Simmons – he'll be joining us there. And so will Detective Chief Superintendent Thompson from the National Crime Squad," he added.

"Are they taking the case away from us?"

"Dunno. It sounds like it, though; but I don't expect Phil Connors to give in without a fight.

"Let's go and find out, shall we?"

We didn't speak on the way back to the station. Obviously we were still angry at each other following our altercation earlier. I was damned, though, if I was going to hold out an olive branch, however childish that might seem. It also crossed my mind that, if we were removed from the case, then it might be no bad thing, given Jim's nonsensical idea to use Connie in a honey trap. Or was I just being bitchy, I asked myself.

CHAPTER FIFTY-FOUR

Detective Chief Superintendent Thompson and I established an immediate understanding – we took an instant dislike to each other! He wasn't a man you could easily like. The chief wasn't merely big; he was huge and grossly overweight. He must have been around six four or five, and weighed in the region of 18 stone, dwarfing everyone else in the room. I put him at no more than mid- forties – young for a DCS. His hair was thick, as were his eyebrows, framing dark, intense eyes that appeared to be constantly glaring at you. Everything about him was overpowering: his heavily jowled face, his bull-like neck, perched on immense shoulders. I imagined his appearance was something he had learnt to take full advantage of. It came as no surprise, either, to discover that he was completely chauvinistic, making little attempt to disguise his contempt of women officers. I drew an immediate comparison between him and our old DCI, except he was much senior in rank.

I was reminded of a passage in a book my mother once passed on to me to read, called *The Moon's a Balloon* (the autobiography of David Niven), where he said: "Have you ever had the feeling things are so bad, they can't possibly go any worse? And then they do!" I could only think David Niven must have crossed paths at some time with the chief! I was also curious to discover how Jim and he would interact. I didn't have to wait long to find out.

There were eight of us around the table, including the DCS and Dr Simmons. The superintendent was present, along with Frank Kewell, Peter Corkhill and Peter Durning; Jim and I completed the assembly.

After the perfunctory introductions the DCS said, in a voice as gruff as his demeanour, "I want you to understand that I am here solely as an observer; it's not my intention to replace the officer-in-charge on this case. However, as you all know, the Police Authority per se is coming in for an awful lot of flack, not just from the various media but also the many institutions that have a vested interest in child abuse cases. As a result, questions are being raised at ministerial level in London, and I've been assigned the task of providing answers. I trust you people here today will be able to answer those questions to my satisfaction."

"And if we can't?" Jim asked, a distinct chill in his tone.

"You're not going to make this difficult for me, Chief Inspector, are you?"

"No, sir. Not at all. I just don't appreciate having my intelligence insulted by having patronising bullshit dumped on me."

"Jim!" Superintendent Connors interjected. "Can we calm down here? We have a common objective in solving this case; getting unnecessarily defensive is not the right way to go about that – don't you agree?"

Jim shrugged and waved a hand towards everyone around the table. "All of us here have worked our balls off, day and night, to achieve that, Phil. I don't think it's being defensive to react when a senior officer from Scotland Yard is suddenly brought in over our heads unannounced, and patronises us. Don't you agree?" he added sarcastically.

The superintendent's face coloured at the obvious slight, whilst DCS Thompson's facial expression remained belligerently unchanged. He was well prepared for a fight; I was glad it wasn't me who was taking him on.

"Let's cut the infighting, shall we?" he barked. "I'm not here to criticise the West Midlands force, nor to step on anybody's toes deliberately, but – whether you like it or not – London intends to raise the profile of this case nationally, and I've been sent here as part of that exercise. Now, it'll make my job a lot easier if I do have your co-operation, but, with or without it, I fully intend to complete my job, and if anyone doesn't like that, or finds it in any way unacceptable, then I suggest you make your position known here and now.

"Chief inspector, I'm sorry we got off to a bad start, and I hope we can correct that. Your excellent endeavours in this case are, believe me, well documented, and I trust you'll accept my word that I've no intention of undermining you. Why don't we agree that I'm here purely to supplement both yourself and the superintendent? So, are you willing to put your reservations to one side and see if we can work together?"

Jim nodded his agreement. "Since you put it like that, chief – yes, I can accept that. Where do you want to start?"

The sigh of relief from each of us was distinctly audible around the table, and I felt the tension easing. It was clear, however, that Jim still regarded the presence of the DCS as interference, and I wondered just how long this temporary truce would last.

"I've been going through the various reports on the case," the chief began, "and I have to say they're very thorough and professional. However, there are one or two matters that are puzzling London regarding to the source of some of your information. Now, in the normal course of events, no one would dream of questioning this; but, since (as I've already said) this is a case of national – if not international – import, these questions need to be answered."

"We'll do our best, sir," Jim conceded. Personally I wasn't so sure. Why did I have the distinct impression he was fishing in the murky waters of psychic phenomena?

"Good. Well, let me start at the very beginning, may I? With the disappearance of the child called Alice, Alice Newton, back in '99. That was when your force made the startling discovery of a burial ground in the woods, when, in your search for the missing child, you uncovered a total of seven bodies – including, I might add, that of the child, Alice. Am I right so far?"

We all, other than Peter Durning, nodded.

"So, that would be my first question. Who gave you the tip-off where to look for the body? You see, it's puzzling, because the only person who'd possibly know of the bodies' existence would be the killer – and he'd be unlikely to tell you, wouldn't he?"

Before Jim, or the superintendent, could respond, the DCS picked up the thread again. "Then we had a long period of 'apparent' inactivity on the part of the paedophile, didn't we? Just over four years, in fact. Then, another child goes missing. Let me see..." (he examined his notes in the file) "...Yes – here we are: a Josephine Marsden, abducted from outside her school in Solihull. That would be – what? – Three months ago, or thereabouts?"

"Is this absolutely necessary?" Jim asked.

The chief glowered at him, as if it were Jim who was now insulting *his* intelligence.

"Indulge me, Chief Inspector, will you? All will be revealed presently. Now, where was I? Oh yes; Josephine Marsden. Now, it is fully explained how you found the child's clothes in that particular field as you did. And I can also understand how the Marsdens came to know their child was dead before you did. Nothing particularly esoteric about either of those incidents…"

"Oh, Christ!" I thought. I was right. This is where he was leading us.

"But this was followed by the abduction of the child, Lucy, from the children's playground a couple of weeks ago. The question – again – that is puzzling us, and – again – it is not covered in any of the reports, is how could you possibly know what make of vehicle the assailant was driving? There were no direct eyewitnesses, other than those already mentioned in the file."

Once again Jim tried to interrupt and was stopped by the raised hand of the DCS.

"Bear with me a little longer. Next we come to the events of the last few days. The discovery of the bodies in the old coalmine shaft. Now, once again, according to your file records, we have evidence of yet another amazing piece of detection work. Someone, unnamed, happens to give the force a tip-off, that in the wilds of Derbyshire, a mile below the surface, you'll find the bodies of another 11 children, including the missing Josephine Marsden – murdered, no doubt, by the same perpetrator as the other children."

He leant back in his chair, looking every inch like a predatory gorilla, and bunched his huge hands together, almost as if he was trying to make them disappear. For a moment I had a vision of him, naked, climbing on top of me, not so much for sex but to crush me to death. Momentarily, I felt myself unintentionally giggling.

"You find something funny in all this, Sergeant?"

"No, sir," I choked. "I'm sorry; I was distracted."

He glared at me, making me feel very small.

"So," he continued, "we now come to the question of the girl – Connie Rowden, isn't it?"

"I was beginning to wonder what I was doing here," Paul said. "Is that what this is all about? ...My patient?"

"If you like, yes. But there's a lot more to it than that, doctor, isn't there?"

"Perhaps it would be more helpful, Chief Superintendent, if you were to get to the point, instead of indulging in sophistry," the superintendent said caustically.

"The point is, my dear fellow, that on the one hand we have a whole range of seemingly unexplained phenomena going on - no file notes, in fact no record of any description where they came from, and on the other hand we've a young lady being afforded the highest possible security for her personal protection, again with neither formal justification nor explanation. Now, if we add this catalogue of events together, what do we have?"

"Is that a rhetorical question, sir?" Jim asked, an expression of pure innocence on his face.

"Don't fuck with me, Chief Inspector! You know exactly what I'm getting at. Let me make it crystal clear for you. This station's under siege from the world's media; but so's London, and we're determined to make sure the British Police Authority doesn't end up the laughing stock of the Western world.

"And in case any of you might think we're completely stupid, let me point out that one or two questions were raised at Scotland Yard when you found the first burial site. The only reason the matter was never followed up was because you managed to contain the publicity at an acceptable level. That's no longer the case; as I've said, we now have to treat this as an international issue, and we don't deal with cases of this magnitude by delegating them to the local force. That would be irresponsible of us. So, we need answers to those questions, namely: where did your information come from regarding the events I have outlined? Just who is this Connie Rowden? And are our two concerns interrelated?

"Is that succinct enough for you, Superintendent? Or do you still believe it's sophistry as you pretentiously put it?"

The superintendent cleared his throat nervously, and then shook his head in disagreement.

"You said you were going to make it clearer, Chief, but, I'm sorry, it still isn't clear to me," he commented. "You're surely not expecting us to reveal the sources of our information, are you?"

"It isn't clear to me, either," Frank added. At the same time I noticed that Peter Corkhill was also shaking his head. Jim, on the other hand, remained silent – as I did, on the basis that I didn't think the DCS was particularly seeking my response.

The chief superintendent sighed, as if he were disappointed. "Okay," he replied. "Since you people obtusely refuse to understand the subtle approach, I'll spell it out for you by removing the sagacity."

"Bloody hell!" I thought. I wasn't half hearing some fancy words since I started on this case!

"Someone, somehow, has been furnishing this force with information regarding these killings, including the whereabouts of burial sites, that could only have originated either from the killer himself – which we have already discounted – or from sources of, shall we say, an esoteric nature. Then a mystery figure appears in the name of Connie Rowden – let me see... Yes, here we are," he said, after checking his notes once more. "She was hospitalised in Forest Hills psychiatric hospital in '99 – coincidental year that, wasn't it? – where she stayed till only a few months ago, when she transferred to Ashworth House, a psychiatric halfway house establishment. She's resided there, with full police protection, up to today, when a murder occurred in the building; the murder, in fact, of the housekeeper – without, I might add, any apparent motive.

"Now, I appreciate you haven't yet had the opportunity of filing a report on this matter, but – and please tell me if I am wrong – here we have yet another coincidence involving the ubiquitous Miss Rowden.

"I'll finish my preamble with one final and decisive point. As of today, the West Midland force is no longer in a position to maintain its veil of confidentiality over this situation, because, gentlemen – and Sergeant," he said, pointing towards me "– the cat is literally out of the bag. Unknown to you, your CID's been under investigation for some time now, by a television documentary company intent on publicly disclosing your various methods of detection, including – I might add – some detailed aspects of the role of your Connie Rowden."

Jim glanced across at me and a look of understanding passed between us. Evidently we were both thinking the same thing; it had to be the persistent interviewer at the burial site – the one who wanted to know where our tip-off had come from.

"We in London know this to be true," the chief continued, "because the television company's asked to interview the commander of the

National Crime Unit, and we have already been given a brief on the format.

"There," he said on a point of conclusion; "that should be clarification enough – even for you people. Now I demand some answers. Who'd like to begin? How about you, Doctor? This young lady is presumably still your patient; what can you tell me about her? And, more importantly, how exactly does she fit into the scheme of things?"

"Can I say something first?" I interjected.

He nodded assent. "If you must, and it's relevant," he said curtly.

"Well, I'd like to know, Sir, if Connie – Miss Rowden – is likely to have her name splashed over the front pages of the newspapers and on television in the very near future. Because, if she is, it'll put her in an extremely dangerous position; it's not just her safety, it's *her life* that'll be at risk."

The chief leaned forward intently. "The very purpose of my presence here, sergeant, is to cut right through this obscure crap you insist on peddling and get at the truth. And if this young lady's life is placed in jeopardy it will be entirely down to your secretive code of practice. So, I demand you tell me just what the hell you are talking about. And again, if you don't mind, I prefer to begin at the beginning." He pointed a finger at me – threateningly, I thought. "Tell me who this bloody girl is, will you?"

So I told him. From the very beginning, which is what he had 'demanded', and I watched his face remain totally impassive throughout my statement. From time to time he made a note of certain things I had said, which no doubt he would refer back to later, but other than that he didn't interrupt.

I led off with my first meeting with Connie's mother, and how that had moved on to her leading a search party into the woods and straight to where the septic tank was that contained the bodies of the seven children. At no time did I make any attempt to apologise for my involvement, nor for my subsequent friendship with Connie. I explained to the chief the nature of her visions, and the dramatic effect they had upon her, and how the discovery of the bodies in the woods had caused her breakdown. It was only on hearing this that he interrupted.

"Is that correct, doctor?" he asked Paul.

"Yes. She experienced a disassociative fugue as a direct result of the trauma."

"Do you mind explaining exactly what that is – in layman's terms, I mean."

"In essence, it means that a part of the memory area of the brain shuts down completely, in order to block out any painful or intolerable experiences. It's the mind's way of coping with a traumatic stress situation. Sometimes that particular part of the memory never returns – and so far that's the case with Connie."

The DCS looked at Paul in bewilderment. "Surely, you're not telling me you kept her in a psychiatric hospital for over four years because she was suffering from amnesia?"

It was Paul's turn to glare at him, as if he couldn't believe anyone could be so stupid. "Don't be ridiculous," he snapped. "The child was totally dysfunctional in the beginning, displaying all the symptoms of cataleptic collapse. It was more than a year before she could speak, and even today she has absolutely no knowledge of the events before her breakdown. And" (this time he was the one to point an accusing finger at the DCS) "she remains mentally fragile, and the type of publicity you just referred to could induce a further and intractable mental disintegration."

"Thank you, Doctor," he said acidly. "Continue with your statement, Sergeant."

I took him through the various phases of my relationship with Connie, including the vision she had experienced of Josephine Marsden's abduction, followed by her insight into the clothes left in the field, and then on to the subsequent vision of Josephine's body being dumped down the mine shaft. I told him also of the vision she had had, in advance, of the incident in the park when Lisa was abducted, and how Connie was able to describe the vehicle involved, including the type, the colour and a partial registration number. And, more to the point, how she was subsequently proved correct in every detail.

I then took the DCS through the process of elimination we had adopted in identifying the abandoned coalmine used as the burial ground for the 11 murdered children. Finally, I recounted Connie's abject terror of the killer, how she was convinced he knew who she was, and how he was intent on killing her, adding that this was the principal rationale in providing her with round-the-clock police protection.

When I had finished I sat back in my chair and let out a deep breath at the stress of reliving the experiences again.

There was silence around the table. I noticed the superintendent had lost all colour from his face, whilst Jim sat there silent and with a grim expression. Paul leant across from the other side of the table where he was sitting and gave my hand a reassuring grip. Frank was staring at the DCS, openly hostile, and even the two Peters gave me an encouraging glance.

"You seem to be the principal 'agent provocateur' in all this," the chief said. "Would that be true?"

I nodded, feeling at the same time there was nothing left for me to say.

"And you, Superintendent? Were you aware that all this was taking place? In fact, perhaps it was you who sanctioned it – would that be correct?"

"No. He did *not* sanction it," Jim said harshly. "In fact, to be fair, the super refused to be involved in any of what you describe as 'esoteric nonsense'. I was the officer who took the responsibility, and I was the one who sanctioned it. So, if you want to blame someone for this, I'm your man."

The DCS ignored him. "Please answer my question, Superintendent, will you?"

"If I sanctioned it, then it was by omission. And the reason there's no reference in the official reports to Miss Rowden's contribution is because those were my specific orders. What the DCI's told you is essentially accurate; of course, I knew about the girl's psychic input, but I chose, from a formal point of view, to disregard it. Does that fully answer your question, Chief Superintendent?"

"Yes. Quite. However, your disregard of the full facts is now likely to backfire, not only on you and the West Midlands force, but also on the police authorities. And we must find a way of dealing with that satisfactorily."

"How do you suggest we achieve that?" Jim asked. "We can hardly falsify the records, can we?"

"I'm not advocating we go that far, no. But I don't see the harm in updating the files retrospectively. Do any of you?"

"Wait a minute, Chief," the superintendent said. "Am I understanding you correctly? You want us now to belatedly introduce this young lady into the case records, as a kind of addendum?"

The DCS thrust his face belligerently towards the superintendent, who visibly flinched at the perceived threat. "Did this young lady, Connie Rowden, play a somewhat vital role in the proceedings, or not?"

"Well, yes. We've already conceded that."

"And you chose to overlook this because you believed it might be – shall we say – embarrassing, for the force, if it were ever revealed you'd involved a psychic in a serious criminal case?"

The DCS took the ensuing silence as an acknowledgement he was correct. "So, enlighten me, Superintendent; which do you find the more embarrassing? A partial admission of the truth, however uncomfortable that might be, or a revelation by a national television company that you deliberately omitted key elements of the investigation from the police records?"

The superintendent swallowed, as if he were having difficulty breathing. "I don't believe you expect me to answer that." He looked over towards me. "As the chief points out, you're the principal character in this charade, so I'll leave it to you to correct the records accordingly."

"When you do," the DCS said, "keep your litany to the minimum; in other words, Sergeant, no embellishments. Understood?"

"Sir? Would you mind elaborating on that?"

I received another glare, this time in exasperation. When he spoke again it was slowly and deliberately, as if he was speaking to a retard. "What I require you to do, Sergeant, is to make reference in the official records that this police department used the services of a psychic in the hunt for the killer; not altogether uncommon these days in detection procedures, in my experience. That, I believe, will just about pass the test of credibility.

"However, what you must not do – insofar as the records are concerned – is formalise the information you purport to have received from this girl's visions. I can accept an oblique reference to it – in other words, you were given some convoluted guidance as to the whereabouts of the burial sites – but you must say that it was police detection that was entirely responsible for identifying them and not some medium's imagination. There, is that sufficient briefing for you, Sergeant? Or would you prefer I did the job for you?"

"It couldn't be plainer, sir," I conceded, trying not to let him intimidate me.

"And police protection for Connie?" Jim demanded.

"You withdraw it. Totally and immediately. Weren't you listening, Chief Inspector? We have to divert the limelight from this girl by reducing not only her involvement but also the importance of her contribution. Have you got that, Chief Inspector?"

"Jesus!" I thought, as I felt my world spinning out of control. It's an open invitation to murder. This guy was completely remorseless; he couldn't give a shit about Connie's safety. All he was concerned with was saving the face of the police establishment; he didn't even appear to be that anxious about apprehending the killer. Not once had he mentioned that as being the primary objective in prosecuting this case. Well, fuck you, Mister Detective Chief Superintendent!

I was about to say as much when Jim, bless him, addressing the superintendent, said: "When Miss Crossley has finished updating the records, Superintendent, I'd like to formally insist that she goes on indefinite sick leave. It's patently obvious to me that she still hasn't recovered from her injury and she needs more time to convalesce."

The chief superintendent frowned at this, as though it were some kind of imposition. "That's a domestic matter, surely? You don't need my approval for officers' sick leave."

"I'll second that," Paul said. He then pointed a finger admonishingly. "I warned you about overdoing things, Angie."

"And if it's alright with you, sir, I'm *au fait* with Miss Rowden's involvement, and I'd be happy to correct the files," Frank added for good measure. He then glanced at me and said, "So you can get off straightaway, Sergeant."

"Is there something going on here I should know about?" the DCS growled.

"Sir." It was Jim again. "If you care to check the files again you'll discover that Sergeant Crossley was recently the victim of a pretty vicious attack; she sustained a severe blow to the head that put her in hospital. I think she needs a break."

"Thank you, sir," I said, before any further comments could be passed. I then got the hell out of there, with a surreptitious parting wink from Jim.

I collected one or two personal files from the incident room, ordered a squad car to take me to Jim's apartment, and at the same time placed a request for my own police vehicle to be collected from Jim's. I would use Jim's spare car whilst I was at his apartment.

All the way back I kept thinking what an inhuman bastard the DCS was. He had shown not one ounce of compassion for the traumas Connie had endured, and not one expression of gratitude for all the assistance she had given the police. I was only grateful I didn't have to report directly to him; it would be a very short-lived relationship. On the other hand, Jim had shared an identical feeling to mine when he created the situation where my friend was not abandoned to her own resources. It was simply out of the question that Connie's police protection should be removed, regardless of what that SOB had declared, but, undeniably, it would have to be scaled down from its present level. In turn, that meant I would have to be with her night and day, but I resolved to equalise the contest with the paedophile by furnishing the two of us with an essentially improved protection system.

CHAPTER FIFTY-FIVE

Connie was out when I let myself into the flat. She had left a note saying she had gone shopping with Steve Harrison (I had made sure she had sufficient funds to re-equip herself with clothes) and as it was late-night shopping she wouldn't be back for some time. So I twiddled my thumbs for a while and made a couple of telephone calls. Eventually I took myself off in the direction of Bilston – a small town on the outskirts of Wolverhampton.

The house I was heading for was situated in the heart of the Caribbean district, and the man I wanted to speak with was a native of that part of the world. I was lucky; I'd already checked that Henry was at home that evening.

"Unexpected pleasure, Sergeant," he grinned at me when he opened the door. "Is this a social call?"

"Piss off, Henry," I grinned back at him. Henry was the local fixer – a black, five foot six piece of dynamite, bursting with energy. If ever you wanted anything, either hardware or information, he was the man to see. He was also something of an outrageous character, with his bright, colourful clothes, eccentric mannerisms and exaggerated West Indian accent. And he had the whitest set of teeth I think I had ever seen – something he was constantly displaying. What was not commonly known about Henry was that he held an honours degree in electronics from Wolverhampton Technical College. Had he pursued a worthwhile career, by now there is no doubt he would have been a senior executive with one of the computer companies. But Henry preferred his own way of making a living; he insisted it was less boring!

I followed him into the house and along a darkened hallway into a dimly lit lounge. He appeared to be alone in the house, which suited my purposes. Beckoning to one of the lounge chairs, he asked, "So, how can I be of service to me favourite policewoman?"

"I'm the only policewoman you know, Henry, so you can cut the bullshit. I want something from you."

"Well now, why I am not surprised? Are you calling in old favours, Sarge?"

"You're damned right I am. What I am after is a tracer, but one with an extended range. Does such a thing exist?"

"You mean like a personal 'bug'?"

"You've got it."

He scratched his chin thoughtfully. "It depends whether you want it on a vehicle or on someone's body. Now, a car be no problem, 'cos you can carry the receiver in your own vehicle. But a long-range transmitter on a person is quite another t'ing. I'd have to think about that, Missy Crossley. When are you needing it?"

"Yesterday, Henry. That's how long you get to think about it. And for a person, not a vehicle. Can it be done or not?"

This time he played with his Rastafarian locks for a few minutes, and then rolled his eyes as if he had just emerged from the jungle and was glimpsing civilisation for the first time. "Anything's possible, I suppose," he continued. "But there ain't nothing available like that on the market, right now. I got to modify something for you. It won't be easy."

"I realise that, Henry. That's why I'm here. When can you get it done for me?"

"Fuck me, Sarge; you wanna miracle? 'As quick as I can' is the answer. Is that soon enough?"

"Tomorrow, Henry, dear Henry. I'll call by late afternoon tomorrow. Don't let me down, will you? This is very important."

"And very illegal," he commented, with yet another of his wide grins. He held his hands out defensively as I made a move towards him. "Joke, Sarge; just my lickle joke. I'll do me best for you, I promise. You come on by tomorrow; I'll have somethin' for you."

* * * * * * * * *

In fact, my visit to Henry had not been entirely prompted by the DCS's dictates about Connie; it was something I had given thought to for some time, in particular my concern at the paedophile's ability to penetrate the police screens almost at will. I was worried he might go for Connie by way of another abduction, probably when we least expected it. What I needed from Henry was a device that, in the event Connie was snatched, she would be wearing that would assist me in tracing her over an extended distance. I just prayed that Henry could produce the results.

When I let myself into the flat, Connie was already there with Pauline Wilkins. So was Jim, which surprised me; I didn't expect we would have a full complement after today's instructions. Not surprisingly, Jim looked absolutely exhausted; he could hardly keep his eyes open.

"I've arranged for Pauline to spend the night here with Connie - purely as a friend," he informed me. "But from tomorrow you and I are on our own; I've put Connie in the picture, so we all know what we've got to do."

"Thank you, Jim," I said, genuinely meaning it. "Has the DCS left?"

"Has he hell! He intends to stay put for the duration to make sure we don't fuck up any more. From now on he handles all press statements and interviews, and he insists on overseeing our progression of the case. It's going to be like having Dracula permanently on our shoulders. You're okay, though, Ange; you're well out of it. But I still expect you to keep involved, even if it's only at the end of the telephone.

"Now, if you don't mind, ladies, I'm going to bed before I collapse. And if the phone rings, Ange – don't answer it." He pointed towards Pauline. "And that goes for you too, young lady; none of you are supposed to be here."

"Night, Jim."

I made sure all the doors were locked and bolted, the CCTV Cameras were functioning as they should be, then quickly followed him, feeling a little guilty about depriving him of the master bedroom. But I was whacked myself, so I left Connie and Pauline to their own devices.

CHAPTER FIFTY-SIX

The next morning Connie and I left Jim still sleeping whilst we went on a further shopping expedition to complete her wardrobe. Pauline quickly made off in her own car. We spent most of the day in Wolverhampton, exhausting my credit card, and had lunch at a very nice bistro in the centre. I then put Connie in the picture about my visit the previous day to Henry's, and what my plan was – assuming it was workable. She thought the idea of wearing a tag was quite exciting; that was, until I explained my anxieties about the killer, when she visibly paled. I didn't like having to do that to her but it was a preferable alternative to complacency.

Later that afternoon, accompanied by Connie, I knocked once again on Henry's door, and was welcomed by the same incorrigible grin – as if he hadn't seen me for years.

"Come in, come in, Sarge," he chuckled, leading the way again.

"Any luck, Henry?" I asked after we were all seated in the lounge.

"If you only knew the t'ings I have to go through for my favourite policewoman," he preambled.

I said nothing, knowing he would get to the point only when it suited him. The appearance of his cat – a large, overweight and no doubt thoroughly spoilt ginger tom – diverted Connie's attention. He had jumped on her knee immediately he spotted her and began rubbing himself against her hand.

"Well, missy, after a lot of ingenuity – and genius too, I might add – I believe I have the very t'ing you are looking for." He went over to a bureau and retrieved a small box from one of the drawers.

"*Voilà!*" he exclaimed in triumph. "Just look what clever old Henry's rustled up for you."

The box contained a small, wafer-thin card, about an inch square, rather like an electronic computer board.

"Now, if you let me have your mobile for a few minutes, I'll key it into this device. Then, you can not only follow the person wearing it from a distance of three miles, you will also be able to hear any conversations taking place."

I handed him my mobile, and he began disassembling it, vaguely humming some Caribbean reggae tune as he did so. It took him only a few minutes to complete the task. "So who's a clever boy, then?" he said, handing it back to me.

"You are, of course, Henry. You are a natural born genius. Now, all you have to do is show me how it works."

"Well, the bestest way of all would be if the wearer agreed for you to fit it into the heel of a shoe. Then, all it would take is the click of a tiny switch, and it be connected to your mobile. I've also added, if you look, a tiny direction monitor to your phone so you can follow the signal. But, I dunno who you be buggin' - how you install it's up to you."

I gestured towards Connie. "She's the *buggee*," I confirmed. "And here" (I pulled from a plastic bag a pair of new, flat-heeled shoes that we had bought that morning) "are the shoes!"

"Man, you've thought of everything! You'll have to give me about half an hour to play with these," he said, holding up the shoes. "And my tools are in the back. So, why don't I show you the kitchen and you make yourself and the little lady here a nice cup of Jamaican coffee? Genuine Blue Mountain stylee."

"Lead the way, Einstein."

He was grinning broadly again as we followed him into the cramped but serviceable cooking area he called a kitchen. But he was as good as his word; in little more than the time he had stipulated, he was back with the shoes.

"You're lucky these ain't stilettos," he remarked. "Anyhow, here you go, Sarge. All done – just the way you wanted."

"What do we have to do to turn it on, Henry?"

He turned the shoe over and pointed to a micro switch placed on the inside ridge of the heel.

"You just click this, like so, and – bingo!"

My mobile immediately began ringing. "No," he said, as I instinctively went to answer it; "you don't answer it, babe. It's gonna ring three times and then you are automatically connected to the trace."

Which it did. Henry then pointed out the display on the mobile, which was now lit a bright green colour, highlighting a tiny arrow that was pointing towards Connie.

"So, you can follow her, and at the same time listen in to any conversation. Go back in the kitchen, darling, and say something out loud, will you?"

Her voice came through loud and clear, as if it were a normal mobile phone conversation.

"And how far did you say the range of this is, Henry?"

"Give or take, it's about three miles. Three beautiful miles!"

"There's just one slight problem, Henry. How will I know where she is, or how far away we are from her?"

"Well, you won't know exactly how far away you be – 'cept you know it can't be more than three miles. And where she is? You keep following the green arrow; it have a tiny magnetic compass always pointing to the north, and it change colour the closer you are – until you're on top o' her, when it goes to red."

"And how long will the battery last?"

He scratched his chin thoughtfully. "I reckon you'll have about half the normal life of your mobile phone battery; what's that? ...About eight hours in all? So, estimate half that and you'll be fine."

I kissed him on the cheek. "Henry, you truly are a genius."

He touched his cheek and then grinned again. "Two conditions, Sargie. One, this repays all favours to date and we don't say nuthin' to no one? Agreed?"

I nodded. "And the second one?"

"When you've finished with this little baby you let me have it back. I can make a fortune outta this sweetheart."

"I agree, Henry. And I hope it'll be sooner than you expect." I took hold of Connie's hand to lead her out of the room. "Bye-bye, Sweetie. See you soon."

* * * * * * * * *

I quite enjoyed the next few days with Connie. We had the flat to ourselves during the day. We didn't see a lot of Jim during the evening either; he seemed to be permanently at the beck and call of the DCS and I missed him. And when we felt like it we went shopping in Birmingham, or sometimes went to the cinema. One day we caught the train from New Street station and spent a very pleasant day in London, shopping, sightseeing and taking in one of the many musicals at a theatre in the West End.

Wherever we went I insisted Connie wore the same pair of shoes. We tried the gadget out that time in London, when I gave her a ten-minute start and then I had to see if I could find her. Just in case I couldn't, we had pre-arranged where to meet. It was unnecessary; the device led me straight to her. And we found ourselves giggling again like a couple of schoolgirls somewhere in the heart of Soho.

Sadly, the good times ended when we both attended Sheila's funeral. Funerals are not, of course, intended to be joyous occasions, but I found this one particularly distressing. When someone you love has been suddenly and horribly deprived of life, the emotions that come to the surface are unlike those of a normal bereavement, where eulogies are read and family and friends remember all the nice things the deceased has said and done in his or her lifetime. This was more the weeping and gnashing of teeth, through a mixture of grief and rage at the violation of a relatively young woman. It was horrible, to say the least, and one of the most affected by it was Connie, who, in some juvenile way, wanted to hold herself partly responsible – despite my pleas to the contrary. I just hoped she wasn't developing her old habit of self-guilt again.

The whole sad affair was heavily policed from start to finish, in the unlikely event the killer would wish to witness the results of his barbarous deprival of the right to life. Both Connie and I ended the service in tears; this was our friend we were burying, not some unknown victim of a vicious predator. The best I was able to manage in the form of sympathy was to squeeze the arm of Sheila's mother.

"I know," she said tearfully; "we're not supposed to bury our children, are we?"

I shook my head and had to walk away, completely choked with the emotion of it all.

Of the killer, so far as we could tell, there was no sight of him anywhere in or around the cemetery. As we were leaving at the end of the service, Jim came over for a word.

"We don't seem to be getting anywhere," he commented. "In fact, since that pompous arsehole turned up we've come to a complete standstill."

I presumed he was referring to the DCS, although I couldn't reconcile his arrival with the lack of progress.

"What about the media, or the television people and that documentary he threatened us with? Any developments there, Jim?"

He appeared decidedly uncomfortable at the question, as if he were keeping something from me.

"That's what I wanted to tell you both. Channel Four's inserting a special documentary on the case this Friday evening – prime time. Evidently the commander of the National Crime Unit has decided, in his wisdom, to grant them the interview they were after; so they've got the full Monty."

"Is Connie's name mentioned?" I asked with a certain trepidation.

He nodded his head in confirmation. "Apparently we all get a mention, Ange – pictures too. Oh, and we all get a hell of a slating, from what my informants tell me. I suppose it's only to be expected, if you think about it. This monster," (he gestured towards Sheila's newly opened grave site) "apart from poor Sheila, has murdered 19 innocent children that we're aware of, and despite everything we've done the bastard's still at large." He shrugged; almost an acknowledgement of failure, I thought.

It was at this point that Connie decided to take up the cudgels, for reasons I could only put down to the unjustified guilt she was feeling over Sheila's death. "Angie told me some days ago, Jim, that you had an idea trap him by relaxing my police protection. Do you still think it might work?"

He shook his head. "No, I'm no longer as convinced. Oh, it might have seemed like a good idea at the time – to me, anyway, although (as I'm sure you're already aware) Ange here was vigorously opposed to it. Now I think it'd be too dangerous. The idea was to reduce your cover, but only visibly, to persuade him you'd become an easy target; behind the scenes it would, if anything, have been strengthened to ensure we got him. But now we haven't got a behind-the-scenes unit to handle it. In fact, we've got bugger all... Just us three left to cover your protection."

Connie looked thoughtful for a while, as if she were studying the implications of Jim's analysis of the situation.

"I'm sure you're right," she said eventually. "But, if this telly programme's going to blab about my bit in the investigation, they'll be giving this fucker everything he wants to know on a plate?"

"I'd be a liar if I said it hadn't crossed my mind," Jim admitted. "But what exactly we do about it is a different matter. For starters, no one knows where you're living – and the TV people aren't going to reveal that. And you've got Ange with you all day and night, with me, and young Harrison, backing her up at night. Short of having a squad car with armed officers outside the door 24/7, I don't see what else we can do. And a plan along the lines I had in mind is not something that is open to improvisation. Have you any thoughts on the subject, Ange?"

"No. I admit the documentary's a worry – something we could all do without – but, I agree with you, it's hardly likely to provide our killer with any information he hasn't already got. So, I suggest we sit tight, and do nothing more than we're doing already. How about you, Connie? You've obviously got some ideas; care to share them with us?"

"Yes. Why not let it slip that I'm staying at your place, Jim? If we give him that piece of information it's bound to persuade him to make a move."

Jim and I let out deep, simultaneous sighs at the suggestion.

"Connie! This ain't the movies, you know," Jim said; "where everything you want to happen goes according to plan, and the 'goodies' always win. This is real life, and we're dealing with a clever and vicious murderer. And call me old fashioned, but I don't think they play by the rules. You're talking about a totally unacceptable risk; I wouldn't even let my hairy-arsed coppers take a chance like that without highly trained and professional back-up people. Nope – it's completely out of the question. Anyway, all that aside, can I remind you you're still a minor. At least for a few more days. So, 'keep your head down' is the best advice I can give you, and leave the police work to the police. Okay?" he ended, smiling.

"S'pose so," she conceded. "It just seems a pity to waste the opportunity. Oh, and by the way, you two, there's no reason why you should know this, but on Friday of this week I cease to be a minor –as you put it."

"She'll be 18 on Friday, Jim."

"I know. You've already told me God knows how many times. How could I possibly forget?"

"You know?" she said excitedly. "Great! Are we going to celebrate, Angie? I mean, do I have any money to take you guys out somewhere? ...Somewhere really nice?"

"You won't need any money, Connie. It was going to be a surprise, but I don't see any point now you've brought it up yourself. We've arranged a dinner party for you at Alphonso's for Friday evening."

"You have? Fantastic! Who else is coming?"

"Well, we've invited Paul – he's really looking forward to it – and, of course, there's Jim and me. Oh," I added, as if it were an afterthought, "I thought you might like Steve Harrison to come along as well. Shall I ask him?"

She thumped my arm playfully. "That'll be fab, Angie." She waved her arms in the air like a football fan. "I'll be an adult!" she cried. "Can you believe that? ...For the first time in my life, I'll be an adult!"

Jim was still chuckling when he left us to return to the station to meet up with his antagonist, the DCS. I couldn't work out why, but I was left with one of those uneasy feelings. Call it intuition, call it mistrust, but something was telling me that Connie had some devious scheme in mind. Whatever it was, I would bet my life it would be dangerous – for her!

CHAPTER FIFTY-SEVEN

The morning of Connie's birthday we found ourselves yet again under siege from an army of media and television crews parked outside the front of Jim's apartment building. The intercom system in the hallway was constantly buzzing, as was the house phone.

I flicked on the teletext to see if that could provide a clue as to just what the hell was going on, and there it was, in headline format:

Police employ the services of young psychic in hunt for child killer

Not only did it clearly spell out Connie's name, with a preview of the television documentary due for transmission that evening, it went on to specify that she was currently being 'safeguarded' in the Birmingham suburb of Edgbaston at the apartment of Detective Chief Inspector Robbins, together with Detective Sergeant Crossley, for her own protection.

"Oh, fuck!" Jim exclaimed when he read it. "How the bloody hell did they get hold of that?" He was grim-faced and patently furious at the disclosure. "If I get my hands on whoever did this they'll wish they had never been born."

I pointed towards the bedroom I was sharing with Connie. "I suspect you'll find your informant in there," I said dryly. "No doubt sleeping like a baby."

Jim glared at me, aghast. "You're kidding me, right? What crazy idea prompted her to do that?"

I shook my head in frustration. "I should have warned you, Jim. I'm sorry. I had a gut feeling she was planning something stupid, but I never guessed she could be that irresponsible. She obviously thinks by revealing her whereabouts she can help us trap the killer. The question is: what the hell do we do now?"

"Christ knows! I need to think." He paced about the flat, cup of coffee in one hand and mobile phone in the other. "Frank," he shouted in the phone; "you've heard, have you? Listen; get a squad car round here *pronto*, will you. I've got to try and shift the bloody press mob away out of here. Yeah; soon as you can. Thanks."

"You can't just order them to move," I pointed out. "And, even if they do, they'll be back the moment your back's turned."

"So, what do you suggest? Ignore them?"

"Why not? If you try to move Connie away from here they'll only follow us. Why not play it cool? Insist you don't know what they're talking about. Then, if Connie and I stay put all day, they'll eventually lose interest." I shrugged – an expression of resignation. "I don't see what else we can do. And, anyway," I added, as an afterthought, "the best thing you can do is to deny it; otherwise you really *will* have the DCS on your case."

He gave the matter some thought, still pacing around the room in a temper. "Okay. You're right. We might just get away with that. I can't think of an alternative, anyway, so we'll go with it. I'll go down and wait for the squad car – say a few words to them."

"You'd better calm down a bit first, Jim. You won't convince anyone in that foul mood."

He gave me a quick peck on the cheek. "I'll be alright, Ange. But keep away from the windows, won't you? I'll try to think of a way to get you out of here later." He gestured towards the bedroom. "And tell that little sod I'll wring her neck when I get hold of her. Oh – and wish her a happy birthday for me!"

Initially, I don't think the approach worked too well. The phone still didn't stop ringing for the first hour after Jim had left, but at least the porters were managing to keep the press outside the building, so the intercom was silent. I woke Connie with one hand around her throat.

"This is what Jim is going to do to you when he gets hold of you!" I whispered.

"What? What's going on, Angie?"

"Don't play the little innocent with me, young lady. You know exactly what's going on, since you're the one who's caused it."

She sat upright in the bed, sleep still in her eyes and her hair all tussled. She rubbed her eyes and looked at me in confusion.

"Angie; honest – I don't know what you're talking about. What's going on?"

"The press camped outside the front of the building is what's going on. You trying to tell me you had nothing to do with it?"

"No!" she protested loudly. "I don't know anything about it." I saw her bottom lip begin to tremble, and she looked so crestfallen I couldn't help but believe her. "Angie! Please. Why would I want the press to find out where I'm staying?"

I leant forward and kissed her forehead. "Okay, I believe you. And I don't know how or why, Connie, but someone's found out you're here and blabbed to the media. The only thing I can think is someone followed you here from the college. No doubt one of those fucking vultures outside. Anyway, I'm sorry I blamed you – I thought you might've had some crazy idea of making yourself the bait. And a happy birthday, Sweetheart. Welcome to the adult world."

At least this prompted a smile. "Thank you, Angie. Are they still there – the press?"

I nodded. "Jim went to talk to them, on his way out. He's going to deny you're here, so it looks as though we're stuck indoors till they've disappeared."

"I don't mind. We'll find some way to spend the time until this evening. We're not cancelling the party, are we?"

"Good God, no. We definitely are not cancelling. But if that lot" (I nodded towards the window) "are still hanging around, we'll have to think up some seriously sneaky way of getting us out of here. Maybe Jim'll come up with an idea during the day. Come on, young lady; you get dressed and I'll make you a birthday breakfast."

Connie and I spent the morning spring-cleaning the flat; God only knew when it was last done. I wouldn't have minded but I happened to hate housework; still, I told myself, we were living there, so it was as much in our interest to have the place clean and tidy. At one stage I left Connie to it whilst I went off to make the coffee. Now, *that* I didn't mind doing!

Just when I felt boredom moving in, my mobile went off. It was Jim, checking on the media.

"Has she admitted the leak?" he demanded.

I let out a sigh. "She denies it, Jim. And I believe her. Connie agrees it would've been irresponsible to inform the media where she's staying."

"So how did they find out? Another bloody psychic vision?"

"I don't know, Jim. I suspect either Connie or one of us was followed here. But I don't think it matters now, anyway. Any way you look at it, we're stuck with the problem. The question now is: what we do about it?"

Have they gone yet – the press?"

"Hang on; I'll take a peep out of the window."

There were only two of them left and they didn't appear to be terribly interested – which was probably understandable, considering the weather; once again, it was, quite literally, pouring down.

"There are two of them left, Jim," I informed him. "And, thankfully, they're getting soaked. Shall I invite them in for coffee?"

He growled something indecipherable, then said, "That's two too many. Christ knows how we're going to get you out of there during daylight. I reckon as soon as you show your face the rest of them'll start coming out of the woodwork."

"Did they buy your story this morning?"

"Yeah. Grudgingly, but most of them did. That's probably why the television people have fucked off – I'd guess those two out there are stringers."

"How did you get on with the DCS?"

I could almost see him shrugging. "I effectively told him to piss off – as we agreed. Connie's not at my place and that's the end of it, as far as he and I are concerned. And I'm not responsible for press speculation. But that's another good reason for you both not to show your faces outside; if he finds out I've been lying he will happily lynch me. Are you okay there, Ange – for the time being?"

"Don't worry about us, Jim. We're busy doing some overdue housekeeping – I never realised just what an untidy sod you are! Any further developments, by the way?"

This time I distinctly heard him sigh. "No. But this morning I managed to persuade the TV interviewer to contact her producer, and he's agreed to splash the photofit on tonight's *Crimewatch* programme.

And I've also given them the bastard's real name. It's time Arnold Brownlaw suffered some anxiety of his own, don't you think?"

"Good idea. What about tonight, Jim? I've already assured Connie there's no way we're going to cancel her dinner party. So, how you going to help us escape?"

"Well, I agree about not cancelling. What I thought we'd do is to send a squad car there to collect you for about 7.30, and at the same time I'll have a taxi waiting for Connie at the side of the building, by the fire exit. Peter Corkhill has already contacted a local taxi firm and put them in the picture. I can arrange for the security staff to open the side exit, so as the squad car, with you inside, pulls away from the building the taxi can set off in a different direction." He paused, presumably to give me time to consider his plan. "So, what do you think?" he then asked.

"Sounds like a plan, Jim. I don't see why it shouldn't work. So, we'll all meet up at the restaurant at about eight, then?"

"Yeah. If you don't hear from me again, I'll see you both at Alphonso's later. Enjoy the housework!"

One of the things I made a point of doing during the day was ensuring the battery on my mobile was fully charged. Better to be safe than sorry, I thought. I made Connie and myself a late lunch – I wasn't very good at cooking, either! Then we settled down to watch an afternoon film on the telly.

Later, I had a snooze and then took my turn, after Connie, for a long soak in the bath, after which we dressed for the evening. Connie looked exceptionally pretty, wearing the outfit we had purchased during our shopping expedition to London. It was a short, elegant black evening dress, with a slightly plunging neckline; personally, I thought it made her look older than she needed to, but Connie insisted that was exactly what she wanted. Fortunately, the special shoes we had bought in Wolverhampton, before returning to Henry's, went very well with the dress. She blushed when I told her how lovely she looked. I made do with one of my evening trouser suits; perfect for the evening, but slightly below Connie's level of elegance. She was, after all, the star of the occasion.

I glanced out of the window just before 7.30, to see our two stringers were still waiting patiently for their non-existent story. It was still raining, but not as heavily as it was earlier; more like a persistent drizzle.

CHAPTER FIFTY-EIGHT

Our exit from the building and into the cars was timed perfectly: me into the police car – driven, as it happened, by WPC Pauline Wilkins – and Connie out of the fire exit at the side of the building and into the waiting taxi. One of the stringers shouted something at me as I was getting into the squad car. I wasn't clear what he had said, but it wouldn't have mattered anyway; I simply ignored him.

"Evening, Sarge. Alphonso's, isn't it?"

"Hi, Pauline. Yes, Alphonso's. How long have you been with the motorised unit?"

She smiled enigmatically. "Oh, I'm not with them permanently. Inspector Kewell allocated me the car when he asked me to collect you this evening. It's Connie's birthday party, isn't? What is she – 18? How lovely. I can hardly remember my 18th…"

On and on she chatted – probably through nervousness, I thought. Then we found ourselves stuck, for what felt like an age, in heavy traffic on the Birmingham ring road. I checked my watch: it was coming up to eight o'clock. Connie would probably be there by now, having taken a different route to the restaurant. Moments later my mobile went off, and as I fumbled for it in my bag it suddenly stopped. Then I heard Connie's voice say: "This isn't the way to Alphonso's, and I don't believe you're a taxi driver. Who are you? Where are you taking me?"

I felt the blood drain from my face. "Oh no, no, no!" I pleaded with the gods above. "Don't let this be true!"

"Sarge? Are you all right? Is that Connie on your mobile?"

I ignored her, instead checking the signal from the phone. The display was brightly lit and the tiny arrow was clearly pointing north-eastwards – away from the city centre. Someone was saying something to Connie, but I couldn't hear it too well because of Pauline's wittering.

"Shut up, Pauline, will you; I'm trying to listen."

"I think you know who I am," a man's voice was saying. "And it's no good trying the door – it's locked."

"My worst nightmare?" I heard Connie say in a hoarse voice. Then the man laughed; a harsh humourless laugh that sent a shudder through me.

"You don't seem very afraid," the man said.

"Should I be? After all, I've been expecting you; it just took you longer than I thought."

"Oh, you *should* be afraid, little one. You should be very afraid."

Then I heard what I thought was a shuffling in the car, and Connie was saying: "Will you take that fucking knife out of my throat? ...Unless you intend to kill me here in the car. And would you mind telling me where exactly we are heading? I don't like mysteries."

I closed my ears to the angry reply, but not to the thud of a fist striking bone that followed. Oh, Christ! Why did she choose to sit in the front with the driver? I reached across to grab hold of the radio.

"Come in, Central. Car four here; Sergeant Crossley"

"Acknowledged, car four. Do you need assistance?"

"Yes. Patch me through to DCI Robbins, will you. Urgently."

"Wilko."

Then Jim's voice came on the line. "Ange? What's the problem?"

"Jim – that taxi you sent to collect Connie? It's fucking fake. It's the paedophile – he's snatched her!"

"Snatched her? How do you know that? She can't have been in the cab more than 15 minutes."

"Jim, please; listen to me. She's carrying a tracer – it's linked up to my mobile. I can hear her talking now to the killer."

"Sweet Jesus!" he gasped. "Where is she now? Have you got a direction finder on her?"

"Yes. The car's heading north, moving slightly east. I think it's heading towards the M6 in the direction of Walsall."

"Okay, Angie. Keep following. I'm arranging for some patrol cars to join up with you. Stay on the line while I check out this taxi business. I don't suppose you can communicate with her?"

"No. It's only one-way. I'll keep listening."

"No!" I heard Connie sob as I broke the connection with Jim. "All I know is that for some sick reason you made me a target."

"Think about it, bitch. It'll come to you eventually."

Connie was clearly injured, going by the difficulty she had in speaking.

"Is...is it because I can see you? ...In my visions? Or do I know you from somewhere?" There was a distinct tremor to her voice now, as if she had suddenly realised that even though she would know I was following her, she could still be in danger.

Again the harsh guttural laugh; it had a kind of maniacal quality to it that sent shivers through me.

"You know me alright, little one. And, I promise you, before the night is out you'll remember me."

I indicated to Pauline she should follow the direction the arrow was pointing. The incident had certainly shut her up; all she seemed able to do was cast scared glances at me from her driving position.

The radio crackled again, and Jim's voice came through. "Ange. I've got some information on the taxi driver. He's a regular, been with the company for five years, and he's 52 and got grandkids. So, it can't be him. The only thing I can think is that our man picked us up on the police band when Corkhill ordered the cab this afternoon. He must have intercepted the driver and commandeered the taxi."

"What about the original driver?"

"Dead, probably. I don't think this shit's going to leave any witnesses – do you? Where are you now, Ange?"

"Coming up to the motorway. I'm sure he's heading for Walsall."

"Has Connie given us any more clues? You know: who he is, or where they're headed?"

"No. But she's being incredibly brave. I heard her tell him to take the knife out of her throat! But I'm afraid, because of that, he struck her in the face. I don't think she's badly hurt, but she is having problems in speaking."

"Yeah. I was afraid something like that might happen. This guy is an out and out psychopath; Christ only knows how he will react. Listen; I've got three patrol cars waiting at the motorway exit to Walsall. We know now at least what car he's driving, and I've also passed on the registration number. An armed response vehicle will meet up with them there in a few minutes. Ange, I do believe we've got him, thanks to your unorthodox tracer."

"Where are *you*, Jim?"

"In one of the patrol cars. I'll be waiting for the bastard. Keep in touch."

The only sound coming from the taxi after that was Connie trying to keep her breathing normal. Then there was the sound of braking, followed by the same guttural voice. "This is where we get out, bitch. Come on – move!"

"W…where are we? Why are we stopping here?"

"Strip!" he ordered. "Take off all your clothes. NOW!" he screamed. "Either you do it or I will."

There was a pause followed by another thud, and then a scream of pain from Connie and the sound of her hitting the ground, coinciding with a loud cry of, "Oh. No!" Then came a tearing noise – apparently the sound of her dress being ripped off. By now I could hear Connie sobbing. Next, I heard the sound of a boot striking flesh, and I realised she was on the ground being kicked. I felt the hatred boiling over inside me, and an overwhelming desire to kill him myself.

"Faster!" I urged Pauline. We're going to lose him."

"Not so tough now, are you?" the sneering voice said. "You've a nice body, though I must admit. I'm looking forward to getting my hands on it. Now, get up, you fucking bitch, and take off those shoes. Didn't you hear me? I said everything." This command was followed by yet a further blow. Then: "Take the fucking shoes off – do you people think I'm altogether stupid? I've an idea you're wearing a bug of some sort, so, unless it's up your fanny, it's staying here. My own car's just over there. Come on. *Move!*"

There was silence for a moment, then I heard Connie say, partly in a whisper, partly in a sobbing voice, "Angie, I'm remembering. We're going to his house in Sutton Coldfield – it's very big, and it's on a hill. I can't say…"

"I said: 'Get up!' bitch."

The last sound I heard was a long yell from Connie – no doubt he was pulling her up from the ground by her hair. Then total quietness. I urged Pauline towards the by now stationary direction arrow on my mobile. It took us something like ten minutes, though, to locate it; the bastard had pulled the taxi into a narrow lane, and we had to reverse a couple of times before we found it. Not surprisingly, it was empty, with Connie's torn clothes strewn across the rear seat. I choked back a tear when I spotted that her bra and knickers were included.

I immediately contacted Jim again.

"What's going on, Ange? You should be here by now."

"We've lost him, Jim. He knows."

"What are you talking about, 'We've lost him'? How can we lose him unless he's found the trace? Has he? Is that you're trying to tell me?"

"He guessed she was wearing one, so he's forced her to strip off – everything, including her shoes. He's left her things in the taxi and transferred over to his own vehicle."

"Didn't she say anything? Anything at all?"

"I think he's hurt her badly, Jim. She could hardly speak. She did say something about Sutton Coldfield, but it wasn't very clear. Look; why don't you stay there, in case he's still heading in that direction, and I'll head off to Sutton Coldfield – see if I can't spot them."

"What a fucking disaster!" Jim snorted over the radio. "No, Ange. I'll leave two of the cars here, and I'll head towards Sutton Coldfield from the opposite direction to you. We'll meet up later."

I urged Pauline to put her foot to the floor, and I switched on the siren as we approached the motorway. I decided to bypass the Walsall turn-off and take the ring road to join up with the Sutton Coldfield connection.

"Which part are we heading for?" Pauline asked me.

"How the hell do I know? Does it make any difference? We just keep going until we see a house on a hill; a big house, I'd guess."

"No. It's just that I've got relatives round there. I know it quite well."

"You wouldn't happen to remember a big house on the top of a hill, would you?"

"Well, I do know of one big house. I'm not sure it's the one we're looking for, but it *is* perched on the top of the hill."

"God bless you, Pauline! Let's give it a go, shall we? I'm in your hands now."

The patrol car put on a sudden surge of speed, which threw me back in my seat and had me hanging on for dear life. Pauline had all of a sudden lost her timidity and turned into something of a rally driver; but who the hell was complaining? We screeched along the main road into Sutton Coldfield at 90 miles an hour, with siren blaring and cars pulling hurriedly onto the pavements to get out of the way. I wasn't sure now just how much of a head start he had on us, but estimated it must be around 15 or 20 minutes' advantage.

We entered the beautiful tree-lined avenues in the approach to the town almost in a blur. I barely had a glimpse of the mansion-like properties set deep from the road in their one- or two-acre sites. Without doubt this was an area for the extremely wealthy; we were screaming through it as if it were something from hell – which in some way, I supposed, it was.

The car took a sudden sharp turn to the left, causing me to bang my head on the side window. I didn't dare say anything to Pauline; the last thing she needed at the moment was discouragement. We were climbing towards the top of a hill, I noticed, and for the first time I started to worry about weapons. We literally had nothing with which to defend ourselves.

Finally, she stopped the car at the top of the hill. All I could see were the bright lights of Birmingham across a valley, on the not too distant horizon. It was a breathtaking sight, but not the one I wanted: there were no houses in the immediate vicinity.

"Oh, shit!" Pauline said irritably. "Wrong street."

Again I decided not to say anything. It would have achieved nothing anyway, and might just have panicked her. She turned the car around and we tore back down the hill towards the main road again. A sharp right turn, cutting across the traffic virtually on two wheels, then a determined Pauline righted the vehicle, without flinching a muscle, and pointed us back in the direction of Walsall.

"Don't worry, Sarge; I've got it now. We're two minutes away."

A half a mile further, another right turn – almost colliding with a local bus in the middle of the road – and we were climbing once more. And there it was: a forbidding-looking property that I could just make out through the protection of trees, standing about 400 yards back from the road. She turned off the siren and unhesitatingly pulled into the driveway, shrieking to a halt at the front of the house. There were no lights showing and no vehicles in view.

"Do you think this is it?" I asked Pauline, worry seeping from my voice.

"I'm pretty sure this is it," she confirmed. "Are we going round the back, Sarge?"

"*I* am. *You* are going to stay here and let the DCI know exactly where we are. Okay?"

"Sure. But, for God's sake, be careful! That man's a maniac."

CHAPTER FIFTY-NINE

I eased myself around the side of the house, ignoring the crunching sound my feet made on the gravel path. It was far too late for subtlety. There was a garage at the side of the house; the door was partly open, so I went to examine it. From the feel of the engine of the car inside, whoever was driving it had only just arrived; it was almost hot.

At the back of the property I saw a light on in what had to be the kitchen. I tried the door and felt it easing under the pressure, and found myself in a kind of laundry room facing a slightly open door where the light was coming from. Quietly I let myself into the kitchen, not knowing what I might come across. It was empty, and as silent as the grave – which caused me again to wonder if this was the right house. Then, at the rear of the room, I noticed a darkened passageway leading into the bowels of the house. I withdrew my torch and, keeping it low to the ground, I entered the passage. There was another light protruding from a slightly open doorway at the end, and as I came nearer I saw it was a doorway with stone steps leading down to the cellar. Every instinct within me urged me to get the hell out of there and wait for the arrival of the second patrol car. And then I thought of Connie and the terrors she would be going through, and what he might be doing to her down there. However reckless, I took the only decision possible and began to descend the stairs towards the light.

Partway down I heard the voices: one of them, which caused me to freeze against the wall, was definitely Connie's; the other, the same nightmarish voice I had heard through the mobile. I was horrified at the things she was saying.

"Why are you doing this to me, Daddy? Mummy promised me you wouldn't do it again. Ooh, no; please, Daddy – you are hurting me."

I stood on the stairs frozen in shock. Her father? I was told some years ago he had died in a car crash. Why? What was the point in telling me that?

"Now, now, my little darling; you know you don't mean that." The sneering voice said. "You used to like your daddy doing this to you, didn't you? It was only that bitch of a mother of yours who interfered and spoilt our fun. Come on, sweetie – tell the truth; you love it really, don't you? And when I've finished there's another little treat in store for you … you see, my dear, you now have to pay for all the trouble you've caused me. You do understand, don't you? Thanks to you and your fucking visions my pleasures are almost at an end."

The sound of weeping followed; it was a ghoulish, horrifying sound – a mixture of sobbing and squealing with pain – and I found myself paralysed with shock and revulsion at the thought of what was taking place below me.

Then I began to realise why they had kept his existence a secret. That was the shocking part. He was the one who had molested her as a child. He was the one who had raped her and driven her mind into a retreat.

For all these years we had hunted a monster whilst, unknowingly, we had his daughter in our care.   And neither she nor we had had the beginnings of an idea. He, then, was the cause of the disassociate fugue Connie had suffered.   It was not solely due either to the trauma of uncovering the mass grave in the woods, as we had all thought, but also from the sexual abuse this evil monster had visited on a little girl – his daughter, for God's sake! And now her memory had returned, accompanied by all the vivid images of the violent, depraved obscenities he had committed.

But her current recollections were of the eight-year-old child who had had to endure the nightly terror, rather than the adult she had now become.   Listening to her speaking, through the closed door, was like listening to a child.   It was as if she had regressed into the world she had inhabited when still living with her father; as if she was reliving the events of that time.   I shuddered from an amalgam of my own fear at the reality that men like her father actually existed and outright rage that anyone could do those things to their own daughter.

I remained transfixed on the cellar steps, trying to make some sense out of the thoughts racing through my head.   The visions she had experienced?   Was that something she had inherited from her father? Hadn't Connie said, a number of times, "He can see me"?

Was this a shared phenomenon?   If so it would clearly explain why he couldn't allow her to remain free; he must have been afraid that her memory was slowly returning, and in that event would identify him. In that instance I also remembered something Paul Simmons had said to me some years ago: that we would find the origins of her trauma in her family environment. But, then, that wasn't supported by Connie's assertion that she had inherited the gift from her grandmother.

I had never cursed my incompetence more than I did at that moment. I was standing there, on the stairs, rigid with shock and the on point of being violently sick, but totally unsure how I should proceed. In the end it was cold anger that emerged the winner, especially as I felt the penetrating sobs from my young friend tormenting me.

Silently I retreated back to the kitchen and hastily, using my flashlight and searched through the drawers until I discovered a large carving knife, which I gripped with a new resolve. Then I hurried again down the steps and without hesitating I pushed open the door to the cellar. I couldn't help myself; what I witnessed and experienced there caused me to let out a feral scream, the like of which I had never before heard, and from which I felt I was totally detached. It will haunt me for the rest of my life.

Arnold Brownlaw – I will always think of him by that name – was lying naked on top of an equally naked Connie, very evidently penetrating her, and very evidently enjoying his depraved sexual act. I saw that he had his hands around her throat, and was beginning to squeeze the life from her. He had a grotesque expression of lust on his face; his mouth was gaping wide open, whilst saliva trickled down to his chin. His eyes appeared to have lost focus; he was immersed in his world of madness – until he heard my scream. Then he regained a degree of control; I saw his head come up, and watched him withdraw himself from Connie. He climbed off the small bed and came towards me, oozing pure hatred, coupled with a sense of pervading evil. I had an overpowering sense of malevolence cloaking his whole body.

I know I should have concentrated on him, but I was paralysed with the horror of it all. Then the sight of a child's body behind him distracted my focus. She was lying there, naked and dead, but in perfect repose, as if she had been prepared for a requiem ceremony. I guessed it was Lisa – the girl from the playground. She seemed to be at perfect peace, even though her throat and vulva were badly mutilated. Above her, and all around the walls of the cellar, a variety of trophies were displayed: photograph after photograph of naked children. Dead little girls in a variety of obscene poses, positioned by the killer especially for his album. Most of them appeared to be silently pleading for mercy, as though they were aware of what was to come. Others had their faces screwed up in agony. This then was what Paul was referring to when he mentioned trophies. These pictures, hanging on the wall around the room, were Brownlaw's trophies of his evil acts.

As my attention was diverted, I sensed rather than saw Brownlaw leap at me and make a grab for the knife in my hand. I stood virtually paralysed, tears streaming down my cheeks, still attempting to absorb the enormity of the scene into my shocked consciousness. It was pure instinct, and perhaps some training, that prompted my reaction. As he knocked the knife from my hand my foot came up reflexively and kicked him hard in the groin. He fell to the ground, clutching his testicles in agony and screaming obscenities at me, as I, in turn, was pushed backwards heavily, against the wall, my already sensitive head impacting with a sickening thud against the hard concrete. I felt the blood trickling down the back of my neck as the room started to spin and my focus start to distort, and I desperately tried to maintain my balance.

"You're the other fucking bitch, aren't you?" he squealed in pain. "How did you find me?" I then heard him scream. "You had no right to find me." Slowly he tried to climb back to his feet. "Well, now you're here you can join the party – there's no way out of this place. Connie," he gasped, looking towards the bed, "get the knife. Hurry! We can't let her get away."

I watched Connie, in a dreamlike state, climb slowly from the bed, almost as if she was unaware of where she was or even that she was naked. I noticed her jaw was badly swollen and displaced from where he had punched her. She walked over towards the knife without speaking and picked it up from the floor. Then her head turned towards me and I saw just a flicker of recognition in her eyes. By now Brownlaw had managed to painfully struggle to his feet. My vision of the scene kept distorting, and I felt I was on the point of passing out.

"Hurry, you stupid BITCH !" he screamed at Connie. "Right. That's it. Now, give it to Daddy." He held out his hand towards her, and then took a step nearer. Before I knew what was happening, or could do anything to prevent it, Connie thrust forward viciously with the knife and sank it deep into his stomach. In absolute horror, I watched her deliberately withdraw the blade and then plunge it into his abdomen again. The blood from his severed artery was spurting all over her naked body, from her breasts down to her lower abdomen, and into her crotch, changing the colour of her pubic hair from blonde to a deep, unnatural red. She was completely oblivious.

"Daddy…Daddy…Daddy…" she said, over and over, in that child-like voice, repeatedly plunging and plunging the knife into him. "I said for you not to do it again, didn't I? And Mummy warned you too, didn't she? You know she did."

Brownlaw had a look of sheer astonishment on his face. "I'm your father; you can't do this," he whimpered in unconcealed agony. This merely prompted Connie to thrust the knife once more into his now eviscerated bowel. I watched, almost in fascination, as his intestines began spilling out from the wounds, and I witnessed his gaze turn from bewilderment to horror, then to intense fear. It was as if he had experienced a sudden and graphic vision, at the precise moment he was about to die, of the eternal damnation waiting to welcome him.

I turned my face away from the nightmarish scene and felt myself throwing up, no longer able to control my reaction. My legs giving way followed this, and I sank to the floor in deep shock. My whole body was trembling.

I watched in a kind of blur as Peter Conway pulled Connie away from her father and took the knife from her. The last thing my consciousness noticed was what a pathetically small man he was. Lying there, dead now, drenched in his own blood, his eyes still open in disbelief and looking so innocuous, I was left with the impression we had caught the wrong man. It just didn't seem possible that this insignificant and disembowelled little man, with his by now shrivelled penis, could have possibly committed all those atrocities.

CHAPTER SIXTY

The events that followed are still confusing to me. I vaguely remember there being a lot of bodies in the cellar, and a great deal of shouting from fellow officers. I was still half collapsed on the floor – with blood streaming from the back of my head – and feeling like death myself when I heard someone – it might have been Jim- asking me if I was alright. I thought at the time it was a pretty stupid bloody question, although I wasn't capable of telling him so. I couldn't see Connie's face; she was surrounded by uniformed figures, although I did notice someone had covered her naked body with a sheet from the bed.

I distinctly recall half sitting, half lying, on the cellar floor, flooding with tears at this indescribable tragedy, but the next thing I was aware of was being carried on a stretcher into an ambulance and on my way to hospital.

I was informed later that I had suffered a severe skull fracture – infinitely more serious than my earlier concussion. This time I felt so unbelievably shitty I was unable to argue with the doctors. I remember lying there just wishing I was dead, drifting from an overwhelming sadness and trying to come to terms with what I had witnessed in that cellar. I was simply unable to comprehend the events that had taken place.

Later, after I was able to stem the tide of incessant tears, I moved into a deep depression, which made me feel that life was no longer worth living. I, too, had suffered a kind of bereavement that night.

Jim came to see me regularly, of course. He told me that the majority of officers thought I was some kind of a hero; personally, he felt I had been bloody stupid in not waiting for him to arrive. He was very curt and matter-of-fact, almost as if I had become a complete stranger. I could not care less either way. I was too consumed with my own wildly oscillating emotions. Perhaps it was my disorientation, but I also sensed there was a coolness between us, as if something else had died in that cellar. Oh, he did inform me, as an aside, that the DCS was going to recommend that 'silly cow' for a bravery medal!

This time they kept me in hospital for almost three weeks following surgery, during which, I was later informed, a small metal plate had to be implanted into my skull for long-term protection. It was then that I realised I would never again be able to take up active police duties, so forcing me to reconsider my future.

During my time in hospital I did manage to ask various people – including Jim and Paul Simmons – about Connie, and what would happen to her now. I came up against a stiffening reluctance on the part of everyone I asked to give me any information. Jim did confirm, though, that Paul was pretty well spot on with his profile of the killer, even down to his conclusion that he would, in all probability, collect trophies of the victims. That didn't stop him from constantly reminding me that, as a procedure, profiling was never intended to replace police work, merely to assist us. Nonetheless, it did prove invaluable. It wasn't until I was actually discharged from the hospital that I was able to complete the whole story about the circumstances following Brownlaw's death.

* * * * * * * * *

The first discovery the police made was the body of the taxi driver. They found it in a ditch not far from where Brownlaw had abandoned the taxi. His throat had been cut.

Forensics evidently spent a great deal of time in the cellar gathering samples and DNA. They were able to confirm very quickly that the body of the little girl in the cellar was indeed that of Lisa, the six-year-old from the playground. They also confirmed that Brownlaw's DNA matched the samples they had recovered from other sources during the investigation, including that found on the clothes of Josephine Marsden. He was also directly linked to the body of one of the children found in the pit in the woods.

Further investigation into Brownlaw's background uncovered no new evidence, other than that his neighbours knew the killer, vaguely, as Harold Davidson, and that bank accounts – with substantial deposits – also appeared in that name. He was also in possession of various credit cards and a driving licence in the same name. Apparently, shortly after his mother's deaths, and his inheritance of the millions she in turn had been left by her industrialist husband, he had decided – for reasons we could only speculate on, never prove – literally to disappear as Arnold Brownlaw.

It was Jim's suspicion that he had murdered his own mother, and his disappearance brought an end to any further investigation that might have followed. Enquires produced little additional information on the man; nothing was established about his education, his career or even his own family. It suggested a convincing argument that, in reality, he was indeed Arnold Brownlaw. Harold Davidson had appeared instantly out of nowhere, almost simultaneously with Brownlaw's disappearance, which did lend some credence to the suspicion that it was Brownlaw who was responsible for his mother's death.

The total number of murders this man had committed was never factually established. We had already identified 19 children, making a total of 21 victims including Sheila and the taxi driver, and the obscene trophy photographs of the children on the wall seemed to confirm these numbers. We would never be able to prove that he murdered either his mother or Sylvia; suspicions alone were irrelevant in law. And then we had to ask ourselves: how many more children were there likely to be? We would never know, and personally I don't think I really wanted to know. I truly had had a sickener of it all.

The end result was that a full enquiry was called for, and granted; one of the Appeal Court judges was chosen to oversee it. The relatives of the victims were promised that it would be comprehensive and there would be no closing of legal ranks.

And, finally, there was Connie, and what became of her. There was no question of a trial, as two eminent psychiatrists, in addition to Dr Simmons, testified that she was totally unfit to plead. As a result, she was committed indefinitely to a penal psychiatric hospital, but from the evidence of all the doctors there was no likelihood of her ever-regaining sufficient mental competence to be considered for release.

On more than one occasion I tried my best to visit her, but I was refused permission. I was once allowed, however, to 'view' her from the glass window of her room, and it brought back memories of the early months at Forest Hills, when she spent her days sitting on the floor in complete silence and in a foetal position, recognising no one and communicating with no one. It was more than I could bear. After all we had shared together, the prospect of that poor girl spending the rest of her life trapped in the darkness of her mind tormented me. Once again, the intense hatred I felt for her father boiled to the surface. He had completely destroyed her life, along with the lives of so many others. I remember leaving the hospital in tears and wishing with all my heart that he *had* killed her.

* * * * * * * * *

Shortly after that I met up with Paul Simmons again, who did his best to explain what had happened to her. It was Paul's medical opinion that, because of the sexual abuse by her father, Connie had begun to lose touch with reality so as to escape from the trauma. What then followed, from the discovery of the bodies in the woods, was that something within her, some psychic recognition, realised who the murderer was, thereby forcing her to retreat into a fugue state because of her mind's inability to cope with the awful truth about her father. Paul had always suspected that somehow her family was involved, and that was why he had been so hesitant about releasing her from Forest Hills. He knew that all it would take would be one catalyst and she would slip back into the world of her childhood. In short, Connie was permanently damaged, and would never experience a stable adult existence. And, of course, he was proved correct. That is precisely what happened to her that night she was abducted.

She had a brief moment between lives, when she remembered that part of her childhood when she lived with her father in the big house in Sutton Coldfield – that instance when she was able to tell me where they going; then she was lost for ever. As Paul said, it wasn't the Connie I knew who killed her father; it was an eight-year-old child. And that is how she would remain forever – as a child.

It was so, so sad, and the only comforting aspect to it all was that, however unwittingly, Connie had obtained true retribution from her father, for herself and all the other victims he had brutally murdered. After all, what greater retribution could there possibly be than an awareness of his own death, paralleled with a glimpse of the eternal hell waiting eagerly for him on the other side?

EPILOGUE

All this occurred a few years ago – five years, to be precise. Having accepted a generous disability pension I left the police force almost immediately following the completion of the enquiry, when, everyone was relieved to learn, the police were exonerated from all responsibility. Cold comfort, perhaps, for the parents, but they were finally able to bury their children with the dignity they had awaited for such a long time. As for myself, I politely refused the offer of a bravery medal; I had never felt less brave in my life, and my emotions were still on a roller coaster. In fact, I spent two years as a private patient of Paul Simmons, when he treated me for what he named 'reactive depression'. Even today, all these years later, I cannot imagine I will ever be whole again, and I still need, from time to time, to restart a course of anti-depressants.

I saw Jim only occasionally after I left the force, but the chemistry between us had disappeared since that night in the cellar. I believe that both of us were damaged by that awful experience, and things could never quite be the same between us. We remained friends, but more in a perfunctory manner than close. Eventually I heard that he had married, and apparently he now has a young boy. I am glad for him; he is a thoroughly decent man. I believe, also, he has made Superintendent; deservedly so, in my view.

I have now lived at Warwick University for the past three years. After taking my doctorate I was granted a postgraduate position as an associate professor lecturing in criminology. I am currently about to take my finals in forensic psychology. Eventually, I hope to become an expert in criminal profiling, and perhaps, in time, even work for the FBI in the States. It's a subject I have never lost interest in; it was the hands-on front-line duties, and the personal horrors and suffering associated with them that compelled me to leave the force. That and, of course, the reality that I would never be permitted on active duty again – and I couldn't ever imagine myself sitting each and every day pushing paper.

* * * * * * * * *

I will be 31 next month, and still single. No boyfriends, no lovers, although I have had my moments. And, no, I am not gay – although, to be truthful, I have never been tested! I manage to lose myself in my work. I decided to write this story in the belief that it might prove to be cathartic: help me to purge old ghosts. Sadly, I was mistaken. I don't believe the demons will ever let me go, and I have still only partially come to terms with the macabre events I witnessed that night in the cellar.

I will always miss Connie – the Connie I knew and loved and was close to. There isn't a single night that passes without my thinking of her, sometimes with dry eyes, more often than not blinking back a tear.

I know I will never forget her, and I will always wonder whether her psychic powers might have blossomed even further had she not suffered those terrible traumas. What I do know is that Connie was constantly haunted by her gift, and lived in almost permanent dread of it surfacing. That she was a true psychic I have no doubts whatsoever. I had more than enough evidence that the visions she did experience were indisputably real; they actually did happen. The brutal murders of the children; the discovery of the two burial pits; and, of course, her accurate prediction that Reg, the police artist, was terminally ill. Sadly, Reg died only a matter of months following their meeting at Forest Hills.

It did occur to me, over time, that possibly the mental suppression of her father's existence, and in particular his sexual abuse of her, was not as powerful as her psychic gift, and that it was he, in fact (out of his desire to find and punish her), who was responsible for its surfacing from her subconscious. It was a thought, but I guess now I'll never know.

My prayer each night for Connie, my dear, dear friend, is: "May God bless her and for ever watch over her."

****

AUTHOR'S BIOGRAPHY

Vincent Cobb was born and educated in Blackpool and spent most of his working life in the travel industry. Eventually he moved to London, where he became 'joint managing director' of Thomson Holiday, the giant package tour company, before moving on to head up Club 18-30. His first book, *The Package Tour Industry*, was published last year and recounts his many personal experiences in the early days of travel – some humorous and some terrifying.

The author lives in the Home Counties with his wife, Pat. *Nemesis* is his second work of fiction and follows his earlier success with *Leave a Light on for Jesus*, a disturbing story of abuse and betrayal.

Other books by Vincent Cobb

The Package Tour Industry

Leave a Light on for Jesus

Contrition

Retribution

www.ingramcontent.com/pod-product-compliance
Lightning Source LLC
Chambersburg PA
CBHW020247200626
46816CB00001BA/169